A Random Act of ...

Also by Sophie Jenkins

*The Forgotten Guide to Happiness*

# A Random Act of Kindness

## SOPHIE JENKINS

**avon.**

Published by Avon,
A division of HarperCollins*Publishers* Ltd
1 London Bridge Street
London SE1 9GF

www.harpercollins.co.uk

A Paperback Original 2019

A catalogue record for this book
is available from the British Library

ISBN: 978-0-00-828183-0

Typeset in Minion 11.5/14.5 pt by Palimpsest Book Production Limited,
Falkirk, Stirlingshire

Printed and bound in UK by CPI Group (UK) Ltd, Croydon CR0 4YY

**MIX**
Paper from
responsible sources
**FSC™ C007454**

This book is produced from independently certified FSC™ paper
to ensure responsible forest management.

For more information visit: www.harpercollins.co.uk/green

Dedicated to Rowena Jenkins
19.10.1931–3.12.2018

# LOT 1

*A Chanel-style black-and-white cotton tweed suit with bracelet-length sleeves, double 'C' gilt buttons, chain-weighted hem and matching skirt.*

Most stories start with action. This isn't one of them. Mine starts with indecision. It's a warm Sunday evening and I'm dragging my wheelie case over the cobbled stones of Camden Market, pondering the big issues of my life. Can I really make a living selling vintage dresses from one small stand? Should I call in at Cotton's Rhum Shack to cheer myself up before going home?

The din of the case rattling on the cobbles is attracting some negative attention from passers-by in an annoyed 'What the hell is that noise?' kind of way. It's a cheap black suitcase, with nothing going for it except that it's big enough to carry my stock of frocks.

I come out through the imposing arch of Stables Market onto the busy Chalk Farm Road and I stand on the kerb, still undecided. Quick drink? Across the way, the lights in Cotton's Rhum Shack are gleaming. It's snug and inviting, located between a music shop and one selling white crockery. Right now, there's a gap in the traffic and I've got the chance to dash across. Still, something makes me hesitate. It's been a long day and I haven't sold much so the case is heavy. If I turn right past the Lock and trundle my case along the towpath, I'll be home. I can hang up the dresses, kick off my shoes, undo my fitted jacket and relax. Simple choice. Drink, or home?

Before I reach a decision, a woman coming along the pavement catches my eye. I see her now exactly as I did the first time we met, in a series of close-ups – the scarlet lips, the little Chanel suit, the black silk turban covering her dark hair, her sharp little face, faux pearls, a black patent handbag with intertwined Cs hanging from the crook of her elbow. She wears the outfit as naturally as if it's her skin. It is the perfect fit. With the tick-tick-tick of her heels, she's a combination of sound and vision – that confident, moneyed walk; chin tilted upwards, completely self-contained except for the way her eyes flick slyly towards me to gauge the effect she's having.

I've imagined this moment for a long time.

I feel a surge of happiness and forget about the Rhum Shack. This is my chance to thank her, I decide, for the way she changed my life one day a few years ago.

I was very down at the time; stuck in a dark place. What turned me around was that she noticed me, a total stranger, when I thought I was invisible; she saw through my misery to the person I wanted to be; she told me in a few kind, well-chosen words how to be the person I *could* be.

I want her to see my transformation.

Transformation!

What a word.

It's the best word in the English language.

She made me realise that we're not fixed, rooted firmly in our inadequacies, but that we can change who we are whenever we choose; we can pick up the kaleidoscope, shake it and transform ourselves again and again. We can choose the way

2

we face the world. We can choose the way the world sees us.

I'm smiling; I can't help it. I wish I'd been the one who'd dressed her all up in black and white with those bright red lips.

As she gets closer she, in turn, is studying my outfit with equally blatant curiosity, from my shoes to my confidence-boosting slightly masculine Prince of Wales check jacket with shoulder pads and the nipped-in waist.

I lower my white sunglasses and my eyes meet hers.

She briefly raises one fine eyebrow and smiles at me approvingly.

I love that smile. It makes my day.

'Darling, you startled me, you know!' she says warmly. *Dahlink, you stertled me!* . . . Her accent is German or Austrian, strong and precise. 'That suit! So chic! Suddenly, it's 1949 again – I thought I was dead all of a sudden, bof! God knows, I've practised, but *here*?' A train thunders over the bridge and she looks around, then winces and covers her ears at the trailing noise until it fades.

She folds her arms and looks at me again intently from head to foot, then works her way up once more – shoes, knees, skirt, jacket – and she nods her approval. 'Perfect.' She adds in a whisper from behind her slender hand, 'Except for that suitcase, of course.'

This time around, she's not looking at me with gentle compassion but with humour.

I look at my scruffy case and laugh. 'Grim, isn't it? But it's practical.'

'Oh, *prektikel*! Well then!'

Does she remember me? If she doesn't, I'll take that as a compliment because it's a sign of how much I've changed.

Suddenly, her expression changes to one of alarm.

'Oh! My bus is coming!' she says. 'Excuse me! Goodbye!'

The number twenty-four is coming up under the bridge and she spins around and hurries in her heels towards the bus stop, pearls jingling, her handbag swinging from the crook of her elbow. Waving at the driver, she reaches in her bag for her travel card. In her rush, she's dropping her money. Coins are rolling over the pavement, spinning in all directions.

I crouch to gather them up for her. The number twenty-four bus comes alongside us, gusting warm fumes, and she hurries onto it.

'Wait!' I call, picking up as much of her cash as I can, but she doesn't hear me, so I grab my case and step onto the bus just as the doors are closing. I've forgotten just how heavy my wheelie bag is. Before I can hoist it on board, the doors momentarily close on my arm.

As I yelp and let go, the driver opens the door again and a dark-haired, broad-shouldered guy in a pink floral shirt and jeans grabs the case by the handle before it falls to the ground. 'It's okay! I've got it!' he says.

I sum him up at a glance. Not the fact that he's good-looking and his eyes are deep blue; that's just a quirk of nature and not a good indicator of character. What I notice is that his pink shirt is crisply ironed and he's wearing tan leather shoes polished to a shine. For that reason, I immediately trust him.

'Thank you!' I say gratefully, then I hurry up the aisle to the woman in the Chanel suit and hand back her money.

She looks from me to her empty bag with great astonishment – what? Her cash has been trickling out of it? And I've been picking it up as it rolled away? 'Ach, you are kindness itself!' she says, kissing her fingers and scattering goodwill my way.

Good deed done, I go to get off the bus, when I suddenly realise that the man in the pink shirt hasn't got on behind me. I wonder where he is and what he's done with my suitcase.

4

And then I realise he's taken it.

Not straight away – I'm a trusting sort of person and I have to double-check before it sinks in. First of all, I think wryly, ha ha, wouldn't it be ironic if he's run off with it when I'm here doing a good turn? And then I turn to the driver: 'That man who had my bag, what did he do with it?'

The driver shrugs and puffs out his cheeks sympathetically then closes the doors.

'Stop, I'm getting off,' I say in a panic.

He opens the doors again, so I jump off the bus and look up and down the road with insane optimism as the bus pulls away.

The opportunistic thief has gone and stolen my case.

I lean against the high stone wall of Stables Market, taking deep breaths and pressing my heart back under my ribs.

This great, indescribable sense of loss comes over me, closing my throat with grief.

Gone. Stolen – my beautiful clothes; the clothes that are my livelihood and my dreams.

# LOT 2

*A Paul Smith gentleman's pink slim-fit floral shirt,*
*size medium.*

Once the initial wave of shock passes, I straighten up and force myself to think about things rationally. I mean, that suitcase is so hideously noisy that no thief in his right mind would want to drag it for any distance. And who wants a load of old clothes, anyway? (Apart from me, obviously.)

First, because of the noise of my rickety case, I'm guessing the man wouldn't have gone far. He'd probably nip down one of the residential side streets, out of sight, and find a quiet place to rummage through the contents of the bag, to see if there was anything in there worth keeping. And when he found that there wasn't, I reassure myself, he'd dump it and walk away.

Guided by instinct and a bit of local knowledge, I head to Castlehaven Road, where there's a large triangle of overgrown grass surrounded by wooden benches, known optimistically as The Gardens, which is usually deserted.

Today it's busy. Circling each other on skateboards are three boys – for a hopeful but disappointing moment it sounds just like the wheels on my case. On one of the benches, two tanned and amiable drunks are making philosophical conversation through the medium of Carlsberg Special Brew lager.

The kids watch me suspiciously as I walk around the perimeter of the garden, eyes alert, holding firmly on to my handbag and visualising my scattered clothing fluttering in the long grass like injured birds (this is how sure I am I'll find them).

But I don't find them. On the path, the boys circle like sharks. I leave the gardens and walk slowly back to Chalk Farm Road, knowing I should keep on looking but also knowing in my heart how pointless it could be. The guy with my case could have headed straight for the towpath, or for the car park in the superstore, or down any of the other side streets, or he could have gone straight home. I think about my pathetic gratitude as he'd held my case for me while I triumphantly dashed onto the bus to hand the old lady her money back. That's what you get for helping someone out, I reflect bitterly.

Back on Chalk Farm Road I look across towards the market. Miraculously, I suddenly see that pink shirt as he reappears right at the entrance to the Stables with my suitcase. 'Hey!' I yell. 'Excuse me!'

'Hey!'

We're shouting across the traffic and waving our arms at each other.

'Wait there!' I'm dashing across in my pencil skirt, dodging cars – this is the way to cross a road in London: assertively. 'My bag!' I say warmly and with happy relief until I see he's holding a small shaggy brown dog on a lead. I feel a familiar rush of fear and I keep a distance between us. I've got a thing about dogs.

'Sorry,' he explains. 'I let go of the lead when I saw you struggling and my dog went back into the Stables to investigate the remains of someone's burger. When I came back and I couldn't see you, I kind of thought I'd better wait here, you know, as it was the last place we saw each other.'

I don't know what it is about that sentence that melts my heart. It's as if we're old friends and that's what we do, we come back to the last place we saw each other.

'Thanks. Really. You don't know what it means, to get my case back. It contains all of my best stock.' My voice is wobbling with relief. He's got a beautiful face. His nose is big and noble. He looks trustworthy and somehow sensitive, and his deep blue eyes never leave mine. The pink shirt sets off his tan. And he's clearly kind. I grab the case, using it as a shield between the dog and me. 'Thank you,' I say to him again, because I'm still so relieved at getting it back.

'My pleasure.' He holds out his hand. 'David Westwood.'

'Really? Any relation to Vivienne?' I ask, studying him with interest.

His blue eyes narrow as if he's shortsighted and trying to focus. 'Vivienne?'

'She's a fashion designer. Same surname.'

He laughs and shakes his head. 'No, sorry. No relation.'

'I'm Fern Banks.' I jerk my head towards the entrance. 'I work here.'

'I guessed that when you talked about your stock.' He looks interested. 'So, how's it working out for you?'

'It's early days,' I reply; this is the reassuring fact that I hold on to in the quiet times.

'I've got my name down for a stall.'

I give a shiver of serendipity. 'Really? What are you selling?'

'Light boxes.' His gaze leaves mine for a moment. 'I'm having a career change,' he adds.

There's something defensive about the way he says it that makes me glance up at him curiously, but I'm just happy that he's not selling clothes; I've got enough competition as it is. And I'm still buzzing from getting my case back, so I say, 'There's a stall going next to mine. It's small, though.'

'Where exactly is it?'

'It's right next to the entrance to the covered market.'

He looks down at my case thoughtfully. 'But there's no storage, right?'

I shrug. 'True.' I feel a bit disappointed, even though it makes no difference to me whether he's interested in the stall or not; I don't know the guy and I'm just trying to be helpful. All the same, I really want him to take it. Nothing to do with his looks; anyway, I'm in a relationship. 'My boyfriend thinks it's a good spot because there's plenty of through traffic,' I hear myself say, just so we're clear that my motives are entirely innocent. Then I inwardly cringe – first, because I sound like the kind of woman who needs reassurance from a man about her decisions and secondly, calling him 'my boyfriend' makes me sound adolescent.

Ideally, David Westwood would look devastated at the news I'm not single, but instead he nods and says seriously, 'Through traffic is very important. Actually, I'm trying to get a place indoors, in the Market Hall.'

'Oh, lovely!' I say with deep insincerity.

'My girlfriend, Gigi, says the atmosphere is really friendly in there. And of course it's under cover.'

*My girlfriend, Gigi.* So here we are, two strangers making it absolutely clear that we're all coupled up so that there can never be any misunderstanding about our motives.

I knew a Gigi at school and I'm just about to mention it, when I notice that the shaggy brown dog is getting restless. It gets to its feet and stretches before sniffing with great deliberation around his owner's shoes. As if he can sense my gaze on him, he suddenly lifts his head and looks directly at me, his eyes alert under two blond eyebrows.

I look away quickly, feeling my heart rate rise. I try never to make eye contact with a dog, in case it sees it as a challenge and goes for me, so I wrap things up quickly, while I've still got the chance. 'Well, David, thanks again for your good deed, minding my case,' I say briskly. 'I appreciate it.'

He looks bemused. 'You're welcome.'

The dog is tugging him towards Chalk Farm Tube, in the general direction of Cotton's Rhum Shack. So that settles it. I'll go the other way: straight home.

David Westwood raises his hand to wave goodbye; he walks away with his pink shirt flapping in the breeze.

I'm still looking at him, when he unexpectedly turns around.

'Hey, Fern?'

'What?'

'I'd better watch myself, hadn't I?' he says, laughing. 'You know what they say, right? No good deed ever goes unpunished.'

# LOT 3

*Black one-sleeved asymmetrical dress, rough stitching feature,
labelled Comme des Garçons, Post Nuclear collection, 1980.*

Home is along the Regent's Canal towpath; a one-bedroom
basement flat in Primrose Hill. The flat isn't actually mine –
my parents own it. It's easy to get to, situated between the two
Northern line stations of Camden Town and Chalk Farm. It's
a ten-minute walk along the canal from Camden Lock. It used
to be my father's pied-à-terre during the week and when he
retired I moved in as a sort of tenant, to 'look after the property', as they put it, on a temporary basis until I save enough
for a deposit for my own place. The emphasis is on the word
temporary. However, I haven't yet told them I've been fired
from my dream job as personal stylist in a large department
store, and that getting my own place has become an ever more
distant and unlikely prospect.

In the meantime, I'm very grateful to live here.

The walk is beautiful in the early mornings; cyclists say
hello, walkers smile, the air is fresh and the shadows of the
bridges cast cool stripes across the towpath. The sky is filled
with gulls shrieking like the sound of the harbour when the
fishing boats come in. At night, though, it's a different place
– the smell of dope hangs in the air, empty lager tins bob

on the glossy canal and the bridges are lit up with violet lights.

The decor in the flat is early 21st-century modern; this is my father's taste: Barcelona chairs, glass console tables, a built-in glass wine rack and a flatscreen TV. The flat isn't very big, but it has a brick-lined utility room that stretches under the pavement on the street, which I use as my walk-in wardrobe. The living area is divided between the kitchen at one end and the lounge at the other, with a hallway leading to the bathroom and bedroom. The bedroom is in an extension and looks out on a small L-shaped garden with raised decking and palm trees, which my father created in the new millennium when he heard on *Gardeners' Question Time* that summer droughts would turn all gardens into deserts.

Since then it seems to have created its own microclimate. The hardy banana plants bear fruit, stubby little bananas that I've never been tempted to eat, then having thrown their energy into fruiting and fulfilling their mission, they give up and die and a new plant grows. All this happens without any help from me apart from a quick swaddle in the winter with gardening fleece.

The foliage is pretty to look out on and it's fairly low maintenance. My father rings me up now and then to remind me to do the 'brown-bitting', as he calls it, which means cutting off the dead bits so that the palms look respectably green – it's something I generally put off until just before my parents visit.

What else? I've got good neighbours. Above me lives Lucy Mills, an actor. The top floor is occasionally inhabited by a retired Welsh couple who travel a lot.

As well as my pitch in Camden Market, I sell clothes online. As a hobby it was fun, but as an actual source of income it's not going that well, to be honest. The main problem is, I don't like sending dresses out into a void. I like to know the person they're going to; their shape, their colouring, their temperament.

The returns are a problem. Basically, women are now a different shape from what they used to be. And even though I write down the measurements of each garment along with a 'will this fit you' exact measurement guide, people really can't be bothered to use a tape measure – does anyone even have a tape measure these days? I give the approximate equivalent dress size (this will roughly fit a size 10 or 12), but even if it does fit, that doesn't mean it'll necessarily suit a person. If shoppers like the look of something onscreen, they'll give it a try and then send it back if it's not suitable. This means that my income is worryingly unstable from day to day. It's not a good feeling to be solvent at the beginning of the week and then over the next few days have to return the money and go back to square one.

And people aren't always honest. Sometimes the clothes come back worn, or splashed with red wine, or smelling of cigarette smoke. And if I point this out in a phone call they'll argue that I've 'sold them as preowned so obviously . . . blah blah blah'. And that's the reason for the one-star stroppy reviews that say if it had been possible to give less than one star they would have, because I was rude or reluctant to refund the money.

One of the main selling points of wearing vintage is that the piece is a one-off. It's also one of the main drawbacks; the popular dresses are snapped up quickly and that's another reason my ratings are low – it's often down to disgruntled shoppers.

It's hard work being self-employed, but since I lost my dream job as a personal stylist, this is my plan B. And that's where I'm at now; trying to make it work. My long-term aim is to have a solid customer base of people to shop for. I love that feeling you get when you see a garment that brings to mind a person, when you find a dress that's totally them, and all you want to do is reunite them.

In Camden Market at the weekends, it's crazy. One month into my new venture, I've had a couple of really good days, which keep me going. A lot of gorgeous girls come through looking for something original to wear – model agency scouts find a lot of new faces in Camden – but the customers I like best are the ones who are shy and uncertain and who dress for comfort in safe colours: grey, beige, brown. They look warily at my stall as they hurry past, and then come back and try not to catch my eye. What keeps me going is when they find something and suddenly see themselves through new eyes. They are my dream customers.

Unfortunately, I don't come across them very often.

I trundle the case up the horse ramp from the towpath and halfway along my street, I bump it down the steps to the basement.

The first thing I do is hang the dresses up in the utility room under the pavement. There's no storage at my stall, which means I have to pack and unpack my stock every day.

While I'm getting on with this, vaguely thinking of my encounter with David Westwood, I hear myself saying *'Any relation to Vivienne?'* in that cringy way and David Westwood laughing, *'No. Sorry.'*

And then my thoughts switch to the old woman wearing Chanel and red lipstick, model slim in her black-and-white Chanel suit, perfect in it, and that approving expression in her eyes when she saw me.

Unpacking a Comme des Garçons dress that still hasn't sold on the stall after a month, I shake the creases out and put it on my mannequin, Dolly. With her moulded black hair and rosebud lips, Dolly seems particularly supercilious and unhelpful today. I bought her from Blustons in Kentish Town when it closed down. Blustons was famous for the Fifties-style showstopping red-and-white polka-dot halterneck dress in the window that Dolly modelled wonderfully for many years.

I move Dolly into the light and photograph her for the website. My phone rings and I pick up to my father, who tells me they are having dinner with the Bennetts and that they'll be staying at the flat overnight. Oh joy!

First, this means I'll be sleeping on the sofa. Secondly, I'll have to tell them that I've lost my job – I've so far managed to put this off for a month by keeping our phone calls short.

There's nothing wrong with my father; he's a decent enough guy and he'd probably understand if I told him the whole story. But my mother's a different matter. I'm always uncomfortable with her, never able to relax. She modelled in the Seventies, at the time when models dictated the popularity of women's fashion, and my love of clothes has totally come from her. She never reached the worldwide popularity of models Jerry Hall and Christie Brinkley, but for a while she moved in the right circles, and the glitter and glamour of those times has never faded for her – she still has every copy of *Elle*, *Cosmopolitan* and *Vogue* magazines in which she featured.

When it became obvious in my teens that I was too short to be a fashion model – I overheard her tell a friend, regretfully, that I'd inherited my father's looks and her brains – I thought it would please her if I studied fashion design. But at St Martin's, the more I found out about the great designers, the more certain I was that I could never equal them. As a daughter, I'm an all-round disappointment and losing my job doesn't help.

To take my mind off my worries, I call my boyfriend, Mick, who's in Amsterdam with his band, just to say hello. It goes to voicemail, so I leave him a message to say hi.

Mick and I have been dating for nine months in a friends-with-benefits kind of way. We met at Bestival on the Isle of Wight. He's got red hair and a beard that covers most of his very beautiful face. He's a sound engineer and spends a lot of time travelling. Sometimes I meet up with him somewhere like Hamburg or Paris, and when he's in London he stays over and we have fun together, but other than that, I don't know where the relationship is heading, if anywhere. We both like it the way it is. He's keen on the idea of free spirits; figuratively and literally – no commitment and drinks on the house. His job means that he's not home a lot, but I don't mind. Honestly, it suits me, too.

In a flurry of activity, I make up my bed for my parents with fresh linen, do a bit of desultory tidying, spray the place with Febreze, and then I go shopping for vodka, Worcestershire sauce, tomato juice and celery so I can make some Bloody Marys to welcome my parents with. It's 'their tipple', as they put it, and because of the tomato juice element they knock it back as if it's a health food, which is fine with me.

As a family we like each other a lot better after a drink.

I start watching television and around ten thirty, I give up on my welcoming committee duties and fall asleep.

I wake up as I hear them coming down the steps sometime later and listen to the key rattling in the lock. In my lowest moods I decide I'll ask for that key back, 'for a friend', an excuse I've used before, but they seem to have a little stash of them in reserve in case I absentmindedly forget who owns the place.

With a wide smile of welcome, I jump to my feet and there's my father in a Burberry trench coat, carrying an overnight bag and holding the door for my mother, who comes in with her cream hair blending with her fur-trimmed cream cape, fluttering, elegant and distant.

'Hi! Hi! Come in!' I say, even though they're already very much inside.

I don't recognise my mother at first. Without a shadow of a doubt, even despite my habit of scrutinising everyone, I would have passed her in the street.

My father has mentioned my mother's 'tweaks', as he calls them, and I realise that one of them has involved filling the dimple in her chin. I have the very same dimple and now she's got rid of hers . . . What does that mean? We both have the same wide mouth too, only hers is now poutier, even though she'd pouted perfectly adequately with the old one. And her eyes, which had been large and round, are smaller, as if her real face is sitting some distance behind the one she's currently wearing. She has the eyeholes of Melania Trump.

She looks me up and down without a word, taking in my pencil skirt and white silk blouse. If she could have frowned, she would have. She recoils with a gasp when she sees Dolly. Overreacting is an affectation she's developed.

'You've still got that ugly old thing,' she says.

I cover up Dolly's ears. 'Don't offend her, she'll come and get you in the night.'

My mother pretends not to hear.

'Bloody Marys,' I say cheerfully, sweeping my hand in the direction of the kitchen island as if I'm introducing them to each other.

'Thank you, darling,' my father says, putting his hands on my shoulders briefly in what passes as a hug.

'It's warm in here,' my mother remarks in a troubled way. She looks around with the restlessness of discontent, fanning her strange and unfamiliar face. 'Isn't it warm?'

It isn't, actually, because the heating went off at ten, but my mother's menopausal, so I agree with her. 'It's been very sunny today and hot air sinks, doesn't it?'

'It rises,' my father says.

'It must be affecting us on its way up again,' I say brightly. Honestly, I've no idea who I am when I'm with my parents. They seem to bring out my inner inanity. When I'm with them, they're the grown-ups and I regress to some attitude of despicable girlishness that isn't really me at all.

I stir my drink with my celery stick, mixing in the spices and turning it dark brown. Wow, it's strong.

They sit on the sofa with a sigh and I perch on the footstool opposite them with an eagerness I don't feel. 'How are the Bennetts?' These are the old friends they've had dinner with.

'Oh, you *know*,' my mother says dismissively. 'Ruth drinks too much.' She pulls her cape around her and gulps hers down. 'How's work?' she asks with an emphasis on *work*. Her voice is hoarse and it catches in her throat. 'Still dressing people? However would they manage to go out in public without you?'

That's sarcasm, that is, but it gives me the chance to look at her properly without appearing to stare. 'How would they go out in public without me? Naked, I suppose,' I reply, also with sarcasm.

'Have people got no taste of their own?' my mother asks.

I take a large gulp of my drink and wipe my mouth with the back of my hand in a show of reckless bravado. 'Well, you don't have to worry about people's taste anymore, because I've been fired.' I'd been dreading breaking this bit of news to them but now, ta-da! It's done!

I brace myself for some yelling, because being with them is as nerve-racking as living on the edge of a volcano, but unusually for my parents they seem at a loss for words.

'Fern, Fern.' My father closes his eyes and shakes his head in despair. He looks more resigned than surprised. 'You were *fired*? Why?'

I give them the short version of the story.

'When did this happen?'

'A month ago.'

'And you're only telling us now?'

They glance at each other over their drinks. I've confirmed their deepest fears about me.

'What are you going to do?' my father asks. 'Are you getting Jobseeker's Allowance?'

'No.' I wipe the condensation off my glass with my thumb. 'I'm concentrating on my vintage clothing company. I'm a fashion curator.'

'Really?' My mother looks at me with a flicker of animation and for a moment we connect briefly with a small spark of mutual passion that makes my spirits lift.

My father, too, looks hopeful. 'You've got business premises?'

'I've got a stall in Camden Market,' I tell them.

They freeze. It's as if we've got some kind of satellite time-lapse going on; it takes them a few seconds for the horrible implications to sink in.

All empathy wiped clean once more, my mother says suspiciously, 'You're telling us you're a market trader?' as if it's some elaborate story I've made up to make a fool of her.

I take a business card out of my wallet, which depicts me standing against a wall of flowers in a Sixties minidress. 'Look!' I say. 'That dress is Pucci. You had one like that, didn't you?'

She knows I'm trying to get around her and she doesn't reply.

Some vague desperation for that old connection makes me persevere. 'Gorgeous, isn't it? Marilyn Munro was buried in Pucci, you know.'

'I'm assuming not in this specific dress.'

Ha ha, she's hilarious, my mother.

She reads the business card slowly, at arm's-length, too proud for reading glasses. 'Fern Banks Vintage.' She hands it back to me and sighs, summing up my enterprise with her own brand of snobbery. 'In other words, you're selling people's cast-offs.'

That hurts.

I reply lightly, forcing a smile. 'That's one way of putting it.'

'And you hope to make a living this way?' my father asks.

'Yes, I do. I never pay over the odds. I look for styles and buy diffusion lines, nothing too out there, just clothes for women to look good in.'

'As opposed to?'

'Look . . .' I'm talking too fast and too defensively, I know, but I want them to understand that this is something I can make a go of. 'This is something I'm actually good at. And I'm building a decent client list.' I'm stretching the truth a bit here, obviously. But it's early days.

A deep weariness has come over them.

*See?* I think bitterly. *Dressing people up in a department store doesn't seem such a bad job now, does it?*

My mother expresses her disapproval by emanating a dense and disappointed silence.

I play with a button on the Barcelona footstool. The silence is just starting to get uncomfortable, when: 'How's Mick?' my father asks casually, breaking it.

That didn't take long, did it? 'He's fine! He sends his love.' I say that to annoy them. It's not the kind of thing that Mick would do, send his love to my parents. They've only met once, briefly, on my birthday, and he wasn't what they wanted for me. What he thought of them, he didn't say. He never gives them a second thought.

They digest my comment for a moment.

'Your mother and I have been talking about the flat,' my father says, crossing one leg over the other.

'Oh, really?' I feel nervous, as if I'm no longer on solid ground, and I stare at his feet. For a moment I think that what I'm seeing is his pale bare ankle, but no, he's wearing beige socks.

'The reason we're keeping it in our name, apart from the issue of capital gains tax, is because we feel it's financially safer. For you, you understand,' he adds.

'How so?'

He and my mother exchange a look.

'Have you thought,' my mother says, 'that Mick might simply be out for what he can get?'

This is a brand-new put-down out of a whole array of criticisms. I mean, Mick couldn't possibly like me for my company, my looks and the fact the sex is good, could he? No. He's after my flat. Correction: *their* flat. I take another mouthful of my drink. My eyes water. It hits the back of my nose like mustard powder. It's more like a punishment than a cocktail.

'He's got his own house,' I point out. 'In Harpenden.'

That shakes them.

'Actually his *own*?' my father asks dubiously.

'Yes. Actually his own.' I've got a decent imagination, but even I couldn't invent a house in Harpenden.

My mother gives me the look she uses when she suspects me of lying. I think of getting up to show her photographs of it on my phone, but I change my mind and sink back down again because honestly, it's not worth the effort.

I crunch on my celery stick and look at her face with those new, strange eyes and wonder what my father thinks about it. The work she's had done ages her. Only people afraid of losing their looks have that kind of extreme appearance, the kind that makes them look stretched and plumped and filled and tightened. When you see a face like that you immediately put them in the category of the middle-aged. When I was a personal stylist I saw the same shiny foreheads and immobile mouths on a daily basis. It rarely made women look young. It made them look as if the humanity had been taken out of them.

My parents are leaning towards each other on the red sofa, still recovering from the Harpenden house revelation, forcing them to come up with some new reason for protecting me from Mick or protecting the flat from me. Time to change the subject.

'I saw an interesting woman today. You'd have liked her,' I say to my mother. 'She was wearing Chanel.'

'You sold her Chanel?' My mother brightens, visibly impressed. 'Is she anyone we'd know?'

She's got the wrong end of the stick, but I don't want to ruin it, so I smile brightly. 'I'm afraid I can't say. Client confidentiality. Can I refresh your glass?'

Vodka, tomato juice, Worcestershire sauce, Tabasco sauce, celery salt, fresh celery. Glasses refreshed, I sit down again on the red footstool and the hit of my drink is so strong that for a moment I have the horrible feeling I'm going to topple off it.

'Is she a television personality?' my mother persists eagerly, hankering after the days when she, too, was a name and hung out with the stars.

I smile enigmatically, not wanting to ruin it for her.

'I can guess who it is,' she says smugly, mollified by her own imagination.

The doorbell rings. In my semi-drunk state it doesn't sound like the doorbell. It sounds like an alarm, harsh and urgent and motivating, and the three of us are galvanised out of our alcohol-numbed torpor into action, struggling to our feet in uncomprehending panic.

'Who is it?' my mother asks, keeping her voice low as if we're in hiding.

I open the door and it's my upstairs neighbour, Lucy. She comes in full of drunken merriment. 'Hey! I saw your light on and I—' She suddenly notices my parents. 'Oh, hello!'

I can guess what my mother is thinking behind her frozen face. She hates people who drop in unexpectedly. She thinks it's the height of rudeness.

'Bloody Mary?' I ask Lucy.

'Ooh, yes. Is this a party?'

Lucy's got curly blonde hair and the kind of cheerful superficiality that actors are good at during those times when they're not talking about a new role. They take acting seriously, but they treat life with a very light touch, which is a welcome relief if you belong to my family. Lucy's wearing a black unstructured asymmetric dress with a lot of zips. Comme des Garçons. I know because I sold it to her. She's playing Lady Macbeth at The Gatehouse and she still has her stage make-up on. She's electrified with post-performance adrenaline.

Lucy's ambition is to direct. She's been in all the best crime dramas: *Scott & Bailey*, *Silent Witness*, *Endeavour*, *Shetland*. Whenever she's in something, she invites me upstairs so we can watch it together on her flatscreen TV and she points out the flaws in the acting, things that I'd never have noticed – like when someone fluffs a line, or winces before the knife's been raised, or fails to respond to the scene.

And that's the way she's looking at me now, slightly critically, as if I'm not playing the part of host very well, so I introduce her to my parents and while I mix another jug of Bloody Marys she fills us in on how the night has gone. The theatre was packed. There had been a heckler. The audience was so caught up that at the end there was a long, thick silence after Malcolm's closing lines.

'Malcolm McDowell?' my mother asks hopefully, ready to claim acquaintance because he bought her a drink once.

'*Malcolm*. Duncan's son,' Lucy says. '"This dead butcher and his fiend-like queen".'

My mother's disappointed. 'A dead butcher?' she echoes, confused.

'He's talking about *Macbeth*! The fiend-like queen – that's me. And they're holding up Macbeth's head and this orange light comes over them – it's like an Isis video. Cheers!'

Lucy brings a whole new element to the night. There are some things that my parents will only say to me, which shows some kind of loyalty, I suppose, so the conversation stops being personal. Lucy sits on the footstool and I sit on the Barcelona chair while my parents loll on the sofa. We've reached the hazy stage of drunkenness where words become particularly meaningful.

Lucy's still talking about the play and her excitement about the concept of the 'Pahr off sgestion'.

We're momentarily perplexed but rooting for the concept anyway. 'Par? Path?' I prompt helpfully.

She takes a couple of shots at it.

'Parf – parf –.' She takes another sip of the drink to clear her head and leans forward. 'Power of suggestion,' she says, exaggerating the words at us as if we're deaf. 'The three Weird Sisters, psychics as we call them, I play second psychic as well . . . anyway, the thing is, they put the idea into Macbeth's head. They plant it there. Hadn't occurred to him to become the Thane of Cawdor before then but he thought, you know what? I can do that. See what I mean? It's dark, right?'

'Aha! Brainwashing,' my father says.

'Not brainwashing.'

'Visualisation,' I say.

'You see?' Lucy asks happily.

'They didn't read the future, they just gave him a goal to aim for,' my father says.

'Yes!'

My mother's face turns my way. 'What are your goals, Fern?'

'To make a success of my business.'

She remains unimpressed. 'That's *it*?'

'Well,' I shrug, 'the Thane of Cawdor thing's already gone.'

My mother hates flippancy. 'She had so much promise,' she says, turning to Lucy for support. 'She's thrown it all away. She needs to do more with her life.'

'Why does she?' Lucy asks. 'She's got a nice life. You've got a nice life, Fern, haven't you?'

'Yes.' I want to hug her.

My mother says icily, 'She's got a *market* stall.'

Cheerfully unaware, Lucy replies, 'I know. Great, isn't it? There was a waiting list and everything! She was really lucky to get it, weren't you, Fern?'

My mother's not used to people disagreeing with her. She glares at Lucy from the depths of her narrow eye sockets. When Lucy remains oblivious to the silent death stare, my mother stands up and announces coldly, 'I'm going to bed.'

Retires: hurt.

'Goodnight,' we say in unison.

As she stands, the fur on her cape quivers as if it's alive – *and about to throttle her*.

The thought comes into my head with no particular emotion or malice.

My mother goes through the door that leads to the bathroom and bedroom and closes it quite firmly.

'Was it something I said?' Lucy asks, surprised.

My father looks at his watch. 'My word! It *is* getting awfully late. It's almost midnight.' He puts his glass down and stands up.

I stand up, too, and he gives me a hug, a proper hug, and for a moment I feel his soft, shaved cheek against mine.

He says goodnight to Lucy and follows my mother to bed.

'Insane!' Lucy whispers thrillingly, widening her eyes at me after he's gone. 'Are they always like this?'

I think about it. 'Actually, yeah.'

'What has she got against market stalls?'

I shrug and try to laugh it off. 'She was hoping I'd be a model, like her. And then, as I'm only five foot five, she was happy to settle for me being a fashion designer.'

'Oh, I get it. You're not living up to her motherly expectations. "What are your goals, Fern?"' Lucy says, in an accurate imitation, and adds in her ordinary voice, 'And that whole Malcolm McDowell thing – what was *that* all about?'

'She met him when he was in *Caligula*,' I say gloomily. 'But nothing came of it. That's my mother. Always hoping for the best and always disappointed.'

We stare at each other for a moment and then for no reason at all, we suddenly start to laugh, muffling it with our fists on our mouths.

'And the dead butcher bit. Did she think Macbeth actually *was* a butcher?'

The tears are rolling down my face. 'Don't!'

'"She had so much promise and she's thrown it all away . . ."'

'Stop it!'

'You know what?' Lucy says, giggling weakly. 'You should do stand-up. You've got enough material.'

'I *could* do stand-up.'

'That'll teach her. This could be your Thane of Cawdor moment.' She wipes her eyes and raises her glass. 'Happy to help.' She looks at the time and finishes her drink. 'I'd better go too, I suppose. Time to take my Night Nurse medicine.

I'm incubating a cold.' To prove it, she sneezes into the elbow of her black dress. Her zips jingle.

'Bless you,' I say, dodging out of the way as she checks for damage – I don't move far enough to be rude but I do try to get far enough away to avoid the germs that might have escaped around her slim arm, because what could be worse than catching a cold at this crucial time in my business career?

(Plenty, as it turns out.)

I see Lucy out into the cool night and she totters up the wooden steps, waving all the way, then curses softly for a few moments outside her front door while she finds her keys.

I lock the door and stand in the now spinning centre of the flat that I live in, with my parents tucked up in the bedroom, my friend safely upstairs.

I wonder if the night will have repercussions. My mother's very good at keeping a grudge going, but she can only keep it going as long as we're together and they're going back in the morning.

I brush my teeth in the kitchen sink then make up the sofa, switch the lights off and wrap myself up in my duvet.

Surprisingly, I sleep well.

# LOT 4

*A sky-blue silk satin Sixties-style A-line dress with
bracelet-length sleeves and feather trim to neckline and cuffs,
scalloped knee-length hem, unlabelled.*

I wake up next morning wound up tightly in my duvet and
all the events of the previous night come tumbling back into
my head, starting with the alarming fact that my parents are
asleep in my bedroom.

The sun is flickering in my eyes, the light filtered by the
lacy green leaves of the tree fern in the garden. The sky is a
clear blue and it was a frock of that same pure, uplifting colour
that lost me my dream job.

At least I've told my parents now, so that's one problem out
of the way.

I'd been dreading telling them – it's true, my mother's had
many disappointments in her life, not just the fact she ended
up marrying my father instead of Malcolm McDowell because
she failed to become as famous as Jerry Hall. I've disappointed
her too, and I'm not sure it's anything I can put right.

I studied fashion at St Martin's, but not just to please my
mother – I genuinely had ambitions of becoming a fashion
designer. Like her, *because* of her, I've always loved clothes.
I've been buying vintage clothing since my early teens.

I enjoyed studying the construction of the pieces as much as wearing them.

But in my final year, compared with my fellow students, I knew that I didn't have the imagination or the vision to design clothes that were often avant-garde and unwearable for the average person. I lacked the sheer sense of performance that it takes to bring a collection to the catwalk. To be honest, I'd been winging it anyway, because my passion is for clothes that make a person look good. Otherwise, what's the point? Me, I always choose style over innovation.

After graduating, I spent a few years in fashion sales and I was thrilled when I landed the job as personal stylist in a large department store in Oxford Street.

One of the first things we needed to know about a client was their budget and then we were encouraged to stretch it – although, not all our clients were rich.

There are many reasons why people need help shopping for clothes. These days, people are less confident about their appearance than ever. Sometimes they don't have the confidence to try something new. Sure, they can choose the labels that also have a line of accessories like beaded bags and matching hats, but although it makes shopping easier, it's self-defeating in a way. There's always the risk that someone else is going to show up wearing exactly the same thing and that they'll both have to spend the whole occasion keeping as far away from each other as possible to avoid looking like middle-aged twins.

Fashions change. Partners aren't always helpful enough – or patient enough – to give an honest second opinion. After two outfits, a man will say that anything looks great, just so that he can be done with the whole boring business and go home. Friends aren't always tactful and those who follow trends are the worst. There's nothing more demoralising than shopping with a fashionista who pushes into the dressing room, tries on the stuff that her friend has just turned down and looks fabulous in everything.

As a personal stylist, my job was to make my clients look in the mirror and see themselves differently. I was supportive, admiring and knowledgeable. For a period of two hours, I was the perfect friend; bringing coffee or prosecco, zipping and unzipping, encouraging them to *own* the clothes – can you sit in it? Eat in it? Dance in it? And then I'd get them thinking about accessories: bags, shoes, scarves, pendants, fur cuffs, sunglasses – the beautiful final touches that *make* a look. It was a brilliant feeling to see a woman admiring herself in the mirror with happy disbelief – and keep on looking. For me, that was the ultimate job satisfaction. I discovered I, too, had the ability to see women through their own eyes and boost their confidence by transforming them into someone new.

The client who got me fired was an elderly man shopping for his wife. His name was Kim Aston. He arrived for the two-hour appointment, a neat, slightly built man about my own height, wearing a suit and a bright, multicoloured silk tie. His greying hair was short and swept back from his forehead.

He looked nervously at the glittering chandeliers and the ornate chairs and faced me with a frown. 'I was just about to leave,' he said as soon as I introduced myself.

'Are you in a hurry?' I asked.

'No. It's just that—' He looked up at the enormous chandelier again as if its blatant, lavish extravagance was putting him off. 'I didn't think it was going to be so—' He shrugged and tailed off.

I smiled understandingly, because I knew what he meant. Our department was ostentatiously luxurious. Cream carpets, mirrors, drapes. We were selling the experience: this is what it's like to be rich and have a personal shopper, a valet, an attendant, someone to admire you and to make you look the best you can be while you sit back and enjoy it then hand over a credit card at the end. We were selling the promise that all this could be theirs. And for two hours it *was* theirs to enjoy. But Kim Aston found it intimidating and I could understand that, too.

I said, 'Would you prefer coffee or tea with your glass of champagne?'

That's how we did it. We took it for granted that the client would have coffee or tea and a glass of champagne, to relax.

'Tea, please.'

I tapped in the order on my iPad and led him through to the dressing room where the clothes I'd chosen for his sick wife were hanging.

On the telephone he'd been quite sure of what he wanted. Loose-fitting dresses, elasticated waists, silky fabrics and bright colours – size 14, he thought, or maybe a little bigger. I'd chosen six for his wife that I thought she might like, based on the image I'd built of her, but in the dressing room I realised I'd got it wrong because he looked at my selection anxiously, as if he'd already bought them all on impulse and realised he'd made a terrible mistake.

My colleague Mario carried the tray of drinks in and put it on a gilt, glass-topped table next to the cream velvet and gilt chair.

I handed Mr Aston his glass. There was nothing like a glass of fizz to boost the confidence of a wary shopper.

He held it at eye level and stared through the bubbles as if he were in a dream.

'You said your wife likes bright colours,' I said, 'but if you'd prefer a more muted palette, I do have some things in mind

34

that fulfil your criteria. What do you think of this? It's silk jersey, very comfortable to wear and not restrictive,' I said, showing him a red-and-blue Diane von Furstenberg wrap-around dress.

He smiled faintly as if amused. 'We've been married forty-five years,' he said. 'It goes by very quickly.' He looked at me closely. 'You're too young to know that yet. It's all ahead of you, all that potential. For my wife, she's reached the finish line and she's having her bottle of water and her banana.'

I laughed, because it was a nice way of putting it.

'She's still interested in fashion,' I said, 'which is lovely.'

He sighed. 'I'm not sure that she is interested in fashion. She's not *fashionable*,' he said thoughtfully, sipping his champagne, 'she wouldn't enjoy being called that at all. She's a very practical woman. She's always had short hair.' He looked at me as if expecting me to comment favourably on this example of her practicality.

'It's often best to stick with a hairstyle that you know suits you,' I pointed out. 'Some women have the face for it.'

'And it dries quickly,' he said. 'She has it trimmed every six weeks.'

'Good! So it keeps its shape.'

He put his drink down and took the dress from me. His face softened. 'Don't get me wrong, I *like* this one,' he said, worried he'd offended me, holding it up high as if his wife were a tall woman, a woman he was used to looking up to. 'But no. This isn't it. It's rather plain, you see.'

I smiled. I wasn't done yet. 'I'll put it over here,' I said and then I showed him a shocking-pink shift dress with fluted sleeves that was very pretty.

He studied it for a long time, his face expressionless, and finally he gazed at me doubtfully. 'Do you try these on yourself?'

'No. I mean, not unless I'm looking for something personally.' I let the dress hang. 'This fabric is very flattering.'

'You have to wear black, I suppose. All the staff seem to be wearing black. That's the uniform, is it? Black?'

'It is, yes.'

He nodded. 'I've noticed that. The trouble with this is the sleeves. See? These sleeves, they don't seem very practical. They dangle.' Again, he looked at me quickly. 'I was thinking in terms of housework, loading the dishwasher, cooking.'

Once again, I adjusted my image of his wife. She obviously wasn't too ill to do housework. 'This is more of a going-out dress,' I said. 'Does she get to go out much, your wife?'

'She does when she can. She's got two friends about the same age as herself, Mercia and Betty, and they like their classes. University of the Third Age, have you heard of that? No? A lifetime of knowledge and a wealth of experience. Tai chi, watercolours. They had an exhibition in the library.'

'This floral dress is by Chloé. It's a bit looser in style; it's a relaxed fit. It's great that she gets out. Do you paint, too?'

Mr Aston laughed appreciatively. 'No, I don't. I haven't got an artist's eye. The women don't want us hanging around with them; although Betty plays golf sometimes when the weather's fine. Golf is my hobby; although I haven't much of a golfer's eye, either. They've been good friends to Enid. What other frocks have you got there?'

'This is a beautiful silk jersey by DKNY.'

'Animal print,' he said doubtfully. 'I don't know how Enid would feel about animal print. She might find it a little common.' He sat on the cream velvet chair, looked at the dresses and took a deep breath. 'Have you got something a bit more special, with some kind of embellishment? Feathers, ostrich feathers?' he asked hopefully.

He'd taken me by surprise. 'You mean a cocktail dress?' He

hadn't mentioned it in his brief, but this is how it was some-times, clients had to find out first of all what they didn't want before they decided what they *did* want. 'You don't think that any of these are suitable for your wife?'

He shook his head. 'I keep thinking of a frock that feels *special*,' he said, his face creased with the difficulty of trying to explain. 'The kind of frock that'll give a person a lift. A dress to make the eyes sparkle.'

I liked him. 'I know exactly what you mean. I'll put these away for now and bring something more suitable for evening. More champagne?'

Mr Aston held up his glass. He was beginning to relax at last, but I couldn't help but wonder whether the practical, short-haired Mrs Aston would appreciate a feathery cocktail dress as much as he seemed to think. It was difficult to judge without meeting her personally. I'd never had anyone shop by proxy before.

I carried the dresses out and asked Mario to refresh Mr Aston's drink while I searched our stock for cocktail dresses and feathers. We had a black feather cape and an ivory ostrich feather bolero and I chose a couple of little chiffon dresses to go with them then headed back to the dressing room.

Mr Aston looked up hopefully, but his face immediately fell.

'They're not quite what I had in mind,' he said, stroking the ostrich feathers wistfully. 'But they are beautiful, there's no denying it.' He sighed deeply.

I felt I'd let him down. 'From all the things you've seen, Mr Aston, is there anything you'd like to look at again?'

'No . . . I don't think so,' he said wistfully, 'but I'm very pleased that I came.'

'Your wife will be disappointed,' I said. She wasn't the only one. I was disappointed myself.

'I'll relate the experience to her in detail,' he said, finishing his wine and cold tea and looking around him as though he was memorising it for her.

I didn't want him to leave yet. I wasn't used to failing with a client. I always had a sense of what they wanted but, more importantly, under normal circumstances I usually knew fairly quickly what would suit them. And, suddenly, it came to me. And after one hundred minutes together, I suddenly felt in tune with Mr Aston's wife's taste.

Don't get me wrong; I was scrupulously fair about it. It was only when I'd absolutely exhausted all other in-store possibilities that I'd suggested the under-the-counter deal.

I'd recently bought a satin sky-blue dress with a feather trim and a scalloped hem from a charity shop and it was his wife's size, a 14. It was a playful dress and as I'd passed the window, the beautiful blue had made me smile. I guessed it was from the Sixties and I wondered if Mr Aston was nostalgic for the days of his youth, and whether the dress was a message, a compliment to his wife, Enid. The dress was to say to her: *this is how I see you.*

I showed him a photograph of it on my phone.

'Oh, that's more like it.' He brightened immediately. 'I'd like to see that,' he said.

'The thing is, it's from my personal collection,' I explained, 'but we could meet up somewhere for you to have a look at it if you're interested.'

'When?'

'This evening, if you're free?'

'Here?'

'Not here but – where would suit you?'

'St John's Wood.'

'Carluccio's, then?'

And that's what we did. We met in Carluccio's.

He did love the dress, as I knew he would. He loved the frothy abundance of delicate feathers, the innocent blue, the rich gleam of the satin. He thought it was perfect. We did an under-the-counter deal.

He was so pleased that he wrote a lovely letter to the store to commend me on my kindness, thoughtfulness and total dedication to my work. And as a result, I was dismissed for gross misconduct. It was ironic that after that moment of triumph, I lost my job.

Anyway – where that memory came from is the fact the sky, from the sofabed where I'm lying, perfectly matches the colour of that feathery cocktail dress.

I get up reluctantly and put the kettle on, swaddling it with tea cloths to muffle the sound of boiling because the longer my parents sleep in, the better, as far as I'm concerned.

I start thinking about the woman in Chanel and that look in her eye that said, *aren't we wonderful!*

I've seen her twice, so I think she's local. It's possible I'll see her again. She's hard to miss.

Consoled by the idea, I quietly make myself a mug of instant coffee, black, and retreat to the sofa.

I can hear whispering and the creak of the bedroom floor, and slippered feet padding to the bathroom. I hear the bathroom door closing. After a few moments, the lavatory flushes.

I stare warily at the slowly opening door.

It's my father.

'Morning,' he says, rubbing the bags under his eyes. 'Your mother would like to know whether you've got Alka-Seltzer.'

'Ah. I have.' I've got a whole kitchen drawer dedicated to ailments of all descriptions. I'm very susceptible to the power of the placebo effect. Once I've bought something from the pharmacist, I miraculously find I'm cured of whatever it was that was bothering me. As a result, the Alka-Seltzer has passed its sell-by date, but I drop the tablets into a glass and add water.

'Aren't you working today?'

'I have Mondays and Tuesdays off. They're the quietest days.' The tablets fizz and tumble merrily up and down in the glass, and my father takes them back to the bedroom.

I get dressed, put the duvet and pillows away, and rearrange the fruit bowl on the table, ready for breakfast.

I've taken the croissants out of the freezer, so I heat up the oven and make real coffee in the KRUPS coffee machine, because they both detest instant.

I can hear Lucy walking around in the flat above me. I've always liked the sound of neighbours – it's friendly.

Next thing I hear is my shower switching on, and twenty minutes later my mother emerges and sits by the table. She stares out at the garden without looking at me to make it clear she hasn't forgiven me for working on a market stall.

I feel the old sense of dread at her disapproval coming over me. But I can make it work, I know I can. I'll prove it to her that I've made the right choices in life.

I make her a coffee and put the croissants on a baking tray while she continues to pretend I'm invisible. It's quite nice, actually, not having to talk. Like breakfast in a silent order at a monastery.

My father comes in and drinks his coffee in silence, smiling at me a couple of times to show who's side he's secretly on while publicly showing his alliance to her. Not that I blame him; he has to live with her, after all.

They leave about ten and I hug my father and kiss my mother on her plumped-up, wrinkle-free cheek, then I wave them off feeling suddenly light-hearted at being free.

Once they've gone, I turn on my laptop and see that I've had some new orders in. A couple of the clients are names I recognise from my database and one is new. I wheel my clothing rails out of the utility room and into the lounge because the utility room is too small to stand up straight in.

I'm looping a price tag from a wooden hanger, when my contact lenses start to bother me. I blink. Everything seems hazy and my eyes begin to itch. I squeeze them shut and wonder if I've caught Lucy's cold already. Is that possible? I go to the bathroom and drip Thealoz eye drops into my reddened eyes and feel much better. Back in the lounge, though, they get worse again. I look around. The room is strangely misty.

There's a loud thudding overhead from Lucy's flat. I hear her front door open and slam, and down the outside steps she comes, boom-boom-boom! And she's thumping on my door with her fists. 'Fern!' she cries dramatically. 'Fern, are you in there?'

I open it, standing well back in case she sneezes on me again. 'What's up?'

'My flat's on fire,' she says breathlessly, eyes wide, damp hair clinging to her forehead. She's wearing a black towel. That's it. Just the towel.

'Really?'

To confirm it, my smoke alarm goes off, so I grab my phone, trench coat and my red lipstick. After shutting the door to muffle the noise, we dash outside and up the steps into the street. We stand together on the pavement, hanging onto the black railings and staring at the house nervously, looking for flames.

A middle-aged man comes towards us with a black Labrador on a blue retractable lead. His eyes settle on Lucy, barefoot and clad in the black towel. Then his gaze rests on me for a moment and swiftly returns to Lucy before he politely passes us without a word.

'Lucy, here, take my coat.'

'No, thanks, Fern. It's a better look to be standing outside a burning house wearing a black towel, dramatically speaking.' She looks up at her window again and nudges me with her elbow. 'Have you called the fire service yet?'

I put my hand in my coat pocket, feeling for my phone, and hesitate. Out here in the fresh air, the house looks perfectly normal and I happen to know that Lucy just loves a drama. Well, she would, being an actor. I can't see any smoke or flames and I wonder if it's burnt itself out already.

'Lucy, how big is the fire, exactly?' I ask her sceptically.

She stares at me through the damp blonde strands of her fringe. 'What do you mean, how *big* is it? Fires spread, you know! They spread like wildfire. Hence the saying.'

'Mmm. Mmm. What's the difference between a fire and wildfire?'

'Give me that.' She grabs my phone from me and phones the emergency services.

Staring up at her sash window, I can now see grey smoke opaquing the glass and leaking out around the edges, fraying the sky above our heads. Down in the basement beneath it, I can see clearly into my lounge and my heart jumps a beat. 'Hey! My clothes are in there!'

'Don't do it, Fern!' she said, holding me back ineffectually with her free hand. 'It's not worth it!'

'My stock! It's all I've got,' I say as I dash back down the stairs and let myself back into the smoke-alarm-screaming din of the house.

I'm just going in for the clothing rails, but once inside the flat, the noise sends my adrenaline up a notch. The atmosphere has turned from a haze into a smog. I look at the ceiling and see smoke rings coming out of the spotlights. I struggle to push the clothing rail through the door. The wheels brace themselves against the doorframe, reluctant to leave.

Above the scream of the smoke alarm I hear the duetting wail of the fire engine and the squeal of an ambulance, and above them both, I hear Lucy frantically calling my name with varying emphasis and increasing volume as if this is her last chance for a BAFTA.

Still grappling frantically with the clothing rail, which not long ago had come through that same gap without any problem, I start to cough. In the end I give up and unhook my most expensive pieces then hurry into the hall just as an axe splinters a panel of my front door.

'Oi!' I open it, coughing, full of indignation because I'm going to have to pay for that. 'What did you do that for? I was just about to open it!'

'You could get yourself killed,' he says. 'Get out, now!'

So I do.

I find Lucy sitting in the back of an ambulance having her oxygen levels tested. I look at her bitterly. She's clutching her black towel around her and sobbing beautifully; it's heartfelt but not overdone. The paramedic tests my oxygen levels too, and we're both declared fine with the slight disapproval that the medical profession reserves for malingerers. We get out of the ambulance again and I nurse and juggle my dresses like heavy babies.

It's weird – when you're wearing them the clothes are so light you never notice the weight. But carry a few of them in your arms or in a suitcase and they take on a surprising mass density.

A car pulls up and a *Camden New Journal* photographer gets out with a reporter. And of course when they see Lucy, their jaded expressions totally disappear, because this is a story that writes itself: Lucy in her towel and me in my Lauren Bacall trench coat, scarlet lipstick freshly applied, trying to save my livelihood.

Lucy tells them breathlessly how I dashed into the burning building to save my frocks and in return, appalled by my own recklessness, I tell them how grateful I am that Lucy came to alert me. Then we pose against the backdrop of the fire engine and then against the railings. The photographer vapes so as to get the full smoke effect in the shot and then they reluctantly drive away again in a hurry as a traffic warden approaches.

The paramedics leave and after a while the fire officers take Lucy to one side to talk to her. I can't hear the conversation, but the end result is that Lucy and I can go back into our flats, so I head back down the steps, breathing in the damp and smoky air.

Lucy comes after me and taps my shoulder. 'Fern, it's all my fault, you know,' she says in a small voice.

I look up at her over my armful of clothes. 'Is it? What do you mean?'

She says miserably, 'You know I've got this cold?'

'Ye-es.'

'I was just trying to ease my nasal congestion,' she says as if that explains everything.

I mull it over. 'And?'

'And – the thing is, when I poured eucalyptus oil on the coals of the sauna it ignited in a ball of flame. Apparently, that's what happens.' She shrugs in amazement. 'Who *knew*?'

'Who *knew*?' I stare up at her in disbelief. 'Oil's a fuel, isn't it?' I fleetingly marvel at the fact she has a sauna in her flat.

Back inside, my lounge is ruined, dark with soot, the floor is wet, and it smells of damp and wood smoke.

I rush my rescued clothes through to my bedroom, because that room is still mercifully fresh, then I go back into the lounge, open the windows. With my heart breaking, I inspect the clothing rails for damage. It's not good.

Tears fill my eyes.

The gorgeous clothes that I've so carefully collected are ruined.

The gelatine sequins on my 1920s flapper dresses have dissolved. The colours on my tea dresses have run; my silk dresses are watermarked. Hundreds of pounds worth of stock, ruined. Even worse, I haven't got around to renewing the contents insurance. I come to the sickening realisation that my parents are right. I can't be trusted.

Ironically, my rejects on the rails under the pavement are untouched by smoke and water; these are the clothes with perspiration stains under the arms, torn hems, missing bead-work. The wear and tear that makes the difference between vintage and jumble.

I go back into the lounge and stare around me, devastated.

Wood smoke is a smell you can't get enough of in the autumn. It's the smell of freedom. It's so romantic that you feel you should bottle it.

When it's your home, the novelty quickly wears off. It's so acrid that it clogs my throat. I get out the Febreze and spray it liberally, then I light a Jo Malone candle and call Mick for sympathy.

Mick is concerned and also intensely practical, and that's one of the things I like about him. He listens to my tale of woe and then he asks, in his warm, deep voice, 'Is the electricity still on?'

I switch on the light cautiously with my elbow. 'Yes.'

'Good. You want to hire a dehumidifier to dry the place out,' he suggests. 'Make sure you wipe down the walls to get rid of the soot and take the clothes to the dry cleaners so that you can decide afterwards what's salvageable.'

I hold the phone tight against my face and look around at the ruined room, which has become a travesty of itself. 'Okay,' I say with a wobble in my voice.

'Fern,' he says gently, 'you're all right. That's the main thing.'

I nod, even though he can't see me.

'Do you want to stay at my place? My neighbour has a key.'

For a moment, escaping to his house in Harpenden seems a wonderful option. But I need to be here to get things sorted. 'When are you coming home?' I ask.

His voice moves away from the mouthpiece. 'When are we back, mate? The tenth?' He says in my ear, 'The tenth. Not long.'

'It's two weeks too long for me. I miss you,' I say, desperately hoping he'll tell me he'll come back earlier.

He hasn't seen this needy side of me before. 'Yeah,' is his hesitant reply.

After the call I go into the bathroom and lock myself away to cry in private, devastated about my ruined dresses. I'm feeling lost and totally alone.

As I sit on the loo, absorbing my tears with tissues, I hear an apologetic cough above my head and glance up. Argh! I pat my heart.

'Fern?' Lucy's looking down at me through the hole that has burnt through her floor and my ceiling.

'What?' I say tearfully.

'About this hole,' she says. 'Look, I'm going to put a sheep-skin rug over it, okay?'

That's the problem with actors. It's all about the illusion. 'Okay. Now, could you just please leave me be,' I plead bleakly.

'Sorry,' she says and drags the rug into place. The dust captures the light as it floats lazily down.

# KIM

Meeting Fern Banks on our secret assignation in Carluccio's was the riskiest, most exciting thing that I've done in years. Life was thrilling again! The secrecy! The lies I had to tell Enid!

And the shame of telling them!

My married life is comfortable and to a lot of people that would be an enviable state of affairs, because who doesn't long for comfort, the comfort of the familiar? The older I get, the more the sharp edges rub off my emotions. I've got used to love and a kiss before bedtime, a shorthand for intimacy, a desultory declaration of attachment. I know how to deal with the embarrassment of slicing a shot in a round of golf, of believing the World Wide Web traps people like flies, of watching crime dramas that show people having sex.

Enid used to spare us that by turning the TV off at that sort of thing. She held the remote at the ready, like a gunslinger in the Wild West, permanently prepared to shoot, but I'm in charge of the remote now. If Enid's eyes are closed, I mute the sound and I watch it with my emotions removed. In old age, I've become used to most things.

Enid used to wear stockings once, but now she wears knee-highs. She calls them popsocks, but if you ask for a popsock in Marks & Spencer, they don't know what you mean. They're knee-highs these days. Same thing, different name. I used to be in the flow of things once, but now I feel as if I'm standing still and life is rushing past me and I'll never catch up with it, I'm too old.

I've never had to shop for clothes for Enid; she's not the kind of woman who needs a second opinion. Enid's taste in clothes is conservative but feminine. One thing we both agree on is that trousers on a woman over seventy are invariably unflattering and unnecessary – unless, of course, one is a farmer; we're not unreasonable people.

She knows what she likes. Her clothes are well-made. They'll 'see her out'. I listened to her saying that phrase in dismay. I wanted to buy her something worth living for, but it's a tall order, to buy something to raise the spirits of a woman who's unwell.

When I arranged the appointment with Fern Banks, I began by looking at everything through Enid's eyes, by getting into Enid's head. I can't say I started out with a vision of what I wanted; it just gradually formed in my mind by a process of the elimination of what wasn't suitable. It had to be special! Exciting! Evocative of a time when life was full of expectation. Oh, that frock was elusive!

Meeting Fern Banks in Carluccio's meant leaving Enid for a second time and telling her more lies. I said I was going to the golf club and although I don't go there much since Stan died, Enid didn't question it.

When Fern showed me that blue dress, I knew immediately that it was the one! I felt alive again. I was tingling with excitement that I hadn't felt in a long time! It turned the clock back!

After I bought it, I took it home and as I went through the door, Enid was calling me.

I felt so guilty that I hid it in my golf bag.

# LOT 5

*A pale pink crêpe dress, fit-and-flare style, circa 1975, with plunging neckline and tie waist.*

Taking Mick's advice, I hire a sixteen-litre dehumidifier to dry out the flat. I mop the floors and wash the soot from the walls.

When I go to buy milk, Mr Khan, the newsagent, reassures me that it's a well-known fact that it's only possible for a human to detect a smell for a short amount of time before the nose gets used to it, but sadly that isn't true at all.

I put my front door panel together using outdoor wood filler and my Monsoon loyalty card, which is perfect for smoothing. Despite my efforts, it doesn't look exactly as good as new, but at a cursory glance it doesn't look as if it's been hacked in, either; and it'll look better once it's dry and I've painted it. This isn't something I want to bother my parents with if I don't have to. They're sure to make a crisis out of a drama.

That's where the good news ends.

When I pick up the clothes from the cleaners, the woman is apologetic. They've done their best, but now that it's dry, the gorgeous little fuchsia pink wool suit has shrunk a few sizes. Interestingly, the lining hasn't shrunk at all and it billows like parachute silk out of the sleeves and below the hemline. The Twenties cocktail dresses are drab and insubstantial without their sequins. Their seams have frayed and come undone. I feel a wave of panic coming over me. A few hundred pounds worth of clothes and now they're worthless, unsaleable, and I've just spent a large part of my savings having them cleaned.

When I get to the market at nine o'clock on Wednesday, my suitcase is noticeably lighter. To boost my confidence, I'm wearing a black-and-white check Fifties shirtwaister with padded shoulders and a wide black patent belt. My hair has a side parting, with a heavy wave falling loose over my right eye. It's a look I've taken from Lauren Bacall in the film *To Have and Have Not* with Humphrey Bogart, 1944; ballsy, feminine, utilitarian. My lipstick is MAC: Lady Danger; my favourite bright, true red. My outfit makes me feel able to face the day ahead.

In our shady alley, a light breeze is snapping the canvas walls, carrying with it the mellow sweetness of the breakfast waffle stand.

As I pass it, I notice that the stall next to mine is in the process of being set up for the ten o'clock opening time. It's lined with black fabric, and wooden and Perspex boxes are stacked up neatly inside. There's no sign of the new occupant, though.

I unpack my suitcase, store it under the counter and hang up my surviving dresses, grouping them out so they don't look so sparse. Humming to myself, I fix my banner, Fern Banks Vintage, on the skirt of the stall.

As I'm working, someone comes up behind me.

'Morning, neighbour!' he says.

I turn to greet him and to my surprise, it's David Westwood. Oh, he's gorgeous! I'm struck dumb by his ridiculous good looks. His hair is short at the sides, longer on top, thick and wavy, springing up from his clear brow. His eyebrows are straight and stern. He's wearing black, which makes him look edgy, and I like edginess in a man. His eyes are the deepest blue. Probably contact lenses, I tell myself.

'Hello! What are you doing here?' I ask, feeling flustered and breathless and entirely losing my Lauren Bacall calm.

'I thought about what you said about through traffic,' he replies seriously.

'Did you? Well! Good. Welcome to the neighbourhood.' I'm feeling uncharacteristically buoyant at having a friendly stallholder next to me. We can look out for each other, watch each other's stalls as we're having a quick break . . .

'Have you got a minute?' he asks.

'Sure.'

He beckons me over to his stall. 'Take a look at this.'

With the flick of a switch, the rows of boxes, the source of his illusions, disappear and a constellation of stars shines brightly – the stand has been transformed into the night sky and suddenly we're staring into the universe.

'What do you think?'

'Wow.'

'Yeah.' He looks pleased and he hands me a light box to look at.

I take a neighbourly interest. It's five-sided, wooden, with the light fitting inside.

'See the way the sides fit together?' he says, smoothing it with his thumb. 'These are dovetail joints.'

'Nice!'

'And then . . .' He slots into the front grooves two removable dark blue acrylic panels with a pattern of holes drilled through them. Switching it on, the light shines out to create two constellations side by side.

'Neat. I suppose the idea is to sell the whole set of boxes, so that a person could have a whole night sky for themselves, is that it?'

'No, this is just the display. They're star signs. Like, for instance, you're Virgo and if you happened to know a Sagittarian, I'd slot this one in. See? They make a great engagement present. I can also personalise it with lettering underneath and the date.'

'Romantic,' I say dryly. 'I'm not a Virgo.'

He shrugged. 'Yes, well, you get the idea.'

Putting my face closer to the light box, it *is* like looking at the night sky, if you imagine you're looking at it through a very tiny window or maybe a skylight in an attic. Or through two windows, because what we've got here are two bits of the night sky that aren't necessarily next to each other. I'm not sure how I feel about him meddling with the universe. It doesn't seem ethical. I tuck my hands into the pockets of my dress. 'What star sign am I?' I ask him brightly.

He looks up, frowning. 'What?'

'My star sign. Have a guess,' I encourage him. I scoop up and shake my Lauren Bacall hair then let it fall over one eye. 'The hair is a clue.'

'Virgo.'

'You've already said that! *Virgo?* Why would a Virgo have hair like mine? It's a mane! I'm nothing like a Virgo. I'm a Leo!' I nudge his foot. Charlatan.

'Good for you,' he says cheerfully.

I look at him doubtfully. He seems a down-to-earth kind of person and not the kind of guy who'd be selling myths about horoscopes.

'Can I ask, do you believe in this kind of thing, star signs and stuff?'

'No,' he says.

52

'Eh? Oh.'

'You?' he asks.

'No! Per-*lease*. Of course not.' That would make Mick and me completely incompatible, because he's a Scorpio, like my mother. 'I mean, obviously I read my horoscope, who doesn't? But I don't believe in it as such. It's just for fun, isn't it?' I'm expecting him to argue the case for the defence, but he looks at me impassively and doesn't reply, and I worry I've offended him. 'Obviously, I don't know the science behind the constellations,' I add. 'I mean, what's the point of knowing about the stars?'

'Navigation?'

'Oh, navigation,' I reply as if it goes without saying.

He takes a cloth out of his pocket and as he wipes my fingerprints off the wood, he says, 'Luckily, Fern Banks, not everyone is cynical like us.'

Cynical? I don't know where he's got the idea I'm cynical.

As he polishes the Perspex, which is as blue as his eyes, he says, 'It's nice to believe in something, though, isn't it? Everyone likes a guarantee; the belief that things are meant to be and they're not just random occurrences. It's good to believe that you're destined to meet that person for a reason – the reason being true love, right? Otherwise . . .'

'Otherwise what?'

He looks at me from under those dark, straight eyebrows. 'It could be any man, couldn't it? Any man with a decent income.'

Now *that* is cynical. Despite the stops and starts, I feel I've been keeping up with the conversation up until right now, when suddenly he seems to be talking about something else entirely.

I decide to go along with it. 'In other words, these light boxes symbolically convince people they're destined to stay together,' I say, grinning to show I get the joke. It seems artistic but at the same time, cheesy.

'You're romantic, right?' he says.

'No.' I'm not the slightest bit romantic, honestly. You only have to see Mick and me together to know that. And I'd absolutely never buy him a light box with two constellations in it, not even ironically. 'What makes you think that?'

'I suppose it's because of your clothes. They're romantic, from a different era. You look like that Bogey woman.'

'Thanks.' The words that no woman wants to hear.

'Hang on . . .' he's clicking his fingers '. . . it's on the tip of my tongue. That Hollywood actress. Humphrey Bogart's wife. Bacall! Lauren Bacall!'

'Oh, *that* Bogey woman, Bacall. She had wonderful style, didn't she? Shoulder pads give such a great figure!'

For a moment his gaze skims over me and he looks away again quickly.

There's a sudden awkwardness between us and I go back to my stall. I'm easing a dress over Dolly's head, when I realise that David's still watching me.

'That's vintage, is it? What's the difference between vintage and second-hand?'

Dolly looks slightly indecent with her dress around her waist, as if she's been caught drunk in a public place, and I tug it down quickly to spare her feelings.

'The price.'

'So how much is this one?'

'One fifty.'

He laughs out loud – against his tan, his teeth are white and slightly crooked, giving him a roguish appeal.

'What's so funny?' I ask. 'This could be a wedding dress – see this colour?'

'Pink, isn't it?'

'Pink! It's not *pink*,' I tell him. 'It's blush. It's a great shade for a bride.' I lift the hem. 'Look at the quality. It's hand-stitched – look at that! Where else could you get a hand-stitched wedding dress for a hundred and fifty pounds?'

'Don't ask me,' he says. 'Good luck,' he adds, as if I need it, then he unfolds a chair, picks up a book and looks for new ideas for his light boxes.

Good luck? What's that supposed to mean? I could think of plenty of sarcastic comments to make about light boxes, if I was that sort of person. You can't use them as a light and you can't use them as a box, so good luck to him, too.

A young Japanese couple wearing matching outfits come up to his stand and I retreat into my dresses and unfold my stool.

The couple's interest in the light boxes seem to have a knock-on effect, because a woman wearing a multicoloured floor-sweeping skirt stops to see what they're looking at, and then another couple nudge in, and I sit and watch while David Westwood starts on his astrological patter, which involves words like 'air signs' and 'moon in Taurus'.

I hadn't expected him to have a patter but there he is, pointing out the constellations and how these had looked to the ancients like twins, and here, the fish. And he throws in a few more facts as well about light years – and here is the large light box in which they can see the individual stars more brightly. Yes, he can pack it safely, he says, and lo! he produces some cardboard which, with an origami flourish, he makes into a box. Meanwhile, the woman in the long skirt is texting her niece to find out her fiancé's star sign and the other couple are wanting a set for their bedroom. (*Aquarius, I'm going to say, but I think I'm on the cusp . . .*)

I mull over what David said about the right man having a decent income, disagreeing with him in my mind. A decent income doesn't figure in things at all. I have no idea how much Mick makes, and I'd never in a million years ask him. It's just about the least important thing in our relationship. I like him because I get him and he gets me; generosity of spirit is vital, the same sense of fun is a must and mutual lust a priority. It's not a lot to ask, is it? Who'd go for a man just because he has a decent income? A brief vision of Melania Trump flashes through my brain, but that's just cynicism, because who am I to judge? For all I know she and Donald might have an amazing connection.

I watch the people go past.

There's not a lot of space in this alley. It's narrow; it acts like a funnel. But occasionally in the flow of the crowd a woman will catch my eye and in a flash I'll know exactly how they feel inside the things they're wearing. I know as surely as if I am them. I know when a baggy top hides a good figure and when dark colours are worn to blend in. I recognise the elasticated waist that's snug around the belly. I understand the apologetic walk, the wistful glance, because I've been there myself. These are the women who I hope will linger at my stand – but, regretfully, they hardly ever do because it's impossible to wander around and browse. You just have to stand there in full view of me and look; and I know they're afraid the clothes won't fit them. They don't think my lovely dresses, even when they catch the eye, are meant for them. And worst of all, they worry that I might be pushy. We both have our roles, the seller and the buyer.

I generally pretend I haven't seen them, because the first thing I learnt on this market stall was not to scare people off.

Which is why I don't look up when a shadow falls over me and I hear a shriek. 'Fern Banks!'

'Gigi!' I squeal back. I recognise her at once – Gigi Martin, who I was at college with until she left mid-term and got a job as a junior in a hairdressing salon in Camden.

'You haven't changed a bit!' she says.

I seriously hope she's just being polite.

'You neither!' I say. In my case, I'm being truthful. She's model-slim in a polka-dot top and green skinny jeans. She's got a mass of frizzy pink hair.

'How's it going? Man, you're absolutely rushed off your feet,' she says, laughing.

'I *know, riiight*?' I reply ruefully.

'Dave looks as if he's doing all right, though.' *Dayve*, not David. 'So this is what you do now?' she asks, looking up at my diminished stock. 'Have you sold everything?'

Looking at the stall through her eyes I feel a shiver of panic. I don't want to think about it. When I'd been saving my clothes from the fire, I'd obviously saved the most expensive, but maybe that hadn't been my best idea. I should have kept some of the cheaper things, the kind of thing that a person would buy on impulse, just because she liked it, without having to think about it and come back later. 'My upstairs neighbour had a fire in her flat.'

'Fern! You're kidding!' Gigi covers her mouth with her hand. 'And all your clothes got burnt?'

'No, they got wet. This is the stuff I rescued.'

'Oh, Fern! You're insured though, right?' She unhooks a flowing pink fit-and-flare dress and holds it against herself, looking down. 'What waist is this?' she asks.

'Sixty-six centimetres.'

'It's beautiful. Seventies?'

'Yes, mid-Seventies, I'd say.'

'Hey, Dave?' she calls. 'What do you think?'

My neighbour in black emerges from his parallel universe. He grins at Gigi and glances at the dress. 'Very nice.'

'"Very nice."' She laughs and holds the pink dress up to look at it. 'That's all he ever says, Fern – very nice.'

He looks from Gigi to me. 'Do you two know each other?'

'We were at Camden School for Girls together, briefly. You were a shy little thing, weren't you, Fern? Always drawing stuff in this little black book of hers. He's the same.' She jerks her thumb at my neighbour. 'You're always drawing, aren't you?'

'Yes,' he replies. 'Always.'

The way Gigi is talking implies it's some weird quirk that we share, but David doesn't seem bothered.

She's still holding the pink dress.

'Do you want to try it on?' I ask hopefully. I've devised a way of closing the stall off with a muslin drape and crocodile clips.

She gives David a quick look. 'Yes, why not. But I'll have to be quick, though; I've got Pilates.'

I'm glad she's said yes. I want to see it on her. This is one of those dresses where the genius lies in the cut of the fabric and the way it hangs. It counterbalanced the androgyny of the styles of the Sixties.

Gigi pulls the dress on over her jeans, but it looks lovely on her with its plunging neckline and the fluid curve of the skirt. The pink is the same shade as her hair. She undoes a couple of the little covered buttons down the front to show her cleavage and she poses for us both with a hand on her hip. It was made for her.

'Gigi, you look gorgeous,' I say sincerely, my hand on my heart.

'Dave? What do you think?'

'You look like a stick of candyfloss.' His face softens. 'Yeah. Gorgeous.'

She turns the label over to look at the price. 'You take cards?'

'I do.'

As I reach for the machine, she touches some other dresses and looks at them briefly but puts them back. She pouts at him, ducks back under the curtain and takes the dress off. She's satisfied.

Once she's paid, she bundles the dress into her bag. 'Guys, I've got to go; I'll be late for class,' she says, kissing David enthusiastically on the mouth. 'I'll see *you* later.'

We watch her leave – I can see her pink hair bobbing above the crowds.

When she's lost from view, David turns to me. 'How many light boxes has that just cost me?'

'Ha ha!' Hopefully, he means it as a joke.

He gazes down the alley for a moment as if he thinks she might come back. Then he asks, 'What was she like at school?'

I smile. 'The same! She was such a laugh. She put my new jacket on a friend's dog once and it ran off and . . .' I cut the story short, because he doesn't need to know I was too scared to go after it and I never saw the jacket again. 'I never wanted to sit by her in class, though.'

'Why not?'

'She never stopped talking. I couldn't concentrate. I used to get yelled at on account of her.'

'Fern – you were a geek!'

'I know.' I grin at the thought and add truthfully, 'She was way too cool to hang out with me.'

'Small world,' he says.

'Yeah.' I give him a sideways glance. 'You're the astrologer, you'd know.'

The flow of people through the market has ebbed suddenly.

Times like this, I wonder what the hell happens, where they all go. The place is like a huge maze, with certain crucial landmarks like giant sculpted horses, blacksmiths, ATMs. Even so, I still get lost. So do they.

'Is it always this quiet?' David asks.

He sounds anxious and I try to reassure him. 'In the week it's mostly tourists. And the kind of tourists who come to Camden Lock . . . well, let's just say you can't get a lot in a backpack. But at weekends, it's brilliant. The place is absolutely heaving. You'll be amazed.'

'Yeah.' He shifts restlessly, looking at the empty stalls on either side of us.

His mood has changed since he saw Gigi and I don't really know why. Maybe he, like me, is suddenly seeing his stall through her eyes; not as a dream but in cold reality.

As though he's read my mind, he says, 'I'm not sure about this alley, Fern. If somebody wants to come back to buy something, they might never find me again. I need a bigger unit. Somewhere with storage.'

I nod. As I'd been the one to tell him about the stall going free, I feel a certain amount of responsibility for the location. 'Maybe it suits my needs better than yours,' I tell him apologetically. I don't add the main reason that it suits my needs is that it's cheap.

He looks at my feeble display of dresses and gives me a quick smile. 'I guess it does. Gigi's been away for the weekend with more stuff than that.'

The smile softens it and he doesn't say it in a mean way, but my doubts come flooding back. As my parents pointed out, I'm not a businesswoman, I'm a market trader. I've got little stock and even fewer customers and I'm running out of funds.

Feeling a bit sick about it, I say, 'David, you know that day

60

that we first met? And you said no good deed ever goes unpunished? Is that something you really believe?'

He looks amused. 'Touch wood, I've been all right so far.'

I haven't, though.

David goes back to his side of the canvas and sits down, stretches his legs and opens the book on astrology.

Without him, I'm at a loose end. I sit down, too, and write a list in my client book to distract me from my self-doubts:

> Cato Hamilton
> Church sale
> Car boot sale
> Tabletop sale

This list will be the foundation of my new strategy to get more stock.

It's dead here now and the time is dragging. I need an energy boost, a sugar hit. 'David, please could you watch my stall while I get myself something to eat?'

He looks up from his book. 'Sure.'

'Do you want anything?'

'That's okay, thanks, I've got a flask.'

'Oh, fine.' Obviously, he's a practical guy with his dovetail joints and stuff. Of course he's going to have a flask. 'Won't be long,' I tell him and I make my way along the maze of cobbled lanes past the vaults, winding through the steamy stalls selling sizzling street food. It's exciting, like being transplanted to another continent. Here, with the profusion of smells and multitude of languages, it feels like anywhere but England.

I cross Camden Lock Place and call in at Chin Chin Labs for a liquid nitrogen ice cream. I like the process, watching the chilly vapour freeze the cream, choosing the flavours and sprinkles.

Cutting through the West Yard, I lean on the humped black-and-white Roving Bridge to eat the ice cream. It's a sunny day and the place is busy. Beneath me, clumps of green weed undulate gently on the surface of the sluggish canal.

By the time I finish off my cone I start to feel more optimistic. I'll get new stock. I'll message everyone on my mailing list. I'll begin a new push for sales. I'll make a name for myself.

David has started to pack up when I get back. It's early, just gone five, and the market doesn't close until seven.

'How did you get on today?' I ask him.

He looks at me blankly, as if he's distracted. 'It's all relative, isn't it?' he says after a moment. His eyes are tired, but he smiles. 'There's no pressure, that's the main thing. You can't put a price on that, right?'

The way he says it makes me wonder what's been going on in his life, because he doesn't sound that convincing. I want to ask him, but before I can he's gone back to packing away his stall.

The following evening I pick up the *Camden New Journal* from the doormat, where it lies surrounded by Pizza flyers and taxis offering trips to airports, to find Lucy and me on the front page, standing outside our house. She with her black towel wrapped around her looking amazing in a cloud of the photographer's apple-scented billowing smoke and me looking shocked and enigmatic in my trench coat, my hair falling over my right eye, holding my beautiful dresses like a wartime heroine.

Compared with me, Lucy looks terribly underdressed. Compared with her, I look ridiculously overdressed. I'm not sure what prompted me to grab my raincoat, apart from it being Burberry. I had some vague notion of it being appropriate for an emergency, I think.

The important thing is, we look good and neither of us looks particularly traumatised, despite the headline: 'Actress and Fashion Curator in Sauna Trauma'. I like my low chin-tilt. I don't remember adopting it at all, but then I realise I was trying to keep the clothes from falling.

I go back outside, hurry up the steps and ring Lucy's doorbell.

Lucy flings her door open. 'Hey, Fern! Come in,' she says cheerfully, picking up her copy of the *Journal* from the mat. The word 'Welcome' is really faded. It's literally outworn its welcome.

'We're on the front page,' I say, unfurling my paper to show her.

'Oh, *great!*' She looks at the photograph critically for a moment or two and reads the headline. 'Actress? Act*ress*?'

I try to look sympathetic that the paper didn't call her an actor, but I'm secretly thrilled at being called a fashion curator in print. I read it aloud for Lucy's benefit:

'Actress Lucy Mills escaped from a blaze in her sauna on Saturday afternoon. Lucy, who's currently starring as Lady Macbeth at The Gatehouse theatre, Highgate, said, "It's a miracle we got out of there alive." Fellow resident, Fern Banks, curator of wearable vintage fashion at Fern Banks Vintage in Camden Market, lost a sizeable amount of irreplaceable stock in the blaze. "I hope my company will survive this. I intend to be like a phoenix rising from the ashes."'

I glance at Lucy. 'Uh-oh. It sounded good when I said I'd lost a sizeable amount of stock, but now people are going to think I've got nothing left to sell,' I comment gloomily. 'And they'd be right.'

'Don't worry about it. What you have to do is give it a couple of weeks and call the *Camden Journal* to tell them you actually *are* a phoenix rising from the ashes. Get your name out there before everyone forgets it. They always like a good story for the inside pages. You can do an advertorial, with local people rallying around you.'

I like her optimism. 'Good idea! Sounds expensive, though. But I'll think about it, because as we're on the front page,' I point out, 'they might put me rising from the ashes on the front page, too.'

'Aw, Fern. Trust me, they won't. Because a fire's bad news. Rising like a phoenix is good news. They never put good news on the front page – who'd buy it?'

Which is a sad indictment of life today.

We study the article once more in silence.

'Have you forgiven me yet?' Lucy asks in a small voice when she comes to the end of the column. 'I feel really bad about it.'

'Yes, of course,' I reply, giving her a hug. 'After all, it was an accident. The fire officers made more mess than the fire did, what with chopping bits out of my door and the water damage,' I point out ruefully. I don't believe in bearing a grudge – I don't want to be like my mother.

But it is a big problem, all the same, and it's adding to my worries.

So far, the loss adjusters are reluctant to pay out for the hole between our flats, because they see the fire as an act of negligence on Lucy's part, and the estate management isn't happy with the fact she's got a sauna at all.

I haven't told my parents about the fire yet, because one way or another, going by past experience, they're going to blame me for it. Ideally, if I have my own way, they'll never find out.

But if the worst comes to the worst and we have to pay for it ourselves, I can't afford to go halves with Lucy to mend the hole. My priority is to get more stock to sell. The whole 'rising from the ashes' bit is all very well, but without stock I'm not going to have a business left.

'I've arranged for the flats to be thermo-fogged,' she says after a moment.

Apparently, thermal fogging is a kind of deodorising method of blasting out the smoke smell, replacing it with something citrusy and nasally acceptable, despite being toxic to aquatic life.

'Great! No more smoke smell!' I'm very happy about that. Obviously not the toxic bit, but I love the idea of the flat smelling citrusy for a change.

Back at mine, determined to do as much as I can to put things right, I make a coffee, get my paintbrush and go outside to paint the front door. I'm kneeling on the doormat, when my phone rings in my back pocket. I balance my paintbrush on the pot. It's a number that I don't recognise. Spam, at a guess, but I answer it just to be sure.

It's a woman. 'Fern Banks Vintage?'

'Yes, that's me,' I say warily. 'Who's this?'

'Chalk Farm Library. Just a moment, I have a call for you. Here you are.'

I'm perplexed. I have no idea why Chalk Farm Library is calling me. I'm not even a member. 'Hello?'

'Hello?' The voice is high-pitched and accented, vaguely familiar. 'Is this Fern Banks who's in the paper today?'

'Yes,' I say again, getting to my feet because I've been kneeling for ages on the bristles of the doormat and they're prickling my knees.

'Good! You're the woman who stopped the bus to give me my money back. You see, I recognised you from your picture.

You have a very distinctive style. My name's Dinah Moss. M-O-S-S,' she repeats with emphasis. 'And you're Fern Banks. B-A-N-K-S. You see how it is? Moss, Fern, Banks.'

I laugh – I can't believe it. Something good is happening at last!

'Now, I see from the paper that you have a business as a curator of fashion, I understand?'

'Yes, that's right!' I reply brightly.

'I'm ringing to invite you to tea to thank you and I'd also very much like to show you my collection of haute couture. It's evident to me that you're a woman who'll singularly appreciate it.'

The words thrill me. Haute couture is dressmaking perfection, with garments made from the most extravagant fabrics, in the most intricate designs, with meticulous detailing and the finest needlework. And she thinks I'll appreciate it! (That's understating it slightly.) Haute couture is stratospherically out of my price range so it's my equivalent of treasure. 'I'd *love* to come to tea.'

'Ah! We're agreed! And also, I have a business proposition for you that I believe will interest you. But I won't talk now; I'm in the library. So, now I have your number. And you take my number, too,' she says imperiously.

'I'll get a pen.' I go into the shadowed, smoke-scented flat to find one and she gives me her home number. I read it back to her and write it down on my wall calendar with her name next to it, smiling to myself: Dinah Moss. Moss, Fern, Banks. We agree to meet on Monday afternoon, my day off.

'Excellent! Goodbye. I'll look forward to it.' Her voice fades as she says to the woman on the desk, 'Here you are, I've finished now.'

The call ends and I put the phone back in my pocket. I have to say, I'm excited about the phone call, because Dinah

Moss who wears Chanel says I have a very distinctive style and a compliment always means more coming from an expert.

I try not to speculate about the business proposition.

I have a good feeling about it, all the same.

From time to time over the past few days I've been mulling over David Westwood's comment that no good deed ever goes unpunished. Not that I'm superstitious or anything, but the fire did come shortly after my good deed.

More than anything, I'd like to prove him wrong.

# LOT 6

*A blue cotton day dress with five bowling-pin-shaped wooden buttons, fitted waist, patch pockets, size 12, labelled with Controlled Commodity symbol (CC41) to comply with government rationing controls, 1941*

Sunday is a sunny day and the market is busy. However, sadly for me, I'm not busy at all. I was hoping to sell the last of my stock on my practically bare stall so that I'd have the funds to resupply, but the lack of choice is putting people off.

Gratifyingly, a few people recognise me from the article in the *Camden New Journal* and sympathise about the fire, but not enough to buy anything. I get them to write their contact details in my client book before they go.

I lean on the counter and watch the constant shifting tide of people flow past as I listen enviously to David Westwood's sales patter above the noise, lifting my face to the warm sun, whiling away the time thinking up a patter of my own.

And then, suddenly, the mysterious lull occurs and the market is quiet again.

Mick has a theory that any lulls in conversation in a pub or restaurant occur at ten to or ten past the hour, so I check the time. Sure enough, it's ten minutes past five and I feel a sudden fond urge to ring him and tell him. I'm just getting out my phone, when David casts his shadow over me.

'That was *crazy*,' he says, pushing up the sleeves of his black T-shirt, his mood buoyant. He's grinning, high on success, and looks up at my rails. 'How did you get on?'

'Fine,' I tell him, grinning back. I don't want to ruin his mood.

Most people would take this statement at face value and I assume he has, too, because he strolls back around to his side. Then he returns with a single blue acrylic panel and holds it up to the light for me to look through.

'This is what the constellation of Leo looks like,' he says.

As I lean over the counter to look, chin in hand, I can feel his warmth radiating through his black T-shirt.

'Yeah?' I squint at it, trying hard to make something of the random holes. How the ancients got a lion out of that, I'll never know. David's tanned thumb is holding the Perspex, and I look at the pale crescent of his nail. 'Nice!'

'This is the tail, see?' he says, slowly tracing the shape of a lion to the rump, down a leg, along the back and up the neck to the mane and the muzzle and the chest.

Our faces are so close that I can smell him, clean and fresh, even on this hot day in the dusty city. I swallow so hard my throat squeaks. 'So that's Leo,' I say hoarsely, the holes leaking sunbeams along my finger.

'This particular lion has golden fur. It makes it fearless and indestructible.' He shifts his face a little to look at me and he's still holding up the Perspex, its blue colour deepening his eyes and shading his face. 'You'll be okay,' he says seriously.

Without warning, I feel as if I'm going to cry. I'm nodding agreement, pressing my lips together to stop the trembling. 'Yeah, I know.'

He straightens before I do. 'Anyway,' he says. 'That's Leo.'

When he goes back to his stall I feel as if the earth has shifted underneath me. To ground myself, I do what I was intending to do a few minutes before. I call Mick.

'Hey, Doll,' he says in his rich, soft voice.

I can hear music in the background and I know he's home.

'When did you get back?'

'This morning. I got a lift with Roscoe.'

Roscoe's a member of the band. 'That's good,' I say wistfully, staring at the glow of the sun through the canvas roof.

'I was going to call you. What are you doing tomorrow?' he asks.

I smile. 'Nothing.'

He chuckles softly. 'That's where you're wrong. Let's make a day of it and go—'

'Oh!' I interrupt him quickly, suddenly remembering about Dinah. 'Actually, I *am* doing something! I'm meeting a woman about a business proposition. But that's not until the afternoon, anyway.'

'Ah, hell, Fern. Can't you do it another time?'

Through the corner of my eye I can see David's legs outstretched on the cobbles, his polished shoes gleaming, and I lower my voice. 'Well – not really, no, Mick. It's *business*. How about we make it Tuesday?'

The volume of the music increases. What time is this to be partying?

'I'll get back to you, Doll,' he said and hangs up.

I laugh merrily once he's gone, in case David's listening and thinks my love life is as much of a failure as my business. 'Bye!' *Damn*. I'm a Leo. I'm fearless and indestructible, I tell myself firmly, putting my phone away.

Utilitarian glamour – that's the look I'm going for as I head to Dinah's for tea. Dinah's house is in Netherhall Gardens, a quiet, residential part of Hampstead with large, impressive red-brick houses, architectural plants and electronic gates. I'm thinking of reminding her about the first time we met. The way I look at it, the first time was chance, the second time was a coincidence, but I feel in my optimistic heart that this third meeting is meant to be.

Dinah's house has a brown wooden gate and a crazy-paving path leading to the front door. I ring the bell and she opens the door immediately as if she's been standing behind it waiting for me to arrive. She greets me graciously, posing with one arm on the doorframe and looking very Coco Chanel in a little cream silk shift dress accessorised with a cascade of faux pearls. Her dyed black hair is curling slightly around her sharp jawline; her lipstick is bright scarlet.

She, of course, is scrutinising me in turn. I've dressed very carefully for this business meeting in a navy shirtwaister with square shoulders and a narrow belt. I'm posing, too. I've rolled back my fringe from my face, very Forties, and with my peach blusher and red lipstick I look as healthy as a land girl. Dinah beckons me in and we bond immediately over a familiar subject.

'I like your look,' she says approvingly. 'Although you gave me a start when I first saw you with that suitcase. There was all that dreadful rattling noise and it unsettled me. I'm a person who's very susceptible to noise.'

'Sorry. It's a cheap case and one of the wheels is coming off.'

'Oh,' she says, spreading her hands, 'and there's a hole in my handbag; it's come unstitched!'

There's something in the way that we've just swapped stories of our shoddy goods that makes us both laugh.

'It's being repaired now,' she adds gravely, 'at the Handbag Clinic.'

'Good. I'm afraid there's no hope for my suitcase. I'm going to have it put down.'

She nods seriously. 'Put out of its misery; yes. I think that's best – it looked a sorry thing.' Her mood brightens. 'First of all, before we have tea I want to show you something that you'll appreciate as a curator of fashion. Come. Always one must put pleasure before business.'

We climb an oak spiral staircase, which leads up to the first floor.

Dinah takes me into a windowless dressing room with mirrored wardrobes on all three walls. She invites me to sit on a large ivory velvet ottoman. The chandelier throws pools of rainbow light on the polished floor. With a flourish, she touch-opens each of the wardrobe doors in turn. Our reflections disappear and the interiors of the wardrobes glow with lights.

Dinah's smiling, more to herself than to me. 'This is my collection,' she says shyly.

'Wow.'

It's like falling into my favourite dream. Her clothes are hanging in muslin garment bags that shroud the dresses inside them. Each garment bag has a vinyl pocket with a Polaroid of the garment tucked into it. I'm seriously excited by these wrapped-up delights, impressed by the care she's taken to look after them, and I'm filled with a rush of anticipation.

She laughs gleefully at my expression. 'It's taken you by surprise, hasn't it?'

'Yes!' I'm looking at the Polaroids and through the muslin bags I can see the vague but enticing outline of her clothes.

She sweeps her hand along them carelessly but possessively, like a lover, and looks at me coquettishly over her shoulder. 'I have a question for you. How would you catalogue a lifetime's collection of couture like this?' she asks.

Is this something she wants me to do? My heart is beating fast with anticipation. Oh please, yes, I'd do it in a heartbeat. 'I guess I'd do it by designer and by era,' I say, wondering if this is the actual interview.

'That's exactly what I do,' she says approvingly. 'I keep them all in chronological order, in the order I was given them by my dahlink husband.'

I'd like a husband like that. 'Really? Going back to when?'

Again, she turns her head to look at me, her hands on her hips, raising her eyebrows briefly, enjoying my surprise.

'Let's see how clever you are, shall we? Tell me, what was the style in post-war nineteen forties?'

I laugh. 'Come on, that's too easy. I'm wearing it. Utilitarian, flannel, no more than five buttons due to clothes rationing, two pockets—'

She wags her finger at me. 'Shame on you, Fern Banks! I'm talking about couture! Here! Look!' She pulls out a bag, unzips it and takes out the garment to show me.

I can't believe what I'm seeing. It's a wasp-waisted jacket over a corseted black silk dress with a midi-length full pleated skirt, so boned and perfectly structured that even on the hanger it holds the shape of the wearer – it could probably stand up by itself.

*Christian Dior.* I'm stunned, lost for words. My skin prickles with adrenaline. I've only ever seen this ensemble in books and, unexpectedly, here it is, a museum piece hanging in a wardrobe.

Dinah thrusts it into my arms and chuckles. 'Go on! Take it! Feel!' she says. 'Don't we always have to feel?'

Seeing my hesitation, her smile fades and suddenly her mood changes. She says sharply, 'The cat got your tongue? Tell me about this!'

She's testing me. I might, after all, be a fake. 'Well, it's obviously . . .' I hardly dare to say it. 'It looks like – it's in the style of Christian Dior's New Look collection. Spring nineteen-forty-seven, right? La Ligne Corolle. After the war he wanted to move on from the relaxed, practical frocks that women were used to and he chose the corseted, exaggerated cinch-waist styles.' I'm looking under the skirt at the seams, at the finish of it. I glance uncertainly at her, trying to read her expression, wondering what this is all about, what exactly my role is.

She relaxes again. 'Of course, you're quite correct,' she says languidly, swatting away my words with her hand as if they're not important anyway. 'It also has a hat with it. I have it in a box.'

Fascinated, I hold the Dior at arm's-length. It's like looking at something incredible, like a sunset, and trying to put a price on it. I've got an idea how much this outfit is worth. Probably six figures. Does she?

My speechless admiration amuses her. She laughs and takes it from me – she has other things to show me and she shares in my delight. I get a glimpse of the most beautiful fabrics: chiffon, crêpe romaine, crêpe marocaine, crêpe de chine, gossamer, moiré, organzine, shantung, brocade, velvets in jewel colours – emerald, amethyst, turquoise, lapis lazuli, ruby, sapphire, ivory; dresses so beautiful that I groan in pleasure.

'They're all here,' she says with great pride, spreading her arms wide. 'The best of the best. Dior, Givenchy, Balenciaga, Laroche, Schiaparelli.'

The names are poetry to me.

Dinah pauses and glances at me conspiratorially. 'And Chanel.' She raises her hand. 'No, don't say it! I know you're wondering, *Chanel*? How *could* she? Well, I forgave her in the Fifties.'

'You did? For what?'

Dinah frowns and her expression hardens. 'What do you

think? For cosying up to the Germans during the occupation, of course. Everyone knows she had an affair with that diplomat, the Baron.' She shrugs. 'But she was cleared of being a collaborator, so what can you do? Maybe, after all, it was just sex. I chose to forgive,' she says haughtily, sliding the hangers along the rails. 'Look! Here's a Grès that might interest you.'

'Madame Alix Grès,' I say, showing off my knowledge, and Dinah pats my cheek sharply but approvingly.

'Of course, dahlink. Madame Alix,' she says fondly. 'Who else but us remembers her anymore?'

She pulls out the gown, in Grecian draped and pleated ivory. It's breathtaking, a miracle of construction, the pinnacle of elegance. As she holds up the hanger, her arm trembles with the weight; it's heavy, lavish with fabric. I want to hold it. Hell, I'd kill to wear it.

'You like it, huh?' Dinah shakes the hanger so that the dress shimmies gracefully. 'See how it hangs? Magnificent, isn't it?'

It takes my breath away. 'I've seen one in the Victoria and Albert Museum. I never thought I'd get to hold one.'

Dinah smiles. 'How about you try it on? Would you like to?'

'Really? Yes, please!'

'Don't worry, I won't look,' she says, turning her back to me, but as soon as I step out of my dress she turns around and issues a series of stern orders.

'Here, slip that arm out of your bra strap, see, it's one-shouldered. Undo the side zip – no, not there, it's on the right. Don't step into it, pull it over your head. Okay, wait. There.' Dinah's tugging it into place, her cold fingers rough against my skin.

The gown slides down my body as cool and silky as a waterfall.

'This hooks onto this – stand still, will you!' She jerks me almost off my feet. 'That shoulder isn't straight – pull it up. There. Okay. Look at me.'

I turn to face her.

Her face softens and she clasps her knuckles to her mouth, her chin crumpling, tears shimmering in her eyes. 'So beautiful,' she says softly. She shuts a wardrobe door with the toe of her shoe. 'Look at yourself in it.'

I stand tall, shoulders back. My reflection shows me as my very best self – the person I dream of being. The gown is a masterpiece of design, the definition of elegance. The fabric knots in the front and falls from my hips, Grecian and feminine. I step forward in it, and the chandelier's reflection sparkles beneath my feet, the folds caressing my legs and ankles. It's the sexiest dress I've ever worn. It elevates me to a new state of being. No one could possibly feel ugly or inferior in this gown. If it were mine, I'd keep it and it would give me permanent confidence and I'd never take it off.

I turn to look over my shoulder, seeing myself from the back. 'Oh, Dinah.' It's the most surreal experience of my life. 'And you've worn all of these,' I say to my reflection, trying to comprehend what it must be like to own these clothes.

'Yes, of course. They exist to be worn,' Dinah says airily. 'Well, you know, in those days, my husband and I, we socialised.'

I shake my head in disbelief. 'It's amazing to imagine. It's like another world to me.' But the thing is, I *can* imagine it. 'Do you ever wear them now?'

She shrugs nonchalantly. 'Now and then, if there's an occasion. Weddings; dinners; we attend wearing our best and doing nothing more energetic than picking up a fork.'

She gestures for me to turn and, reluctantly, I stand still and raise my right arm for her to unfasten the gown. She helps me out of it then I put my navy blue day dress back on and become myself again, trying to ignore the anticlimax.

Dinah tucks the clothes away, taking time to put them back in the right order. Then she straightens them and briskly closes all the wardrobe doors, and the two of us stand side by side with our sunray of multiplied reflections in the mirrors.

She looks at herself critically in her knee-length cream Chanel, one hand on her hip, and tilts her head. 'How do I look?'

'Fabulous,' I reply.

She grips my hand. 'You think I'm beautiful?'

I almost say yes just out of politeness but she asks the question so intently that I consider it seriously. She's not beautiful, actually, although on first impression I thought she was. Her eyes are large and close together, like a lion's eyes. Her dyed hair is neat and wavy, her nose is narrow and her mouth well shaped in that bright red lipstick so similar to my own. She's not beautiful, that's not the word at all, but she is striking.

'Come! It's not difficult! It's a yes or no question,' she says brusquely.

What kind of question is that to ask someone who's practically a stranger, anyway? 'You give the general impression that you are.'

This makes her smile.

'Good! The impression is what counts! And now, let's have tea.'

Once again, I find myself wondering about the nature of the business deal. I'm eager to find out what it is and return to the fantasyland of haute couture.

She leads the way back downstairs and we go into the far end of the dining room. Facing the lush green garden is a seating area with two worn sage green velvet armchairs and an occasional table piled with Sunday supplements. On the mahogany sideboard stands a seven-branched candelabra, a Jewish menorah.

She's laid a butler's tray with china cups and saucers, milk and sugar cubes, and she goes into the kitchen then comes back with a teapot with a felt tea-cosy.

She pauses before pouring and looks at me steadily. 'In Chalk Farm, you stopped the bus for me so that I could be reunited with my money. I'm grateful for that. So now it's time for me to do something for you.' She has a sharp and lively gleam in her eyes. 'Let's talk business,' she says, pouring the tea. 'It's what you've been waiting for, isn't it?'

'Obviously, I'm curious,' I reply, my heart thumping with excitement.

'Do you know of a place called Morland Street?'

'Yes.'

'Oh, good. There is a post office there, do you know it?'

'Yes, I do.'

'Next to the post office is my husband's tailor shop. It's a big shop; you can't miss it. You know the one I mean?'

I shake my head.

'Well, it's there, anyhow. He also offers dry-cleaning but,' she pulls a face, 'that's something that he farms out to another company and there's no money in it. Dressmaking is what he does best.'

She's lost me. I have absolutely no idea where this conversation is going, but I nod.

The tea is dark and very strong; I can taste the tannin on my tongue. I take the sugar tongs and put in a couple of sugar lumps just for the novelty value. Now it's very sweet, too.

'Tell me, who do you use for your alterations?'

'What?' Yikes. She's got the entirely wrong idea about me.

I don't need a tailor. My thoughts keep returning longingly to those rows of garment bags lined up in the wardrobes. *Dior, Chanel, Grès* . . . 'I don't offer that kind of service. My clients get it done themselves if they need to.'

She sucks her breath in sharply and tuts. 'But you're a curator of fashion. You need a good tailor for couture. My husband was in the atelier for a French fashion house. You know the word atelier?'

I nod. 'It's the workshop where the dressmakers stitch the garments.'

'Exactly, yes. You know how important that job is, the dressmaking?'

'Sure, of course.'

'Well then. Before the war he was with Chanel and after coming here as a refugee, he worked for Norman Hartnell, so you see, he has credentials. He's been in the rag trade all his life and between you and me,' she says, lowering her voice, 'his life has been a long one. Listen to me. He's the best. I can recommend him to you.' She grips my wrist, pulling me towards her. 'You helped me out and now I'm helping you out, as a friend.'

This is what happens when I big myself up; it's very misleading. 'Dinah, I'm so sorry, I've given you the wrong impression,' I confess. 'I don't sell couture. I sell vintage, retro, ready-to-wear.'

'Ready-to-wear?' Dinah recoils and cups her hand around her throat. For a moment she sounds like my mother. She sits back, dismayed, breathing in heavily through her nose before coming to a decision. 'Well, look at you, you're just starting out, you're young. No problem. Here's how I can help you. No – hear me out. This is what I'm suggesting,' she says, clicking her rows of faux pearls like worry beads. 'You could offer a bespoke service for your clients to get the perfect fit for their ensembles. Moss knows how frocks are made, the generous seams for alterations. He can let things out and take them in, no problem. His shop has a dressing room and a nice golden looking-glass. You can bring your clients to him to be measured. This will suit my husband because he's a friendly man – not too friendly,' she says hastily, 'don't worry about that; naturally, he's respectful.'

*The perfect fit*, I think, watching the steam rise from my tea. The tea is marbling the inside of the china cup. 'Dinah—'

'You'd be bringing in work for him, you see? And he'd have the company. He likes company. You get to our age and our friends are dropping dead, or they're not allowed to drive, or they move in with their middle-aged children, or they lose their minds entirely and dribble all day. You can put the cost of the alterations on the price of the garment. Bespoke fitting. What do you say?' she asks eagerly, raising her fine black eyebrows in a question.

I glance over at the polished dining table with all those chairs around it, getting caught up in her vision. But with a surge of excitement, I think: actually, it's not a bad idea. Bespoke fittings could be my USP. 'I *love* the idea, Dinah, and it's definitely something I'm *interested* in,' I say carefully, 'but since the fire I'm a bit low on stock.'

The sun comes out from behind a cloud and for a moment as she holds her cup her hands are bathed in light, her veins purple under her translucent skin. She stares at them without expression for a moment and she sighs deeply. 'I'm old, and all I have left is my beautiful wardrobe,' she says sadly, appealing to me directly with her bright eyes. 'It's everything to me. Dahlink, you must understand, I need someone to look after it when I've gone; someone who'll love and appreciate it.'

My heart leaps in shock. Does she mean me?

I know I'm being manipulated, even though she's doing it so charmingly. She knows my weaknesses; she's called me perfectly by letting me try on the Grès gown. I try not to think about it and, mustering up all my integrity, I tell her, 'Museums and private buyers would pay a fortune for your collection.'

She bangs her cup down in a sudden flash of anger. 'Museums and private buyers? My gowns need to be worn, not stared at!'

'You're right.' Deeply uncomfortable and out of my depth, I finish my tea. 'Okay, well, I'll keep the alterations idea in mind,' I tell her and I pick my bag up from the floor.

'Of course!' she agrees graciously. 'Naturally, you must see his shop first, before you make a decision. Go any time. Anytime you like. He'll be there.'

'Thank you.'

She tugs at my arm. 'But why wait? Go now. I'll call and tell Moss to expect you,' she replies firmly as she sees me to the door.

The reason I go directly to Morland Street is out of curiosity. Moss has worked for Chanel and Hartnell, and my vision of the tailor's shop is entirely influenced by Dinah's throwaway line about the dressing room and the golden mirror. I'm intrigued.

This is the reality of it: the shop is a large space cut in half along its width by a full-length wooden counter on which there's a handwritten sign on a piece of card: *cash payment only*. The dressing room is in the left-hand corner, with a faded velvet curtain for privacy and a faded red rug on the floor. There's a long rail affixed to the wall on the other side of the counter and hanging on the rail there's a fake fur coat. Behind the counter is Moss's cutting table with a modern sewing machine and a quantity of brilliant coloured threads. The place is shabby rather than elegant.

Moss greets me morosely. His hair is longish, coarse, collar-length, brushed back from a face dominated by dark bushy eyebrows. He's overweight, but on the other hand, in his black jacket and tie, he has the upright bearing of someone important, some who knows he is *someone*.

'Hello, I'm Fern Banks,' I tell him. 'Your wife—'

'Yes,' he says, looking at me from under his wild eyebrows without enthusiasm. 'She told me to expect you.' His voice, like Dinah's, is heavily accented and his face is stern. He has a jug of filter coffee brewing and he pours two cups for us then leans on the counter and sighs deeply. 'What's the weather like now?'

For some reason I feel obliged to look through the window, even though I've only just come in from the street. 'It's a bit chilly, for May.'

'Chilly, is it? It's quiet. So, tell me,' he says softly, confidingly, as if it were a secret just between the two of us, 'how's business with you?'

I shrug. 'Not great.'

'Dinah tells me you buy cheap and sell cheap.'

It sounds awful put like that and I feel I have to defend myself. 'I buy cheap and I sell competitively,' I tell him, but it doesn't come across any better. I look up at the lonesome fur coat while Moss gazes out of the window at the passing cars.

'It's easy come, easy go,' he says. 'People buy rubbish these days and if it doesn't fit properly, who cares?'

'I know. Crazy, right?' I'm totally with him on this subject. 'Why buy cheap and mass-produced when you can buy quality vintage?' I literally drool over some of the details on the clothes that I sell; for instance, the little tabs that hold the bra strap in place under the dress – how lovely, how thoughtful is that?

'Huh.' Moss leans on the counter heavily and gives a long and heartfelt sigh.

His eyes are distant, as if he's remembering better days.

Neither of us says anything and the silence seems to drag on. It's so quiet that I can hear his watch ticking.

'See what I'm telling you? How quiet it is?'

He sounds defeated and it's a feeling that I'm beginning to recognise. 'Dinah asked me to come because—'

Unexpectedly, he chuckles. 'Yes, she saw you in the paper, saving all of your frocks from the fire. Exactly the kind of thing she, herself, would do. Her clothes are her babies. "Look, Moss, this Fern Banks, she's a woman who loves her clothes," she tells me.'

I laughed dryly. 'I didn't manage to save all of them.' I find myself telling him about the Twenties and Thirties cocktail dresses whose sequins have dissolved or melted, and the wool suit that has shrunk to a smaller size than the lining.

'A tragedy,' he comments.

'Yeah,' I agree, straightening my teaspoon in the saucer.

'To fix them is almost impossible. Who has the time to sew sequins?'

'Exactly.'

'It is a challenge.'

'I know.' But something in his tone makes me look up at him.

His face is impassive, but there's a gleam in his eye. He straightens a cufflink and says, 'You need a good tailor.'

He's right. With a sudden epiphany, I say, 'I *do* need a good tailor!'

For the first time since I entered the shop, he smiles. 'Obviously, to make a judgement I'd have to see these garments for myself. To you, they're ruined, but,' he shrugs in an exaggerated way that reminds me of Dinah, 'maybe for me I'll see a solution. For example, I can re-line the suit, alter the seams, maybe put a little contrasting panelling in, that won't be a problem. The sequins, well, it depends.'

'I'll bring them in for you to look at. It's worth a try, isn't it?'

'Of course,' he says.

'Okay, then.' I pick up the cup and sip it. 'Blimey.' The coffee gives me an instant hit and makes me shudder.

Moss has gone all morose on me again. 'This shop is in a busy street and look at it,' he points out, even though the street is empty. 'My wife didn't tell me about the repairs. She tells me that you want to bring your clients here for a bespoke fitting. And also while they're here you may bring items for them to look at, in addition, to catch their eye.'

Eh? 'I didn't exactly say that. That's not how my business works,' I explain to him. 'I sell things online and in Camden Market and that's my living.'

'Women buy frocks from you without trying them on?'

'Yes.'

He stares at me for a moment and shakes his head in disbelief.

I glance around the place again, trying to see how it could be with a bit (a lot) of money thrown at it. There's the huge window front, which is a plus. The wooden floors are scuffed, but they could easily be polished. The large rug is faded but it could be replaced. Maybe a couple of mint green bucket chairs and a little glass-topped table for coffee – or prosecco. It just needed a little TLC. New drapes on the dressing area would make a big difference and maybe if he propped another mirror against the wall – it's all about the look, right? The trouble is, it costs money and by the looks of it, Moss hasn't got any, either. 'What do you usually charge?'

'Who can say? It depends on the amount of work. Someone's

paying a hundred pounds then a little more on top of that is easy to find. Bring your damaged frocks in, I'll tell you what I can do.'

And there it is again – the spark of ambition fizzing in my head; something different that I'd have to offer, that'll make my business stand out from the rest. 'That sounds fair enough.'

We shake hands and I glance surreptitiously at the fur coat on the rail.

I hesitate by the door. I change my mind about asking him how many alterations he does in a week because I suspect the answer is going to embarrass us both.

# KIM

There's a picture of Fern Banks in the *Camden Journal*. She's surrounded by billowing smoke and hugging her saved frocks to her heart, and she has that look in her eyes that I recognise from the couple of times I've met her; the look that says she knows me better than I know myself.

Staring at Fern in the paper, I'm trying to avoid seeing the hearse through the window.

The undertakers have come to take Enid. She went quietly in the night with no fuss and no last words. But when she didn't say good morning to me, I knew.

They're moving about upstairs. There's no point in me getting in the way. That's that, then. I am eighty-five and a widower.

I'm frightened of being alone. I'm a widower and I've lost my wife. What I need to do is, I need to get a new one. I know a lot of widows. All of Enid's friends are widows. I don't mind which one it is. I'm not looking for love or looks or even conversation, I just want someone in the house, moving about, someone to put the kettle on for. I do my own laundry. I don't need looking after.

What the bloody hell is all that bumping?

Aye, the stairs are narrow, I should have told them about that. Didn't think to. They can see it for themselves.

'Kim?'

Kim, is it now?

The lad comes into the sitting room. Young enough to be my grandson; bright, healthy-looking, and he's working in the undertakers. Says cheerfully, 'Sorry to trouble you, but we might have to take that door off the bottom of the stairs to get her out. It's that right-angled bend.'

If it's not one thing, it's another.

'Rubbish, lad! I've taken wardrobes and beds up and down these stairs without taking the door off. You telling me you can't get my wife down here? There's nothing of her.'

He looks at me with sudden concentration as if he's translating my words from a foreign language.

'Yeah. Okay. We'll have another go.'

I follow him into the dining room, where the door to the stairs is open and the edge of a trolley is wedged in the doorframe.

I stand on the bottom step next to the lad and take a quick look. Enid's strapped tightly to the trolley, underneath a red blanket, as if she's not dead but just chilly and likely to spring off it at any minute, protesting at the damage to the paintwork. I shake my head – if she were alive now, there'd be ructions.

'You want to back up a bit, you won't get it through at that angle,' I tell the lad.

He gets hold of the trolley. 'Back up a bit,' he tells his dad. They back up and disappear from view.

A muffled voice asks impatiently, 'Now what?'

I've never had a high opinion of myself. Didn't make it to grammar school – it was the technical college for me. But the older I get, the more faith I have in myself because people don't know how to think for themselves anymore. That's what's wrong – they don't have to figure things out – they get a google to do their thinking for them. I haven't got a google. I do things the old way. 'Hold her vertically,' I say.

'Okay, Kim. Gotcha. You go back in the sitting room, leave it to us. We'll call you when we're done.'

I smooth my hand down the waxed woodgrain of the door. Take the door off? How did they think that would help? The door opens outwards. They'd have to take the doorframe off.

Standing in the dining room, I can hear grunts and curses up the stairs; they're more like builders than undertakers. To them, it's just a job.

'You're having the funeral in the crem,' the lad says when he reappears in the doorway and sees I'm still there.

'The *crem*?' I say. He's too lazy to stick another four syllables on it.

'Crematorium,' he says helpfully and he backs up the stairs again.

Enid would have hated them.

She always thought that I'd go first. We both did. All her friends are widows and some of them had a new lease of life after their loss. I'm not saying she was looking forward to her widowhood, but she was pragmatic about it. She liked to make the best of things.

The husbands went in various different ways in their own time: heart attack, cancer, mobility scooter accident. Stan broke his hip on a golf course after Christmas. He'd tripped over the rake in the bunker, stayed there overnight and got hypothermia while his wife, Betty, thought he was in bed with her all the time. She'd been at watercolour classes, painting flowers. She'd undressed in the bathroom, tiptoed into bed, woke up the next morning, made him a cup of tea and saw he wasn't there, after all. Surprise of her life, she said, to see his side of the bed empty.

Enid thought it was the way he'd have wanted to go, on a

golf course. She was wrong about that. I know Stan. Stan wouldn't have chosen to die in a bunker, out of all the ways to go.

On a green, maybe. Stan was competitive.

But if he'd broken his hip on a green somebody would have seen him and there wouldn't have been a rake to trip over in the first place.

Betty had a shock when she read through his will, because he wanted his ashes scattered in the Himalayas. But by the time she read it, he'd been buried in East Finchley Cemetery.

It was a bit of a puzzler why he wanted to be scattered in the Himalayas. Betty couldn't fathom it. He didn't like heights or travelling. I think it was Stan's way of having an adventure to look forward to.

Enid thought he'd wanted to spite Betty, because even if Betty had read the will earlier, she'd have had all the worry of getting him there. Enid had a cynical view of people. She was always alert to people's motives.

In a marriage, it rubs off.

Stan was happily married to Betty, though.

Perhaps I could be happily married to her, too.

There's a thud then a rattle from somewhere in the house.

'Nearly done,' the lad tells me as they push Enid through the hall.

There we are, then. I sigh.

Since Enid died, I've sighed a lot. I've caught myself doing it.

The boss comes back for a last word to tell me that Enid will be available for viewing twenty-four seven until the funeral.

'Viewing?' I say. I don't want to view her. After she passed I couldn't even recognise her. Her face had relaxed and smoothed out, and she didn't look herself at all. I tried to find some features I was familiar with, but even her nose looked different.

I'm not saying there was anything funny about it; she was in her bed and it was her all right, but she just didn't look anything like my wife, Enid.

'Sometimes people like to say goodbye,' the undertaker points out, leaning against the door. 'So that option is available if needed.'

It was possible that her friends would want to say goodbye. I could take Betty and Mercia to see her. I'm not sure she'd like it. It would be personal, like watching her sleep.

I watch the undertakers drive away and I go back into the house.

It's proper empty now.

On the table there's a glossy business card that reads: *House Clearance. Proprietor: Cato Hamilton.*

I face life head on, always have. I go back upstairs to the bedroom and look at the empty space. Then I push my feelings aside and I think right, okay, let's get on with it. Her bed can go, for a start. I could get rid of both the beds and buy a new double for myself to sprawl around in.

I open the wardrobe and swish my hand against her pleated skirts. Her clothes can go, too. I sigh because it feels as if I haven't got enough air in my lungs to breathe; I have to keep gulping it in and letting it out.

Enid was always very particular about her clothes. She hung them up on silky padded coat hangers and she never wore slacks, always skirts and dresses. She thought of slacks on a woman as sloppy dressing. I was glad about that because I like the dresses. Trousers hold no novelty to me, but looking at her dresses was always a thrill.

I can wear any of her clothes now without her catching me or finding out. Looking in her wardrobe, though, they are still *her* clothes. There's a difference between looking at them and claiming them. Everything that used to be Enid's belongs to me now, but they're still Enid's really, even though she's no longer got any use for them.

Without even thinking about it, I take off my shirt and put on one of her blouses, white with gold buttons and long ties to make a bow. It's too small for me and I can't fasten it, but I pose in it and look at myself in the cheval glass. I see an old white-haired man in a lady's blouse, but I feel cool and elegant and it smells of her. I don't know what the smell is, she wasn't one for perfume, but it's a smell I recognise as being her smell.

I feel a gust of longing for her that almost knocks me off my feet.

I console myself with the thought that I can wear my sky-blue cocktail dress now. It's hidden at the bottom of my golf bag in a Sainsbury's carrier. I won't have to worry that the feathers are moulting. But the thought doesn't bring any relief, because . . .

*She's going to catch me*!

I know she's not, but that's how it feels.

I stand very still and listen.

It's dead quiet except for the humming of the fridge.

I remember Betty saying that Stan hung around the house for three days after he died. This seems unlikely, because surely the first thing he'd have done is told Betty not to bury him and to take his ashes to the Himalayas.

Anyway, I can get no enjoyment from wearing Enid's blouse after remembering that. I'll try it on again in three days' time. So I hang it back up again, put my shirt back on and once more I'm at a loose end in my empty house. I ring Betty. 'The undertakers have been,' I tell her.

'Oh, Kim,' she says. 'Poor Enid. Poor you.'

'Yes, well. No use brooding. I'm going to ring a chap called Cato Hamilton to clear her belongings.'

'Kim,' she says quickly, 'it's far too soon to get rid of things. George might want them. Don't do anything you'll regret. Just try to go on as usual for now.'

George won't want them. He has his own things. 'I can't go on as usual without her.'

'No. Of course not.' She's quiet for a moment.

'Do you want anything of hers?' I ask.

'Kim, if you want my advice, you'll wait a bit.'

I grunt a laugh. 'Why? In case she comes back?' I can hear Betty suck in through her teeth at my admittedly tasteless remark. 'I'm sorry. I don't know what's come over me,' I say apologetically.

She breathes out a forgiving sigh. 'Grief affects everyone differently,' she says. 'I expect it's different for men. The sentiment, I mean. I didn't feel right getting rid of Stan's clothes. I felt it wasn't enough that I'd lost him, I was giving away what little of him I had left. I gave his watch to my granddaughter's boyfriend and when they broke up, I regretted it, but she was heartbroken and I didn't like to bring it up. I know I sound rather mercenary, but I still think of tracking him down now and then, you know, to ask for it back. I wouldn't mind paying him for it.'

I nod. 'You should do that,' I tell her.

'Young people don't wear watches anyway.'

'Don't they?' I doubt this is true, but the sense of the world getting away from me comes over me strongly. I want to ask her what proof she has of this.

'If you do use Cato Hamilton, he's young but he's very fair. Presentable, too. I tested him out with Stan's Tantalus in the mahogany case that holds the three crystal decanters. Stan had it valued just before he died. He always fancied taking it to the *Antiques Roadshow* but he didn't want to be made a fool of. Funny, isn't it?'

'What is?'

'The way Stan was still carrying on as normal, little knowing . . .' She trailed off.

It wasn't funny at all, to my mind. That was the whole point, wasn't it? He was taken unawares. If Stan had known he was going to die on the golf course, he wouldn't have gone to play golf. 'Go on about the Tantalus,' I said.

'He offered me a good price. I didn't give it him, of course, but he took Stan's safari suits and all those old books he had, and my nose has cleared up ever since; I think it was the dust, you know.' She laughs, sounding bright and happy.

She hears her own happiness and apologises, remembering I'm now Kim, the widower.

'If there's anything at all you'd like of Enid's before I call him,' I remind her. 'Any of her clothes or anything.' I look around the room. 'Ornaments.'

'You mustn't think like that. Your life isn't over, Kim. It's still your house and you still need ornaments.'

No one needs ornaments. Enid had lost her enjoyment of them, too. They were a burden, more work, but she couldn't give them away because the cranberry glass was her mother's, the Royal Doulton was an investment and the Portmeirion bowl looked pretty with oranges in. 'I like pretty things, Kim,' she used to explain, as if it were some quality peculiar to her.

And it wasn't just the ornaments. We have more glasses than two people could ever need. I don't know why we have so many. We're not party folk.

And we have two dinner services, even though a one-course meal only needs one plate each. And a tea service, even though we only use mugs. Saucepans? Enough to feed an army. I'll get rid of the lot, let someone have them who'll use them.

'Kim? Are you still there?' Betty asks anxiously.

'Yes.'

'Of course, it's no business of mine. You must do what's right for you, when you're ready.'

I've only got myself to think of now. It's a bleak thought. 'Thank you, Betty.'

# LOT 7

*A calf-length green and gold pleated velvet skirt, Jaeger, circa 1990, size 10, along with a white silk pussycat bow blouse with gilt buttons, blouson sleeves, size 10.*

On Wednesday, it's pouring down. I've dropped off the damaged clothes at Moss's tailor's shop and I've got a strong feeling that at last, things are looking up.

Back at the market, the cream canvas awnings flap wetly. David Westwood is sitting on his chair, head down, engrossed in sanding something, possibly a dovetail joint. The rain is bouncing off my umbrella and he looks up at me with a flicker of interest, thinking I'm a customer.

'Morning,' I say brightly over the sound of the rain, hating to disappoint.

'Hi, Fern,' he says with a smile. He blows the dust from the wood and smooths his hand along it.

I stand and linger a bit longer, but he's concentrating on his work again, at home in his universe of stars.

There's something about that kind of single-mindedness that I find really attractive in a man.

I see it in Mick when he's working and his world, his existence, becomes all sound. But then I wonder if I'm just getting my emotions mixed up and it isn't admiration, it's jealousy, and because I'm attracted to him I want him to concentrate his attention on me. Mick, I mean, not David. Obviously.

I move on to my stall and poke a puddle of water out of my awning with my umbrella then stand back as it gushes along the cobbles. I wonder whether it's even worth setting up in this weather. There's nobody around. Our customers are all staying dry in the Horse Tunnel Market.

I sit on my suitcase and my phone rings. It's Cato Hamilton, returning my call.

Cato's an ambitious antiques trader in his late twenties who does house clearances. He has, in my opinion, an individual MO, because he's got contacts in the funeral trade who leave his flyers and business cards at the deceased's, and Cato waits for a response from the grateful executors. He's got a 20 per cent hit rate; being a stoic he's pleased with that. His personal style is the weekend-in-the-country look favoured by auctioneers: tweeds, soft flannel shirts and cords in autumn colours – berry red, straw yellow, purple heather, as if he's just coming in after a tour of the estate, his fair hair very slightly windblown. He's got a whispy fair beard that he's convinced will fill out in time.

He sells me the clothes because he hasn't got any interest in textiles – too specialist, he says. I keep the ones I want, give the high-street wearables to charity and take the rags for recycling.

We first met outside the Angel Comedy Club in Islington on a cold night in January, clapping our hands and stomping our feet to keep warm. This was our opening conversation:

ME: 'Great! We'll be first in! Yay!' (Holds out hand.) 'Fern Banks.'

HIM: 'Cato Hamilton.'

ME: 'Ha ha ha! Seriously? Cato? Your parents must really love *The Pink Panther* films!'

HIM [aloofly]: 'No. They're Stoics.'

But we had an hour to kill just queuing and in that hour we found an area of mutual interest, which he described endearingly as 'the search for pre-owned treasure'. In his case it's an old master and in mine, a couture ensemble with a label discreetly hidden in a seam and no sweat marks.

'Hi, Cato,' I say cheerfully, shouting above the patter of rain on the canvas. 'Have you got anything for me?'

'Can you read Arabic?' he asks.

'No.'

'Oh. Right, what have I got? I've got some men's clothing here, if you're interested. Safari suits. Must be, ooh, about nine or ten of them. Large. I've had them a while, so I can give you a good deal on the price.'

I laugh. 'Nine or ten safari suits?'

'He was a bit of an armchair traveller, this guy. Collected adventure books but he never left the country, his wife said.'

Making him promise to keep me in mind, I then google the local churches to find out when their sales are on. Primrose Hill, Belsize Park and Regent's Park are areas that regularly enjoy sharing the distribution of wealth. Naomi Watts is happy to hear from me. Her church has started a weekly clothing sale on Sunday afternoons during the summer, at the same time as they serve teas in the garden. I can't make Sundays – they're the busiest days in Camden Lock – but it helps to be practical.

'Come on Saturday night for sorting,' she says, 'and maybe you could bring your Allen keys. The clothing rails need tightening up.'

'Will do!'

I've just put my phone back in my pocket when it rings. It's Mick, who I haven't heard from for a week. He sounds cheerful, even at this time of the morning, and we flirt a little.

I love his deep, decisive voice. He's got the kind of voice that makes everything sound like an indecent proposal.

'Quick call. I've got two tickets to the Jazz Cafe in Camden Town on Friday. Are you free?'

My stomach flips and I grip the phone tightly. 'Oh, I'm free,' I say breathlessly.

He laughs and we agree on a time to meet, then off he goes.

Mick's phone call restores my energy. I watch the raindrops bouncing off the cobbles and I squint at the sky. The dark clouds are fading to silver grey. I pay another visit to my neighbour. 'Hey, David!'

He looks up at me, eyebrows raised in query, watching me loitering under my umbrella.

'I think the rain's easing off.'

He looks at me a little longer and when he realises that I've come to the end of my statement, he says, 'Oh, good,' and goes back to his sanding. He's got one of those little fold-up silver mesh baskets and he drops a piece of used sandpaper in it then cuts himself a fresh piece.

I like watching him work. 'That was Mick on the phone,' I tell him, in case he thinks I'm staring at him because I fancy him. 'He's been on tour.'

'Good,' he says again.

'So, where did you and Gigi meet?'

He looks up patiently. 'In an Argentinian steakhouse.'

'Really?'

'She was trying to get a vegetarian option.'

'Oh, okay. And then what?'

He puts the woods down and sits back in his chair with his hands behind his head. 'It was love at first sight. Wham! It hit me right between the eyes.'

'Wow. What was she wearing?' I asked, eager to fill in the details.

He pulls a face. 'I don't know, something, some kind of skirt, I expect.'

It's not the most satisfying love story I've ever heard. Maybe he's not telling it right. 'Usually, love hits people in their hearts; but you felt it between the eyes, did you?'

'Fern, that was a joke. I don't believe in love at first sight.'

'Don't you? Me neither.'

'But I found her interesting and slightly . . .' He tails off thoughtfully and shakes his head.

'Slightly what?' I prompt.

'Unknowable,' he finishes. 'Still waters run deep.'

Gigi, in my opinion, has about the stillness of a Jacuzzi on full power, but obviously I could be wrong about this. I don't know her that well.

'That's why I'm doing this,' he says, gesturing around him. 'I was a headhunter until I met Gigi. I've spent the last few years finding perfect people for perfect jobs and now it's my turn. Thanks to Gigi, I'm following my dream.' His face creases into a smile and his eyes meet mine. 'It's a good feeling.'

'Yes, I can see that,' I say, realising I'd completely under-estimated Gigi's empathy.

There's the splash of high heels in puddles and to my surprise, Dinah Moss is coming along the alley wearing a red raincoat, a black trilby, black stockings and red patent court shoes. (And it works.)

She sees me and waves happily. 'Fern Banks!' Coming under the awning with David and me, she lowers her red umbrella and flaps it wildly. 'This weather!'

'What on earth are you doing here?'

'I've come to thank you. You have given Moss a new interest in life.' She looks at the stall in dismay. 'What's this with the boxes? Where are your clothes?'

'Next door, but it's too wet to open up. We haven't seen a soul yet, apart from you.'

She tuts, disapproving of my attitude. 'This one's opened up,' she says to me, jerking her thumb at David.

He grins at me smugly.

I snort. 'Yes, but he hasn't sold anything, has he?'

Dinah blanks me. She turns her back on me and holds out a wet hand to David. 'Let me introduce myself. Dinah. Dinah Moss.'

'David Westwood.'

'Now, David, explain to me about these interesting boxes. Is it a game?'

David goes through his spiel and asks her when her birthday is. It turns out that both Dinah and Moss are air signs, both apparently capable of the power of the hurricane or the delightful caress of a summer breeze. 'Gemini, Aquarius, you and your husband have perfect compatibility,' he tells her.

'It's true! How we met was destiny, fate, true love,' Dinah agrees passionately.

David picks up his box of drilled Perspex sheets and slots them into a box. 'Now this is Aquarius, the water carrier. Look, you can see him bending forward with the jug in his hand—'

'And I can see the water pouring from it!' Dinah says excitedly.

'That's right! You've got a good eye for the heavens. And this is Gemini. See, they're holding hands.'

'I see it!' Dinah says.

David says gently, 'See these big stars in Gemini? This one's called Castor and this one's called Pollux. In Greek mythology, they were the sons of Leda.'

I'm staring out at the rain and only half listening as he starts telling the story of Castor and Pollux. I roll my eyes. It's all a load of pollux, if you ask me.

For a self-confessed cynic, he's very convincing, and his voice is gentle and almost hypnotic. As he talks about their perfect compatibility, Dinah agrees.

'I was wearing scarlet lipstick and Moss said I was beautiful and asked me to dance. What do you say about that?'

'I'd say he was absolutely right,' David replies.

She swats his shoulder. 'Oh, you! You are a charmer! I wasn't beautiful, but he made me feel beautiful and I loved him for it then. I love him for it now,' she said firmly, tossing her head as if he's challenging her. She turns to look at me and says ecstatically, 'Fern, you've met Moss. You know the man only, but I still see the boy. I'd do anything for him and he'd do anything for me. He's my sunlight, my joy! I look after him and he looks after me.' It's a declaration of love and in the dark shadow of David's stall, her face is radiant with happiness.

It's depressing, that's what it is. My relationship with Mick seems horribly superficial in comparison.

I wonder what David's thinking. He's frowning, too, and he's still holding the light box tightly. The whites of his knuckles are powdered with wood dust.

'And now Moss has work,' she says, winking at me and pinching my cheek. 'Thanks to this one.'

I yelp as the blood flows into it like a blush.

'So now, Mr Westwood, I'll take this box as you've explained it so well. You have something for me to carry it in?'

David wraps it up carefully and puts it into a brown paper bag.

Once Dinah has paid, she brandishes the bag in front of my face. 'You see? He's open, so I bought something. That's how it works. Maybe if you were open, I'd buy something from you, too.' The rain is dripping from the brim of her hat and she's very wet.

'Where exactly are you off to in this weather?' I ask curiously.

She looks surprised. 'I came to see you, because you and Moss, you're in business now.' She pulls me towards her and says in my ear, 'You won't regret it. I'm telling you, my dear, it's a good decision. I promise you, you'll get your reward.'

And there it is again: no good deed ever goes unpunished is an obvious lie.

Dinah tucks the parcel under her arm, opens her umbrella and steps back out into the rain.

I watch her splash along the cobbles, slender legs and red shoes under the red umbrella. I'm disturbed by her promise, because the reward's not my motivation. I don't want her to think it is.

'She's a character, isn't she?' David says, breaking into my thoughts. 'Is she German?'

'I think so.'

'How do you know her?'

I tuck my hands in my damp pockets. 'That day you and I first met, and you grabbed my case as I dashed onto the bus, I was giving her back the money she'd just dropped.'

'Really?'

His gaze seeks mine and our eyes lock meaningfully. His don't look so blue now; they look deep and black as the night sky.

He says, 'The three of us were aligned on that day. Do you realise, Fern, if it wasn't for that . . .'

I hold my breath and finish the sentence in my mind – *we'd never have met.*

But he carries on cheerfully, 'I'd be warm and dry in the Market Hall right now.'

# KIM

It's raining. I've got the lights on. Enid kept me on the straight and narrow for sixty years, and now that she's gone and I'm home all alone, I think about her clothes all the time. When I try them on they feel as cool and gentle as her touch. I can't concentrate on anything else. They're a guilty obsession. They're all I can think of. I'll be glad when Cato Hamilton takes them away.

Let's get this straight – I don't want to *be* a woman. I've never thought I was born in the wrong body. I'm not tormented by it. It's more like the feeling when you want a scone with jam and cream and you look in the fridge and there's no cream. You hanker after it and settle for a scone and jam but it niggles and takes the enjoyment out of eating. Because it's better with cream.

Being in the house without Enid is better when I'm wearing her frock.

This one is hers, the one I've got on. It's purple and very tight on me; I struggled to fasten the zip. Enid was slim, with the appetite of a sparrow. She deplored greed. Enid was a model of restraint and I always admired that in her.

The doorbell rings and I stand motionless. I've got half a mind not to answer it, but I haven't spoken to anyone for two days, so I pull on my plaid dressing gown over the frock to answer the door.

Mercia's standing on the doorstep wearing a transparent rain hat over her fair hair and lobster oven gloves. She's carrying a lasagne in a Pyrex dish and she's startled to see me in my dressing gown.

'Ooo! Did I disturb you?' she asked, full of concern.

'No. Come in,' I tell her.

'It's still hot, but if you're not going to eat it now you might want to pop it in the microwave for a couple of minutes. I'll take it through to the kitchen.'

She comes back still wearing her oven gloves. She smacks them together and barks like a seal, which makes me laugh.

'Tea?' I ask her.

'Lovely!'

Under my robe, the frock tickled my shins as I walked to the kitchen. I feel daring and uneasy. Enid would have something to say about me entertaining a woman in my dressing gown, never mind what was underneath.

I carry the two mugs into the sitting room and I fling open the curtains. The window's freckled with rain. There's a fine layer of dust on the windowsill, as fine as face powder.

Mercia's sitting down and I notice she's wearing lipstick, pink and pearly.

Enid stopped wearing make-up at around the time that her hair started to go grey. She said she felt a fool in it, at her age. 'I look like a pantomime dame,' she said crossly, looking at herself in the magnifying mirror. 'I'm not trying to attract a man, after all. It's different for Mercia.'

Mercia has been widowed for many years. Her husband Bertie was buried in the South China Sea. He died on a cruise. She never showed any sign of wanting another husband. She takes holidays at regular intervals – organised tours by coach or train – although she's given up on cruises for obvious reasons. She always looks nicely put together.

I sit opposite her and my heart's beating so hard that I can hear it thump in my ears like waves on the beach.

She smiles. 'You're looking . . .' She doesn't finish the observation. Something has caught her eye and her smile fades.

I know immediately even without looking that my purple frock is showing. I cover my knees quickly with my robe.

Mercia raises her eyebrows. She doesn't meet my eyes for a few long moments while she keeps her thoughts under control.

I gulp my tea down quickly, even though it's hot. Suddenly, I can't breathe properly. My ribcage won't expand. I'm suffocating. The frock is too tight.

I see black spots floating before my eyes, just a few at first, as if it's snowing soot. It turns into a blizzard that blots Mercia out. I can feel my muscles weaken.

I'm dying.

I imagine the voices of the paramedics: *this old guy wearing a frock so tight he suffocated himself.*

Concerned, Mercia's voice comes from a great distance. 'Are you all right, Kim?'

I shake my head frantically and tear off the dressing gown.

She gets to her feet and I plead with her, 'Mercia, don't go! Could you unfasten it? I can't breathe!' I'm struggling to stand, gasping shallowly like an old fool while Mercia comes behind me and tugs at the zip fastener.

'Can't get a grip on it; I've got a touch of arthritis,' she says grimly. 'Have you got a paperclip? Or a shoelace?'

The blizzard of spots blots out the room and I can feel my thoughts draining from my head.

'Oh! Hang on there, Kim,' she says. She dashes off and comes back with a pair of scissors. 'Hold still!' I can feel the cold blade against my chest as she cuts straight down the bodice of the frock, through my chest hair.

Released, I gulp air in gratefully and my ribs expand. I sit down, panting and flexing my shoulders, and the spots gradually clear from my vision like midges in sunlight. I'm too ashamed to look at her.

As I put my dressing gown back on, Mercia starts to giggle.

'Honestly, I don't know how you ever got into it,' she says.

She's laughing at me. I look down at my white-haired chest. Pathetic. I close my dressing gown and knot the belt tight.

'Sorry, Kim,' she says. 'Didn't mean to laugh. I wasn't laughing *at* you. Politically incorrect and all that. It's just . . .' Another giggle escapes. 'It's as if you had the vapours.'

'The vapours?'

'Swooning. Like a Victorian heroine in her corsets.'

'I shouldn't have sat down in it. I shouldn't have had the tea.' *I shouldn't have worn Enid's dress.* Reluctantly, I force myself to look at her through my shame and I ask, 'What's going to happen now?'

'In what way?'

I stare at her for a moment. 'People talking.'

She raises her eyebrows again and blows out sharply through her nose.

I've offended her. I watch her drink her tea. Soon, the cup will be empty and she'll go. I can't wait for her to go.

She puts the cup carefully down on Enid's favourite coaster, which has a blue sailboat on it. 'Shall I tell you the secret to happiness, Kim?'

'Go on.'

'You've got to move with the times.'

'Move with the times,' I repeat.

'Nobody cares about this sort of thing anymore, Kim. It's different now. Things have changed. Boys can wear skirts as part of their school uniform. Where have you been for the past few years?'

I've been here, with Enid. 'I didn't think that sort of thing had anything to do with me,' I tell her.

'Never mind. It's never too late to learn,' she says, getting to her feet. She glances at me and presses her lips together, squeezing back a smile. 'Although, if you're going to make a habit of it, you might want to buy yourself clothes that fit.'

Her kindness fills me with gratitude and I nod, seeing her face through a film of tears.

'Don't forget to eat the lasagne. Keep your strength up,' she advises.

After she's gone, I eat the lasagne, but my shame still hangs over me and I've got an evening to fill, so I empty Enid's wardrobe into black bin bags and call Cato Hamilton.

Delivering myself from temptation, Enid would say.

# LOT 8

*Black velvet opera cape with large padded collar and pink silk lining, hook fastening, full-length, circa 1936, unlabelled.*

Now that Moss has magically and skilfully restored my dresses and suits to their former glory, business has picked up again. Before I restock on Friday night, I spray the flat with Moth Stop, because when I opened my wardrobe door a movement caught my eye and to my horror, I saw a little brown moth fluttering out of sight into a wool jacket.

Fabric moths look so innocuous, like tiny folds of delicate tissue paper, but their one job is to reproduce and they're good at it, so they like to be part of a gang. The moths do the breeding not the eating and their larvae are pretty, almost decorative, like fine silver silken threads. The larvae, too, have a mission in life, which is to eat. It's the larvae that do the damage. I'm not talking about a snack here. One small hole in a garment isn't too bad. But these little grubs treat it more like a running buffet; a little bit here, a little bit there, a quick look at what its neighbour is having and a speedy wriggle to a new spot.

Their secret weapon is they look so surprisingly innocent, but like most insects they're totally dedicated to a cause. Forget cedar balls. Cedar balls don't bother them in the slightest.

Moths will happily reproduce using cedar balls as furniture. Professional and expensive fumigation works in the short term, but once the larvae find a good source of food they'll eventually come back and carry on where they left off.

What kills them best are old-fashioned mothballs, those little pungent white balls that dissolve and gradually give off a gas that poisons moths – and, incidentally, repels snakes, bats and squirrels, gives susceptible people anaemia and puts off customers.

The war between clothes moths and me is ongoing.

I stick some pheromone moth traps around the flat to gauge the degree of the infestation and spray the place liberally with pesticide. Then I go along to St Mark's Church, where they're setting up for the Nearly-New Clothing Sale.

I like working in the vast holy emptiness of the church and I like the organiser, Naomi Brown. She's a tall, slender woman with an eye for the asymmetric in hems, sleeves, necklines and hairstyle, who greets me warmly because I've brought my Allen keys to tighten up the clothing rails that invariably develop a lean.

The church is sunlit, jewelled with stained glass, highlighted with gold-leafed angels, and we're watched over by a solemn Virgin Mary holding a chubby toddler.

There are lots of bags on the floor – bin bags, carrier bags, designer shopping bags –and that's when the excitement starts, when we begin to unpack. There might be a Primark dress in a Selfridge's bag and a John Galliano suit in a bin liner.

Since the popularity of vintage, more people have become experts on the subject. The charity shops keep the labels and sell them at a premium price. The jumble sale has been dropped for 'nearly new' and Mary Portas is the Queen of the High Street, so the church nearly-new sale is always popular for bargains.

I like this kind of redistribution of wealth and I'm happy to be on this side of the church door instead of queueing early outside with other dealers; they're the first people in line for any sale. We pitch up early and have an eye for a bargain, but what got me on this side of the door was my knowledge about fashion and how much things ought to be sold for. I always offer a fair price. As helpers, we get first choice and first refusal, which is a huge plus.

Naomi's an expert, not only on fashion, but also on the people who bring the clothes. She knows the importance of provenance, she likes people and she also knows interesting facts, such as that Jesus's clothes had no seams.

Not only that, but the lack of seams in his robes had also been foreshadowed in the Old Testament years before – it was that big a deal. I love that kind of detail. Little-known fact: the Bible's big on clothes.

Some of the items I recognise from previous sales, because the church also acts as a clothing swap for disciplined people who believe in the one-in-one-out method of minimalism.

I unearth a tan fringed leather poncho, a gold leather cowboy shirt and a matching skirt. I come across a Comme des Garçons dress, which I show to Naomi Brown, and she says that Joan Fielding, a psychotherapist, has brought them in.

'Post-nuclear' seems a surprisingly chaotic choice of dress for a psychotherapist – it's black, with mismatched sleeves, random slits and raw hems, but who knows? It might have been the owner's idea of sartorial humour.

I'm interested in the Comme des Garçons and I fall in love with a Le Smoking-style evening trouser suit, which I buy with a compulsive feeling that if I didn't, I'd regret it. I know I will find a buyer for it.

I also like a full-length black opera cape lined in pink silk that I can see Gigi wearing, with her love for the dramatic.

Naomi prices the four items for me and at 8 pm we call it a day and have a glass of wine each before heading home.

As an added bonus, Cato turns up at my place on Monday night with a consignment of orange-bin-bagged clothes from someone who'd recently passed, and a bottle of Romanian wine.

'You're going to like these,' he promises, dumping the bin bags in the centre of the room. He tosses his tweed cap onto Dolly's head.

The bags sigh as if punched and slowly exhale the dying breath of floral scent.

He sits on the edge of the red sofa, gripping his moss green cord-clad knees in anticipation. 'This lady was a padded coat-hanger kind of gal,' he says, because I've told him that I judge people by their coat hangers.

It suddenly occurs to me that David Westwood probably uses wooden ones. I'm not sure why I keep thinking about him. 'Good,' I say, contemplating the mound of bags warily. There's nothing quite as exciting as going through old clothes, but sometimes there's nothing so disgusting, either, and I never know which it's going to be.

By arrangement, Cato brings all the garments for me to sort – and that includes stiff underwear, grub-eaten wool, stained pyjamas and the soiled laundry that people assume they'll tackle at some time in the future when they're ready to, not realising how time-consuming dying is.

Or maybe they do realise.

Maybe they realise then they sink back into their soft pillows and think, what the hell! Let someone else deal with it!

Let's face it, it's got to be one of the main perks of dying: the knowledge that keeping your possessions in order isn't your problem anymore.

'Okay! Let's see what we've got,' I decide robustly, ripping open the bags and upending the clothes on the floor while Cato finds my wine glasses and unscrews the cap on the bottle.

'Ta-dah! Oooh!' I say, admiring the promising orgiastic huddle of entwined velvet and silk, or possibly acrylic and polyester.

Cato stares at the pile with interest, wedging the bottle between his knees.

He generally takes my word for it whether the clothes are designer or not, and he's learned that Jonelle is actually John Lewis and Florence and Fred is Tesco, not a couture label.

'Her husband just wanted her things cleared. He doesn't want to keep anything of hers; no jewellery, nothing. He says he's not sentimental that way.'

One thing I've learned over the years is that 'one size fits all' is a myth, in clothes as in life. I look up and meet Cato's pale green eyes.

'I suppose grief hits some people like that. They don't want to be reminded of what they've lost,' I comment, draping the clothes on the chairs.

Bottom line – there's no smell of mothballs and the dresses are pristine. If clothes are the outward manifestation of a person, this woman was squeaky clean and had impeccable taste. 'Look how slim she was.' The clothes' previous occupant favoured long pleated skirts in rich colours, pussycat bow blouses and jersey dresses, Jean Muir for Jaeger. My eyes light up. I have new stock!

As I unfold them I notice that one of the dresses, a purple wool crêpe, has been unevenly cut down the front with a pair of scissors. I smooth it out and wonder whether she was trying to remodel it. But it looks wildly haphazard and freehand. Sacrilege! 'Eww, it's covered in white hairs.'

'Maybe she put it on a dog,' Cato says. 'Possibly a greyhound, from the shape.'

'Don't!' I shudder at the thought. I put the ruined dress to one side and hold up a long green-and-gold printed velvet skirt. Loving it. It falls to my ankles. 'She was really into pleats, wasn't she?' I say, checking the label. 'I *love* pleats and pussycat bows.'

'Do you?' Cato asks with sudden interest. 'I didn't think they'd be your kind of thing. They look a bit Thatcherish to me.'

'True . . . they are a bit Thatcherish,' I agree, quickly playing it down – it's always a mistake to be too eager with Cato during negotiations. 'She's tall, too. But so *neat*.' I take a gulp of Cato's Romanian wine and glance at him for corroboration. 'She *was* neat, right?'

'Oh, absolutely.'

'You know what they say? Clothes are the outward manifestation of our inner lives.'

'Who says that?'

'Er – I do.' That's what I believe. The woman these clothes belonged to had abandoned her earthly body for dimensions new, but she'd left something of her personality behind and it resonated positively with me.

'Our outward manifestation? Oh, I like that,' Cato says, dabbing his mouth with a monogrammed handkerchief – not his monogram though, I notice. 'It's very philosophical.'

'Thanks.' I'm really pleased with the contents of the bags. The summer is coming but the days are still cool, perfect for the mid-season gravitas of velvet and silk. I'll choose an outfit for myself, too, to wear on the stall as an advertisement for my new stock. I can feel a whole new persona coming on thanks to Cato. I'll be cool and well groomed and prim. 'I'll give you thirty for the lot.'

Cato chokes politely on his drink and gives me an injured look. 'Come *on*, Fern, play fair. You *love* them.'

'I only love them with thirty pounds worth of love. Like you said, they're a bit Thatcherish. It's a niche market. And they're a small size.'

Cato holds his wine glass up to the dim light from the window and contemplates it thoughtfully. His pale wispy beard blurs his jawline, giving him a saintly aura. 'You can have the lot for a hundred.'

Now it's my turn to be appalled and I close my eyes wearily. 'Pass me the bottle, will you.'

He tops up my glass. 'I've read the labels. Some of these dresses are Jon Mweer,' he says in a dubious French accent.

'Jean Muir. She wasn't French, she was British. Forty.'

'Eighty.'

'Forty-five.'

'Fifty.'

I do a double-take. 'Fine, that's fair, fifty then.' There will definitely be a profit in it for me. I open a packet of Marmite thins – don't let anyone tell you I'm not a good hostess. Marmite thins are a great invention. I make them look artistic on the plate. I've been watching *MasterChef* and it's all about the presentation.

Cato and I do our familiar riff on how hard it is to make money doing what we're doing and we reassure each other that really we're doing it because it's our passion. Which is true, but we've still got to live. 'How long are you going to give it?' I ask him.

'Five years. You?'

'More like five months, ha ha,' I say merrily. 'We've just got to get *known*, haven't we? I'm scraping by at the moment, to be honest.'

Cato glances discreetly around this Primrose Hill flat that my parents own. 'Same,' he says. 'Scraping by.' He chinks his glass against mine. 'It's just a matter of discovering one good thing; one sleeper . . . something with provenance that'll make a fortune . . .'

'Just one beautiful garment,' I say thoughtfully. 'There's this woman I met recently. She's got this wardrobe and it's so wonderful, Cato. And the thing is, she *knows* how lucky she is,' I say with the intensity I get when I'm halfway to being drunk. 'She *knows*.'

'That's what I'm saying,' he replies. 'Once you have a passion . . .'

I'm excited, lying on the floor with my wine and a whole new wardrobe of clothes to admire. I'm looking forward to turning myself into a human mannequin, teaming the gold-and-green pleated skirt with flat brown brogues and a white silk shirt with a pussycat bow, enjoying their sheer loveliness.

Happily, I don't realise it's a decision I'll turn out to regret.


Before I keep my date with Mick at the Jazz Cafe, I change the sheets, shave my legs and paint my toenails. I can't wait to see him. This date will eclipse my inexplicable crush on David Westwood and get him out of my head. It's always exciting meeting up with Mick again because we've never been together long enough to get bored, so it's like a series of first dates, where we look at each other closely, enjoy the novelty of being together, feel each other up under the table and fall in lust all over again.

It helps that in appearance he's absolutely nothing like David Westwood. Mick has got shaggy red hair, a short red beard and the palest blue eyes I've ever seen. He's distinctive. He's average height but he's got the flawless, innocent face of a Da Vinci disciple and with his beard – really, he's impossible to overlook. And nobody did overlook him until a couple of months after we met, when he shaved his beard off on impulse and I didn't recognise him.

It wasn't just me. Not recognising him, doormen at clubs that he'd gone to for years ignored him, his mates asked him to his face where he was and he travelled around perfectly anonymously until he grew the beard back and became visible again.

He smokes roll-ups with narrowed eyes and taps out drumbeats on tables, but he's also kind and funny, which is why we're still together.

Obviously, I'm dressing to impress him in my new clothes. I wear the silk blouse with a pussycat bow and the green-and-gold pleated skirt. It feels elegant as it swirls around my bare ankles and it makes me walk taller. I team it with my brown brogues and tie my hair up in a high ponytail.

Being the trendy place it is, it's hard to stand out in Camden Town, which is one of the area's most endearing features in my opinion. Even the most outrageously dressed people will find they're just one of many, so as I happily walk from the flat, down Parkway to the Jazz Cafe in the cool evening air, velvet skirt billowing, I'm feeling pretty good about myself.

I can see Mick waiting for me in the queue, his copper hair burnished by the sun, and I sneak up to him and tap him on the left shoulder then feint to the right – it's a joke we play on each other.

He turns around with a big smile, which instantly fades as he looks me up and down.

Instead of the admiring hug and kiss that I'd been anticipating, he takes a quick step back, rakes his hand through his hair, looks me up and down once more and says, 'Fuck me! Who made you granny all of a sudden?'

To display the clothes successfully I've accessorised with a pair of tortoiseshell glasses. 'Gorgeous, aren't they? Feel!' I said, grabbing his hand and smoothing it down the pleats of my skirt around my thigh.

But he's not laughing at all and he pulls back. 'No, seriously, Fern. Take the glasses off. You look weird.'

I feel my confidence drain, replaced by self-consciousness and uncertainty. The magic goes out of me – the warm breath of velvet against my legs, the shivery touch of the silk against my arms, and all I can think now is: do I really look that bad? Rallying, I conclude that no, of course I don't. I just look different from what he's used to. This realisation is followed swiftly by annoyance and I fight back, folding my arms. 'You look weird as well, Mick, actually. What's with the T-shirt?'

Mick looks down at himself as we shuffle forward in the queue. We're right behind a group of girls looking at their phones.

'What are you talking about? This is my Status Quo T-shirt,' he says. 'I always wear it.'

It's true, he does always wear it, but it feels as if I'm seeing it for the very first time because now it doesn't accessorise with what I'm wearing. We don't look like a couple at all anymore. We look like random strangers in a queue. We clash, horribly. We're totally mismatched. 'What you need, Mick, is a tweed jacket and brogues,' I tell him, thinking fleetingly of Cato, who would, as it happens, coordinate with me perfectly.

Mick stares at me blankly and rubs his pale blue eyes. When he looks at me again, they're narrowed and watery and even more naked.

'I don't get it,' he says, giving me the once-over as if confirming his initial impression. 'What's going on, Fern?'

'Nothing's going on,' I tell him. 'It's my new look.'

'But it's an *old* look. You look like a National Trust life member.'

'Thanks.'

The girls in front of us in the queue stop playing with their phones and turn around to see what a National Trust life member looks like. I glare at them disapprovingly over the top of my glasses.

When I met Mick at the beginning of last summer at a festival, I was going through my Kate Moss phase; fringed shorts, boots and floaty tops. He liked the free-spirited image because it complemented his own, which is ageing rock star. His T-shirt collection is from gigs that he's been to and the logos are so faded from washing that you have to be really committed to work out the image on them. Just to make it clear, despite the rock star T-shirts, I've never viewed him as merely an accessory – I genuinely like him. Or did.

Which is why his criticism hurts so much.

In my frayed shorts and boots I used to slouch a bit, but now I'm walking tall, as if the previous owner still inhabits her clothes in spirit. Standing straight makes me a couple of inches taller than Mick and when he goes to put his arm around my shoulders, he has to reach up a bit. He gives up and pulls the ends of my white pussycat bow.

'Hey!'

'That's better,' he says. 'Undo a couple of buttons and let your hair down.'

I'm deeply outraged. 'Mick, I'm not used to men telling me how to dress. In fact, I think there's something unpleasantly controlling about a man who judges a woman's wardrobe.'

Call me cynical, but most men only notice a woman's clothes if they're short and bodycon. In a situation like this they have two stock responses (*delete where applicable): 1) Wow! You look hot! 2) What? I didn't even notice her!

So, I tie the floating white ribbons into a bow again and we shuffle nearer to the door in an atmosphere of hostility. The bouncer nods in acknowledgement and Mick shakes his head wearily then does something with his eyes that makes the bouncer look me up and down. He smirks.

'Oi! I *saw* that,' I protest, elbowing him, but just then he lets us into the Jazz Cafe and the argument is put on hold for a while.

Despite the music, which is good and loud, and the drinks that keep coming, and the fact we have a table and food, the night doesn't go well. Mick barely looks at me. I resent his attitude. I keep playing the conversation over and over in my head – *granny???* – and I formulate so many counterarguments to his criticism that it feels as if we've been yelling at each other all night.

When it's over and we're back outside in the dumb, raucous hustle of the late-night crowds, I fold my arms and look at him accusingly.

'Fern.' Mick says my name and takes me in his arms very lovingly. 'This is crazy.'

'I know.' I nestle into the soft right angle of his neck and shoulder with a sigh. His beard smells of mandarin and cedar-wood. I'm ready to forgive him. 'I've missed you so much. I can't believe we're arguing.'

'I've missed you, too,' he says in his lovely deep voice. He kisses me softly and gives a wry grin. 'Just promise me you won't wear this ridiculous look again. Not when you're out with me.'

And suddenly it all flares back up again, and we're back to square one. 'Mick! Argh! You can't tell me what to wear!'

'Whoa! Easy! I'm not telling you what to wear. I'm just saying that you look better in other stuff – what's wrong with that? I'm just being honest. Anyway, don't you think it's super-ficial to be so fixated on the clothes you wear?'

'Now who's fixated? Don't *you* think it's superficial to be judging me on them?'

'I'm not judging you, am I? Come on, Doll, let's go home.'
He puts his arm around me.

I brace myself. 'No.'

He laughs. 'No?'

'Not until you apologise.'

'Apologise for what? Laughing at your dress sense?'

This is the thing – his comments hurt so much it's like a physical pain. My emotions are bashing around in my head and I can't control them, even with logic. Fashion is my thing, my area of expertise, my specialist subject, and I should be able to rise above it because what does he know about style? His clothes are all jeans and band promos.

But I can't let it go. He's mocking the part of me that I'm most proud of and I'm all ready to hit back hard. 'Mick, if you're not going to apologise you can go back to Harpenden tonight. I just don't want to talk to you anymore at the moment.'

He frowns. This is where he should back down, apologise and beg me to forgive him. Instead, he looks at his watch. 'Okay. Fine. Have it your own way, if that's how you feel.' And he heads quickly for the Tube to King's Cross so that he can catch the last train home.


'You're uncharacteristically quiet,' David Westwood says to me the next morning, emerging pale-faced from his personal universe like the man in the moon to offer me some coffee from his flask. He's brought an extra cup. I'm deeply touched.

I fill him in on the reasons for my misery. 'It's our first major argument. Although Mick would probably agree with me that we've never gone through the stage of actually being in love, I've always been pretty fond of him,' I say, playing with my pleated skirt.

*Fond?*

The new clothes from Cato are hanging up around me on my stall and I start to wonder if I really have turned into another person altogether, because 'fond' isn't a word that I'd normally use.

'Why don't you just wear something else instead?' David asks reasonably, moving his teak chair closer to my stool.

'Because! I like the power of transformation. It's my super-power; my own personal airbag to defend me from people,' I explain. 'Everyone has an airbag, even if they don't realise it. Maybe it's jokes or sex or superiority or alcohol, something anyway to use as a buffer between them and the world. With me, it's clothes. I could tell you other stuff like my name is Fern Banks and I have this stall, Fern Banks Vintage, and my hair is dark blonde, but these facts are subject to change, so I'm just describing myself the way I am now, today. Tomorrow, who knows?'

David's sitting there drinking from his steel flask lid – it's a strange juxtaposition of images because he's so startlingly good-looking you always expect him to be drinking Dirty Martinis. 'Yes,' he says.

I take that to mean he agrees with me. Encouraged, I expand on my hypothesis. 'See, in my opinion the art of reinvention is one of the best things about being human. It's what separates us from animals because, let's face it, despite their intelligence, you never see a dolphin in fancy dress. A dolphin would never wear a cow outfit because a dolphin has no conception of a cow. A dolphin knows what it is and sticks with it.' I'm passionate about this and I really want him to understand.

He looks at me thoughtfully through the steam of his coffee for what seems like a long time and I wonder if maybe there's the potential for a deep connection between us. If he and Gigi don't work out, I mean. But she'd be crazy to let him go – he really is incredibly good-looking.

Finally, he responds. 'You lost me at "dolphin in fancy dress",' he says.

I'm at home scrolling through the Tallulah Young Auction Catalogue on the screen. Tallulah Young specialises in vintage and retro fashion and I'm looking for anything with an affordable guide price when my father calls. He's not happy. He leaves out the niceties and plunges straight in, as formal as a lawyer.

'I understand from the managing agents that there's been a fire in the flat,' he says. 'It would have been courteous of you to have informed us yourself, in the circumstances; the flat not actually being yours.'

'Well, it wasn't in our flat, it was in the flat above.'

I can hear my mother prompting him in the background.

'Yes, yes,' he says briskly to her, and then to me, 'Our bathroom ceiling has had to be repaired, has it not?'

When he's annoyed he talks like that, in senior civil servant language.

'It has. But it's okay, Dad, the building insurance covered it.'

'And I understand the front door was damaged. Do you realise it could have resulted in compromised security?'

'Well, not really, it was just a bit of the panel. Anyway, it's fixed now.' It's not going to help if I tell him it was repaired by me. At times like this, I've found it's best to say as little as possible and let my father get it out of his system. It's just a matter of being patient, so I carry on looking at the auction items on the screen while he continues to lecture me.

'We, your mother and I, feel that you're taking a very irresponsible attitude, Fern. Not just towards the property but towards your life in general.'

Here we go. I put down the mouse because this sort of talk always scares me.

I'm absolutely aware that without their support my life would be a whole lot harder – and I'm really grateful, but at the same time I also feel permanently at their mercy because they could withdraw their help at any time and all my ambitions suddenly seem precarious. 'Sorry,' I say. 'I got the place cleaned up. I didn't want to worry you.'

The apology calms him down.

'In future,' he says, 'whenever something like this happens, just tell us, that's all I ask.'

As though it's a problem that's going to keep recurring.

'I'm sorry,' I say again, contritely. 'I definitely will.'

I can still hear my mother hectoring him in the background, but I think the whole conversation has taken it out of my father, because he ends the call suddenly without saying goodbye. I don't think retirement is suiting him that well; being with my mother twenty-four seven takes a lot of stamina.

Almost immediately the phone rings again and I almost don't answer it, but this time it's not my father, it's Mick.

'Hey, Doll. Let's call a truce,' he says.

I'm so pleased it's him and not my parents that I'm super friendly. 'Truce,' I agree.

'Good, because I've booked us a few days away on a mini-break.'

Hooray! All is forgiven!

'So where are we going?' I ask, curling my hair around my finger.

'South of France,' he says in his deep, seductive voice. 'Cap d'Agde. Plage Port Nature.'

'Sounds amazing.' South of France . . . Bardot country. He's *totally* forgiven.

'Don't pack much,' he warns.

I'm really excited about our romantic trip and drop it into the conversation with David over our breakfast croissant of ham and cheese. I check the weather and it's hot in the south of France.

To show Mick that I, too, can compromise, I take his advice and travel light, packing a white bikini, my biggest sunglasses, a couple of A-line cotton shift dresses and a wide-brimmed white straw hat.

When we meet up at the airport, we're a bit cautious with each other, a bit polite, holding back warily following our first real argument. We've pushed, we've found ourselves on the edge of the precipice, and now we know where the boundaries are we're making sure we stay well behind them.

His innocent pale blue eyes take me all in approvingly. He doesn't mention my yellow shift dress, although he can't resist making a crack about my large straw hat, ducking underneath it to see if there's enough room for two.

He's wearing a white linen suit and a navy linen shirt. 'You look amazing,' I tell him, delighted that he's taken my criticism of his black T-shirts to heart. 'Very French and chic.'

'You think? It's my "trying for an upgrade" kit,' he says.

All he's carrying is a laptop bag. He's travelling even lighter than me.

He flips the brim of my hat. 'Think of what we'll save on beach umbrellas,' he says as we wander around duty-free, me buying SPF 50 sun lotion and squirting myself with perfume samples and him looking for his favourite tobacco.

He signs me into the lounge on his Priority Pass. He travels so much, he sees it as a challenge to get the most value out of it. We debate which is the best breakfast drink, Bucks Fizz or a Bloody Mary, and he brings me ham, cheese and bread rolls and we add more orange juice to our prosecco, then more prosecco to our juice. It's fun and mega romantic.

It's quite funny – the Bucks Fizz completely breaks down

the reserve between us. We've survived our first big argument and now we're stronger than ever.

On the plane we have another Bucks Fizz because I firmly believe, from personal experience, it's impossible to get drunk on prosecco. We giggle and test each other on the details of the safety card. We practice the brace position. We lean forward as far as our seatbelts will allow to check out the exits. And I ask him about the resort. 'Plage Port Nature sounds lovely. Environmentally friendly,' I say.

Mick strokes his red beard and then looks out of the window at the clouds. 'Probably, yeah.'

I'm hyper with happiness. 'You know when they ask you to use your towels twice to save water, do you think it's just because it's cheaper?'

'Not *just* because it's cheaper.'

'No, not *just* because.' I stroke the cool sleeve of his shirt. 'I can't believe you got all your clothes into a laptop bag,' I marvel. 'You look so nice in linen. You look as if you're the head of some major international criminal organisation, in a good way.'

'A friendly criminal, you mean?'

'Yeah, a friendly one.' He's so nice that I've almost completely forgotten about David Westwood. He's gone to all this trouble for me, for us, and I'm beginning to think I could love him. And you know something else? I think he could love me.

A couple of hours later, I'm sitting on the bed in our hotel room with the sea view in my lovely buttercup-yellow shift dress hyperventilating.

'You could have told me that Plage Port Nature is a *nudist* camp.'

'Naturist,' Mick says, as if it makes a difference.

'And this is supposed to prove a point, is it? Naked people everywhere? It's disturbing.'

I'm so gullible. How did I not realise what he was up to? How come I didn't spot that the purpose of the trip was to make a point? The instructions not to pack much should have been the clue.

'Come on, Fern. Give it a try,' Mick says, kneeling in front of me and holding my fingers tightly while he looks deep into my eyes and gives me an urgent team talk. 'It'll be fun. We can be our true authentic selves. You and me. Look at me!'

Resentfully, I look into his sincere eyes and he looks so handsome, with his milk-white skin and his burnished hair and his mandarin and cedarwood scented beard. I shake my head. 'I can't believe you're doing this to me.'

'I want to prove to you that clothes aren't important; they're really not. It's the person inside them that counts. You with me?'

'No, I'm not!' Despite what Mick thinks, clothes are nothing to do with vanity. 'Clothes are everything! It's all about the look – peacocks, robins, those monkeys with the red arses, lions' manes – it's all about sex, Mick! It's about attracting and being attractive! It's pollination!'

He grins and slides his hand under my dress. 'Yeah . . . fancy a bit of pollination, Fern?'

I push his hands away. 'What? Are you *kidding* me?'

'Relax,' he says, backing off quickly. 'Listen to me. This is what we're going to do. We're going to get undressed and then we're going for a paddle, understand?'

'I suppose so,' I say.

And so we undress for the occasion and go naked to the beach.

I say naked; I accessorise with my large round sunglasses,

flip-flops, my wide-brimmed hat and a stripy navy-and-white canvas tote bag which is large enough to hide behind.

It's a big beach. We set our things down on the perfect spot for sunbathing – ten metres from anyone – and work up the nerve to go for a naked swim.

I entirely lose my frame of self-reference, being naked.

Nothing wrong with the human body or anything, it's just that without my clothes, my armour to define me, I honestly don't know who I am.

I'm a snail without a shell, lost and unformed; I feel peeled and skinned, vulnerable, as if my internal organs are on display. I'm living the dream, the one that no one ever wants to live, where I find myself naked in public.

I want to cover up and hide my dismayed heart, my twitching liver and my grinding guts, and clothe myself once more in the armour of fashion.

Mick is completely unsympathetic. He crouches beside me, freckling in the sun, and says this is what we came for, this is the whole point of the trip, so that I can see how completely unimportant clothes are.

So reluctantly, after psyching myself up, I follow him on the long walk across hot sand to the sea, meandering around bare bodies starfished everywhere in shades of pink and brown, smooth and freckled, some with pubic hair and some waxed to a shine. It's impossible not to look, or be looked at.

Hugging myself, I follow him nonchalantly at first and then as the heat of the sand burns my feet, I speed up, swearing and hopping over the searing sand into the icy surf.

Gasping with the shock of the cold, I go deep so that the water's up to my shoulders. I'm happy now, clothed by the sea. I'll just stay in the water all day until everyone goes home.

Wow! Against the dazzling blue water Mick is luminously pale. *Luminously.*

I breaststroke towards him, where he's still standing in the shallows with the foam lacing around his ankles. 'You know something, Mick? This is the longest I've ever seen you naked without an erection.'

Bad mistake. When I tell him that, he gets self-conscious, turns his back and tries to crouch in the waves. He mistimes it horribly.

'Look out!'

A wave hits him at the back of the head, knocking him off his feet, and he springs up, choking and blinded by his wet hair. Then the wave ebbs away, leaving him pale and floundering in the shallows.

I'm floating with my hands behind my head, my bare breasts breaking the surface, watching him with a smirk. 'Come over here.'

He shakes his head, scattering drips like a dog. He flinches as the foam hits his legs. He cups himself miserably. 'I can't, Fern. I can't swim.'

I laugh. 'Really?' I stop floating and start to tread water. 'You're serious?'

He doesn't bother to answer.

'Aww, Mick! How come you've never learned how to swim?'

'I just never have, okay? My mother tried to teach me on an ironing board, but it was no use, I couldn't get the hang of it.'

You think you know a person and then they come up with a story like this. I tilt my head back in the sea, feeling the cold grip my scalp like a hair band. I'm intrigued about the ironing board. 'Was the ironing board an improvised surfboard?'

'No, she was teaching me how to do the crawl in our lounge, you know, the arm movements.'

This is wrong on so many levels. I'm bobbing up and down

in the waves, feeling the sun hot on my head, trying to work it out. 'No one starts with the crawl on an ironing board in the lounge. Why didn't she take you to the pool with a pair of armbands like everyone else?'

'She's scared of the water, too,' he says.

I breaststroke towards him, feeling a little superior and also more loving, because I'm seeing a vulnerable side of him that I didn't know he had. 'I'll teach you how to swim. Forget the ironing board. I'll show you how to float.'

'With my hands behind my head?'

'Yes, good, isn't it? It's like lying on an invisible airbed.'

Mick shies back fearfully at every slapping wave. His shoulders are hunched and his dark body hair clings like weed. When he's chest-deep, he clutches me and I turn him round and put my arms under his armpits then tell him to relax, to let the water take his weight. He's surprisingly heavy.

'Can you feel it holding you up?'

'No! Don't let me go!'

'I won't! Trust me!'

All around us in the turquoise sea, people are swimming, shouting, playing ball, doing naked handstands and generally enjoying themselves while Mick, on the other hand, is flailing around wildly, fighting for his life. I move my hands from his armpits to his shoulders and he sinks like a stone.

'Relax!'

'I can float if I keep one foot on the floor,' he tells me.

'That's not floating, that's standing.' I'm determined to persevere. The sun is blazing down but the water's as cold as peppermint and I'm really enjoying myself. 'Try it on your front. You stay there and then just push off and glide towards me.'

He looks at me fearfully. 'Come closer. Closer than that. Come to where I can reach you.'

'Then you're just basically falling on me, aren't you? You kind of need to push forward. Push! Just try it. I'll count to three.' I hold out my hands and after a couple of false starts he musters his courage and makes as if to glide towards me. He churns his arms and legs and goes straight under. I pull him back up and he coughs and hawks and blows seawater out of his nose, hanging on to me in obvious distress. Our bodies create a warm cushion of air and, clinging to each other, we're carried up and down in the waves.

'I think I can feel it holding me up,' he says after a bit.

'Yes, you will. Take a deep breath, fill your lungs. See? You're higher in the water now. Your lungs are your internal floating device. Now breathe out.'

I let him go and he sinks slowly then he breathes in again and rises up.

'Huh!' he says, keeping his beard above the water. 'I've got an internal floating device.'

'Let's try again. I've never met anyone who just sinks,' I tell him. 'Feel the water taking your weight. Try to lie flat as if you're stretching out on a bed of nails. I'll hold your shoulders. Keep your head back.'

'Bed of nails. Okay.' He's biting his lip, tilting back with his arms outstretched, rocked by the sea.

'I'm hardly touching you now. I'm going to take my hands away, but if you sink, I'll catch you.'

I take my hands away. It's a triumph.

'I'm doing it!'

'I know!'

We hold hands and float as happily as jellyfish for a long while, and eventually, immensely pleased with ourselves, we plod back to our towels – unselfconscious now and lightly coated in salt crystals – to lie on the sand by the tote bag and hat.

Away from the cooling turquoise of the sea, I prop myself on my elbow to look at him fondly. His beard is frosted with salt. 'Mick, you look really red.' I press my hand firmly on his abs.

'Ow!'

It leaves an alarming white handprint, so I say helpfully, 'I think you need to cover up.'

Oh, the irony.

He sits up and looks at his fiery body then compares it with mine, which is pale gold.

I'm fine, of course. I'm wearing my factor fifty. 'What factor did you use?'

'I didn't bring any. I was going to ask if I could borrow yours but then we were going for a paddle so I thought I'd wait until I dried off.'

I've never realised the awful, debilitating effects of sunburn before. We go back to the room, where Mick stands under a cold shower until he starts to shiver. Despite it, once he's out, he radiates more heat than a wood burner. And he's in pain.

During the next few days I more or less get used to the naturist life: reaching cautiously into the freezer at the supermarket, keeping my knees together in restaurants, avoiding wicker chairs and wooden benches. I even get stronger muscles from holding my stomach in all day.

Mick, on the other hand, is living on paracetamol and sitting miserably under a sun umbrella confined to a small circle of shade layered in wet towels to cool the pain.

He can't bear to be touched.

So much for our romantic getaway.

Without the sex we discover that our authentic naked selves don't get on that well at all. We run out of subjects to talk about. In the evenings, anaesthetised by Jack Daniels, Mick's red skin makes him appear to be in a state of permanent embarrassment. He gets tired of people staring at him and murmuring knowingly: *English.*

And let's face it, a naked, peeling man drumming his fingers on the table doesn't look cool; it just looks insane.

On Monday, we get dressed to go home. It's a wonderful feeling.

Once we're in the foyer fully clothed and ready to leave the hotel – Mick in his white linen suit and me in a shift dress – I study him with renewed interest and the kind of 'Hey! It's you!' sense of happy recognition.

On the flight home, I flick through the duty-free magazine, get my bank card ready for our proseccos and take the laminated safety instructions out of the seat pocket. I always read the safety instructions; I'm cautious that way. I nudge Mick with my elbow. 'Go on, test me.'

He's looking out of the window. He doesn't laugh and he doesn't take it from me.

'What's wrong?'

He turns to look at me, the new skin rosy and pink on his peeling nose, his saintly face deadly serious. 'Fern,' he says in the deep, solemn voice of a newscaster announcing the death of a royal, 'we need to talk.'

It's so unexpected that I don't understand what he's saying. 'What about?'

'This isn't working for me. It's not you, but over the last few days I've realised that we're looking for different things.'

I suddenly feel cold. 'Like what, for instance?' The trolley stops next to me and I'm still holding my credit card. I order two proseccos anyway.

When I keep them both myself, he says, 'Fern, don't take it the wrong way. There's nothing wrong with *you*. It's just the relationship, it's superficial.'

'Oh, *thanks*,' I chip in indignantly. 'Superficial? You'd know all about that. You're the guy who nearly broke up with me because I wore pleats. Idiot.' I proceed to pour one of the drinks and knock it back.

'That's what I mean – you take the whole fashion thing too far. You're really nice, but . . .'

'Obviously not nice enough to spend any more time with, that's the bottom line,' I say, my voice rising. 'You've made me spend the last four days naked and now you're breaking up with me?'

'Shhh . . .'

'You tell me clothes aren't important and when I don't wear any, you *dump* me?' I don't know why he thinks that flapping his hands at me is going to calm me down. 'Don't shush me! So what if people are looking? You *should* be ashamed!'

I grab the drinks and go and ask the cabin crew for another seat, but the flight is full. There's no way that anyone survives the break-up speech feeling better about themselves, so I stomp back to sit next to Mick and tell him to shut up. For the rest of the flight I sit there hating him.

I'm devastated. After all I went through for him.

Resentful, too. I was game, wasn't I? I took up the challenge, I did the naked bit, I gave up wearing clothes for him, didn't I? I put cream on his sunburn, fed him painkillers, and he does this to me?

It's a long, silent and very miserable journey home.

# LOT 9

*Ossie Clark for Radley 'traffic light' dress, midi, yellow, green and red skirt, with black bodice, mid-1970s, with yellow-self-covered buttons and yellow trim, deep plunge neckline.*

In need of a sympathetic shoulder to cry on, I call in on Lucy when I get back and she makes hot chocolates with marshmallows then sits on the sofa in the lotus position, cupping her mug in her hands, while I tell her about the break-up.

I leave out the shameful part, the fact it was a naturist resort, for the same reason that I don't tell anyone I'm afraid of dogs; I always try to hide my weaknesses.

'I didn't even realise you and Mick were that serious about each other,' she says frankly when I come to the end of the story.

My eyes swim with tears. She's right, of course. I've never kidded myself that Mick was The One, but what it feels like is another failure and I've got enough of that in my life as it is. 'I thought we were okay together, you know? That we suited each other. And didn't ask for too much.'

'Aw, Fern. Men, eh. Don't worry, you'll find someone else,' she says. 'Someone better. Smarter.'

'Smarter,' I repeat wistfully, my thoughts jumping to David, who's always smart even in jeans. I've never even seen him with his hair ruffled. 'Maybe I'll even find someone who wears polished brown shoes.'

She laughs. 'That's weirdly specific. Listen, this is the way I see it. Dating is like an audition. You win some, you lose some, but you can't take it personally – it has to be the right person for the part, do you know what I'm saying? Like Christian Bale in *American Psycho*. They wanted Leonardo DiCaprio but, in the end, Christian Bale played the role of Patrick Bateman and smashed it, right?'

I'm not sure where this line of reasoning is going, but I nod. 'That's true.'

'So what you have to ask yourself through the pain is, was Mick the right person for the role?'

I think of all the times my heart lifted when I listened to his gorgeous voice, and the times I met him at airports and snuggled up to the lovely warmth of his beard. But now it's superimposed by the image of shiny brown shoes. God, I realise despairingly, I *am* superficial. I consider her analogy. 'What happens if the person who you really want for the part has already got a part in someone else's production?'

She unfolds herself from the lotus position and sits forward. 'Fern Banks! I do believe you fancy someone else!'

'It's nothing,' I say quickly. 'Honestly, it's just a crush.'

'Come on, who is he?'

'David Westwood.' I even like his name. 'He's got the stall next to mine. He's already in a relationship, so don't look at me like that.'

'But is it serious, though?'

'Yes. Absolutely. She encouraged him to follow his dream.'

Lucy ponders on this for a moment. 'Got to be straight with you, Fern, it doesn't sound like he's the one, either. If you mainly like him for his shoes, I think you're on safe ground, though. There are plenty of brown shoe-wearers in London.'

I'm thinking about these words of wisdom when I get to the market early the next day and my look is dishevelled bohemia; a comforting floral maxidress that covers me up from my neck to my feet. The weather's getting warmer and I'm hoping it'll be busy, to distract me from my heartache. As the sun warms up the canvas, the smell reminds me of festivals, which in its turn reminds me of Mick.

David comes just before nine with his trolley stacked with boxes.

'Good holiday?' he asks with a smile.

'Not really, no,' I say, folding a cashmere sweater. I glance at him quickly, curling my hair around my ear. 'My boyfriend, Mick, broke up with me.'

'Oh.' He looks dismayed. He reaches out and pats my arm slightly awkwardly as if it's something he's not used to doing. 'Sorry to hear it.'

He smells of limes and spearmint and I feel strangely consoled by the gesture.

As he sets up his stall, a woman coming along the alley grabs my attention. She's petite, wearing a red tunic, purple tights, a yellow baseball cap and a scarf in neon colours. It's a bold look, because nothing goes with anything, but what strikes me is that she's not wearing her clothes proudly; there's something self-consciously apologetic about her hunched shoulders that intrigues me.

She starts looking through the rack, pulling out black dresses. She sees me watching her and when I smile, she seems to come to a decision. 'Can I just ask you for a bit of advice?' she says, draping the black dresses over her arm.

'Sure,' I reply.

'The thing is, I'm colour-blind.'

'Ah, that explains it!' I realise it's not the most tactful comment and I'm about to apologise, when she laughs.

'Crikey, do I look as bad as that? Okay, well, I've got a new job and I need a work wardrobe because I can't tell if the clothes I've already got match, you know? I find it hard to work out colours. Can you tell me, what's this tunic I'm wearing, grey or red?'

'Red.'

'Red? And these tights are green, aren't they? Yikes, I must look like one of Santa's elves.'

'They're purple.'

'I never wear purple!' She looks down at her legs. 'I'm wearing *purple*? Shit!'

I start to laugh. 'What colours do you normally like?'

She looks at me through her huge dark pupils. 'Strong colours. Bright colours. But most colours look like mud now and yellow looks like white, so it's hard to tell.' Our conversation is interrupted by a cheery greeting.

'Hi, Fern!'

'Oh! Hi, Gigi!' Her pink hair is tied up. She's wearing a leopard print shirtdress and leopard print shoes. She's holding David's steel flask and she fake-hits him on the head with it.

'Look what you forgot! He's normally so *sensible*,' she says, glancing back at me. 'Aren't you *sensible*, David?'

'Very,' he says impassively, but then he smiles.

I turn back to my customer, who's holding on to the black dresses. She asks to try them on, so I pin up the curtain while Gigi looks gleeful and gives me a double thumbs-up.

The woman comes out and nods. 'Yes, I'll take them.'

But I'm intrigued. 'So you like bright colours but you have to wear black for work?' I ask, knowing from personal experience what that feels like.

'No, I don't have to wear black, it's not the dress code, but I thought it might be the answer to my colour problem. I'll know where I am then. I can't go wrong with black, can I?'

'True. But you don't generally wear it,' I say.

'No, I love colour.' She moves the strap of her bag further up her shoulder. 'I haven't always had this problem with my sight – it came on gradually. My night vision went first. My boyfriend kept asking me why I was driving so slowly and why I was hunched over the steering wheel as if another six inches of vision was going to make any difference. I went to the opticians and he asked if I'd ever noticed that my pupils are always quite large.' She laughs. 'I always thought that was one of my good points.'

I like her, not just because of her honesty, but also by just getting on with her life she's given me some perspective on my own problems. She's still holding the four dresses and I'm thrilled at the idea of making a sale this big, a sale that will put me into profit, but she's so bubbly and open that I really want to help her.

In my peripheral vision I can see Gigi taking a keen interest.

'If it's just the problem of colour, you don't really need a new black work wardrobe, you just need to know what goes with what of the clothes you've already got, don't you?'

She chews her lip thoughtfully. 'True. But my girlfriends aren't much help. They tell me everything looks fine on me, nothing has to match, that nobody cares. But I care, you know?'

I do know. 'Me, too,' I tell her. We like people who are like ourselves and she's definitely like me.

'I love what you've got on. Very Sixties,' she adds, tongue in cheek. 'Did you get up this morning and think, what would Twiggy wear?'

'She'd wear Marks & Spencer,' I reply, laughing. But I've got a plan. 'Have you ever used a colour recognition app?' I get out my phone, click on the app and focus it on her tunic. I show her the screen. 'See? Flame red. You could get some iron-on nametapes and label everything in your wardrobe with the exact description of the colours so that you'll always know what goes with what and what you're wearing. Like if it's pink, you could write down bubblegum pink or baby pink; or blues: indigo, navy, royal, denim, ultramarine, turquoise, topaz, sky, hyacinth, bluebell.' I'm getting carried away with myself. 'Well, it's just an idea, anyway.'

'But not black, you think?'

'No, not black.'

'Yes, okay, that would be amazing,' she says softly, and she hangs up the dresses she's holding and asks for my card. 'Thanks. I'll give it a go.' I get her to write her details in my clients' book – Hannah York – and I'm pleased to notice that I've now gone on to a new page.

Once she's gone, I stretch, feeling absurdly happy that I've been useful. But the feeling doesn't last long. 'What?'

Gigi's smirking, arms folded. She's shaking her head. 'Fern Banks,' she says. 'You're not much of a businesswoman, are you?'

'What do you mean?'

'You just talked yourself out of a sale. She was going to buy those black dresses. Not just one of them, but all of them.'

David blows a puff of sawdust off the wood. 'Gigi—'

She whirls round. 'Yeah, Dave, I know. Tell me it's none of my business.'

'It's none of your business,' he says, but of course, Gigi's right. I could have sold four dresses and I talked her out of it.

The criticism stings, though. She's right. What the hell's wrong with me? I needed that money.

'She wouldn't suit black,' I explain, trying to stick up for myself.

'Who cares? A sale's a sale. What did she write in that secret book you've got there? "Thanks, you mug"?' she asks.

'It's my client book.'

'Let's have a look.' Gigi flicks through it, and I have a flash-back to school when she snatched my sketchbook from me once and held it out of reach before tossing it back to me, safe, I suppose, in the knowledge that there was nothing in it that would interest her.

'Dave.'

*Dayve.*

He doesn't look at her, he looks at me with understanding in his eyes.

'What?' he asks.

'We've got to take her in hand.'

Oh, the humiliation of it. 'I don't need taking in hand,' I protest.

'Trust me, you do, doesn't she, Dave? My friends are always buying vintage. They make special shopping trips to some old flea market in Paris – you could put their names in your book, for starters. I know! Tell you what! You should come to my birthday! Dave, shouldn't she come to my birthday?'

'I don't think—'

'Dave, tell her she should come. It'll be fun! Bring your boyfriend!'

'Shut up, Gigi,' David says.

She gives him such a death stare that now I feel obliged to explain.

'My boyfriend and I have just broken up,' I tell her.

She looks as dismayed as if she knew him personally. 'Aw, Fern! Why?'

'Incompatibility,' I mumble, praying that she'll drop it and leave me alone.

'Well, that's it. You're coming to my party,' she tells me in an
'I'm not taking no for an answer' tone of voice. 'We've got the
place for the weekend and it's got a lake and swans and' – she
waves her hand vaguely – 'sunsets.'

Gigi, all abrim with self-confidence, is unlikely to understand that I'm not that crazy about partying at the moment,
especially with strangers. While I'm thinking up another way
to refuse, she says, 'And I need to find something gorgeous
to wear. Is this new stock?'

Gigi looks through the clothes on my rail and at the ones
hanging up – I hope she'll like the Jaeger pleated skirts, because
they've lost their appeal for me. She shows no interest in them
but she likes a Seventies Ossie Clark dress that I bought on
eBay. It's a combination of yellow green and red, A-line, with
a fitted black bodice, form-fitting and sexy. I'm really keen to
sell it quickly.

I pin up the curtain while she tries it on.

When she comes out it's too big on the bust and she looks
down her cleavage as if she's lost something. 'Too loose,' she
says.

Moss! 'I could get it altered for you,' I tell her smoothly,
thinking about her friends, the vintage buyers. Hah! Who says
I'm not much of a businesswoman! 'Is that something you'd
be interested in?'

'I don't know. Maybe, yeah. Depends. How long would it
take?'

'A couple of days,' I say, chancing it. After all, he's not that
busy.

She does a twirl for us in the shady alley and the dress
billows out. She gets warm, admiring looks from passers-by
– she's got that kind of personality.

'What do you think, David? If you can imagine it fits me
perfectly?'

144

He looks up briefly and his face relaxes. He smiles at her like a man in love. 'It's nice.'

'There you go!' she says to me, rolling her eyes. 'Nice.'

I laugh. I've met couples like this before, the ones who act as if they never get on when they really do.

'So, my party. Give David your details and I'll send you the invitation. Otherwise,' Gigi says, with a pathos guaranteed to make me weep with self-pity, 'you'll be spending next weekend all alone. Fun is absolutely the best cure for a broken heart. Isn't that right, David?'

Again, he catches my eye in that deeply sincere gaze. 'Yes. It's a well-known cure.'

He's so lovely. 'Well, actually, I work weekends,' I say, kicking myself because I'd had the perfect excuse right there and I didn't use it.

'It's just a couple of days – Dave's taking the time off, aren't you, Dave?'

'Yes, dear,' he says with exaggerated obedience.

I want to explain that as I've just had a weekend off I have to catch up, but continuing with the argument makes it look as if either I'm enjoying being persuaded into it, or that I've made my mind up and I'm determined not to go whatever happens, and I hate that in a person.

While Gigi changes back into her clothes, I call Moss and between us we arrange a time for the fitting.

'Kiss kiss, kiss kiss!' Gigi says with an airy wave and leaves us to take her Pilates class.

Once she's gone, I've noticed that David and I have fallen into some sort of comfortable, thoughtful silence, the same kind as when a boisterous child falls asleep and calm descends.

He looks at me and smiles, and I wonder if he's thinking the same thing.

# KIM

My son, George, comes here after work, by himself, to see how I'm holding up. He's a good lad.

My fifty-year-old lad.

He hugs me. Pats me on the back. 'How're you doing, Dad?' His voice is muffled.

I pat him on the back. I say into his shoulder, 'Oh, lad.'

He puts the kettle on and while we drink our tea he asks me what needs doing, who I've informed.

I've informed a lot of people. Him first, and the widows, and the undertakers, and Enid's sister who lives in Philadelphia. I spent the day she died ringing people up.

'How about the Pension Service, the insurance company, the Passport Office,' George asks briskly.

'No, no. Not yet,' I add.

'Don't worry, I can do it. There's a way we can do it all at once to save going over the same thing every time.'

My lad, George.

He knows all about this kind of thing. A long time ago, I gave him advice. And now, the tables have turned.

'How about us getting you a computer?' he says. 'It'll make your life easier.'

'Easier, how?'

'It'll be easier to stay in touch with us, and the kids.'

His grown-up children are kids in the same way my grown-up son is my lad.

'It'll open your eyes,' he says. 'There's a whole world out there waiting to be explored. You can find anything on the Internet.'

I grunt. 'Your mother said it was a filthy place.'

George laughs. 'That's because she was a *Daily Mail* reader. You only find what you look for, so don't worry about that. Have a look at my laptop.'

He takes it out of his bag, sets it up on the table and switches it on. Suddenly, up pops a photograph of us all last Christmas, sitting around his table, six laughing adults, twenty-four glasses, red wine on the tablecloth, party hats askew, cracker trinkets scattered, the crumbling ruins of a Christmas pudding on a plate. Takes me by surprise. 'Where did that come from?'

'It's my screensaver,' he says, tapping the keys. 'Right, Dad, what in the world would you like to know more about?'

It's a tall order.

'The Himalayas,' I say.

'The Himalayas generally, or do you want a holiday there?'

'I don't mind. What have they got?'

'Both . . . either,' he shrugs. 'Here you are, here's a holiday company – look, you just click on it. See?'

'As quick as that,' I say.

'Or look, here, here you've got all the facts about the Himalayas or the Himalaya. See?'

I'm impressed. 'What else has it got?'

George laughs. 'You name it, it's on the Internet. If you want to take up a new hobby, this is the place to look.'

Golf is my hobby, but I haven't played since Stan went. Stan was a better player than me. We saw the game differently – for him it was about beating me, and for me it was about getting out of the house for a few hours and having a drink on the nineteenth. Partly, it was that for Stan, too, getting out of the house for a bit, having a break from being a husband for a few hours.

Stan's view was that games should be played to win. He could remember a club competition hole by hole, telling me about every shot. He was a fanatic. Never forgot a drive.

'I might go back to the golf club,' I say.

Tap-tap-tap-click, and there's the clubhouse and the opening hours and the greens. And despite what the *Daily Mail* says, no sign of anything that would make Enid blush.

'Anyway, Dad, it's worth considering,' George says.

I decide there and then. 'No need! I'm going to get one.'

George turns his head from the screen to look at me and he smiles; surprised but pleased. He's a good-looking lad. 'That was a lot easier than I expected,' he says. 'We'll get you an Internet connection and you're sorted.'

'I've decided to take up new things,' I explain to him.

He smiles again. 'Good for you. It's never too late to learn.'

I know what Enid would say.

Without Enid I have no motivation to do anything. The dishes pile up and the dust gathers. I work my way through the tins in the cupboard. Oxtail soup, cream of tomato, minestrone, peaches in syrup, garden peas, baked beans, fruit salad.

Next day, Betty comes round with Mercia. Betty's tall and wearing a beige hooded raincoat. Mercia's short and wearing a blue cagoule with the hood up; it's tied tightly around her face.

'Going hiking?'

'Keeping my hair dry,' she says, unpicking the cord under her chin. 'Just had it done.'

I'm a widower with two blondes at my door. Not bad for an 85-year-old. Enid wouldn't dye her hair. Left it as God intended and it was as white as mine at the end. It's unlucky for Betty and Mercia that Enid's gone first, because come Judgement Day she'll make sure Betty and Mercia have their trumpets taken from them for the sin of vanity, which she deplored.

'Come in,' I say and they follow me into the hall.

'How are you? How are you *really*?' Mercia asks me softly, tapping my arm.

I turn back to look at them. They're full of kindness.

I've missed kindness, and suddenly terror and loneliness fill me. 'Would either of you marry me?' I plead. Then I start to bark. I can't call it crying. The noise blares out of my chest and takes all of my energy away. I fall to my knees. I can't stand.

'It's the shock,' Mercia says.

'I'll put the kettle on,' Betty says, hurrying to the kitchen. 'It's hit him hard.'

'Find some brandy, Betty,' Mercia calls after her.

I run out of air and raise my head to suck it in. Bark it out again hoarsely. Ashamed of the noise. Grief possessing me. On my knees and too old to get up. Too old to cope. I roll sideways, a commando roll, coming to rest against the cold wall.

Mercia bends over me with a glass. 'Sit up, Kim.'

Rocking.

Holding my knees and rocking.

Moaning and sighing. Ah, me.

They help me up and I open my eyes to take the glass. The brandy is in one of the best glasses, lead crystal, which we never use.

It's still got the red label on.

'Go on, drink it up,' Mercia says. 'It'll do you good.'

It's like drinking hot pins. It prickles and burns my throat and my head then, suddenly, it brings calm – the storm is over.

I'm ashamed that I asked them to marry me.

And of the spectacle I made of myself.

But they don't seem to mind, not the way that Enid would mind.

They don't tell me to pull myself together.

They look at me, worried and sympathetic, and go into the kitchen to fetch the tea.

'It's harder for men,' Mercia says.

'Oh, I don't know,' I say.

The teaspoon rings in the mug.

'We're having a lick of brandy in it,' Betty calls to me.

A lick of brandy.

We go into the sitting room and we all sit forward, leaning on our knees as if we've got secrets to tell.

And I'm worried again.

When they finish the tea with the brandy in it, they'll go.

I don't want them to go. I'm crying. I'll keep them here all night with my tears dripping in my drink.

'It gets easier,' Mercia tells me, patting my knee.

'You get used to it,' Betty agrees. 'I miss Stan, but I talk to him a lot. You should talk to Enid, Kim.'

I will. I'll say to her, 'Enid, what time will you be home? Do you want a lift?'

'You can still enjoy life. Do things that you'd never do together – that helps, doesn't it, Betty?'

'Yes, that helps. Do something completely new.'

They both lift their mugs at the same time and tip their heads back a little to finish their tea. I feel the terror rushing through my skull. They're going to go.

'Is there anything you want? Biscuits?'

I nod.

Mercia pulls the hood of her blue cagoule carefully over her hairstyle and ties it around her face.

I walk them to the door.

'Bye, Kim! Bye! Look after yourself!'

I nod because I've got no say in the matter. What choice have I got?

# LOT 10

*Zandra Rhodes 1970s 'Field of Lilies' printed chiffon gown, aqua, full sleeves, deep v-neck with deep aqua ribbon sash belt.*

I've arranged to meet Gigi at Moss's shop to fit the Ossie Clark dress.

She's late. Moss and I wait for her in awkward silence and I wonder if she's going to turn up. Embarrassingly, seeing it through her eyes, the place is shabbier than I remember. The lonesome fur coat is still hanging on the rail.

Finally, she strolls unhurriedly up to the door and as she comes in I see her looking around, eyebrows raised. To her credit, she makes no comment.

Moss is wearing not just the suit, but a black tie, too, and he's taciturn but impressive. With Gigi he's very proper. He introduces himself and asks her, with stiff formality, to kindly put on the frock.

Amused, Gigi flashes me a smile and goes into the dressing room. A couple of minutes later she's out again, tugging at the front of the dress. 'See? Way too big.'

Moss smiles secretively. He has a row of glinting gold pins along the lapel of his jacket that he wears like medals. He starts pinching, tucking and pinning the dress with sure fingers, standing back now and then with a critical gaze.

Gigi stands surprisingly still, for her. 'How long is it going to take to alter?'

'Give me until tomorrow,' Moss says.

We both look at him curiously because, like the conductor of an orchestra, he then stands back on the faded red rug to look at Gigi and – this is what brings the idea of the conductor into my mind – he begins to wave a brisk rhythm in the air as he studies the dress. It's as if he can hear some soaring background music to accompany the image.

I suppose that's the moment I realise what an unusual man he is.

'Turn,' he commands her.

Gigi does a twirl. 'Mmm.'

Finally, he says, 'Now you can look.'

Like Dinah, Gigi has style. She's tall and slim, very pale, and her pink hair is as fine as candyfloss. Even now, barefoot and with her arms dangling loosely, she looks graceful.

The same thought seems to occur to Moss.

'You remind me a little of my bride,' he says soberly, kneeling heavily on the carpet as he pins Gigi's hem.

Gigi looks across at me through her pink frizzy hair and tightens her lips to hold back a laugh. 'Oh, Moss, I love the way you call her your bride.'

He shrugs modestly. 'She's a beautiful woman,' he says.

'It must be wonderful to be loved like that. Are you loved like that, Fern?'

'No.' It comes out more forcefully than I'd intended, bearing in mind she knows I'm not loved at all, and I flush with embarrassment, even though I know she's only said it to charm Moss.

'Me neither,' she says. 'Moss, I hope Dinah appreciates you.'

I look at her curiously. *Me neither*. That can't be right, can it? I wonder if she's just saying it to make me feel better, but there's a crease between her eyebrows that's almost a frown and I wonder if David Westwood's not shaping up.

Not for the first time, I wonder about their relationship. I'd never in a million years have matched these two up together and yet, it was Gigi who encouraged him to leave his job as a headhunter and follow his dream. Knowing his previous occupation puts him in a different light – like finding out your plumber used to be a professional stuntman.

Gigi's attention has gone back to Moss. 'How old is your bride?' she asks, teasing him.

He looks up at her from under his bushy eyebrows. 'Over twenty-one,' he replies seriously.

'I should hope so,' Gigi responds and he laughs. 'You've got a big imagination, haven't you, Moss! That's what makes a good husband.'

She's right about that. I've never thought about it before, but I could never date a man who has no imagination. But there again, a man can have too much imagination and that's not helpful either, especially when he imagines you'll enjoy a naked holiday and never be bothered about clothes again. 'Her boyfriend's a woodworker,' I tell Moss. 'He makes light boxes.'

Gigi rolls her eyes and I wonder if she's regretting telling him to follow his dream.

'I know what he makes. With the stars,' Moss says, pouring us coffees out of a jug. 'My wife bought one as a gift for me. Very romantic. Romance is a good quality to bring to a marriage. How long have you two been together?'

'Almost a year.' Gigi laughs. 'Who said it wouldn't last, eh, Moss?'

'Almost a year,' Moss repeats in wonderment.

'Dave's a nice guy, very practical. He suits me. I mean, if I want fun I go out with my girlfriends.' She goes inside the changing room in the corner of the shop and rattles the velvet curtain across.

While she's trying the dress on, Moss beckons and leans a little closer to me. 'This is it? Just the one customer? There's a guy who wants to sell mopeds here and he'll take over the lease. It's Hamed's son.' He jerks his thumb in the direction of the shop next door. 'Hamed from the post office.'

'Yeah?' I don't know Hamed from the post office, but I get the feeling that Moss is seriously thinking about it and it's not just a line.

I've come to a thick sludge of coffee at the bottom of the cup, so I put the cup down and run my tongue over my teeth to clean them.

The velvet curtains rattle and Gigi emerges from the changing room carrying the dress. She checks her phone. 'Got to rush,' she says. 'Moss, I'll come back tomorrow afternoon to pick it up.' She blows me a kiss and after she's gone, Moss drapes the dress on the counter, shaking his head ruefully.

'Almost a year and she's proud of herself,' he says, chuckling.

'What's so funny?'

'Nyah.' He shrugs. 'Mopeds and scooters,' he says, going back to the subject. 'They're popular with young people now. Mostly the criminals. But still. A sale is a sale.'

'I don't know if criminals buy their mopeds,' I say. 'I think they steal them.'

Moss raises his wild eyebrows. 'Well. Don't tell Hamed. He thinks his son's going to make him rich.' He turns to look at the dress and runs his hand over it so the fabric catches the light as it ripples under his fingers. 'Where did you find this frock?'

'This is from a church sale.'

He pinches the fabric between his thumb and forefinger. He straightens the skirt, smooths it tenderly; this time so subtly that I almost miss it. He says with a smile, 'You know, someone had fun in this in the Seventies. Some girl.'

'I know!' I smile too, because I recognise the feeling of past pleasures shared and understood.

Moss pours more coffee and leans back on the counter. He gives his a stir. 'My bride, Dinah, you open her closets and point to something and she can relive the time like that, like reading a book.' He clicks his fingers. 'She'll tell you where and when I gave it to her and exactly the emotions she felt. Ever heard of that before in your whole life?'

'No.'

'Her life story is in those clothes. It's a great joy for me to see her wearing them like a second skin. My joy is in her joy.' He looks at me with pride.

'They're so wonderful,' I agree. 'She let me try on the Grès.'

'How do you know about the Grès?'

'My degree is in fashion design. It's the most beautiful gown; the construction is out of this world, isn't it?'

His mood changes instantly. Moss taps his spoon sharply on the rim of the cup to get the drips off, silver ringing against china. 'You wore her clothes? Where was this?'

He's so angry that I immediately back off, surprised at his sudden change of mood. 'Just in her dressing room when I went to your house,' I reply defensively, in case he thinks I've been out clubbing in Dinah's prized dress.

Moss looks at me narrowly as if I were blurred and he's trying to get me into focus. He's seeing something in me that he doesn't much like, breathing heavily through his nose, getting his anger under control.

He takes a deep breath and lets it out in a sigh. 'I don't know,' he says irritably. 'I can't see it, you and Dinah. People should stick to friends of their own age. You have friends your own age, don't you?'

'Of course,' I say, taken aback.

'So does she.'

I remember her description of her friends as old and decrepit. I don't understand it. Moss has never been the warmest of people towards me but I haven't done anything wrong, I don't have to take this. 'What's going on, Moss? I'm confused.'

'You have to ask? You've met her. She's particular.'

I feel myself tightening inside, defensive. 'What's that supposed to mean?'

'I mean she's peculiar,' he corrects himself after a moment.

I don't understand. 'Dinah's peculiar?'

'A little, yes. For instance, she feels very strongly about her wardrobe. It's very personal to her. She doesn't like it being touched.'

It makes no sense to me at all; it was Dinah who took me upstairs to show me her collection. It was Dinah who asked me if I wanted to try on the gown. Still, it's not something I'm prepared to argue with him about.

'Her clothes, they're personal.' He frowns, waves his hand at me crossly and turns away. 'I'm old. I can't explain it.'

I suppose he must wonder if he can trust me. And as he bought the clothes for Dinah's collection, he's going to be very aware of their value – if I'd bought them, I wouldn't necessarily want random strangers trying them on either; I get that. Still. His reaction seems a little over the top.

'Fair enough,' I say and I pick up my bag. 'Let's leave it at that, then.'

When I get to the door he says, 'Wait!'

I've had enough but I turn back to face him. 'What?'

'When are you going to bring me more customers?' he asks.

It's not exactly an apology, but it does feel like an olive branch. 'When will you decide about the shop?'

'What's the shop got to do with it? I can fit clothes on people anywhere, makes no difference.'

'That's true.'

He leans against the counter for support. 'For now, send them here, okay? As many as you can; don't worry, I'm not afraid of working hard.'

I nod. It strikes me for the first time that he's a long way past retirement age. Like his wife, it's only his energy that gives him the illusion of being younger.

Maybe working isn't just a hobby for him but a way to stave off loneliness. I start to wonder if it's more than that and if he genuinely needs the money. After all, Dinah's pretty high-maintenance. However, it's not the kind of thing that I can ask.

'Okay. I'll do my best. Thanks for the coffee,' I say and he nods.

He gathers the dress up and stares at it. 'Anytime,' he says tiredly.

# LOT 11

*Lilac-and-black tweed suit, with co-ordinating sleeveless lilac blouse, intertwined 'C' buttons, size 36/10, Chanel-inspired.*

Dinah Moss turns up at the stall late morning, just as I'm hanging up a sign offering Bespoke Tailoring and Alterations.

She sneaks up on me. 'Hello, dahlink!' she says in my ear, scaring me half to death and laughing cheerfully at the heart-stopping effect it has on me.

'Dinah!'

She's wearing a lilac-and-black Chanel suit with a silky lilac shirt and she reads my sign with the studied poise of a model on a photoshoot. 'So! Bespoke tailoring and alterations! You and Moss are a partnership now.'

'Yes.'

She gives a satisfied smile. 'And whose idea was that?'

I laugh. 'All yours, you're a genius.'

Her dark hair is tucked into a black satin turban and she looks like the kind of woman who does charity lunches; well preserved and wealthy. She has the gold chain handles of her repaired Chanel 2.55 jersey quilted bag in the crook of her arm. 'I've been looking at the other stallholders. All these people trying to make a living,' she says, marvelling. 'And you, too, and such a tiny stall to sell from.'

'Small but cheap,' I tell her.

'Ach, cheap. Fern Banks Vintage,' she says, reading my sign. 'It's always good sense to put your name to a business. You have a little chair for me to sit on?'

'I have a stool. Here.'

I unfold it for her and she sits neatly then smooths her lilac-and-black skirt over her knees. 'Tell me, what do you think about Moss? He's a good tailor, don't you agree?'

'Yes, he's amazing. My client's thrilled she can have the dress fitted.'

On the stall next to us, David Westwood can hear us talking. 'Absolutely thrilled,' he calls dryly.

'Ah, there you are, hiding in the dark! Good morning!' Dinah sits forward and waggles her fingers at him coquettishly. 'Handsome,' she says out of the corner of her mouth, loudly enough for him to hear. *Hentsom.*

'The woman Moss is altering the dress for is his partner,' I say, to set her straight.

'Ah. Generous, too,' she replies flirtatiously.

I'm not sure whether Moss's description of Dinah as peculiar was a slip of the tongue or not. She's actually pretty normal. It's him I'm not so sure about. I've met men like him before, the ones who accompany their wives or girlfriends on shopping trips, proud of imposing their taste and sense of style on others. I realise for the first time that the same could apply to Mick; I'm not judging.

It's a sunny day and the light through the awning gives the stall a mellow glow. Above the alley I can see a strip of clear blue sky. It's going to be a good day for shopping.

Dinah sits forward to have another look at David and says in a stage whisper, 'He'll make a good husband for someone. So, what is she like, the partner?'

'Tall, stylish and really friendly.'

It's meant to be an honest and flattering description, knowing that David can hear us talking about her, but Dinah tuts and shakes her head.

'Really friendly? Oh, he has problems, that one. He looks a shy man who keeps his own counsel.'

Luckily, David Westwood's now talking to a customer. He doesn't sound at all like a shy man who keeps his own counsel – he sounds, as always, completely relaxed and convincing.

The market is starting to get busy. I wonder if I need to give Dinah a brief lesson in stallholder etiquette – like not to intimidate the customers – but she turns out to be even better than Dolly at attracting attention.

She poses as elegantly as a mannequin on the stool in her lilac-and-black Chanel suit with her legs crossed, her elbows bent at angles, her chin held high, greeting people as they pass.

Far from finding the attention intimidating, people seem to enjoy the personal touch and start to cluster around my stall. She doesn't intervene while they look; she sits perfectly still, showing nothing more than the occasional alert expression of interest.

As a result, I sell a couple of Seventies midi dresses and a brocade evening coat during lunch, and afterwards, smiling gleefully at each other in the post-lunch lull, Dinah decides to get us some sandwiches.

I'm folding some of the garments, when I suddenly see a man whose face is vaguely familiar coming through the alley. He has white hair – newly washed and fluffed up like a halo – beige trousers, a fine cotton shirt. My stomach tightens with surprise – what do you know! It's the man who inadvertently got me fired: Kim Aston, who I haven't seen since Carluccio's when he bought the blue cocktail dress from me.

He sees me and gives me a smile of recognition. 'Ah! Fern,'

he says warmly, coming over. 'I saw in the *Camden New Journal* that you had a fire trauma. I thought I'd see if I could find your stall and say hello.'

'Good to see you again!' I say, optimistically wondering if he's looking for more clothes for Enid.

'I tried to get another appointment with you at the store, but they said you'd left.' He looks up at the dresses hanging around the stand, frowning. 'And this is what you do now, is it? You sell these clothes here, full-time?'

'Yes, this is what I do now.' I look around, too. No more chandeliers, no soft carpeting, no champagne and tea. 'How's your wife?'

'She died,' he says, his face creasing as though he's perplexed by the idea.

'I'm *so* sorry.'

'Yes.' He nods as if this is something that he's heard a lot. The dresses seem to mesmerise him, and he gazes from them to me and back to them again. He says abruptly, 'Well, I'll be off. I just wanted to say hello.'

'Nice to see you again, Mr Aston.'

He raises his hand in a wave and disappears into the Stables. A few moments later he comes back again.

'You seem a very understanding person.' He leans towards me, looks furtively around and lowers his voice. 'I'm afraid I lied to you when I came into the store. I wasn't looking on behalf of my wife.'

'That's okay,' I say quickly, imagining some flashy ageing mistress in the background. 'You don't have to explain.'

'No, of course not,' he says. Again, he looks over his shoulder and turns back to me. 'I suppose you guessed that the dress was for me.'

I look at him in surprise, wondering if I've heard right and then clearly remembering his nervousness, his hesitation, his growing confidence in what he was looking for. 'I had no idea,' I tell him truthfully.

'No? I wish I'd told you at the time. I've been informed since that that sort of thing is quite acceptable now?'

I can see the eagerness in him and I nod. 'Oh, absolutely.'

His face relaxes again. 'You see, it was hard for me to talk about it because my wife didn't know.' He shakes his head violently as though he's trying to dislodge the idea. 'Good grief, no. I consider that was one of the strengths of our marriage, that she saved me from myself.' He gives a small, self-deprecating smile. 'And I'm a member of the golf club. There would be questions about which tee to drive from.'

I laugh. When a person can make a joke, there's always hope, in my opinion. 'So you never told her?'

'Never. Although, I got close once. That dress – she found a stray blue feather on the floor. She puzzled over it for days. I should have told her then but I couldn't risk her disapproval, and yet . . . she might, like her friends, have turned out to be a woman of her time and understood it.' He presses his lips together and tucks his hands in his jacket pocket, shoulders hunched. 'The truth is, I don't know what she would have thought. I never gave her the chance to tell me.' His voice is full of regret.

'You didn't want to upset her, I suppose.'

All this time, his faded eyes are holding mine. 'Yes. That's one way of looking at it. I want you to know, that dress was what kept me strong through her illness. It was better than brandy for helping me to escape for a time. It gave me the courage to keep going.'

'I know what that feels like.'

Those words make everything different between him and me. He relaxes because he sees it's the truth, the truth that I live by. And I've seen something, too. I'd thought I'd lost my job over something small and frivolous, when in fact I'd been making his pain easier to bear. I feel vindicated and suddenly cheerful.

'It saddens me to think I've wasted my life,' he says, looking at the dresses longingly.

Just then, I see Dinah coming back with our lunch. 'I bought ham croissants,' she announces imperiously and she's suddenly distracted by the sight of Kim.

He's staring at her open-mouthed. For a moment she stands and stares back at him in silence, shielding her eyes from the sun with one elegant hand.

She has much the same effect on Kim as she had on me, because he seems to be seeing some other-worldly revelation. 'I want to look like *you*,' he tells her passionately.

Once again, Dinah surprises me. She laughs, batting away the compliment. 'Dahlink, of course you do.' She looks him up and down. 'Well, you're slim, it's not impossible. And take it from me, a turban is utterly divine to wear. Have you ever tried a turban?'

Speechless, he shakes his head.

She looks into her paper bag. 'I only bought two, so we have to share.' She tears the croissant in half. 'You choose. Give me your phone number and I'll find you a turban. Schiaparelli, dahlink,' she mouths and shares her croissant with him.

# LOT 12

*Mixed lot of three day dresses, circa 1940s, including a pink-and-orange dress with button detail and matching coat; red silk blouse with fan neckline detail; Prince of Wales check suit; bottle-green wool suit with peplum.*

It's Wednesday. The morning light is yellow and melancholy, and the clouds are dusted with cinnamon. It's going to be a hot day and I'm wearing the orange A-line minidress. By the time I've arranged my stall, my flicked-up hair is already going limp.

David Westwood is focused on sanding down an irregularly shaped block of wood. His eyes are lowered and he's got the thickest, darkest eyelashes I've ever seen on a man. I wonder if they're the reason his eyes are such a striking blue.

Somewhere in the yard behind us a busker is playing melancholy Donovan songs on an acoustic guitar. David's sanding to the rhythm of the music.

A gabble of voices: a group of excitable students in bottle-green sweatshirts come down the alley led by a tour guide holding up a Union Jack flag. They file past us as if they're keeping to a schedule.

'Whatcha doin'?' I ask David curiously, watching the fine dust dull the cobbles around our feet. Looks like a departure from the light boxes.

'I'm making Gigi's birthday present,' he says, smoothing the wood with his hand. 'It's a surprise.'

'My lips are sealed.' I'm not sure what it's meant to be. One thing I know, it's definitely not a light box. 'What woman wouldn't want a rustic shelf for her birthday?' I say cheerfully.

He ignores my facetiousness. 'It's a chopping board. I've carved her name and date of birth on it.'

He hands the board to me. It's extremely heavy. But even as a total non-connoisseur of woodworking, I can see that the intricate carving has taken him a lot of time and work. I trace Gigi's name and date of birth with my finger. 'Wow. It's beautiful.'

'I'm going to put flowers along here,' David says, showing me where he's pencilled in the design. I can feel his warm breath against my cheek.

The wood is streaked and swirled with contrasting shades of rich brown. 'Gigi'll love it,' I say admiringly, trying not to sound envious.

He looks pleased. 'It's maple.'

'I like these markings on it.'

'Those are burs. Burwood, it's called. Don't they look like birds' eyes?'

'Yes! Burwood,' I repeat, so that I'll remember it.

'The burs make it brittle and harder to work with, but it's worth it.'

He says it with so much warmth that I smile, because everyone loves a lover and I can see that the effort of working with this brittle wood is his measure of his love.

'Does a lot of chopping, does she, Gigi?' I ask him curiously.

'She will when she's got a chopping board,' he says. He holds it at an angle to the light and turns it over, blowing off the dust. Then he picks up a chisel. Lucky Gigi.

I've been thinking about her birthday present, too. I'm going to give her the velvet opera cloak with the pink silk lining, because it's a striking garment, one that'll make people ask her where she got it (and she can then tell them it was sourced by me).

From Dinah, I'm learning a bit about hustling; I've seen the way her face will light up sometimes when a passer-by picks up a dress, even though they're just looking at it in passing really, and it turns out that, surprise! the dress is Dinah's absolute all-time favourite, and what good taste the passer-by has! Her approval is as sweet and warm as sunshine, and her enthusiasm and friendliness is contagious.

Unlike me, with my paranoia about putting people off, Dinah talks to everyone, even if it's just a good morning or good afternoon as they walk by. And they respond.

Life is good at the moment. After the disaster of the fire, and the absence of Mick, I believe I've come out the other side. A combination of the sunny weather, the bespoke alterations and Dinah's chutzpah means that sales are going well. And it's time to restock again.

The Tallulah Young Vintage Auction is coming up in Clerkenwell and I've gone through the auction catalogue online, looking for retro pieces, searching for a particular look; simple lines, Peter Pan collars, primary colours.

The sale's on a Monday and because Dinah's getting to know my stock as well as I do, I've asked her if she wants to come with me. She's very enthusiastic, so we make our arrangements and I wait for her at Camden Town Tube. It's really busy and I'm looking round for her when I hear her call me.

'Dahleenk! Hey! You there! Audrey!'

I'm embracing the Hepburn look in black Capri pants, a knotted white shirt and a red Hermès neckerchief.

Dinah has dressed up for the auction too, in heels and a

little suit. She frowns at my flats. 'What are those things on your feet?'

'It's what Audrey would have worn,' I tell her. I'm not that impressed with her heels, either. 'Can you walk in those? You do realise it's fifteen minutes from the Tube, don't you?'

'Pah!' she says dismissively. 'Up a mountain?'

On the journey there she asks me plenty of questions about the auction, mostly about how it works financially. She's indignant that both buyers and sellers pay commission, and by the time we get to the auction house, she has all the attitude of a seasoned auction-goer.

She fits in here perfectly, with her polished style and her haughty chin. I look through the racks at the lots I'm interested in, beguiled by the richness of beauty and design. I love the Sixties psychedelic tunics, synthetic black-and-white mod-look trouser suits, pop art shirts with blocks of colour, geometric patterns. I also have my eye on a group of Forties day dresses, easy to wear and sexy, and they suit all ages.

These delight Dinah too and she gleefully tucks her arm in mine. 'They take me back,' she says breathlessly.

I register for a paddle number with which to bid. At Dinah's insistence, we sit in the front row.

Tallulah Young, the auctioneer, comes over to say hello and I introduce her to Dinah. Tallulah's truly passionate about clothes and since I've become a regular at the viewings, she'll often point out things that she thinks I might be interested in.

Despite Tallulah's warm greeting, Dinah isn't impressed with her. Once she's out of earshot, Dinah says, 'Look at her skin – sun damage,' she says, leaning her head towards mine and pointing as if I don't know who she's talking about. 'She looks her age. Her blonde hair is greying and her upper arms are losing tone – why's she wearing short sleeves? Why doesn't she try to appear younger?'

'Personally, I've always admired women who let their hair grow grey,' I say.

Dinah has a different opinion. 'You don't see me with white hairs,' she says disapprovingly.

'That's because you colour it,' I point out.

Dinah's indignant. 'Who says? I suppose it's a good look if you can keep your nerve, but who would want to?'

Dinah has the open curiosity of a child when it comes to people. She's distracted by a woman in her seventies with an asymmetric bob, a geometric structured black-and-white jacket, white plus fours and black-and-white zigzag socks, and black brogues. 'Stylish,' she says.

A couple of good-looking men come to sit a couple of seats down from us. I realise that they're fussing over a white Yorkshire terrier and I get anxious and uneasy.

'Let's move further back,' I suggest nervously. I won't be able to relax while the dog is there.

'Why?' Dinah looks up from her auction catalogue and turns around to look at the room, which is filling up. 'No,' she says, 'I like it here.'

'Swap seats, then?'

'What's wrong with yours?' she asks suspiciously.

'The dog.'

'That thing?' She looks at it over her spectacles. 'What's wrong with it?'

I could tell her I'm afraid of dogs because of their unpredictability, their jumpiness, the barking that's always loud and startling. I'm afraid of them because dog lovers always say dogs can sense fear and that makes me fearful. I'm afraid because dog lovers always tell me their dog just wants to play, even though it's straining at the leash and making a rumbling noise in its throat. And I know about the prey reflex that means that when the fear gets too much to stand and you try

171

to get away, dogs are hardwired to come after you. I don't want to tell her, because she won't understand. People don't.

But Dinah has a fine-tuned sensitivity to mood. She shrugs and without asking any more questions, she gets up and changes seats with me.

The two men fuss over the white Yorkshire terrier until it farts with happiness. The fart spreads slowly and hangs in the air, taking its time to dissipate.

'Disgusting!' Dinah says loudly, fanning her catalogue furiously while I pretend not to notice. 'That's why you wanted to change places?' Someone else catches her eye.

A woman, mid-thirties, pale, wearing a trilby on the back of her head like a halo, military green jacket, jeans.

'Who is that one, Fern?'

'Not sure,' I whisper in the hope that she'll whisper, too.

'Well I don't know about the jeans,' Dinah tutted. 'Strictly for cowboys. But perhaps I like the effect. Oh, that dog! We should move.' She looks around at the windows first and then at the ceiling. 'Fans.'

'Are you warm?'

'For the smell.' She sniffs the air delicately. 'He's done it again. These people and their dogs.'

'Shh,' I tell her, demonstrating with the universal sign of pressing my index finger against my lips.

'Don't worry about it, dahlink,' she says, patting my knee. 'Everyone else is thinking it, too.'

My heart's pounding with anticipation. I now realise it's a bit of a responsibility, bringing her here. The fun of being in Dinah's company is offset by her loud comments and our two different sets of needs. For me, it's business and I hope to get some lots at a good price. At auction, fashion finds its own level, but sometimes items that don't reach the lower estimate can be bought just under the reserve at Tallulah's discretion, and that's where I get lucky. Other lots might attract no interest in the beginning and I think I've got a chance, but once bidding starts it can lead to auction fever; a frenzy of waving paddles that means the garments far exceed the top estimate. There's no way of knowing in advance how it's going to go and the uncertainty is part of the excitement, but I hope I won't leave empty-handed.

For Dinah, it's a fun day out. How long will she want to stay? I wonder.

Having checked online and now in the sales room the first lot I want to bid on is number sixty-eight, which means there's some waiting around. The auction begins. There are maybe twenty of us in the room and some phone lines set up. The screen lights up. Lot number one.

Dinah takes a gold pen out of her handbag, crosses her legs, balances her catalogue on her knee and watches the auctioneer.

Although I've spent a lot of time online picking out the dresses and ensembles that I'm interested in, as the clothes appear on the screen, everything now seems new again and desirable.

As each lot sells or doesn't sell, Dinah writes the price in the margin. The well-known names go for above the asking price, but there are also some surprises. There are no bids for a little gold tweed Yves Saint Laurent suit. The lower estimate is only eighty pounds.

'I wonder what's wrong with it? I'm tempted to buy it just for the buttons,' I whisper to Dinah.

'I looked at it myself,' Dinah says loudly. 'It's full of moth holes.'

'Shh. Now this is ours,' I say to her. 'The lot with the Ossie Clarks. Everyone loves them.'

I bid decisively, but despite stretching my limit, the first dress, a black crêpe dress with a plunging keyhole neckline, goes for four hundred and sixty pounds to a phone bidder, way above the upper estimate and well over my maximum. Overseas buyers, probably. An Ossie Clark/Celia Birtwell for Radley printed rayon dress goes for five hundred pounds. I haven't got a hope of affording them.

The serious bidders, it seems, are there for Chanel. 'The fight of the Chanels,' Tallulah Young calls it as the bids go higher and higher for a pristine purple tweed suit and a jacket with a chinchilla fur collar. Dinah can hardly contain her excitement as a lot of two suits exceeds its top estimate by nine hundred and fifty pounds.

As the hammer goes down she sinks back in her chair, fanning herself with her catalogue.

Disappointingly, we lose out on the op art suits and mini-dresses, but I don't stay despondent for long because our next lot comes up: 'Ten evening/afternoon dresses, mainly 1930s, including black chiffon example, the yoke and sleeves with zigzag inserts of red, a sequinned skullcap, navy blue bias-cut chiffon gown and others, busts approximately 32 to 40 inches.'

My heart is thudding each time I raise the paddle and I'm relieved when I manage to buy them mid-estimate. I feel completely drained. Dinah's absolutely thrilled that we've bought a whole bundle of clothes and she's sitting beaming on the edge of her seat.

Mostly, I'm grateful that I haven't got carried away by auction fever.

When the morning session is over, I nudge Dinah. 'Come on. Let's go.'

Before we leave I pay by bank transfer. We'll go back later to pick up the dresses and in the meantime, we stop for a lunchtime glass of wine and a bowl of olives outside a pub.

Dinah is surprisingly subdued, and she unclips her earrings

and drops them into her handbag. I assume that, like me, the whole process has exhausted her, but as she spears an olive with a cocktail stick she starts to talk about her own collection.

'You know how I feel about my wardrobe?' she says, her excited dark eyes searching mine.

'Yes,' I reply cautiously, thinking of Moss's comments that she was peculiar about it.

'But now I see they're worth all that money!'

'Yes.' I'm surprised that she's surprised.

'I've been thinking. Could *I* sell some clothes in the auction?' She chews the olive thoughtfully.

'You could, of course, but why would you want to do that?'

She lowers her eyes modestly. 'This year it's our platinum wedding anniversary.' She laughs at my surprise. 'I've been married to Moss for seventy years. I want to take him on holiday.'

'But your clothes are part of your history,' I point out.

She smiles. 'True. And for you, with clothes, it's the same, isn't it?'

'Yes. I can define the big occasions of my life by what I wore when they happened, like the fuchsia broderie anglaise dress with scalloped hem for my first day at school. For my first day at uni I wore a yellow PVC raincoat and silver sandals, and I went on my first date wearing a turquoise-and-white dress, chrome necklace and glittery tights that I borrowed from my mother. I attended my first music festival in second-hand Biba and my first funeral wearing my grandmother's Rive Gauche, and I lost my virginity in a lilac John Galliano that I got from a church sale. I like to look right. It lifts my heart. The way I see it: what makes the eyes light up – a gift topped by a jaunty bow or a gift in a carrier bag? It's all in the presentation.'

Dinah laughs. 'Exactly! And do you still have those clothes?'

'No. I've sold them on. It's a way of passing on some of my joy.' After a moment I add truthfully, 'Also, sometimes I just need the money.'

She looks at me carefully, her head tilted, and she raises an eyebrow. 'And it doesn't matter to you that you're selling your history, does it?'

'No, because I remember them perfectly well.'

She frowns. 'Maybe that's enough for me, too.'

I nod, but I'm full of misgivings about the plan. 'What would Moss say when he finds you've sold the things that he bought for you?'

'Dahlink, I wouldn't tell him until afterwards and then it's too late. You must help me choose what to take,' she says, tossing the remainder of her green olives to the pigeons. The birds beat their wings and retreat a short distance, keeping their eyes on the prize. 'Now, remind me what the most expensive lot sold for.'

# LOT 13

*A 1930s bias-cut black satin figure-hugging midi-length evening dress, with red blouson sleeves, size 14/42.*

I've reread the invitation from Gigi to her birthday party, with the location and a request to RSVP. It might be fun. I deserve some fun.

'So,' I say to David. 'Gigi's party. What kind of party will it be?'

David gives me his direct look, his blue eyes meeting mine. He hesitates for a moment and then he says with a smile, 'The usual kind. Drinks, food. Why?'

His dark blue eyes pierce me to my soul.

I look quickly away; it's like looking into the sun. But being unable to meet his eyes is not a good move – it's very shifty. 'I was just wondering, that's all. What are you going to do about your stall?'

'Close it down for the weekend. I booked the house way before I left my job so obviously at the time I didn't know it was going to be a problem.'

I make most of my money at the weekend. And I've just bought those dresses at the auction, which I'm keen to sell on. I'm distracted from my musings by a customer; another smiling face from the past.

'Er, Fern? Hi! It's Bethan,' she adds, to jog my memory.

'Hi!' Bethan hasn't changed much since I last saw her – she's still got short, highlighted hair, and she's wearing cropped jeans and a blue-and-white check shirt. She's somewhere in her fifties and there's a sadness about her, despite her smile.

'Do you remember me? I came to see you a few years back when my ex married again.'

'Of course I remember you.'

She chuckles. 'You threatened to burn my fleece.'

I remember that fleece; the least flattering garment a woman could wear.

'Did I?' I steer her away from David, who's just made some kind of noise, a cross between a snort and a laugh. Honestly, it's surprising I wasn't fired a lot sooner than I was. 'This is my stall here.'

'Small, isn't it? I saw you in the *Camden New Journal*. Not being funny, but you haven't exactly risen from the ashes yet then – this is a bit different from personal shopping. No champagne, I don't suppose?'

I laugh merrily. 'Sadly, no.'

'It's crisis time again. My daughter, Zoe, is getting married and of course *he* wants his new wife to be there. If I had my way she wouldn't go; what's it got to do with her? She's not *her* daughter,' Bethan says heatedly. 'It's sickening. He's making such a big deal of the whole thing because he's paying for it. He and I got married quietly in Tuscany. It was a small wedding with a handful of good friends and it was, you know, lovely. That's the kind of wedding Zoe wants.' For a moment, she turns her head, blinking away the tears. 'But no, he wants her to do it "properly",' she says, drawing imaginary speech marks around the word, 'as if ours was some kind of second-rate way to tie the knot. And his mother loves his new wife because, apparently, she's so *approachable*, and his mother is sure if I

178

make an effort that we'll get on perfectly well. See?' She shrugs miserably. 'Everything's perfect, apart from me.'

"'If you make an effort?", I repeat. 'Why do you have to get on with her at all? That's a big ask, in the circumstances.'

'Isn't it?' Bethan curls her lip and forces a laugh. 'As if it's just a matter of putting my mind to it. The worst thing is, his new wife really is nice. She's got one of those faces that – uch.' She shudders.

I hazard a guess. 'Too much make-up?'

'Ha! Worse than that! She doesn't wear any at all. She looks really innocent and pure, like a cherub or a seraph, but not the ones that just have a head and two wings, I mean the normal-looking ones. And her hair is all – *natural*. She wears organic cotton.'

I've never heard anyone put so much contempt into the word *natural* before. 'She sounds awful.'

Bethan opens her tote and finds a tissue. 'Yeah. She's not though, that's the problem. She's much nicer than I am. How can I fight that?' She blows her nose violently and tucks the tissue into her jeans. 'Sorry. Anyway. Bottom line, I need an outfit that makes me look nice, even if I don't feel it. If I look good and I don't drink any alcohol at all, I think I can get through it.'

It's a tough brief. Nice. I've never met anyone who wants to look *nice* before – I'm not even sure what it looks like. 'Just to clarify – nice like Kate Middleton?'

Bethan shudders. 'No, she's too mumsy. I don't want to look as if I'm just the mother of his child. I want him to look at me and feel at least a pang of regret for Tuscany. But I don't want to look too sexy, either, because that's going to make me look desperate.' Her gaze skims disinterestedly over the clothes hanging up behind me.

I know in a flash of insight exactly what she means and

exactly how she needs to look to give her the confidence to get through the day. 'Don't go for nice,' I tell her. 'You can't out-nice the nice new wife. You want to look a bit edgy, kind of dangerous,' I tell her. 'Believe me, the last thing you want to do is look *nice*.'

'Dangerous.' Bethan smiles, and for a moment her cloud of sadness lifts. 'As if I'm capable of anything. Well I am,' she adds. 'I'm Welsh.'

'Exactly! You want to look so amazing that no one can take their eyes off you. Because they're *scared* of taking their eyes off you.'

Bethan nods. 'And I want people to wonder why the hell he left me.'

'You need a what-the-hell dress.' And I know the very one, the black one with red silk chiffon sleeves. I unhook the dress for her to look at it.

The red sleeves are full and floaty against the black satin and it doesn't look at all like the sort of dress that the mother of the bride would wear to a wedding breakfast (unless she was still wearing it from the night before).

Dinah has turned up mid-conversation, apparently having heard enough to get her interested. 'Wear it with a red hat,' Dinah says, 'a big one.'

'Bethan, this is Dinah, my assistant. Dinah, this is Bethan, a good client of mine.'

Dinah pouts at me, probably because I've called her my assistant.

'A red hat?' Bethan asks Dinah. 'How about a fascinator?'

Dinah lets out a little shriek. '*Not* a fascinator; never a fascinator – it's an apology of a hat. You want a statement hat and red lipstick. Not that pink you're wearing now, which is pointless because you can barely see it. Red. Make sure you leave it on some collars.'

Bethan laughs a real good belly laugh and goes behind the makeshift curtain while Dinah and I wait outside, breathless with anticipation.

Dinah's clasping her hands together. 'And black shoes, not those flesh ones, yuk!' She covers her eyes theatrically. 'Fern, you have some hats in your house?'

'No, I don't sell hats.'

'What can I tell you, we should get hats,' Dinah murmurs under her breath as if it's long been a bone of contention between us.

'Women don't wear hats to weddings anymore.'

Dinah looks askance. 'What weddings do you go to, that they have no hats?'

Just then, Bethan comes out from behind the screen, putting an end to our bickering.

Knees together, a quick wiggle, turning her back to us. 'Could you zip me up, please?'

Dinah gets there first and Bethan turns around then strikes a pose for us. It's then that I know so certainly it's the dress for her that tears spring to my eyes. It fits her like a dream. 'Perfect!'

Dinah isn't so easily pleased. She turns Bethan around, looking at her critically from close to and then stepping back across the alley, all the way to the wall of Stables Market, where she makes binoculars of her two hands before coming close again to smooth the silk over Bethan's hips.

Honestly, I've never seen such a performance in all my life.

'Perfection,' Dinah declares at last, opening up her arms to catch imaginary bouquets from the heavens.

She's incorrigible.

'David, let's have a man's opinion.'

David gets to his feet, turns his clear, intimate gaze on Bethan and raises his dark eyebrows.

181

It doesn't sound much, compared with Dinah's extravagant display of admiration, but Bethan blushes and clutches her throat.

How does he *do* that?

Bethan's excitement shows all over her face. 'I'd never think to wear this for a wedding,' she says. 'Dare I?' She raises her arms and the sun glows through the floaty red sleeves.

'Oh, my dahlink – heh – I'd give anything, truly, to see your ex-husband's face when he sees you.'

'And a hat . . .'

'Tell you what, Dinah'll go hat shopping with you. Won't you, Dinah?' I say, volunteering her.

'Who, me? Well, maybe I could. Why not?'

Bethan smiles, closes the curtain. As she takes the dress off she says, slightly muffled, 'I didn't ask you the price.'

'It's two hundred and fifty pounds,' Dinah says.

*What?* I glare at Dinah, annoyed on two counts: first, because it's not her decision to make, and secondly, because I can't drop the price now.

Bethan comes back out holding the dress. To my surprise, she gets her credit card out and seems okay with the price, but still, it should have been my decision. I wrap the dress up in tissue and she and Dinah make arrangements to meet in Fenwick in Bond Street the following day.

Once she's gone, Dinah sits on my stool, admiring her legs and looking very pleased with herself.

Me, I'm not so pleased. In fact, I'm annoyed. 'You know we've overcharged her.'

Dinah glowers at me and turns away.

After a few more minutes of silence I relent and say, 'I know you're looking at it from a business point of view, but—'

'Business?' Dinah explodes. 'Of course, business! But, more importantly, she *loves* that dress. You saw her. How's she going to feel about it if she doesn't pay much for it? Who feels good in a cheap dress? At her daughter's wedding? With the mother-in-law and the second wife there? She wants to splash out the cash – don't you know anything about women?' She gets to her feet and stalks off.

She doesn't go far. Coming back, she says patiently, 'Huh. It's not your fault. You're no businesswoman, that's the problem. Lucky for you, you've got me around.'

# LOT 14

*Yellow Chloé dress with fitted lace overlaid bodice, cutaway sleeves and silk chiffon handkerchief hem, 1970s.*

'Who better to look after my stall for the weekend of the party than Dinah Moss? She's a bloody good saleswoman,' I tell Lucy. 'I'll probably be able to retire by Monday.'

It's getting dark and we're sitting outside in my garden under the ragged banana trees, drinking cider. The lights are going on in the windows around us. Above us, the navy sky is studded sparsely with stars that are outshone by the city's glow. 'See that there? That's Leo. Possibly,' I add, because they look very faint. 'I recognise it from David Westwood's light boxes.'

'Tell me again why you're going to this party?' Lucy asks suspiciously.

'Because! Because Gigi likes vintage and her friends like vintage, so I'm going to be handing out my business cards and doing a bit of networking.' I chink my glass against hers.

'Oh, is that all? A bit of networking. Nothing to do with the fact that you fancy her partner and want to know him a little better then?'

'Lucy Mills! Shame on you! Of course not! David's totally in love with Gigi. He's making her a beautiful chopping board for her birthday.'

'Why? Is she a butcher?'

'Ha ha!' I say. 'It's made of burwood, which is really hard to work with.'

'Burwood? Get you! Since when have you been interested in carpentry?'

'No, listen, he's personalising it. He's carved her name on it and her date of birth.'

'Oh, he's carved her *name* on it! Why didn't you say so? That makes all the difference.'

Her sarcasm makes me defend him more heatedly than it warrants. 'It's romantic,' I tell her. 'He's put a lot of work into it. Even if she hardly ever uses it, she's going to love it just because *he's* made it.'

Lucy's silent for a moment, mulling it over. 'You think?'

'I would, wouldn't you?' A moth flutters towards us and folds up on the lighted window.

'In that case, lucky her.'

If he'd carved my name on it, I'd cherish it forever. I look longingly up at the dark sky, trying to see it as he sees it, and I feel a shiver of misgiving.

Lucy's right. I've got it bad.


I haven't got a car because it's too expensive for me to drive in London, with the congestion and emissions charge, so I arranged to borrow my mother's motor to drive to Gigi's birthday party in the Cotswolds.

This involves catching the train to Berkhamsted first, to pick up the car from their house. I get there by two o'clock. Shamelessly, as a walking endorsement of Fern Banks Vintage, and nothing to do with David, I'm wearing a yellow off-the-shoulder crêpe-de-Chine long dress with a lace bodice. I've let my hair dry naturally and it's got a bit of a curl.

My mother answers the door. She's wearing a pink Ralph

Lauren cotton sweater and white jeans. Her hair's tied up in a ponytail and she's uncharacteristically pale.

'Hi, Mum.'

She winces, as if I've scraped my fork on her favourite china. 'I'd prefer you to call me Annabel, darling.' After brushing her cheek lightly against mine by way of greeting, she stands back to look at me without comment.

The house is very quiet. 'Where's Dad?' I ask, because since he's retired, they do everything together.

'He's at yoga,' she says and smiles ruefully at my surprise. 'I know! Can you believe it? He says it helps him de-stress. Come on through. I've made us a late lunch. We never have the chance to talk, just the two of us.'

Lunch? I'd imagined grabbing the car keys and staying for a quick coffee, maybe, to be in the Cotswolds by late afternoon, but I follow her into the dining room.

The table is set for two, formally, with white linen. I don't know how long yoga lasts, but my father's obviously not joining us. Through the French windows, the lawn is as bright and precision-cut as a bowling green, the borders are weedless, the laurel bushes shaped into perfect spheres. 'What's he stressed about?' I ask, half expecting her to say me.

'I don't know and I'm not sure he does, either. He's not sleeping very well.'

'Do you want a hand in the kitchen?'

'Sit. It's all ready, darling.' She goes to the kitchen and comes back with a salad of leaves, capers and pomegranate seeds, and a plate of goat's cheese. She sits opposite me and gives a faint smile as she unfolds her napkin.

It's been so long since we spent time together, just the two of us, that the silence is unsettling. 'Everything's all right between you two, isn't it?' I ask.

'Yes, of course. We get in each other's hair from time to time, but retirement is a period of transition. The Bennetts went through the same thing. Francis said at one point he was thinking of committing a crime so that Ruth could only visit him in prison once a week.'

We both smile at this because their old friends the Bennetts are models of propriety.

My mother's smile fades more quickly than mine, though. She chews the salad slowly and mindfully, a habit from her modelling days. I'm guessing that she, like me, is trying to find a suitable topic of conversation.

'Thanks for lending me the car,' I say.

My mother's eating her pomegranate seeds one by one. She looks up at me from her plate. 'Doesn't Mick drive?'

'Mick and I have broken up.'

'Oh, Fern,' she says and puts her cutlery down carefully as if this new disappointment has taken away her appetite. 'And what's going on in the Cotswolds?' she asks.

'It's a friend's birthday. Gigi. We were together in sixth form for a while.'

'I think I remember her. Is she French?'

I almost say yes, because that's how dysfunctional our relationship has become; instead of having a conversation with her, I field her questions by filtering out anything she might disapprove of.

Instead, I reply, 'No. And she wasn't at school long. She left before her A levels to be a hairdresser. But she's going out with the guy on the next stall to me and we've kind of got reacquainted.' When she doesn't react to the mention of the stall, I start to get really worried. 'Why don't you go to yoga with Dad?' I ask.

She takes her napkin off her knee and folds it carefully, smoothing it with the flat of her hand. Her eyes meet mine, briefly. 'He doesn't want me there. He says we should have separate interests.'

Yikes. When I was young, she and I did everything together, we were a unit, inseparable, and my father was the outsider, the man who appeared at the table for supper, who I kissed goodnight and who was off to work before breakfast.

And then when I left home, my parents became the unit and I was the outsider, listening to stories about where they'd been and whom they'd met. Their marriage had always seemed solid to me; the one thing in life I didn't have to wonder about.

And now my father thinks they should have separate interests. That's never good.

My mother's eyes meet mine. I smile reassuringly and hope I don't look as worried as I feel.

As a result of the lunch with my mother, I get to Gigi's later than I'd intended. The pastel timber houses, very New England, have been built around a gravel pit that's been requisitioned as a lake.

I drive into the estate and the gatekeeper points out the faded aqua-green house as he raises the barrier, but I'd have recognised it anyway because of the number of cars parked around it.

I find myself a parking space near a gravel border with large decorative rocks and stones spaced artistically around long fronds of grasses and ferns. I study the house. A couple of children's scooters lie abandoned by the front door.

Leaving my bag in the boot for now, in case I change my mind and want to make a quick exit, I get out of the car. I can hear children squealing with excitement somewhere behind the high fence and I walk up to the house. The door is ajar, but I ring the bell anyway.

'It's open!' David calls and in I go.

He's wearing a blue floral shirt and red surfer shorts, which takes me back to the first day I saw him. 'Come on in, Fern.' His voice is a bit hoarse. 'You look different.'

A combination of excitement and nerves makes me babble. 'It's the hair, probably. And I've got different clothes on. Well, of course I have – I mean, I'm wearing a different look.'

'Oh. Who are you supposed to be today, then?' he asks as if it's fancy dress.

I laugh. He looks different, too; for a start, he's not wearing black, and secondly, he's more relaxed than I've ever seen him. As I follow behind him a little too closely, breathing in his cologne, I remind myself once again that he's been in a relationship with Gigi for almost a year; happy enough to be renting this place for a whole weekend of celebrations on account of her. In other words, he is Strictly Off Limits.

And an amazing house it is, too: open-plan, glass on two sides looking out on the lake, a kitchen island, huge dining table and to the left two separate seating areas, one facing the widescreen television and the other facing the water.

Gigi and her friends are in the kitchen part. Gigi's wearing jeans. Her pink hair is held back by an Alice band. She's holding a champagne bottle up to the light then upends a few drips into a crystal glass before noticing me happily. 'Fern, open another bottle, will you?' Which is lovely, because it's as if I've been there the whole time.

I look around for a fridge and see two open doors. Inside them is a long black granite counter with bottles of Veuve Cliquot, gin and vodka, all lined up, a couple of sliced limes and several shelves of glasses, all reflected in the smoky mirror behind them. It's so extravagantly over the top that I just stand there admiring it for a moment, and then I feel the bottles, trying to gauge which one is the coolest and least likely to explode when I open it. Okay. This one. Peel the foil off the bottle, undo the wire, put the cork up and twist the last bit, pouf! A small, fine spray, perfect, and I pour myself a glass first then take the bottle over to Gigi, feeling surprisingly pleased with myself for carrying out a tricky operation with relative aplomb.

The two friends with Gigi could be models. They seem to be built on the same lines: tall, beautiful, smiley, amiable. The woman in shorts has very short bleached hair and introduces herself as Jenna. The long-haired brunette in the maxi is Alexa.

'Worst name to have in the world, right? "Alexa, close the curtains. Alexa, dim the lights." So much for digital technology. Max thinks it's hilarious, of course. We've changed its name to Computer now because I was getting seriously close to killing him.'

'You should have changed it to Max,' Gigi said.

'Then it wouldn't have worked at all, would it, Max?'

He's come in dripping wet with his fair hair plastered to his head. 'Talking about me again?' he asks. 'I'm looking for a beer and nuts, or crisps, or are there any little sausages left?'

He suddenly grabs Alexa and she gives a high-pitched squeal that makes the glasses ring.

'Max, you're soaking!'

'Who gave the kids water pistols?'

'David,' the women chorus.

David. My abs involuntarily tense at the sound of his name.

'Just wait till he has kids,' Max says. 'He won't be encouraging them to squirt people then, I can tell you. And if we ever have them, he's barred from ever seeing them.'

The children must be Jenna's. I look at her in admiration. How does she manage to have children, keep slim and have no cellulite? How does she *do* that?

She catches me staring at her and she smiles. 'What?'

191

I tell her what I'm wondering about and her smile turns into a laugh. She runs her hand over her short, bleached hair.

'Effort,' she says.

'Oh,' I reply. 'I was hoping it would be something easier.'

'You've got no kids?'

'No. I'm single.' I think of Mick saying: *It's not working for me*.

Jenna cups her elbow in her hand and nods. 'It's hard to find good men,' she says. 'It's hard to know where to look for them in real life, isn't it? It's a chance in a million you'll find them on a dating site, that's for sure.'

Alexa tops up our glasses, holding her dark hair away from her face. Changing the subject away from men, I say, 'I love your dress. Zandra Rhodes?'

She looks surprised. 'Sweet of you. I picked it up at a flea market in Paris.'

Aha! 'Really? Which one?'

She pauses with the bottle over my glass and stares at me speculatively. 'Marché Serpette?'

'Artémise et Cunégonde?'

She laughs and carries on pouring. 'I can't believe you know it! Amazing stall, isn't it? All those wonderful vintage dresses.'

Jenna groans. 'How many times did we go back there, Lex?' she says. 'Not that you're indecisive or anything.'

'It's expensive, for a flea market, don't you think?' Alexa asks me. 'Cleaned me out.'

Gigi's making eyes at me, because this is my opening. 'Fern sells vintage in Camden Lock, don't you, Fern?' she prompts. 'She's got this little tailor who'll alter things to fit. Fern, tell them about Moss. How long's he been married?'

'A long time,' I say with an emphasis on the *long*. 'Almost seventy years.'

'And he still calls his wife "my bride".'

'Aww! Sweet!'

'He's German,' Gigi adds and they laugh.

I laugh too, although I don't know why.

By early evening I'm light-headed. Happy, but definitely slightly drunk as well. I wish I'd paced myself better, but the frequent top-ups make it hard for me to work out how much I've had.

I'm still holding the glass, but the tips of my fingers feel numb and I can't feel it in my hand, so I put it down and ask where the bathroom is.

'Down the corridor, first door on the left.'

In the bathroom, I lock the door and study myself in the mirror. My eyes look big and I'm slightly blurred. My lip balm has rubbed off and I didn't bring my handbag with me – I'm not even sure where it is. I must have put it down when I was opening the bottle of champagne. Surreal.

I've been in a state of low-level drunkenness since I got here. A long time has elapsed since lunch with my mother and my stomach's rumbling.

Back in the lounge, everybody's quiet, overcome with lethargy – even the children, who are watching the TV – and I'm playing with the stem of my glass, watching the way the light catches it, not sure about the wisdom of continuing to drink on an empty head.

I go outside for some fresh air and lean on the glass barrier at the end of the decking and look down at the water.

On the opposite bank, the pastel-coloured houses curl around the water's edge. A swan drifts out from some reeds.

I sit on a sunlounger, trying to get used to the feeling of having nothing to do, which is slightly unnerving, as I'm usually always doing something.

A shadow falls over me and it's David. He sits on the chair

next to me and I look at him, expecting him to say something. I'm struck again by how good-looking he is, David Gandy, male model good-looking, which is something that I haven't mentioned to Lucy.

I'm on the point of saying how lovely it is and how restful and how happy I am to be there, but he hasn't yet said a word himself and for all I know, he's come outside for a bit of peace. I rest my head back and stretch my legs into the evening sun to top up my vitamin D. The yellow silk handkerchief hem flutters and tickles between my legs.

I'm ridiculously pleased he's come to sit next to me, because there are seats all the way round the decking and if he'd really wanted to be alone, he could have gone to sit in any of them.

It's years since I've had a crush on anyone; that intense longing for someone who's unattainable. I close my eyes and listen to the patting of the water against the bank and in the background the shrill voices of the children, high-pitched and excited. *Living the dream*, I think, even though it's never been a dream of mine before to have a husband, children and a house by a lake.

I've never even got as far as imagining living with a man. That was part of the attraction of Mick. I'd imagined our relationship going on forever, being mostly apart but meeting up occasionally, always glad to see each other.

Logistically, there's no room for an extra person in my parents' flat, so I'd have to go to his to start with. And I suppose we'd go down the route of eventually buying a house together, in a commuter belt. But I'm frowning because the whole thing just seems like the worst combination of fantasy and hard work, and I've got enough to do as it is. I lower my eyelids and look at the dazzling water striped vertically by my dark eyelashes.

A loud snore wakes me. My own snore, I realise, because

my throat's tingling as if I've been choked. Yikes! How embarrassing! I wipe my mouth in case I've drooled and swivel my eyes a fraction to look at David, wondering if he heard – and yes, he's still sitting there, grinning at me. I've never seen eyes as dark blue as his – if I'd ever seen eyes like that on a person before, I'd have remembered.

'Sorry about the snore,' I say, laughing at myself, because it's destroyed any possibility of me passing myself off as perfect, which is a bit of a relief, to be honest, because it was an impossible ambition anyway. Snoring has got to be the least sexy noise a body can make, next to a fart.

'Late night?' he asks.

He's got it all. His tanned arm is on the armrest, dark hairs silvering in the sunlight, and he's got smooth tanned hands and naturally pink fingernails, like the inside of shells. His floral shirt fits him perfectly. Even slumped in a lounger, his belly is flat and his shirt doesn't gape. Oh, he's so lovely.

'Well, you know how it is,' I say enigmatically, hoping he'll assume I've got an exciting social life. 'It's so relaxing, sitting here.'

'I'll give it five minutes before Gigi calls me,' he says, turning around to look into the house.

I laugh. I like our easy friendship. For me, that's got to be enough.

'Dave!' Gigi shouts from inside.

*Dayve.*

'Told you,' David says and gets to his feet.

I stay sitting because it might look weird if we both jump up at the same time. But as any infidelity is entirely a product of my own imagination, I get up after a moment, unsticking my dress from the back of my legs, and go back inside into the shady coolness of the house.

We're having home-delivery pizzas for supper. Max has his

pen out and he passes me a menu because he's taking the orders. Gigi asks me to open the wine bottles – she seems to be under the impression that I've got a talent for it. I'm happy to be helpful and it's true, I've had a lot of practice. We lay the table and fill our glasses then wait hungrily for the delivery driver to come.

A conversation starts up about holidays: Sri Lanka, Argentina, Belize.

I find myself looking at David; at the side of his face that's turned towards me, at the line of his cheekbone. He has this particular way of listening, with his eyes slightly narrowed and his head slightly tilted. I move my gaze from one speaker to another, half smiling at the conversation, but he's giving them his full attention.

He's the host, of course.

I reach for some cashew nuts from a horn bowl. And then suddenly:

'Where was your last holiday, Fern?' Max asks me.

I look up at him. He's wearing a black shirt and his hair seems to flare in the spotlights overhead. For a dizzy moment he reminds me of Mick.

'Oh. The south of France,' I say.

He laughs. 'Doesn't narrow it down much.'

'It's a place called Cap d'Agde.' My wine glass is almost empty and I can smell the fumes of the red wine on my own breath as I speak. I should keep quiet but I don't want to be the disappointing guest, the one who doesn't contribute. Anyway, it's a funny story, isn't it? It wasn't at the time, but it is now, after a few drinks. Most embarrassments turned to comedy in time. 'I went there with my boyfriend. My ex,' I add, for clarity.

'What was his name?' Alexa asks eagerly, folding her elbows. 'Mick.'

'Why, do you think you know him?' Max asks her.

'Shh. We have to know his name. It's part of the story, isn't it? Carry on, Fern.'

Suddenly, because they're all listening to me, it seems a bad mistake, embarking on this true confession from the embers of a broken heart. Plus, even now, I don't know what kind of a light that holiday with Mick casts on me. I feel that I've been a bit of a woman of mystery in the proceedings so far and it's a role I like playing. I haven't voiced any controversial opinions or anything like that. I've blended in as best as any stranger can and they really don't know anything about me apart from the fact that I sell vintage. That seems a good place to start.

'So, I sell vintage clothing,' I tell them. But that doesn't really cover it, of course. 'It's a bit of an obsession, I mean – you really never know what you can find and sometimes, you just come across something that's so special, so incredibly crafted that it's just like finding treasure and you get this feeling.' I press my fingers on my breastbone. Alexa's nodding, as if she understands, so I press on. 'The right garment can change the way a person sees themselves. It's not their monetary value necessarily,' I add, slightly breathless from gabbling, 'it's the thrill of finding them and then – how they look, how they make a person look.' I can hear myself desperately justifying it as if Mick's in the room with me. God, I'm talking too much. 'In the forties, if people didn't care about their appearance it was a sign of low morale.'

David smiles. 'Fighting a war, are you, Fern?'

I laugh, although that's how I feel most of the time. I've gone off at a tangent. Someone kicks the table, and for a moment the cutlery rattles and flashes and I steady my glass.

'So,' Jenna says encouragingly, 'you took your vintage clothes to the south of France.'

'No.'

They all laugh, so I try to explain. 'The thing is, basically, Mick never really got the vintage clothing appeal.'

'I'm with him on that,' Max says.

'Shut up, Max. Don't listen to him! Go on.' Alexa's smiling encouragingly, her glossy dark hair spilling over her shoulder.

'And we had a bit of an argument about it, because he hated one of my outfits and I don't like being told what I should wear – by anyone, on principle. And he said that my obsession with clothes was a way of hiding my true self and he wanted to prove that clothes aren't that important. So he booked this holiday for us in Cap d'Agde. I didn't know it was a naturist place. Mick thought that a few days without clothes, going cold turkey, would cure me of the habit and reveal the true me.' It sounds absolutely ridiculous and I find myself giggling.

I glance across at David. He's looking at me curiously.

Max points at me. 'Hang on a minute. Let me ask you a question. Who do you dress for?'

'Myself.'

'No you don't. You dress for attention. Why vintage clothes, though? Why not go to Primark?'

I'm not sure if he's spoiling for a fight or just trying to keep the conversation going. 'What difference does it make?'

He laughs. 'Exactly! You can't tart up a relationship in some nice clothes and hope that it'll look fine. It doesn't work like that. The outward appearance is a sham. It's what's underneath that counts.'

'You sound like my ex-boyfriend.'

He grins. 'Aren't you getting the message?'

Gigi's giggling, too. 'So you spent the whole time naked?'

I nod. It *is* a funny story. We're all laughing.

'Yes, we both did.' I add, 'And he got horribly sunburnt.'

'But apart from the nakedness,' David says, deadpan, 'how was the holiday?'

We're still laughing and I'm wiping away tears because the whole thing seems so bizarre, looking back. I take another mouthful of wine to sober up. Swallow it. When I put the glass down, David's still watching me with that slight head tilt and warmth in his eyes.

'So, this naturist place,' Alexa begins, and then suddenly the doorbell rings and we all spring into action.

Max collects together the money that he's conscientiously worked out will cover the pizzas, plus a tip, David uncorks some more bottles, Gigi dims the lights, someone puts music on and the wine looks black in the subdued light.

We eat the pizzas out of the boxes and the volume of conversation gets louder, seeming to echo off the wooden floors and bounce against the windows until it seems to me that we're all shouting at each other across the table, roaring with laughter. Jenna excuses herself and takes the children to bed.

Like the wine in my glass, the wine in the bottles seems to have drained suddenly, now half full, now empty. I'm astonished by how quickly it's being drunk.

While Jenna's gone Gigi moves seats, so now she's sitting next to Max, winding spiral strands of her pink hair around her finger.

Alexa comes to sit next to me, tilting her wineglass at a reckless angle. 'Amazing place, isn't it? Special. Cost David an absolute fortune to hire, according to Max.'

'It's fabulous,' I agree.

She lowers her voice to a whisper. 'You know why we're here, don't you?' She moves in really close. 'Come here. Listen. Shh. Tomorrow, Dave's going to propose to Gigi. Don't say anything,' she says, slapping me on the arm. 'It's a secret.'

Gutted by the news, I press my finger against my lips to prove my sincerity. 'I won't say a word,' I promise.

'That's the spirit,' Alexa says, looking into my eyes intently. 'It's a surprise. But I think Gigi knows. Do you think she knows?'

I look across at Gigi. She's laughing at something that Max is saying, head thrown back, enjoying herself. 'Maybe. She does look happy, doesn't she?'

'You know why I think she knows?'

'No.'

'Because she's hired a photographer. She wants him to be there to capture the moment.'

'She *definitely* knows,' I say enviously, taking another look at Gigi. 'Wow.' If I knew that David was going to propose to me, I'd be laughing like a drain, too.

This new revelation makes me feel intensely sad. I want to go to bed now and hide my head under the pillow. My bag is in the boot of the car, along with Gigi's gift: the black velvet cloak wrapped in pink tissue. I excuse myself and go outside to get my things, concentrating on walking straight, noisily crushing the gravel in the quiet night, then I take them to my room.

I can hear Jenna talking to her children in a room on the ground floor. Through the window the house next door looms pale against the polished still water and I draw the curtains, brush my teeth, drink water from the tap and lie on the bed, feeling my ribs, checking that my bruised heart is still beating beneath them. I close my eyes and the room revolves.

The noise level coming from the lounge is off the scale, so after a few minutes I give up trying to sleep and get up again. When I come back to the table Gigi's still staring at Max and Alexa's leaning in my pizza box, eyes closed, propping up her head, a smear of tomato smudged on her forearm.

I fill up my glass and take it outside. The glitter-scattered night sky looks huge and black, and I stand still for a moment in the silence, which has a blessed sound of its own.

As if I'm in a dream, I hear someone else coming out into the peaceful dark and I know without turning around that it's David. He comes to stand next to me. 'I've been looking for you,' he says softly.

Back in the house, raised voices; there's an argument going on, political not personal.

'You've found me,' I say, without turning around. I feel as if I'm reading from a film script; this is the way it's meant to be.

It's so dark that the lake is like a deep hole, the quarry that it used to be, and the stars line the bottom of it, mined silver.

As if he's reading my mind, he says, 'It's a celestial sphere.'

'That's poetic,' I breathe.

He laughs. 'But not original.'

'This is an amazing place.' At this moment, I have never been anywhere so profoundly wonderful in my whole life.

'Yes. Gigi chose it.' He adds, 'Before I left my job, obviously. Anyway, that's what I want to talk to you about.' He looks towards the lake. He's quiet for a moment.

I know what he's going to say. He's going to tell me the whole Gigi thing is a horrible mistake. I look up at him hopefully, untangling a strand of hair from my eyelashes.

He says, 'I've got a bigger unit in the Stables yard, from next Wednesday. Setting up every day is a major hassle. But I like the atmosphere and I've got a product that sells, and that's the bottom line, isn't it? The product.'

I frown, because hang on, that wasn't in my script. I look at him over my wine glass, feeling a pang of separation anxiety. I don't want it to end. I was happy to settle for just being friends and seeing him every day. I suppress my disappointment and conceal my despair. 'I understand. It's been lovely having you as my neighbour.'

'Same.' He turns to me and in the dark, his eyes are as black as the lake. 'This is the thing. I was thinking, maybe you and Moss could take half the unit and we could share the rent.'

I hold my wind-tangled hair away from my face and look at him. 'Seriously?'

He returns my look with a calm expression of his own. 'Take your time. Think about it.'

I don't have to. YES! YES! YES! Even though I'm not used to making spur-of-the-moment decisions, and I've been taught to write down the pros and cons and think carefully before taking any action. Even though I've never been impulsive.

So, I ask myself, what's different this time?

Him, that's what. I can't deny it. He's the incentive.

The future that David has got mapped out looks as real as a mirage and I'm scared to test it, but I'm excited all the same, because this isn't the end, this is the future, and I'm still in it.

My gaze drifts to his hand holding his beer, the light from the house silvering the glass, and I imagine how that hand would feel if he reached out and brushed my hair away from my face – my breath comes in a jerk.

See? This is exactly the reason that sharing a unit is a bad, bad idea. But hey! I'm the master of self-control! I mean – despite provocation, both my parents are still alive, so that tells you something.

'You've gone quiet,' he says.

'I'd *love* to share a unit,' I reply.

David laughs; which is lucky because it came out more intense than I'd intended. He punches me gently on the shoulder. 'Good old Fern,' he says warmly, then he turns around and goes back inside the house.

*Good old Fern.*

Hell, I'm an idiot.

I wake up late the next morning to the riotous sound of the children racing each other along the decking outside my window. I keep my eyes shut and try to block out the noise. My thumbnails hurt like crazy. The nail bed is blue and bruised. I stare at them for a moment, baffled. Then I remember Gigi and I putting up a futile hunt for the corkscrew and me impressively doing my student party trick of pushing the cork into the bottle, to applause.

David's words crowd in on me bleakly. *Good old Fern.* What's that supposed to mean? Oh, I know what it means all right. I'm the girl next door, that's what.

I open the drapes and the children are pattering back along the decking, shouting and swathed in towels: two blond boys, a taller, older boy in glasses and a little girl with dark wild hair in a neon pink swimsuit following behind. The little girl stops suddenly and a look of painful disbelief distorts her face. She falls on her bottom, crying loudly, and picks up her foot to look at it.

I wait for someone to respond but the house is quiet, so I grab my robe and open the door to the decking, go outside to help her up.

She stops crying immediately she sees me and looks at me with great suspicion.

'Who are you?'

'I'm Fern. What's your name?'

'Lola.'

'Are you okay?' I ask.

She shakes her head. 'Something pinched me.'

'Shall I have a look?'

She shows me her foot and I can see a dark splinter under the pink skin of her soft, water-wrinkled sole.

It looks like a job for the experts. 'Shall I get your mum?'

She frowns. 'She's not Mum, she's Mummy,' she says firmly, getting suspicious again.

I can see the end of the splinter jutting out of the skin. 'I can probably get it out myself.'

'Is it a pinch?'

I give her my diagnosis. 'It's only a very small pinch.'

She turns and lies on her tummy then bends her legs back. I hold her foot and grip the splinter with my nails and it comes out easily, in one piece. 'All done.'

'Let me see it,' she commands.

'Hold out your hand.' I put the sliver of wood in the palm of her hand.

She looks at it closely for a moment and then looks up at me, nodding. She runs back into the house, cupping it carefully, to show.

I swallow a couple of paracetamol, shower and get dressed in shorts and a halterneck top, with a flowery broderie anglaise smocked dress over the top. I grab Gigi's birthday gift, negotiate the children's game of tag in the hall and go to the kitchen.

A bunch of shiny helium balloons is tied to a chair and birthday cards are propped up on the table.

Jenna's dressed and drying some mugs. Gigi's wearing David's flowery shirt from the day before and spooning instant coffee into two mugs. Her hair is tied in a spiral with a wired velvet band.

'Morning,' she says brightly.

'Morning. Happy birthday! Tah-dah!'

'Ooh! For me?' She puts the spoon down, tears the pink tissue off and holds up the velvet cloak with the shocking-pink lining. 'Gorgeous.' She puts it on, poses for a moment and rubs her cheek against the raised collar. 'Fern, I love it!'

Jenna switches on the kettle. 'Sorry about the kids this morning. I told them to amuse themselves, but I was hoping they'd do it less loudly. What time did you guys go to bed?'

'Four-ish,' Gigi said. 'Dave and I were in the hot tub.'

*Dave and I were in the hot tub.* I'm so jealous, the words stab me in the heart.

I begin to think irrational thoughts. *She doesn't appreciate him. She doesn't understand him.* There are two half-eaten pieces of toast and jam on the worktop. I absently start to eat one and Lola comes running over.

She puts her hands on her hips, full of indignation. 'That's my toast!'

'Sorry, I thought you'd finished.'

Like a baby bird, she opens her mouth to be fed and I push a piece of toast inside. She snaps her mouth shut and runs back into the hall.

Jenna yells, 'Stop running!' She looks at the time – it's just gone eleven. 'Don't let her eat any more, we're having lunch at twelve.'

At the mention of lunch, Gigi gives a shiver and hugs the cloak around herself with delightful anticipation, her eyes gleeful.

I smile back. She's so happy, it's hard to hate her.

'I'm going to get changed,' she says. 'Could you take this coffee for Dave? He's outside. Do you want milk in yours?'

I take the coffees out. David's wearing a lemon shirt with the sleeves rolled up. I sit next to him in the rattan chair. The cushion's damp. A breeze rustles the reeds. He's looking at his phone and balancing a plate of toast on his bare, tanned knee.

'Morning, Fern,' he says cheerfully.

'Morning.' He's so lovely and being with him feel so right.

If I were Gigi I'd love him for his sheer loveliness and I wouldn't care if he was boring at all.

We're sitting in shadow, with the sun behind the house. Across the water, the other houses curve, solemn and empty, no signs of life.

Putting the phone in his shirt pocket, David says, 'Watch this.' He energetically flings a piece of bread skywards over the lake and a flock of dazzling white gulls appears, diving and screeching against the deep blue sky. They're tearing it apart in midair and the lucky winner wheels away with the largest share while the others crash-land in the water and scramble to take their share of the crumbs. It's very entertaining. David waits until they all scatter and the sky's empty then he flings another piece in the air and they instantly reappear and do their aerobatics all over again.

Makes me laugh.

David looks at me and grins, and I can see the creases around his eyes. 'Fun, huh?'

'Really fun,' I agree.

Getting ready for lunch is a major operation.

I can see Jenna bending over Lola. She straightens up. 'Don't move – you need suntan lotion on. Where's your dress? What did you do with your dress?' She goes outside and comes back with a little white linen dress. 'Arms up!' She pulls it over her head.

'I've got the suntan lotion,' Alexa says. 'You want me to do it?'

Lola jumps up and down on the spot. 'Yes, please!'

I feel exactly what I am – very much the outsider – when Jenna hands me my bag.

'Come on, Fern, let's get a head start on them,' she says, straightening her shorts around her slim thighs. 'Alexa, you're in charge of the kids, we're going to bagsy the table.' She puts a baseball cap over her cropped fair hair and we leave the house and walk together down the drive, waving to the gateman.

'Bloody madhouse,' she says cheerfully.

I'm still preoccupied by the little girl. 'Your daughter's cute.'

'She is, isn't she? But boys are easier,' she says. 'More straightforward, don't you think? I think males tend to be more straightforward, generally. That's why I could never seriously date a woman; I couldn't take the twenty-four-hour angst. Of course, men are less emotionally evolved than women, so there's that to consider.'

I laugh. 'Is that a good thing or a bad thing?'

'A little bit of A, a little bit of B. Ben, my husband, hates these get-togethers, which is why he didn't come last night. Said he had to work. He's shy. He'd happily live his life with just him, the boys and a cricket bat. Ben doesn't realise that my genes are in the mix. Given the technology, he'd have had them cloned from himself.'

'Is he coming today?'

'He's meeting us at the pub. I told him we'd be there before twelve. He's going to think we've forgotten all about him.'

We cross the road and go down onto the footpath. Jenna checks her Fitbit to check her step count. 'We've got to be back by three because the photographer's coming. Have you known Gigi long?'

'We were at school together, briefly.' I dodge a piece of overgrown bramble. 'How about you guys?'

'Alexa and I go to Gigi's Pilates class.'

We turn around, hearing voices behind us. David's striding towards us with Lola on his shoulders, a heavy green sports bag bumping against his hip.

'Wait for us!' they yell.

Jenna nudges me. 'Run,' she says, and we leg it as far as a

gate then crouch down behind a hedgerow, giggling and waiting for them to get close. Then we spring out and David roars and Lola screams. They chase us all the way to the pub car park, where a man's sitting at a large table in the beer garden with a reserved sign on it. Jenna collapses, giggling, next to him and kisses him so hard on the mouth that her baseball cap falls off.

Ben is dark-haired, wearing a Tommy Hilfiger navy-and-white striped shirt, a black waistcoat and jeans. He's got black-rimmed glasses and three days' growth of stubble and he gets up when he sees us, but he has eyes only for Jenna.

'Did you see the chocolate I bought you?'

'You bought me chocolate?' she asks with delight. 'Galaxy?'

'No, Minstrels. I hid them in the case.'

'Did you?' She kisses him. 'Oh, Minstrels! I love Minstrels!'

Honestly, I've never felt more horribly single in my whole life. David hoists Lola from his shoulders.

'What you want to drink?' he asks her.

'Apple juice, please.'

'Good girl. Fern?'

'White wine, please, any sort,' I say obligingly, looking at my reflection in his shades.

'Get a Budweiser for Ben and I'll have a white wine, too,' Jenna says.

'Where are the boys?' Ben asks.

'They're coming with Alexa. They'll be here in a minute.'

Ben's eyes sweep over my face momentarily and he glances quickly at Jenna. I remember that he's shy, so I introduce myself and explain that Gigi and I knew each other at school, that David and I have adjacent stalls in the market, and that I came because the party sounded exciting.

'You're going to be disappointed, we're not *that* exciting,' Jenna said. 'We actually thought you'd come to dress Gigi for the photoshoot. It's the kind of thing she'd do, bring a dresser along.'

'I'd have done it, too,' I laugh. 'I wish I'd thought of it.'

Ben says to David, 'What have you bought her for her birthday, David?'

Jenna clamps her hands playfully over her husband's mouth. 'Don't ask that – it's a secret,' she says.

David picks up the sports bag and puts it on the table. 'I've made her a wooden chopping board with her name and date of birth carved on it,' he says.

Ben laughs. 'David, mate!'

'What's so funny?' he asks amiably.

'You've made her a *chopping* board?'

Jenna nudges him. 'Shut up, Ben.'

'Sorry, buddy, but what's Gigi going to do with a chopping board?'

'Chop things up. Trust me, when she sees it her eyes'll light up.'

Ben and Jenna are both looking at him expectantly as if they're waiting for a punchline, a wink, a sign that it's a joke.

David puts the sports bag back under his seat. 'Okay, drinks,' he says, rubbing his hands together, completely unfazed.

Ben goes with him and Jenna and I sit at the table.

Jenna giggles. 'He's such a kidder,' she says fondly. 'He thinks he's kept the ring a secret.'

'Yeah,' I agree.

Lola kneels on the seat next to Jenna and plays with the reserved sign.

'What does this say?'

'It says reserved,' Jenna replies.

'What does reserved mean?'

'It means no one's allowed to sit here apart from us,' Jenna explains.

'And me?'

'Yes, all of us, Mummy and Daddy and David and Gigi and Fern and Alexa and Max and Albie and Rowley.'

'But no one else?'

'No, just us. Very territorial, aren't we?' Jenna says, flashing me a look.

I smile, because actually they haven't been *that* territorial; they've included me and I'm really enjoying myself, not just because of the fact I'm going to eat soon, but also because they're good company, fun company. I'm in love with them all. I get like this over people as well as clothes – when I'm having fun I want to keep it going; I want it to last forever.

David and Ben come out with two trays of drinks and some laminated menus, and the three boys came racing into the garden, followed by Alexa and Max.

'Gigi's on her way,' Max says, putting his phone in his pocket then untying his pink jumper from his neck and pulling it on. 'She's been waiting for the photographer.'

The sunny day has turned breezy and Alexa's laughing and trying to hold her billowing dress down as she comes to sit next to me. 'Stupid frock. Fern, didn't people used to put weights in frocks or something once?'

I put my fingers to my throat. 'Um, well, Chanel puts chains in the hems of jackets to make them hang better. And I think the Queen has weights in her skirts to save embarrassment, but . . . I don't know. I could be wrong about that.'

'Isn't it wonderful to have a style expert who knows these details,' David says wryly and I feel myself blushing.

The boys come running up, chasing a blue football, and behind them is Gigi and a bald man with two Nikons around his neck.

'Here she comes!'

Gigi's wearing the Ossie Clark 'traffic light' dress with the plunging neckline and she puts on an exaggerated catwalk stride as she walks towards us. She stands right in front of David with one hand on her hip, the breeze wrapping it tight around her legs.

'Like it?'

'You look amazing.' He puts his hands on her hips and smiles up at her, a true and loving smile. 'Come and sit here.' He makes a space for her and hands her a glass of prosecco. 'Happy birthday.'

'Cheers.'

She takes the Alice band out of her pink hair and runs her fingers through it. The sun makes it sparkle like angora.

The photographer takes his lens cap off and captures the moment.

Jenna passes her the menu. 'Who knows what they want? No, don't tell me until I find a pen. Anyone got a pen?'

Ben has a pen in his jacket.

'I need something to write on.'

I've got my sunglasses on, listening to the conversation, feeling the warmth on my face. Although my dress is beautiful and airy, the halterneck top is feeling a bit sticky. I feel the tickle of an insect on my neck as I flick it away and look down and notice the flower print is dotted with greenfly. Huh?

I've left my insect repellent at the house. I'm practical that way.

'You're covered in greenfly,' David says.

I look at him over my sunglasses. 'I know.' I should move away from the table to brush them off. It's not cool to sit at a table sprinkled with insects. Again, I feel the opportunity to say something witty and sparkling come and go.

'They think you're a wild flower meadow,' Gigi says suddenly.

'Romantic!' David replies.

It's hugely endearing, the way they laugh at everything, and it's heightened by the excitement, the anticipation of David's grand gesture to come.

I sip my wine and when I next look down, the greenflies have all disappeared. Maybe they've come to some mutual understanding that despite appearances, my dress isn't organic.

Ben begins to write down our order. How many for fish and chips? How many for tuna ciabatta? Thai prawns? Green salads? Sides of fries?

The food isn't the main event; we eat quickly as if it's something that needs to be got out of the way so that we can share in that big secret that's been so badly kept and so enjoyed.

Plates cleared, a waiter comes out with a birthday cake dotted with flowers. Following him is the barman with champagne and glasses.

The candles keep blowing out and we form a huddle around it to keep them alight and sing 'Happy Birthday'. When we start clapping, the breeze blows the candles out again. Gigi says that Dave's always telling her to save her breath and now she has. She divides the cake and we toast her. The photographer's circling the table, getting candid shots, waiting for the moment, THE moment. David reaches under the table and we hear the sound of ripping Velcro and the bag unzipping.

Gigi looks at David with a lovely smile.

Gigi's present is gift-wrapped neatly and topped with a pink bow.

He makes room on the table and puts it down in front of her. 'Happy birthday, Gigi,' he says softly.

Gigi frowns and tears a hole in the wrapping, like a child. In the sunlight, the oiled wood gleams through the ripped paper. She bites her lip and sits back in her chair.

'Carry on,' David says. 'There's more to see.'

He's looking at her eagerly – waiting, I suppose, for her eyes to light up.

The camera shutter is the only sound I can hear. We've all fallen silent. He's seriously miscalled it and he's the only one who hasn't realised it yet.

She doesn't bother to unwrap the paper completely. She rests her chin on her fist and looks up at him. 'What is it?' Her voice is dull, disinterested.

David's still smiling. 'Open it properly! It's a chopping board,' he says. 'It's got your name on it.'

She sits back in her chair again. 'Yeah, thanks, Dave. When I take it to meet all the other chopping boards, I'll know which one is mine.' She scratches her shoulder and looks across the table at us, frowning as if she's forgotten we're there.

'It's maple,' he says. It seems to dawn on him that the gift has gone flat and it's painful to watch.

If the engagement ring exists, I think, now is the time to bring it out. For his sake, I shut my eyes, praying for one.

'Beautiful patina,' Ben says encouragingly after a moment.

David glances at him, his face impassive and dignified.

How could she do this? I'm embarrassed for him.

But Gigi looks humiliated, too. She pushes the gift away from her and knocks her champagne glass over. The prosecco spills onto the board and pools in the wrapping paper.

Max jumps to his feet and dabs it with his paper napkin. I'm still watching Gigi and hoping for just one word to make it right again, for Gigi to look at it properly and throw her arms around him in delight.

But she doesn't.

David puts the wet chopping board in its dripping wrapping paper and puts it back in the sports bag.

No one says anything. It's hard to know what to say.

Gigi gets up and goes inside the restaurant and Jenna follows her.

I'm playing with the stem of my glass.

'She was expecting an engagement ring, buddy,' Ben says, putting his arm around David's shoulders.

David looks genuinely surprised. 'Why?'

'Because you made such a big deal about keeping her present a secret, you berk,' Max says, his pale eyes hard. He's angry and I don't know if this is how they always are with each other, whether this is the normal dynamics of their friendship or not.

'I didn't think we were there yet, in our relationship.'

'*She* was there. She was never going to want a chopping board, was she?' Max said. 'For God's sake, why do you think she got the photographer?'

David shrugs. 'I don't know. Because she's Gigi. Fuck,' he says, resting his face in his hands.

I want to be the one to put my arm around his shoulders. I want to tell him she's an idiot and doesn't deserve him. I want to tell him that I'd appreciate with all my soul the time, the effort, the craftsmanship, the *love* that he's put into it.

I watch Ben slide the empty prosecco bottles towards himself and crowd them together like a visual statement of the amount that we've drunk.

I see David looking towards the restaurant.

The photographer's still hovering. 'Do you want me to stay?' he asks David.

'No. Yes. Hang on a bit will you, mate,' he says, getting to his feet. 'I'll go and talk to her.'

Jenna comes back a few minutes later, fanning herself with her cap. 'Gigi and David are heading back to the house,' she says to no one in particular. She picks up the knife and cuts a slice of cake. 'Anyone else want a slice? It's a shame to waste it.'

The tension has set up a carb craving in me, too. 'How is she?' I ask, holding out a plate.

'Embarrassed and humiliated,' Jenna says, cutting me a large wedge. 'She thought he knew her better than that. That's what they're like!' she said, her voice lifting with frustration. 'They don't *talk* to each other; they both assume they know what the other wants. Like when he'd had a really stressful day at work, Gigi told him to follow his dreams, you know, the kind of thing you say to make a person feel better. And three months later, he's handed in his notice and they're living off peanuts.'

'But David said . . .' I start to protest and then change my mind. I could have misunderstood him when he said Gigi was very supportive. I don't want to take sides.

The only person who seems to notice that I haven't finished the sentence is Max; he gives me a knowing smirk that makes me feel uneasy.

When we get back, David and Gigi have made up. That's how it looks, anyway.

They're down on the jetty with the photographer and Gigi's posing, only it's not a pose, it's completely natural – whether she's hugging one arm, or sitting on the jetty with her feet dangling in the water, or folded up thoughtfully with her chin resting on her knees; all of it is unconsciously elegant and somehow poetic in a way that touches me. Watching her, I try to analyse it and I imagine adopting the same position, but it's a quality peculiar to her.

David's wearing a fresh white shirt and pale trousers that show up his tan and he puts his arm around Gigi's waist. Against the shimmering water they would have looked like the perfect couple, like every Instagram I've ever envied, if only Gigi hadn't abruptly twisted away from him.

He's not quite forgiven, obviously.

A windsurfer tacks across the water, its sail blazing red. I can hear ducks quacking and a swan puts in an appearance in the distance.

Gigi calls me down to join them and suddenly I'm part of the picture. We take our shoes off and dangle our feet in the cold water, disturbing the fish that are hiding in the shade.

Gigi looks across the lake. 'Fern, do you fancy a swim?'

'You can't swim here,' David says. 'There's all sorts of junk in it, it's an old gravel pit.'

She points across the water. 'Look! *He's* swimming.'

'He's not swimming, he's that windsurfer and he's just fallen off.'

'Fuck off, Dave. You're so *sensible*, you know that?' she says vehemently.

'Hey, guys!' We look up as Jenna and Ben come outside and lean on the barrier, arms around each other, all loved-up, making happy noises of appreciation while their children run around behind them.

'We'll have to do something this afternoon or we'll go stir-crazy,' Gigi says. 'We could hire some canoes, couldn't we?'

'Sure,' David replies.

I think about telling them that I ought to go home. It's not exactly that I feel like a gatecrasher, but there are too many undercurrents.

*You can't tart up a relationship with nice clothes and hope that it'll look fine. It's what's underneath that counts.* I don't know if that was just something that Max said to mess up my mind, but it hit a nerve. I know I like David too much for comfort and I can't bear to see him get hurt. I'm losing control of my emotions.

A terrible thought hits me: *You don't just like him; you love him.*

I have an urgent need to get away and think about things clearly, in my own time.

I take my phone out of the pocket of my shorts and look at it intently, as if I've suddenly felt it vibrate. 'Excuse me,' I say, and I leave the jetty and go up the steps past Jenna and Ben. I go to my room, pack my things and make up my bed.

I scribble a thank-you message on the back of one of my postcards, put my stuff in the boot and go back out to find Gigi.

She's alone, lying on a lounger. She smiles and shades her eyes with her hand to look at me as I invent a fairly plausible story about Lucy phoning me about a visit from the loss adjusters. 'But it's been great,' I add.

I had the idea of sloping off surreptitiously, but Gigi gets up and announces to everyone that I'm leaving, and they commiserate that I've been called away at such short notice.

They all come out with me, all bar David, which is both a disappointment and a relief, and they each find a farewell stone to stand on in the gravel border. The children, too, stand on the rocks in the gravel in the garden among the wild grasses and ferns. Before jumping back onto hers, Gigi runs over and gives me a hug through the car window, and they keep waving as I drive away.

# KIM

Time's a great healer. Both Mercia and Betty have told me that, and to begin with I was eager to believe it. And over these many days I've held onto that thought and waited patiently for my pain to scab over, but it's not happening. It's not happening yet. It's the opposite. As the days stretch on, I miss Enid more, and the hole in my life that started off small just gets bigger and bigger.

I've always loved Enid; she was my wife. But I liked her, too. If she were here, she'd have something sensible to say to me and then I'd know how to cope. That was one of her strengths, I could rely on her to do things right. She'd never, for instance, have told me that time's a great healer, I'm certain of that.

I feel abandoned.

Enid didn't choose to go, I know that. She hung on longer than anyone has a right to who hasn't drunk or eaten in five days, and she did it for me – she stayed with me as long as she wilfully could.

And then she left, torn from me, that's how it felt; she gasped with the speed of it.

And now I'm lonely. Loneliness isn't something that fills you up. It empties you.

Her absence has stopped feeling like an adventure, the

adventure of a boy alone in his house. To begin with the kingdom is all his, he has biscuits to open, his mother's shoes to try on, Coty talcum powder to dust down his trousers. The time passes, and he looks through the window and sees the day is growing dark. He begins to wonder . . . when will she be back? And the boy goes to the door and looks out into the empty street in the empty night, standing so long that his bones creak and grind as he tries to conjure her up from the dark.

The boy's question is: who's going to look after me?

'Enid?' I say sharply.

Silence.

I don't know what I'm expecting. I'm not expecting her to reply, that's for sure, and if she did, I'd know I had finally lost my mind. But I'd like something, some sign from her to let me know she's okay and that she's thinking about me; that I haven't been left on my own.

'I wondered if you were here, that's all,' I conclude apologetically. She wouldn't like me hectoring her.

The phone rings – ring ring ring – making me jump, and I hurry over and stare at it as if I've never seen it before, this black rectangle with the blue glow and all the buttons, most of which we don't use. And the noise is like a crying, crying, crying baby, demanding attention, and I'm scared to answer, because when I answer, it won't be her. But if I don't answer it and it stops ringing, I can pretend it was; that she rang, rang, rang, rang, rang me up with advice.

I pick it up. 'Hello?'

'It's me!'

It's not Enid. 'Hello, Dinah.'

'Listen! I'm managing the stall for Fern and its crazy busy here. Kim? I can't hear you! Can you hear me?'

'I can hear you,' I shout back.

'You have to come and help me, because I'm on my own!'

It sounds like: *You hef to komm and hilp me!*

'I'm on my own, too,' I tell her.

She sounds exasperated. 'Of course! I know that! Can you come?' *Kenn you komm?*

'I'm on my way!' I put the phone back carefully in its cradle and the silence hums around me.

Tears of gratitude burn my eyes. 'Thank you, Enid,' I whisper.

Sure enough, when I get there Fern's little stall in the alley is surrounded by people and I have to battle my way through them to reach her. Dinah's arguing with a woman who's trying to buy her purple jacket. They're pulling the jacket by the sleeves.

The woman's shouting crossly, 'It was on the table!'

Dinah's shouting back, 'But it's not for sale!'

'Don't worry, I'm here,' I tell Dinah proudly, pushing through and crawling under the counter to reach her. I've never used those words before in my life, but while I'm down on my hands and knees I find a credit card belonging to a customer.

Dinah clasps her hands together when I emerge waving it.

'Thank God!' *Thenk Gott!* she says. 'I heff been looking for that!'

I retrieve her jacket from the cross woman and in a moment of inspiration, I hand the woman the client book and ask her to write down her details so that Fern can find something similar for her. 'If anyone can, Fern can,' I tell her confidently.

'When will she be back?'

'Wednesday,' Dinah says. 'Come back then and yell at her for a change. Kim!'

'Yes?'

'This skirt needs wrapping up for this lady.' She's now all

221

smiles and graciousness again. 'This *kind* lady. One moment, madame.'

I pick up the long pleated skirt and as I begin to fold it, I stop and take a closer look. Something about it reminds me of Enid. I unfold it again and lay it flat on top of some other clothes. The hairs prickle at the back of my neck, and I stare at it in stunned and miraculous disbelief. Could it be? The purples, the moss greens . . . it's Enid's. I know her clothes as well as my own. It's one of the garments that I gave to that chap, Cato.

Well, then. I look across at the lady who's buying it. She's practically a girl, thirty years or so younger than me, only in her fifties, and she's patient in the melee. I fold the skirt again and impulsively, before I put it in the bag, I raise it to my lips, shut my eyes tight and kiss it.

Though I meant it as a goodbye kiss, the woman smiles and inclines her head, receiving the kiss along with the skirt.

'You're smiling,' Dinah says a few moments later, hands on hips. She's put her jacket back on. Her black satin turban is slightly askew.

I nod. My heart is full. When I was holding the skirt, Enid's skirt, I knew that was Enid's sign to me. But that's between me and Enid.

I'm not going to tell Dinah about my desperate call, or that she was part of the answer.

I'm not sure how she'd take it. I'm sure in her opinion she rang me of her own volition, because she needed help on the stall. She might not like to see herself as a divine emissary, sent by Enid to stop me from being alone.

I start to chuckle at the thought. It doesn't matter, because I know what I know.

Dinah looks at me and starts to laugh, too. She has a high-pitched laugh, a proper tee-hee-hee, very infectious, and she doubles up over the counter. "That mob!' she says gleefully between giggles, 'I thought the stall was going to fall down, didn't you!'

I'm laughing with her and gradually we pull ourselves together. She dabs the tears from her eyes, turning her face up to mine. 'How do I look?'

'Um, your turban's a little jaunty,' I advise, and she takes it off and studies it.

'Here,' she says suddenly. 'This is for you. Remember, I promised it to you.' She places it on my head as gently as a crown.

# LOT 15

*A belted black PVC raincoat, small, knee-length,*
*unlabelled, circa 1980.*

I drive from the Cotswolds back to Berkhamsted. My mother's surprised to have the car back a day earlier than she expected. She takes me into the lounge to see my father. He's watching cricket on Sky Sports. He tears his attention away briefly from the screen to say hello.

She shrugs and gestures to me, a gesture that says – see what I have to put up with!

She goes into the kitchen, her kimono fluttering behind her. The sunlight's coming through the window, illuminating a vase of red tulips.

As she puts the coffee on, I think about the events of lunchtime and wonder what would have happened if one of their friends had actually warned David that Gigi was expecting him to go down on one knee.

Would he have stuck to his opinion that they 'weren't there yet', or would he have done it to please her, to 'make her eyes light up'?

'Wasn't it fun?' my mother asks doubtfully, seeing me frown and probably wondering why I've cut my weekend short.

'Tremendous fun,' I reply, and I describe in detail the house and the restaurant we went to for lunch, and the cake, and the photographer.

'Was he from a magazine?' she asks eagerly.

Despite the fact he wasn't, my mother's happy that I'm mixing with the right sort of people. 'Your father's meeting new people, too,' she adds.

'Yes, well, that's what happens when you take up a new hobby. You should find something new as well; he's right about that.'

'Why?' she asks stubbornly, leaning elegantly against the fridge. 'You and your father are my whole life.'

I'm so shocked by this admission that without thinking, I say, 'No wonder I'm such a disappointment.' I regret it instantly, because her face hardens with disapproval and all the warmth is suddenly sucked out of the kitchen. 'Sorry,' I say desperately. 'I just mean – your life is your life and you've got so much to give.'

'I know what you mean!' she says, her voice vibrating with emotion. 'You make me laugh! You think you don't need me, well, see how you get on without me – and don't bother to come running to me when you want to borrow my car or my money.' She walks out into the hall, slamming the door behind her, and I wince at the thud, which has effectively ended the argument. For a moment I stand there frozen, trying to rewind the conversation.

My father comes to see what's happened and sums it up in a second when he sees my face. 'Said the wrong thing, did you?' he asks gently.

I'm pressing my lips together; I can't even speak.

'Come on,' he says, taking my arm. 'I'll give you a lift to the station.'

I get off the train at Euston and head with my bag to the market. It's almost seven and I'm amazed to find Dinah's still there, and Kim's with her. They're packing up and giggling like two conspirators. Kim's wearing Dinah's black turban.

226

They're happy to see me and I'm happy to see them.

'Hooray! She's come back early! You know why? She doesn't trust us,' Dinah says and that sets them off again.

She's excited to tell me about the sales they've made and Kim shows me the client book.

'We've got a few extra names for you,' he says, flicking through the pages.

I'm thrilled and absolutely convinced that sharing a bigger unit with David is going to make a difference. The business is expanding!

'So tell us, Fern! How was the party?'

'Amazing!'

'Gigi liked your gift?'

'Yes, she loved it!' I'm on the point of telling them about the new unit, when I think it would be better to mention it to Moss first.

Ever sensitive to people's thoughts, Dinah notices my hesitation and says, 'You were going to say something?'

'Yes! I'm lucky to have you as my friends. Tell you what, let's go for a drink to Cotton's Rhum Shack. It's on me. You deserve it.'

On Monday morning I'm meeting Moss at the Paradise Café to tell him about David's idea of sharing a bigger unit. The Paradise Café is a Greek restaurant with pine wood panelling painted in dark brown gloss and streaked to look like mahogany. The effect isn't very convincing, but I suppose if you live with it long enough, you get to accept it. And Moss doesn't come here for the decor; he comes here because it's convenient, Andreas, the dark-haired, wiry owner is friendly and the coffee is good.

Moss sits down heavily, scraping the chair legs on the floor. The lapel of his black jacket is threaded with a bright row of pins. 'You've seen the shop?' he asks me gloomily. 'Ali's moved some bikes in. He's doing MOTs at the back. I'm not happy about it.' He rubs his freckled hands together to soothe himself. 'He says he'll pay me for the extra days.' Moss doesn't look entirely happy with the coffee, either, scooping it up with his teaspoon disdainfully and letting it drip back into the cup. 'Andreas, what *is* this?'

'It's the coffee you always have,' Andreas replies. 'There's nothing wrong with it. Taste it.'

'I just did.' Moss raises his wild, dark eyebrows and lowers them again.

'Time to retire, maybe,' Andreas says. 'Do it while you're still young.'

'Too late, my friend. Anyway, you know how many people drop dead after they retire?' Moss asks. 'That's why I'm never giving up.'

'You'll drop dead sometime, one way or the other,' Andreas points out.

Moss looks at me gloomily. He rubs the loose skin of his face, his eyes glossy black. 'So, now you've got me here, say what you've got to say.'

I fold my arms on the table and sugar grains stick to my elbows. 'Gigi's boyfriend has got a place in Stables Market and we can share with him if we go halves on the rent. He reckons that there's plenty of room for you to put a worktable there and if people want alterations, you'll be there on the spot to measure them up. What do you think?'

His expression doesn't alter. To be fair, he's never been a bundle of laughs, has Moss.

He rubs his hand over his eyes wearily. 'Gigi's boyfriend, the boring man?' he asks with a frown. 'I don't want him bothering me all day with his talk.'

'Honestly, Moss, David's not boring, he's practical.' I realise

I seem to have spent the last few days defending him for one reason or another. 'I think it'll work out really well for both of us. People can browse, there's more room for stock and people are a lot more likely to be interested in alterations if they only have to walk to the back of the shop instead of finding their way to Morland Street.'

Moss lowers his heavy eyelids, deep in thought. He opens them a fraction. 'What's the catch?'

'There's no catch.'

'So why haven't you said yes?'

'Actually, I have – I said yes straight away. It's up to you whether you come in on it or not.'

This is meant to prove that I think it's a great idea, but Moss laughs out loud. 'Is he good-looking, this man?'

'Maybe Greek, if he's good-looking,' Andreas observes soberly over the counter.

We're interrupted by a cheerful, grey-haired elderly priest from the Orthodox Church wearing elaborate gold-embroidered-robes. He's holding a bouquet of smouldering branches.

'Blessings for prosperity?' he asks Andreas, wafting burning leaves towards him.

'Go ahead,' Andreas tells him and opens the till.

The priest chants and cleanses the four corners of the coffee shop with smoke.

'Hey, Father, bring your prosperity this way,' Moss says and the priest obligingly waves the branches over us. Enveloped by smoke, we listen to him going through his rituals and after the final flourish, Andreas hands him a tip. Moss and I follow suit, then we thank him and watch him leave while I try to get the ash out of my cleavage.

'I don't know if it's doing any good. It's got very quiet in here since the last time he came,' Andreas says thoughtfully. 'Still, he has to make a living.'

'If I say no, then what?' Moss asks me, taking up the conversation from where we left off.

'David and I'll go halves.'

'And if I come in, we split it three ways?'

'That's right.'

'Ah. Now I understand.' Moss holds out his large hand and shakes mine. 'It's a deal.'


Lucy comes down to mine this evening because she's blagged a VIP ticket to a film premiere at the British Film Institute IMAX cinema in Waterloo and wants something incredible to wear.

'I'm going with a guy who works for Universal Films. I'll give you a shout out,' she promises. 'We're talking red carpet, press, crowds . . .'

I'm hugely impressed. 'Will you actually be on TV?'

'Well, not officially,' she admits. 'I was thinking more of, you know, photobombing. One way or another, I'm getting my face out there.'

I drag my clothing rails from the utility room and tell her about the weekend. 'You were right about the chopping board. Gigi wasn't impressed.'

'Of course she wasn't! Whoever thought that would be a good idea for a gift?'

'David did,' I say.

'And you did, too,' she says accusingly. 'Honestly. You two, you're made for each other.'

This wonderful thought sends me into a daydream.

'So, how did everything end with David and Gigi?' she asks, pulling out a teal beaded lace dress with a flesh underskirt as iridescent as a peacock's feathers.

'See for yourself.' I get out my phone and show her the photographs that I took.

'Wow.' Lucy scrolls through them. She taps a picture and looks at it closely. 'Fern, he's gorgeous!'

I screw up my nose. 'I know.'

'He shows just the right amount of teeth when he smiles. And he's so *neat* I want to ruffle him all up,' she growls. 'She doesn't look too happy though, does she?'

She gives me the phone back and while she continues to look at the dresses, I take a closer look at Gigi, who actually, now that Lucy has pointed it out, doesn't look happy at all. 'She's pouting. Everyone pouts in photographs.'

'Yes, they pout, but they don't *pout*. She looks more moody than sultry.'

I don't argue with her. There might be hope for me yet.

# LOT 16

*Blush pink dress, 1920s, heavy, French guipure lace, with*
*dropped waist, and silk-lined underskirt.*

Moving day!

The sky is dark and heavy. Cato parks his van outside and he helps me to transfer my rails and clothes from my flat to Stables Market in the rain. When we get to Camden Lock, he stays in the van so he won't get a ticket and I'm dragging my big, rickety case along the pavement for the last time, hopefully.

Moss meets me at the entrance to Stables Market and he's holding a large black umbrella over his black overcoat. His black trilby makes him look like a gangster from a Twenties film.

I'm wearing my belted black PVC raincoat that squeaks as I walk. Moss gallantly takes my arm and holds the umbrella over me. The rain has slicked the cobbles to a high gloss.

David's unit is in the central yard. He's fixing units together with an electric screwdriver, surrounded by boxes. He's wearing white overalls – the only man I've ever seen looking good in them – and he's focused and self-possessed. I feel a sudden nervous thrill at seeing him. In the same way that I can't act naturally around my parents, I can't act natural with a good-looking man and now I'm sharing a pitch with him. It would help if he was missing some teeth or covered in boils and deeply flawed or something. Any of those and I'd be fine.

'Hi!'

He looks up. 'Hello, Fern!' he says and flashes me a smile.

I give an involuntary whimper of longing.

Looking concerned, he asks, 'Is your case heavy?'

'Er, no, not really. The wheel's coming off. This is Moss.'

Moss flaps the raindrops off his black umbrella and props it up against the wall. He shakes David's hand sombrely. 'I've heard a lot about you from Gigi,' he says.

'All good, I hope.'

'Not so much.' Moss shrugs. 'I'll have a look around, if I may?'

'Go for it,' David says, putting his weight on the storage unit to test it.

I follow him, my mac squeaking and rustling, to the back of the shop. The place is pretty big and there's plenty of room.

'If I put some hanging rails in here,' Moss says, 'that'll give me space for my table.'

'Yeah. Nice, isn't it?' It reminds me of my utility room at home. The exposed brick arch is industrial in a trendy way and it's got bags of potential.

Moss is already walking away with his hands clasped behind his back. He's taken a desultory look at the space on offer and now he's standing in the entrance at the front of the shop looking out at the rain, rocking gently from his toes to his heels. He looks at David curiously. 'You seem like a nice guy. I don't know why Gigi says you're boring.'

I cringe.

David laughs. 'Gigi thinks life should be a permanent holiday,' he says.

'Listen to me, take my advice, never let a woman get bored,' Moss says darkly. 'You need to keep surprising them.'

'Is that so?'

'Surprise is the key to a happy marriage. How else would we have kept married for almost seventy years? See this? This is my application to the Queen's anniversary office for a card of congratulations from Her Majesty herself.' He takes a form out of his jacket pocket and shows it to David.

'I didn't know your name was Moses,' David says.

'You come to a country, you have to fit in,' Moss says sternly. 'We're British now.'

Seventy years! Mind-boggling!

I hurry back out in the rain to get the rails from Cato, who's looking in the rearview mirror and tugging on his wispy blond beard to encourage new growth while keeping a lookout for traffic wardens.

My last trip is for Dolly. I hoist her over my shoulder and Cato pulls away in the nick of time, saluting the traffic warden as he goes. In the yard I pass Moss, who tells me he's on his way to get Hamed's son to help him empty the shop.

Back in the unit I start fixing the rails together with my set of Allen keys. It's a noisy business, what with the rails and David's drilling.

David's arranging the light boxes on the new shelves. He seems deep in thought, but that could just be because he's busy.

By the time I've finished putting them together and unpacked the clothes, a couple of hours have gone by.

It's finally stopped raining and I can see the lunchtime crowd gathering in Stables Yard: people eating fish and chips with vinegar, or trays of fragrant noodles. The street food vendors are veiled in steam and I feel some sudden trepidation. There were no food stalls near the alleyway.

One thing I've noticed is that the other vintage stalls are

strewn with signs telling people not to touch the garments. *Don't make me laugh*, I thought when I read them. The first thing a woman wants to do when she sees something she likes is to touch it; only through your fingers can you appreciate the crackle of viscose and the comfort of wool.

But now those signs make perfect sense. What if passers-by wipe their hands on my dresses? All those people are coming through with their polystyrene trays and bags of doughnuts, licking their fingers and – oh look! Convenient!

Maybe I should hand out wet wipes. Would that be rude?

I reposition Dolly so that the blush pink dress is glittering in the weak sunlight and stand guard over her.

David glances at me with a faint half-smile and puts his tools back in a toolbox, wiping each one as he does. He clips the box shut and straightens. I can't help noticing that his white overalls are miraculously untouched by dirt or sweat. How does he manage that? He faces Dolly thoughtfully. 'Fern, isn't this the dress that could be a wedding dress?'

WAH-WAH-WAH! The warning klaxon sounds in my head. 'Ye-es,' I reply hesitantly.

'Don't tell me! It's not pink,' he says, clicking his fingers. 'It's flesh, right?'

'Blush,' I correct him, blushing. 'Why?' I ask nonchalantly. 'Do you want to buy it?'

'This is the thing,' he says. 'I'm looking for a way to make it up to Gigi for this weekend. As you know, it didn't exactly work out as she planned.'

I feel a flicker of trepidation – I think I can see the way this is going. Honestly, what's he like? 'David, you can't buy this for her and tell her it's her wedding dress.'

'Hear me out! It's better than that. First, she loves vintage and secondly, I'm going to book Camden Town Hall and arrange to get married to her, as a surprise.'

Arghh! I blame Moss for this; him and his marital advice. 'No-no-no-no-no! Don't do that! Gigi won't like that at all, trust me.'

He looks at me doubtfully. 'How do you know? No offence, but you told me she'd love the chopping board and we both know how that went.'

'Yes, okay, I was looking at it from my own perspective, because the chopping board is a thing of startling beauty.'

'You think?' he asks, his blue eyes penetrating mine.

'Of course! But the whole wedding business – Gigi's going to want to plan that herself. She'll probably want it in a cathedral, with choirs and bishops and bridesmaids all matching and looking gorgeous. It's not something she'll want you to surprise her with in Camden Town Hall. She'll want to plan it herself. Planning a wedding is the fun part! I'm telling you this as a friend.' I say it hand on heart, without an iota of self-interest.

He frowns and chews his lower lip while he ponders my good advice and I watch him hungrily, wishing I were the one chewing it.

'A *cathedral*?' he says at last. '*Really*? It all sounds a bit conventional, for Gigi.'

'What do you think an engagement is?' I point out in my role as 'good old Fern'. 'She wanted a ring so give her a ring, not a wedding.'

'A ring,' he says. 'What kind?'

'One with a diamond,' I say wearily. 'And take her with you to choose it.'

His face breaks into a smile and Lucy's right, when he smiles he shows just the perfect amount of teeth.

'Thanks, Fern.'

'Ah,' I say, flapping my hand as if it's cost me no heartache at all, 'you're totally welcome. What are friends for?'

# KIM

Dinah's turban is a delight to wear because catching sight of myself in the mirror, the blackness of it reminds me of the thick, dark hair I had when I was young, before age faded me and it started to turn to grey in my forties, silver in my fifties and white in my eighties. Wearing it, I see myself with new eyes, as someone rather dashing.

Sitting together in Cotton's Rhum Shack with Dinah and Fern, the turban didn't so much as raise an eyebrow – and there were plenty of eyebrows that could have been raised because the place was packed. That acceptance is what's given me the confidence to wear it to Kentish Town.

I'm making my way to Poundstretcher for essentials, when I realise it's stopped raining and I fold my umbrella up, feeling joyously young and debonair.

A couple of bulky old ladies are coming out of Better Specs, wearing matching pale blue anoraks and carrying Iceland bags, engrossed in an energetic conversation.

'Would you look at him!' one of them says, her expression as avid as if she's watching a minor car crash. 'Doesn't he look an eejit!'

'Oh, he does all right.'

I feel a moment's sympathy for the subject of their scorn.

'You have to ask yourself, if you have to wear a hat, what's wrong with a flat cap?'

It dawns on me then that I, myself, am the subject of their conversation.

They're big women, standing in my path, blocking my way, and I clutch my umbrella with a terrible feeling of being caught out, exposed.

'You'll not mind us telling you the truth that that's a terrible hat for you,' one of them says to me, and the horrible thing is, she's trying to be helpful.

'That's a woman's hat,' her friend says disapprovingly, jutting her chin at my turban.

They separate and walked past either side of me. I'm breathless with the nerve of them. 'I *do* mind,' I call after them.

'Please yourself,' one of them calls back.

I whip the turban off my head, trying to smooth my hair down while holding the umbrella between my knees, and I briefly catch the eye of a slim, well-dressed woman who's holding the hand of a little girl in school uniform. The woman discreetly inserts a slender, manicured hand inside her bag and as she passes, she drops a coin into the turban.

I look in my hat. It's a pound coin.

It's the most demeaning moment of my life and I hurry home. What I haven't taken into account is that Kentish Town is very different from Camden. Kentish Town is determinedly conventional.

I'm upset to find that contrary to what my friends have told me, political correctness is not as widespread as I've been led to believe. Not in Kentish Town, at least.

Back home, the fridge judders, my shoes thud, my stairs groan as I flee to my room, and for consolation I retrieve the blue feather cocktail dress and hang it up on my wardrobe door.

It's suffered from being hidden in the golf bag. Some of the blue feathers have broken and it's creased, but it brings me a familiar, soothing pleasure along with the ache of shame.

Enid found one of the feathers in our bedroom one evening on one of her good days when she came home from art class. She showed it to me, twirling it between her finger and thumb, and asked me where it had come from.

I'm not a slow-witted man, but I stared at the feather as if I'd been struck dumb, one unnaturally beautiful sky-blue feather; hard to imagine it had once been attached to a bird.

I looked at Enid, expecting her to confront me, but she was waiting for my opinion as to the source.

I could think of no explanation for it apart from the truth, and I couldn't share that with her. But I wish I had. She was my moral compass. Enid and I were as close as a long-married couple can be, and I think of Mercia and Betty, how accepting they are of change, how modern the world is now. I wonder if Enid was like that too, if she had a side to her that I'd never seen, or if she'd expect me to stay strong and keep to the old values.

She was holding the feather by the quill. Her eyes were curious, probing as they met mine. 'It's such a pretty blue, isn't it?' she said.

I nodded and told her I was going to put the kettle on, then I concentrated on going down the stairs slowly, deliberately, in the manner of a man with a clear conscience. In the kitchen I filled the kettle, switched it on, my mind racing. Enid wasn't the kind of woman to let things go without an explanation. I could tell her I was having an affair with someone. Who?

A burlesque dancer?

I could tell her that a window was open and the feather flew in.

But when I gave her the cup of tea, Enid didn't mention it again; I didn't mention it either and she let the mystery go.

And I think the reason she let it go was that she knew it was mine all along.

I've got her ashes here in a mahogany box. Betty says I should scatter them somewhere meaningful, but Enid isn't the kind of person who'd like to be scattered. She was a very together sort of person and she disapproved of littering.

I don't know what to do with the dress. I pace the bedroom, in need of advice, and I sit on the bed and call Dinah.

'Hello, who is this?' she asks piercingly on answering the phone.

Enid always answered the phone by reciting our phone number. I never understood why, because obviously the person calling already knew it.

'It's Kim. I've had a dreadful experience.'

'Dahlink!' she says sympathetically. 'What do you want me to do?'

'I want you to be sensible,' I tell her hopelessly. 'I want you to be my moral compass.'

'I'll come at once,' she says. 'Tell me your address.'

When Dinah arrives, I take her into the parlour. She sits on the sofa in a patch of sunlight, adjusting her dress over her knees, and I tell her about the two women in Kentish Town who made rude comments about my turban.

'So what?' she asks mildly.

'How can you ask that? It was *embarrassing*.'

She takes a Cadbury's chocolate finger from the blue willow-pattern plate. 'These two women, are they people whose opinions you respect?'

'No, but it was the very idea that they had a right to comment about me, to my face.' I can feel my indignation rising.

She purses her lips and changes position on the sofa, propping her elbow on the arm of the chair. After some thought, she meets my eyes and says, 'Kim, I know what it's like to be reviled.'

Reviled. For a moment the idea of not being alone in this consoles me. 'They called me an idiot and said I had a terrible hat. It was the Schiaparelli turban,' I explain, waiting for her to join me in my indignation. 'And then a woman thought I was begging and put a pound in it.'

The fine dark arches of her eyebrows twitch briefly. She gives a faint smile and says softly, 'Kim, you're a very lucky man.'

'Lucky?' This isn't what I want to hear at all. 'How can you say that? I'm weak! Wait here . . .' I dash upstairs to fetch the blue dress and I bring it back down and lay it on her knee. The sheen of the blue satin is dazzling in the sunshine. 'I'm going to give it all up, this side of me. It's the only thing to do, isn't it?'

'This is the dress that Fern sold you?' She gently straightens the broken feathers.

'Yes!' I try to stop my voice from trembling.

'This is the blue dress that delighted you so much that you wrote a letter of praise about her to the store?'

'Oh, Fern told you that?' I feel enormously pleased that Dinah knows this side of me. It's important to be grateful. It shows me in a good light.

'Let me tell you, that letter of praise got Fern fired from her job.'

I'm mortified. 'What? Why? She's never mentioned it!'

'She sold it to you privately from her own collection, didn't she? So you see, for that reason, you should value it more, not because of what it cost you, but because of what it cost her. Listen to me. You asked me to be your moral compass but you're a nice man and I'm sure your morals are fine. Sensible? Now that I can help you with. The world is full of other people, and in the same way that you like some of them and you don't like others, and you judge some and you don't judge others, you, yourself, are going to be liked and disliked and judged and unjudged. What for? If it's not your turban, it might be your age, or your religion, or your culture, or your accent. It's not fair, but that's the way it is.'

She says it with great seriousness, veined hands tightly clasped on the dress on her lap, as if this is something she's dwelt upon in depth and made her peace with.

The silence of the room rings in my ears and I have the strangest sensation I'm shrinking, as if some unconscious realisation of what she's saying is putting me into perspective, as a small man with small problems. *Reviled.* 'Are you a . . . are you Jewish?'

'Yes. I was Jewish, and German.' She puts the blue dress to one side. The corner of her mouth twitches but her eyes are kind. 'So you see, at least with a turban, you can take it off. Kim, I have to go now. Moss will be home soon.'

She stands up and I stand, too.

I see her out and I go back to sit in her seat, in the sunshine, facing the blue dress, which is lolling against the seat cushion like a seductive lover.

# LOT 17

*Opulent gold Versace blouse with GV Medusa-head gilt clasps inset with diamante, 1990.*

Moss is at the back of the shop on his sewing machine, which is giving off a comforting staccato hum. He's working through the dresses on his rail. Business has been steady since we moved a couple of weeks ago, partly because we're easier to find, but also because of the benefits of Moss being right on the spot to measure and pin.

I unfold my chair and come to sit with David in the doorway of the unit. He looks preoccupied. The coloured bunting is slapping gaily against the brick wall of the antique shop. I'm about to ask him whether he's thought any more about the engagement ring, when his phone chimes.

He looks at the caller's name and jumps to his feet. 'Watch my stall for a minute, will you?' he asks and he hurries out through the exit onto Gilbeys Yard.

I'm confused – what's the rush?

'Where is he?' asks a familiar voice from behind me.

She says it so sharply that I jump. 'Oh! Hi, Gigi! He's just popped out for a minute. He won't be long.'

She's wearing ripped jeans, turquoise Converse trainers and a bra top with a black lace cover-up. She's also got the shaggy little dog with her, so I get up and stand behind my chair, fully prepared to use it as a defence if I need to.

'Really? Just popped out?' She's in a horrible mood and she looks at me with contempt, as if I've done something awful to her, as if she'd never jumped off the farewell stone in the Cotswolds to hug me before I left. 'Bloody coward,' she mutters. 'Here, hold this, will you,' she says, handing me the lead.

'Hold it yourself,' I say. 'I hate dogs.' My heart is thumping with anxiety, and I hold my breath and try not to break out in a sweat, because as dog lovers point out, dogs can smell fear – in my opinion, it's an insurance policy, so that if their dog attacks then they'll tell you you've only got yourself to blame.

She laughs suddenly and her bad mood dissolves. 'Fern, you're so funny! How come you hate dogs?'

'It's easy, trust me,' I say darkly.

'Go on, give him a stroke. He's lovely!' Her voice goes all mushy. 'Who's a lovely boy then? Who's a lovely boy?'

The shaggy brown creature on the end of the lead sweeps the dust with his tail and looks up at her with an expression of pure and loving innocence.

Me, I'm steering well clear.

She smirks at me, making it obvious she's totally on the dog's side.

That's the trouble with dog lovers – they've got no empathy or understanding for those who don't share their feelings. 'Personally, Gigi, I think it's weird that people hate spiders. If you pick one up it's like having a tickle in your hand – what's not to like? I know they bite – all spiders bite – but the fangs are too small to break the skin . . .'

'I'm not scared of spiders,' she says.

'Okay. Maybe it's not a very good example. Take something

like a fear of buttons. Buttons don't bite. Obviously, I respect the fear of anyone who's scared of buttons, but I'd never brandish one in their face or chase after them with one, or force them to *stroke* one, Gigi. It's the same as pushing someone off a cliff if they're scared of heights and saying, "That wasn't so bad, was it?"'

'Fern, I honestly haven't got a clue what you're on about. Nobody hates buttons.'

'It's a thing!' I stop right there because the dog starts coming towards me, its nails clicking on the ground. I back away nervously, feeling the fear take hold. 'Can you tie him to the chair? *Please?*'

Gigi gives me a look of exasperation and loops the lead through the slats of David's chair. 'Happy now?' she asks, folding her arms.

'Ecstatic,' I reply with the same amount of sarcasm, watching a polystyrene cup roll in the breeze and come to rest on a drain cover.

Gigi kicks it away with the toe of her trainers.

As I go to pick it up, curiosity gets the better of me. I asked innocently, 'Anything exciting going on with you and David?'

'Other than I've dumped him, you mean?'

I'm stunned. I can't believe it. 'What? How come?'

'He's got it in his head that we ought to get married. Too little, too late is what that is. Anyway, that whole weekend away opened my eyes, Fern. If he wants to marry someone who's going to chop up vegetables on his bloody chopping board, then he's had it. After a year together he still hasn't noticed that I buy my vegetables ready-chopped.'

'But doesn't he want you to choose an engagement ring?'

'I'm not choosing my own ring!' She snorts her contempt. 'It's meant to be a surprise!'

'Gigi, you're going to break his heart.'

Her mood changes. She says regretfully, 'Yeah. I know. Can't help that. Fern, there's something I haven't mentioned. Max has left Alexa.'

I try to get my mind around it. 'Really?' And now I understand. 'Oh, Gigi. You and Max?'

'Yeah. We're going to give it a go. There's always been something there, you know, this chemistry between us?' She smiles slyly. 'And it's good for you, huh?'

'What do you mean?'

'I've seen the way you look at Dave. He's decorative, he's got that going for him. And he likes you, you know? He's always Fern this, Fern that.'

I feel the blood rising to my face. 'That has absolutely nothing to do with anything. I work with him, that's all. He *loves* you.'

She tosses her head and her wild pink hair is as turbulent as a twilight thundercloud. I suddenly see her as the girl I went to school with, the girl who played tricks on me. She pokes me in the ribs with her elbow and grins. 'I bet you'd love that chopping board,' she says. 'Chop-chop-chopping away for him. Good luck.' She starts to walk away.

'Hey! Gigi! You've forgotten the dog!'

Twirling back, she says, 'It's his dog, he can look after it.'

'What shall I tell him?'

'Tell him he's a shit for running off.'

I try to dampen my anxiety as I look at the dog with its black shaggy fur and blond shaggy eyebrows. He's sniffing the air around him, trying to track down the intriguing source of fear.

He looks at me and I glance away quickly in case he thinks I'm challenging him.

I wonder where David's gone. *Tell him he's a shit for running off.*

It's true that he rushed off as soon as he got her call, no doubt about it. I've never seen anyone move so quickly. Poor guy. Well, I can understand it. I hate confrontation, too.

The dog barks and I jump out of my shoes clutching my heart.

Thankfully it's David, coming back through the gateway the way he left, and he sees the dog. The dog wags its tail while David looks at it in a puzzled way as though he's trying to remember where he's seen it before.

For a moment I see his face tense and I think he's going to turn around and walk out again, but he comes back to the stall and I pretend to be busy adjusting the clothing rail and making sure all the hangers face the right way. 'Gigi came looking for you,' I say eventually.

'Did she say anything?' He sounds hopeful and wary at the same time.

Times like this I wonder why anyone bothers with relationships. 'She said you're a shit for running away,' I murmur apologetically. 'Sorry about that.'

He's bereft. 'She's leaving me, Fern.'

'Yeah. Why didn't you stay and talk to her?'

He scratches his forehead awkwardly. 'I didn't want to hear her say goodbye,' he says and his voice is full of pain.

'I'm sorry.' I want to put my arms around him to comfort him, but the dog's watching me. 'Er . . . what are you going to do about the dog?'

'Poor Duncan. She lavished her love on him, made him feel special, the luckiest dog on earth, and now she doesn't want him. He'll be cut up by this.' His eyes film with tears. 'Gigi was – is – the most exciting woman I've ever met. You know that charge you get when you see a person and all you can think about is them, and when you're not with them you're just wasting time until you can see them again?'

'Yes!'

'I had all that and now I've lost it.'

'David—'

'Don't tell me that there's still a chance. I hate that.'

'I wasn't going to.' I was going to tell him he'd find someone else, but I change my mind. It's not what he wants to hear. While he's still in love with her I know there's no hope for me.

Then Dinah turns up. She lets out a little cry and points her finger at David's chair. 'What's *that*?'

'David's dog. Gigi brought it,' I tell her, lowering my voice. David rests his head in his hands. 'She's left me.'

All Dinah says in response to this bombshell is: 'Interesting.'

He looks up irritably. 'What's that supposed to mean, "interesting"? What's interesting about it?'

'Poor you! But you see, she's not interested in hurting you. If she wanted to hurt you she'd keep the dog, no? Don't blame yourself. Some situations, there's nothing you can do to change it.'

The dog has inched out from beneath David's chair and it regards us with an innocent expression, as though he's got nothing to do with it but he's somehow sliding forward through no fault of his own. I get behind Dinah.

'What make of dog is it supposed to be?' she asks David suspiciously.

'It's got a bit of golden retriever in it,' he says vaguely, taking one of his light boxes off the shelf.

'Which bit, the eyebrows?'

I look at the light box in his hand. I wonder what he's going to do now. I wonder if the whole idea of being compatible because of a star sign was just a way of persuading himself that he and Gigi were meant to be.

Moss comes to the front of the shop unpicking the seams

of a gold Yves St Laurent blouse and kisses Dinah. 'My bride!' Against his dark trousers, the blouse pools like molten gold and catches the sunlight.

She fusses over him, picking a strand of gold thread off his sleeve and blowing the cut gold threads away into the breeze.

'David!' The squeak of trainers on cobbles makes me look up. It's Alexa.

Moss touches his trilby.

'David,' she says, bursting into tears.

'Alexa,' he says.

Moss bundles the gold blouse under his arm. 'Sit,' he says to Alexa, pulling his chair towards her. 'Sit before you fall.'

'I don't want to sit,' she replies fiercely. 'Have you seen Gigi?' she asks David between sobs.

Other people's emotions scare the life out of me even more than my own and I glance at David, who's holding his light box and looking at her with a thousand-yard stare.

I don't really know how long a person can cry for. It's years since I've really cried. Even with Mick, I held it in. My head's full of no-go areas, places I steer clear of.

Dinah makes two cups of tea and gives one to David. 'Don't upset yourself,' she says to Alexa. 'Take this.'

This time, she does sit down. She's shaking as she takes the cup and she sips it, closing her eyes in the steam.

Alexa turns to David. 'What am I going to do?'

'I don't know,' he says, squeezing his eyes shut for a moment and pinching the bridge of his nose.

I have a sudden flash of inspiration. 'I've got some really gorgeous dresses in your size, if you want to take a look.'

I realise immediately that it's the wrong thing to say by the fact that she stops crying and looks at me open-mouthed.

'I can't believe you, Fern. You're seeing my heartbreak as a sales opportunity?'

251

'Sorry.' It sounds really cringy, the way she says it. 'I just thought it might make you feel better. It'll protect you, like wearing a hazmat suit. Reinvent yourself!'

She blows her nose irritably. 'What *are* you talking about?'

'Reinvent yourself as someone unobtainable and strong; someone Max can't have.' Suddenly, I'm sounding like an expert on a subject I don't really know much about. Don't ask me where all this insight is suddenly coming from, but one thing I've learnt about life is you've got to have some armour in place against slings and arrows, otherwise it's easier just to lie down and give up.

Alexa has replaced her grief with a different emotion entirely: indignation. 'And that's it? That's your cure for the fact he's smashed my life to bits? I should buy myself something *new*?'

'That's not exactly what I was—'

But Alexa hasn't finished yet. 'Have you any idea how *trivial* you sound?'

David's phone pings. He looks up at me in despair. 'Fern, can you take over the shop for me?'

'Sure.'

'Why, what's happening?' Alexa asks in alarm, getting to her feet.

David rakes his fingers through his hair. 'Gigi's moving out. Come on, Duncan. We're going home.'

The dog comes out from under the chair and follows him placidly through the market.

Alexa hands the cup to me and hurries after him.

Moss looks at me over his glasses with his bushy eyebrows raised and calmly goes back to unpicking the seams of the gold blouse.

Dinah puts her hand on my shoulder. She's looking at me strangely, as if she pities me. 'What you said to Alexa, about reinventing yourself. This is something you like to do, isn't it?'

'Of course. That's the whole point of fashion, isn't it? You choose a different look depending on who you want to be. Take Wallis Simpson, for instance. She cultivated her sense of style deliberately because her clothes made her look beautiful.'

'It's true, she gave the impression of being beautiful without having the face for it.'

'Exactly!' I say happily, feeling that I've made my point. But the truth is, I can't stop thinking about Alexa's scorn when she said I was trivial.

Nor David's expression when she said it.

# LOT 18

*Full-length, psychedelic-print, hippy-style silk jersey dress, late Sixties, blue/purple colour tones, Pucci, size 38/10.*

This evening, as I'm slobbing around in my tracksuit bottoms and an oversized sweater, Lucy comes down full of excitement to see if I've seen the coverage of the film premiere on the local news, because if not, she's taped it, and as I haven't, we go up to hers to watch it over a bottle of wine.

She points the remote and cunningly, against the backdrop of the crowds gathered at the base of the IMAX, there's Lucy, actually on the red carpet wearing – ta-da! – a Fern Banks Vintage piece. The teal really shines out in the spotlights. She's posing with her hand on her hip, just behind the actress Keira Knightley.

'You look amazing, Lucy. Star quality! You look as good as she does. Pity she had to go and stand practically right in front of you.'

'Yes, but watch – watch – see? Did you see that? When she turns you can see my whole head, and a sleeve. That's at least five seconds of my fifteen minutes of fame, don't you think?'

'At least that.'

'It was such fun! Except my date from Universal is never taking me anywhere with him again because when I talked to Holly Willoughby, you know, the presenter? I spilled my drink on her shoe.'

'Lucy! Was she angry?'

'No, she was fine; once I picked the mint leaves off. Even better, she asked me where I got my dress and I gave her one of your cards. I could get used to that kind of lifestyle, you know,' Lucy says, all reflective. 'Free drinks all night. Didn't get invited to the after-party, though. My date gave me the slip.'

'If you get a part in a film, they'll be *begging* you to go to the after-party.'

'I know! I expect it'll be compulsory!'

The doorbell rings. Lucy goes to answer it and comes back wide-eyed and hopping around on the spot with excitement. 'It's him! The chopping-board king! At the door!'

'What? How?'

'Who cares how?' she asks, pulling me off the sofa. 'Go and talk to him!'

I put down my glass of wine and it's true, David's at the door looking uncharacteristically crumpled in a stripy short-sleeved shirt and frayed jeans.

'Fern?' he says, peering at me in the dark. He's slightly drunk.

Argh! I can't believe he's caught me in my tracksuit bottoms. 'How did you find me? I don't even live here – I actually live in the flat downstairs.'

David's rummaging in his pockets for something. He takes out a piece of newspaper and unfolds it laboriously, with great care. It's the picture from the *Camden New Journal* of Lucy and me after the fire. 'See this picture of you, Fern?' he says. 'See the door? It's got your house number on it.' He looks pleased with himself.

I'm surprised and deeply touched he's kept it. 'Well done, Sherlock,' I say. 'Come on, let's go down to mine.'

Lucy's hovering in the background, giving me the thumbs-up and then doing the 'call me' hand signal with her thumb and little finger.

Back in my flat, I put David on the sofa and dash to the bedroom to do a quick change into a 1960s multicoloured Pucci maxidress. I go back into the kitchen, pour two glasses of wine and get out the Marmite thins.

By the time I've arranged them in a fan shape, he's sitting on the sofa with his elbows on his knees. He takes the glass and knocks the wine back in one. He's suffering the thirst of someone who's aiming for oblivion.

I fetch the bottle and put the plate of biscuits between us, feeling absolutely surreal that he's sitting on *my* sofa. I feel very protective of him, both touched that he kept the cutting from the paper and impressed that he used it to track me down. 'How are you feeling?'

'Grim,' he says. He takes a biscuit absent-mindedly and points at me with it. 'You know what I think, Fern? I think the house party was a way of being with Max for the weekend,' he says. 'That's why she was so happy.' He breathes in hard. 'She was never happy just with me.'

My heart's breaking for him. 'In that case, she's crazy.'

He looks up at me hopefully. 'Do you think so?'

'Absolutely,' I say firmly.

He eats the biscuit and ponders for a few moments, rubbing the crease between his eyebrows. 'Fern, you've known her longer than I have – how can I be the man she wants?'

'Don't think like that. You can only be yourself.'

'I don't want to be myself. I'm going to reinvent myself. You've got to help me. You told me I could be anyone I want,' he says accusingly. 'You said I could be a dolphin in a cow costume.'

'Eh? Did I?' I do vaguely remember saying that. 'I didn't

mean you specifically, I meant people in general. I can't imagine you being anyone other than you.'

'I want to be a dolphin.'

'Don't think like that.'

'I want to wear a hazmat suit, like Alexa. I want to protect myself.'

Hearing my own words said back to me makes me cringe. I think of Alexa saying: *Do you know how trivial you sound?* 'Listen, the point is, it'll get better, I promise. I've been through it myself.'

'Yes, you have. With what's-his-name.' He turns to look at me carefully. 'I want to be like you. You told yourself it's fine, it wasn't serious anyway.'

I'd forgotten I'd said that. How much more has he memorised? 'The point is, I'm over it now. And this is what I think about Mick – if we'd loved each other, a long pleated skirt and a tie-neck blouse wouldn't have mattered to either of us, would they?'

He doesn't reply. His head is bent. The Pucci dress is strangely slippery. It's making me slide down the sofa. I'm level with his ear. It's a nice ear. In the gap under his stripy collar I can see the bone of his spine. I want to kiss it.

He says sharply, 'I know what you're thinking.'

I sit up again, alarmed that I'm being so obvious. 'What?'

'You're thinking about the chopping board.'

'No! Not at all! Well – yes,' I lie.

'You're right. If I'd loved her, I wouldn't have given it to her. And if she loved me, it wouldn't have mattered.' He narrows his eyes and moves closer to me as if he's trying to get me in better focus. His gaze is intense. 'See, Fern, when we first met, I thought Gigi wanted the same things, a house, children, a good work-life balance. But you know what, Fern? She didn't really want them. She liked playing with the idea of them, that's all. It was something different, something new.' He slumps back on the sofa, spilling wine on his jeans, and his mood turns gloomy again. 'Or maybe she does want them, just not with me. If I'd known her at all, I wouldn't have taken her advice to follow my dream and leave my well-paid job.'

'Why did you?'

He looks serious. 'I planned it all well in advance. I wanted to impress her with my spontaneity.'

'That's funny.' I giggle then reach for the bottle and top our glasses up, the attentive host. 'Do you regret it now?'

This is where he's supposed to say, *No, because I met you.* He doesn't say it. He says, 'Sometimes. Do you?'

'Miss my well-paid job?' And I think, *No. Because I met you.*

But I don't say it, either. I smile ruefully. 'Yes. I didn't realise how easy it was, going into work, having a regular income. I still get the same excitement and satisfaction now, but the risks worry me. I keep thinking about the weather, wondering what's going to happen when it's autumn, when it starts getting cold and the days are short. That kind of thing.' I slump back. 'No point in worrying. We won't know until it happens.'

'Can I tell you something, Fern?'

'Yes.'

'Buddha said, "Your worst enemy cannot harm you as much as your own unguarded thoughts." Onwards!' he says boldly, clinking his glass against mine. But he doesn't go much further onwards, because right then his thoughts snap back to Gigi. 'Fern, did she ever love me?'

'Of course she did! How could she not help loving you? It's just – she's impulsive. She doesn't think of the consequences. She was like that at school. I think even the teachers were a bit nervous of her.' This new information about his beloved brightens him for a moment. 'Really?'

'So don't blame yourself. And, of course, opposites attract and all that.'

'I never imagined it would end like this.'

It's the most painful realisation in the world that the person you most love and want to be loved by can't do it.

He looks at me. 'Thanks for listening. You're easy to talk to, Fern.'

It's not the first time I've been told that. Sometimes I feel that my role in life is to be some kind of repository for secrets and confidences. I wish somebody one day would listen to me. I suppose for people to do that, I'll have to start talking more.

'I'd better go, I suppose.' He struggles to his feet on his second try and holds onto me to get his balance.

The desperate way he looks at me, I know I'm not imagining it. He can't face going back to his empty home.

'It'll get easier,' I tell him.

'Thanks,' he says. 'You're a good friend.' He kisses me briefly on my cheek.

I shiver, because it's so lovely, so meant to be, and for a moment I can feel the warm imprint linger on my skin. And then as I turn to look at him closely, I press against him and kiss him, my mouth on his, hard and urgent. I slide my hands under his shirt, across his smooth, warm back. I want to be so much more than a friend to him. I want to tell him that he should be with somebody who truly appreciates him, but instead, we're suddenly off-balance and we hang onto each other, with me tripping over my good Pucci gown, and we fall onto the sofa again. A thud . . . and then the sound of wine spilling from the bottle. 'Oh, shit!'

'Got it,' he says, sliding to the floor to pick up the bottle.

I go to the kitchen, grab a tea cloth and mop the floor hurriedly using my bare foot, but the moment has passed.

'What does that say?' David's staring at the clock. 'I've got to go!' Acting as if it's a matter of great urgency.

'Sure.' I walk with him to the front door, and he closes it firmly behind him and my flat is empty again. He's on his way home through the empty streets doing the walk of shame. I resist the urge to run after him.

I sit on the sofa and finish the dregs of the wine in the bottle, alone and apprehensive. Would we have kissed if he'd been sober? Or if I hadn't made the first move? I know the answer to both questions: no.

The next morning, David's already at Stables Market when I get there and Dinah's reading him bits out of the *Metro* as if he's an invalid. He glances at me with a faint smile and continues to look distantly out at Stables Yard.

I'm going to apologise, because I don't want it to ruin our friendship. Come to think of it, those are the exact words I'll use.

I'm desperate to talk to him, but Dinah's still reading the paper, commenting loudly on things that she thinks are ridiculous or outrageous. 'Heh-heh! Why would a person want to knit a twenty-foot scarf?'

I wish I'd brought a book with me. I'm like someone on a blind date that isn't going well, looking eagerly at everyone who comes along the yard just as a distraction – my spirits sinking as they glance away and walk straight past. I'm looking out for my ideal customer – Kate Moss or Paloma Faith or Demi Moore – but she hasn't turned up yet.

Eventually, to my relief, Dinah pats David on his cheek and says she's going to do her shopping in Sainsbury's.

Time for the apology.

But David picks his book up and shuts me out.

I get up and stand in front of the shop and try to see it

through a stranger's eyes. Even though this is something that happens every day – David reads his book and I rearrange the dresses – today, our actions seem forced and unnatural. Already I can't remember what it's like to feel normal with him. To take my mind off it I arrange the dresses in order of colour. I love the rainbow effect and I wait eagerly for customers with my arms folded. There are so many people in the market today the crowds look pixelated.

'You're putting people off, you know,' David comments, using his finger to keep the page.

I unfold my arms. 'I thought you were reading your book.'

'I am.'

I say, all of a rush, 'David, I'm sorry about last night. I know I took advantage, but there's no need to be mean about it.'

He frowns.

Now I'm irritating him. I wish he'd go home and take his misery with him. He's making the hours drag. He's even making the seconds drag.

A girl stops to look at the blush dress that's still on Dolly. I'll be glad to get rid of the dress, to be honest. I'm sure it's not helping David, having it there as a reminder of the wedding in Camden Town Hall that never was.

She's seventeen, maybe. Young, fair, no make-up. Her grey sweatshirt is baggy and hides her figure. She has an unfinished, cautious look about her, combined with the cockiness of youth.

If you've ever tried to coax a sparrow to eat bread from your palm, that's the feeling I have looking at the girl. So I sit back in my chair, close my eyes and listen to a long goods train rattling by so that she won't fly away.

When I next open them, she's taking a photograph of the dress. She looks at the dress in a way I recognise – the same way that I look at clothes, the combination of an intense gaze and a dreamy half-smile.

It's no use – I have to ask. 'Are you a fashion student?'

She frowns as if I've offended her. 'No. Science. I want to study medicine,' she says sternly, tucking a strand of hair behind her ear. 'Why?'

I back off quickly. 'The way you were looking at it, I thought . . .'

'Oh,' she says, cutting me off before I finished the sentence. 'I'm looking for a prom dress.'

'Ah! Do you want to try it on?'

'No.' She clutches her cross-body bag. 'I've only got eighty pounds to spend, max. It's just, you know, I might find something like it, now that I know what I'm looking for.'

She has good skin. Well, she would, she's a teenager. I can imagine her in the dress. Pale, ethereal, pretty.

*I* want to see her in it; *I* want her to see herself differently. 'There's some movement on the price,' I say. 'You might as well try it on. If it doesn't look good then you'll know it's not the style for you.'

'Oh-kay,' she says with a reluctant sigh, as if she's doing me a favour. Which she is.

I disrobe Dolly. This particular beaded dress has no fasteners. It's heavy and dates from the 1920s, drop-waisted, designed to be slipped on over the head. I point her towards the dressing room and wait.

She steps out a couple of minutes later. The cautious look has entirely gone.

As I'm watching her, she's watching me, too.

It hangs perfectly on her and she's tied her hair back at the nape of the neck, giving her an edgy, boyish, Twenties look.

'Like, I can breathe in it,' she says seriously, as if breathing is usually an added bonus where style is concerned.

'It's the shape. You look confident.'

'Well, I am confident. We get taught self-esteem in assembly.'

'That'll be it, then. Turn around.'

She turns slowly and really, it's such a delight to see her wearing it – barefoot, her shoulders back, her head high. *Wearing* it, as opposed to being clothed in it; there's a difference. 'It could have been made for you,' I tell her.

She goes back behind the screen to change, and she comes back with her hair loose over her grey sweatshirt and the dress in her arms. She holds it out to me. 'Thanks, anyway,' she says diffidently.

'You can have it for eighty if you want it,' I say suddenly.

She looks at me warily. 'But that's almost half price.'

'It's never going to look as good on anyone else as it does on you,' I point out.

I can see what she's thinking. She's thinking that there has to be a catch. Only somebody whose thoughts veer that way, someone cautious and realistic, would come shopping for a prom dress alone, without a mother or a friend to share the moment and advise. 'Okay, then.'

'Would you like to sign up for my mailing list?' I ask.

'Okay!'

As she writes in my book – Daisy Redbourne – I take the dress from her. I wrap it in acid-free tissue and put it in a paper carrier bag as she counts out her money. We swap; transaction done.

'Enjoy your prom,' I say.

'Thanks,' she says. She walks away, swinging the bag.

David's watching me. He looks gloomy. 'You just sold my wedding dress.' He's holding his book like a shield between us.

'That's right.'

'You're not really a businesswoman, are you?' he points out.

Why does everyone keep telling me that? 'So what?' I say warily.

'I would have bought it from you last week for the full price.' He closes his book and puts it on the table with a thud. He gives me a crooked smile. 'Of course, if I had, Gigi would have jilted me at the actual ceremony, in front of witnesses, so I should be thanking you, you saved me from that.'

I'm not sure how to reply.

Then he adds, 'About last night . . .'

'Yes?' I'm hopeful that the rest of the sentence is going to be something on the lines of it being the best kiss he's ever had.

'I had to get back to let Duncan out.'

'Oh. Okay. That's fine.'

'I didn't want you to think I rushed off for any other reason.'

'No problem. Thanks.'

I really mean it. The thanks is because I'm grateful he at least had the decency to spare my feelings and come up with a decent excuse.

# KIM

I'm out with Betty and Mercia in Cafe Rouge in Hampstead and we're having afternoon tea, my treat, to thank them for their kindness to Enid, and to me. We've dressed up for the occasion. They're wearing flowery dresses and pink lipstick and I'm wearing my maroon paisley cravat.

We've got seats by the window, looking out onto Hampstead High Street, and we know what we want: afternoon tea with cakes, scones and croque monsieur.

The charming young waitress is French, with dark hair curling around her face. She tells us that for five pounds extra we can have prosecco.

'Ooh,' Betty says.

'I say,' adds Mercia.

I throw caution to the wind. 'Then we'll have prosecco,' I announce.

The prosecco arrives *toute-de-suite*, as they say in France, and we watch the waitress fill the glasses then we raise them in a salute to each other and ourselves.

'Chin-chin,' Betty says with a sparkle in her eye.

'Bottoms up,' responds Mercia.

'Cheers,' I say.

'I do love afternoon tea,' Betty says. 'It revives you at that time of the day when you're flagging, I always think.'

'The meal I've never understood is brunch,' Mercia says thoughtfully. 'I can't fit brunch into my day at all. It's like an overblown elevenses, with pancakes instead of biscuits.'

'It's not elevenses,' Betty says, shaking out her napkin. 'Elevenses comes between breakfast and lunch, whereas brunch replaces breakfast and lunch. Isn't that right, Kim?'

'I think so.' I'm flattered that she's asking my opinion. 'It's American, I believe. Heavier than breakfast but lighter than lunch.'

'Americans don't have tea though, do they? So after brunch, what time would their evening meal be?'

'Oh, gosh . . .'

This conversation is quite exciting, because it makes us feel cosmopolitan, being in a French restaurant discussing American mealtimes.

The cakes, when they come, are wonderful. I feel as if I've never eaten cakes quite this good before. Presently, I notice that our glasses are empty, so we look around for our waitress and I alert her, with more drama than is usual for me, to the unfolding emergency of the empty glasses. She says that for economic reasons, it would be better to buy a bottle rather than three more glasses, especially if we want three more glasses after that.

I must say, I sober up at the idea of buying nine glasses of prosecco in the middle of the afternoon. But, of course, it only amounts to three each, which feels perfectly manageable, or doable as my son, George, would call it, so I agree on the bottle.

Betty and Mercia are looking pink and flushed. I expect I am, too. I feel carefree and young, and even though I wasn't going to talk about Enid today, she pops into my head in case I've forgotten her. *Hello, here I am!*

'Enid would have loved this,' I say, reaching for a scone.

But as I look at the condensation beading on the glass, I think it's more likely that she'd be appalled by my extravagance.

However, the women are nodding.

'Absolutely,' Mercia says. 'To Enid!'

'Enid.'

It's funny how you can be married to someone all that time and not be sure you ever knew your wife all that well.

I'm not sure that I know myself anymore. I feel carefree, more carefree than I ought to feel being newly bereaved, and I split the warm scone and put the cream on, and the strawberry jam. I wonder if all couples feel like this. I wonder how well Betty knew Stan, bearing in mind the mix-up about his last resting place. 'Why did Stan wear safari suits?' I ask her.

She dabs her mouth with her napkin, leaving a trace of pink lipstick with the dislodged crumbs. 'For the pockets,' she says. 'Stan always liked a pocket. It's hard to get shirts with pockets, you know. Stan used to blame it on the smoking ban.'

'Suits have pockets,' Mercia points out.

'Stan gave up suits when he retired. Except for golf club dinners and funerals, that sort of thing.'

They both look at me quickly.

'Sorry. Insensitive of me,' Betty says.

I wave my hand. *Don't worry.*

Cafe Rouge is filling up with mothers and small children. The noise level rises.

'School's ended,' Mercia says, looking around and smiling. But her mind is now on her husband, too, and his clothes. 'The first time I went out with Bertie, he drove us to Brighton in an open-top car that he borrowed. He wore a suit to the beach. After we'd been married about ten years, he took to wearing a white shirt with the sleeves rolled up and khaki shorts with turn-ups.'

'I don't think there was such a thing as casual wear in those days,' I point out. 'My casual wear was my cricket whites and a football jersey for sport. We dressed for the occasion. Casual meant taking off one's tie.' I chuckle to myself. 'For my eight-ieth, we went out for a meal and Enid asked George to wear a tie – he turned up at the restaurant wearing it around his head!'

They laugh sympathetically.

'This kind of conversation should make us feel old, but I don't feel old at all,' Betty says. 'I feel younger than them,' she says, looking at the mothers. 'We don't have their worries.'

I realise that I've never been drunk with Betty and Mercia before. I have an urge to ask them about Enid and whether she knew about my sartorial penchants. I feel it's important to know whether she'd have thought like them, or whether she'd have mocked me like the two women in Kentish Town. If I ask, I have to be prepared to live with the answer. And if I don't, I'll miss my chance because I might never get drunk with them again.

'Penny for them,' Mercia says, and her eyes are kind.

I decide that, all things considered, it's something that I would like to find out one way or another, so I take my courage in both hands. 'Did Enid know that I had a fondness for her clothes?'

Betty and Mercia snap their heads towards each other, wide-eyed.

I raise my glass aloft and stare at the bubbles, wishing I could drown in them.

'It's not anything that we discussed,' Betty says after a moment, 'although she did once ask me if Stan had ever expressed an interest that way. But he was a lot bigger than you, Kim. Nothing of mine would have gone near him.'

Mercia's licking her finger and pressing it on the cake crumbs on her plate. 'She asked me, too.' She looks up at me and laughs. 'You know what Bertie was like. I've got more pictures of Bertie in a dress than I have of myself.'

'Really?' This is news to me.

'Crossing the equator, Bertie always threw himself whole-heartedly into the fancy-dress ceremony. On his last cruise, his *very* last, he did a wonderful Lily Savage in a gold sequined gown and a blond wig – he made a marvellous drag queen. All the British men dressed up as women and had a whale of a time. *Only* the British men, now I think of it. The Americans went as Uncle Sam or Superman. And the Europeans ignored it altogether.'

How unlikely Enid to ask her friends such an intimate question.

She'd allowed me to keep my secrets without judging or prying or disapproving, or at least, without showing it, which amounts to the same; Enid was never usually slow to show her disapproval.

'I sort of guessed it was something to do with you, but she didn't go into it,' Mercia said.

That's a tender side of Enid, an understanding side of her that I didn't foresee. I suppose what I've learnt is that you can't second-guess people. Even with a fuzzy head, it strikes me as being vitally important that I remember it.

# LOT 19

*Turquoise A-line mini dress, Biba, 1960s, medium, with beaded neckline, high set short sleeves.*

It's a cloudy day and I'm dressing naked Dolly in a turquoise Biba dress with a beaded neckline and cutaway shoulders, humming with pleasure at the texture of the silk. A woman with her hair pulled fiercely into a red rubber band is looking at my daffodil-yellow Chloe maxidress with a distant, slack-muscled look of misery and I hope it might be something she loves, something that'll raise her spirits.

A busker is playing Simon and Garfunkel and it's merging with the reggae on the music stall. The smell of onions blows on the breeze.

David's talking to a bearded man about the constellation of Aries; they're debating the compatibility of Aries with Pisces. Pisces and Aries can get on as long as there's room for compromise, according to David.

If you ask me, that applies to all relationships. I still haven't been able to work out what David thinks about the whole astrology business, especially now his astrologically perfect Gigi has dumped him.

The bearded man is showing him an astronomy app on his phone but despite the app, he hasn't been able to find Aries in the night sky, a confession he admits to in the worried tone that suggests he blames himself for mislaying it. David tells him to look for Hamal in the autumn – Hamal apparently meaning sheep boy – and he's pointing it out on a light box, here, the brightest star of Aries. From where I'm standing, the constellation of Aries in the light box is pretty well a straight line. It looks more like a snake than a ram.

I can imagine the ancients lying on the grass looking at the sky. 'Hey, guys, who else can see a ram?'

'Yeah, man, it's a ram, for sure.'

At the back of the shop, Moss is working his way through the rail of dresses waiting to be altered, humming to himself in time with the sewing machine.

I look around for the unhappy-looking woman, but she's gone, to my regret. Glancing at the rail, I notice . . . just a minute! Oh, great. The yellow dress has gone, too.

I hurry into the yard in a rush of anger, outraged at what she's stolen from me, as surely as if she's taken the money right out of my purse. I want to get hold of her and scream at her and snatch the dress out of her hands but as I spin round, she's lost in the crowds. I curse her under my breath, knowing that it's my own fault. I should have kept my eye on her.

I go back to the shop, my heart pounding, trying to get my emotions under control, trying to look on the bright side. Who knows? That dress might be just what she needs. She might put it on, take the rubber band from her hair and find herself smiling . . .

Dinah shows up just then, wearing a black Susan Small dress with diamante buttons. Very chic. She's making obscure hand signals at me like a bad mime artist.

'Morning!'

'Quiet! Where's Moss?' she whispers dramatically.

'Right there,' I say.

'Is he busy?'

'Yes, but—'

'No! Don't call him! This is top secret. Come!' She puts her reading glasses on and smooths out the travel section of the newspaper on David's table. 'Listen to this! "A luxury hotel, set in verdant gardens overlooking the Atlantic Ocean, Belmond Reid's Palace is the ultimate place to stretch out in the sun and relax."' She looks at me brightly over her glasses to gauge the keenness of my interest and continues, '"Over the years this luxury hideaway has honed the art of pampering, earning a reputation as one of the best hotels in Funchal." Five stars, and a pool. You been there?'

'No, but it sounds wonderful. Luxury hideaway. Pampering.'

'Stretching out in the sun.' She lifts her face to the cloudy sky as if she can already feel the warmth on it. 'It's a surprise for Moss. It's for our platinum wedding anniversary. Seventy years.'

Despite the fact I've had it up to here with surprises, it does sound intensely romantic.

'Seventy years,' I say, marvelling. Literally, a whole lifetime.

'Don't worry, dahlink,' she says consolingly, 'your time will come.'

'You think so?' The pure hope that sparks up in me when she says that!

Never one to miss an emotion, she lowers her voice. 'I'm telling you as a friend, let him into your heart.'

I shoot a glance at David, who's now talking to the partner of the bearded man, and they're back on the subject of Pisces, allegedly the imaginative and dreamy signs of the zodiac. 'Let him into my heart,' I repeat. 'I'm not sure what that means. Anyway, he might not want to come in. He might prefer to hang around on the doorstep.'

'Okay, stop with making the jokes. That's why you're single. Men don't like a joker.'

'If that were true, women comics would all be single.'

Dinah purses her lips to show her disapproval of my facetiousness. 'You have my forgiveness,' she says, 'only because I need your help. For this luxury hideaway holiday, I'm going to sell three or four of my Chanel suits.'

My heart lurches with nervous excitement. 'You're kidding!' I whisper. 'What's Moss going to say? He's not going to be happy about that.'

'Of course he isn't! It's insufferably rude to giveaway gifts.' She pats my face. 'Don't worry; he'll be fine. I'm not giving away my favourites.'

Remembering Moss's possessiveness over Dinah's wardrobe, it's not much of a consolation. 'Talk it over with him first,' I advise, seeing as I seem to be so good at giving advice these days. 'He wasn't very happy that I'd tried on your Grès gown and that's putting it mildly.'

'Exactly!' Dinah says as if she's scored a point. 'If I *ask* him, he'll say no.'

'So don't do it.' I'm getting a strong sense of déjà vu. If there's one thing I've learnt recently about surprises, it's that they can go horribly wrong.

'Don't do what?' David asks, coming into the conversation now that his customers have left with his largest size of light box.

'Dinah wants to surprise Moss with a holiday for their wedding anniversary and to fund it she wants to sell her Chanel,' I whisper.

His features soften in a way that makes him look like a kid watching a Disney film.

'Dinah, your marriage,' he says, 'is so romantic that despite everything, it gives me faith in everlasting love.'

'See?' she says to me triumphantly. 'Listen to him! It's romantic!'

'You must have practically been a child when you married,' he says.

Maybe Dinah's right. Maybe I should let him into my heart instead of standing here cynically rolling my eyes.

'I want you to come with me to the auction house to get them valued. You understand what I want?' Dinah says, rubbing her thumb and forefinger together. 'Maximum bucks for this holiday. You know the woman. You'll see she gives me a fair price?'

'Hang on, she's not *buying* them from you, it's up to the buyers bidding on the day.'

The sewing machine falls silent. David looks up. 'Quick! Moss is coming!' he says and he snatches up the travel section, folds it hastily and tucks it under his arm, and we stand around wearing our most innocent expressions.

'Dahlink!' Dinah says to her husband, arms wide and all smiles.

'My bride!'

The deceit of it.

A group of girls comes in and they tell me they're Daisy's friends, and can they, too, have a student discount? One of them buys a red organza top and as soon as they've gone, and Moss is back at his machine, Dinah says firmly, 'So, the Chanel. I have many Chanel suits – I'm not going to miss a couple of them. Tell me, are you in?'

I've got a bad feeling about both it and love in general, to be honest.

David's holding up the travel supplement and Dinah's watching me, arms folded, so influenced by peer pressure, I agree to get involved, against my better judgement, in the plan to fund the platinum anniversary gift.

\* \* \*

I'd be lying if I said I wasn't excited by my impending proximity to so much Chanel. I make an appointment with Tallulah Young to have Dinah's suits valued.

The sun is out and David has moved into the shade. He's eating a salad out of a Tupperware bowl and balancing the lid of his flask on his book. He looks slightly more cheerful today, as if he's starting to feel better after a long illness. The reappearance of the flask is a good sign, I think.

'Has Dinah really got enough clothes to convert into a holiday for two?' he asks.

I pull my stool up to sit next to him. 'Absolutely. She could go on a world cruise, if she wanted. Unbelievable. Worth an absolute fortune.'

'Vintage?'

'Haute couture.'

He laughs then puts the lid back on his salad, pours us both a coffee and looks at me curiously. The light stripes his tanned cheekbone.

'How did Moss make his money? Do you know?'

'He worked for Chanel before the war and then for Norman Hartnell when he came here. Norman Hartnell made the Queen's wedding dress. Before she was actually Queen, of course.' I shouldn't have said that; it might remind him of his failed wedding plans. But David doesn't seem to notice.

He stretches his legs. 'It must be a bit of a comedown for him, working here under a railway arch.'

I watch a family of holidaymakers ambling past in the sunshine, eating Magnum ice creams. I chew the inside of my cheek, thinking about it. 'You could say the same about us.'

He laughs. 'That's true. You're happy though, aren't you?'

I think about it and realise that I am. I look at his light boxes. 'All I need now is a compatible constellation to fit next to mine.' I'm not sure why I say it. Looking for a response, I suppose. Anyway, he doesn't take me up on it, so I wish I hadn't bothered.

On Monday, while Moss has gone to the sports centre for a morning swim, I get the all clear from Dinah and make my way to her house.

Dinah takes me straight up to her dressing-room heaven and we stand in the golden light while she opens the wardrobe doors as she did before.

I swear I can hear angelic music.

She checks the Polaroids on each garment bag before she unzips them and takes a deep satisfied breath. 'These are Moss's birthday presents to me.' She flashes me an ironic smile. 'At my age I can afford to lose a few.' She pulls a bag from the rail and hands it to me. 'This green one can go. Comes with this camisole. I'm not so keen on green; it doesn't suit my complexion. It's 1950s; you can tell by the length of the skirt. Hold it, please.

'This black-and-gold one, too, and the gold blouse; I wore it a lot – good for day and through to evening, you see? Also Fifties. Look at the contrasting lining! Beautiful. This one with the higher hemline, this is Eighties, you can see, when Karl Lagerfeld moved to Chanel he took the hemlines up – *dahlink*, let me tell you, Coco would have turned in her grave! She hated women to show their knees. Maybe she was right; the skirt is a little short for me now. Also this white suit with the black braid. It's not practical anymore; London is so *filthy*.'

Struggling with the suits, I sit down on the ottoman.

'How much would you say so far?' she demands.

'If the last sale is anything to go by, these should make about five hundred each, but as I said—'

Dinah's face lights up. 'That's enough! Good! Let me find

you a good, decent holder for us to put them in and you can take them home tonight; I'll arrange to meet up with you.' She goes out of the room and comes back with an enormous leather suit carrier. Suits packed, we leave the house before Moss comes back from his swim.

I've never personally sold anything at auction because of the steep auction costs. It's more profitable for me to sell direct. So this is a new experience for me and I have the feeling that this is going to change my relationship with Tallulah Young, because she'll realise I'm not just somebody who buys cheap lots – I'm a serious dealer. On the other hand . . . 'What if Moss—'

'Forget Moss!' Dinah says as we wait at the Tube station. She looks so perky and elegant in a little red suit with a white silk blouse and pearl necklace.

She's quite calm, whereas I'm buzzing. She reaches across suddenly and pulls the sleeve of my PVC raincoat, startling me.

'This is nice – and the beret, too. Very nice. And the red lipstick. This coat, how long have you had it?'

'I've had it ages.'

'How much?'

'Thirty pounds from the Sue Ryder charity shop.'

Dinah nods approvingly, pressing her red lips together. 'It's not cheap but also it's not expensive. Makes you look a little like a hooker, but not too much.'

On the Tube, I notice that she's taken my advice and she's wearing flat shoes.

I, on the other hand, have taken her advice and I'm wearing heels.

With a combination of heels and PVC I'm hot and bothered by the time we get to the auction room. I take my coat off, feeling the sweat cool under my arms, which was not the impression I was going for.

We take a seat and wait our turn, the suit carrier spread over our laps. After a short time our names are called and we take the suit carrier over to the table, where Dinah takes her outfits lovingly out of their garment bags. I'm slightly disappointed that it's not Tallulah Young herself doing the valuation but her assistant, Cathy, a woman with long dark hair who's briskly efficient at her job. She examines the labels and looks at the suits with forensic thoroughness, holding them up against the light and examining the seams.

Dinah's playing with her pearls, her nose in the air, her eyes averted, and I wonder if she's starting to regret it.

'Are you okay?' I ask.

'Perfectly,' she says. She leans forward and says to Cathy sharply, 'My husband bought these for me for my birthday.'

'Lucky you,' Cathy says, looking inside the sleeves. She examines the camisoles with equal thoroughness.

I can sense that Dinah isn't altogether happy. She starts fidgeting. 'What are you looking for?' she asks irritably.

'I'm checking them for the condition report. So that we can make the valuation.'

'This one here,' Dinah says, jerking her thumb towards me, 'thinks seven hundred pounds each. She's a fashion curator.'

'That's nice,' Cathy says, looking at me briefly.

I smile ingratiatingly.

She lays the black-and-gold jacket down and checks the label again. Then she goes back to the green tweed suit. Now it's the turn of the white one with the black braid and the A-line Sixties skirt that's too short.

'You looked at them already!' Dinah says in frustration. 'How many times?'

Cathy gets to her feet. 'I'm just going to have a word with Tallulah.'

'Oh my goodness,' I say to Dinah once she's out of the room, 'what if they're worth more than we thought? The Fifties ones have got to be rare.'

'Maybe in that case I'll only sell one,' Dinah says. 'The green one.'

'Definitely the green one,' I agree.

We look at each other gleefully.

Tallulah Young comes into the room with Cathy. She's wearing a sleeveless cotton camisole and culottes, her grey hair tucked behind her ears. She doesn't acknowledge either of us. She, too, looks carefully at the suits and then at the labels, and then she looks at Dinah. Her expression isn't that of someone who's about to deliver good news and I'm suddenly churned with nerves.

'These aren't right,' the auctioneer says to Dinah. 'We can't accept them.'

Dinah turns to me and spreads her hands in a gesture of incredulity. 'What's she saying? I don't understand.'

Me neither. 'What's the problem?'

Tallulah Young says, 'They're couture standard, beautifully constructed, but the label's wrong.'

I'm confused. 'In what way?'

'You're blind,' Dinah says, her anger rising. 'My husband bought these for me many years ago.'

'I'm sorry,' Tallulah says.

I stare at her, utterly baffled by this development. 'Are you *sure*?'

'Perfectly.' She turns down her mouth in a gesture of sympathy. 'I'm afraid there are a lot of fakes out there.'

Cathy begins to move the garments from the table, draping them over the chairs we were originally sitting on.

'Hey!' Dinah says to Cathy. 'Stop that!' And to Tallulah: 'Fakes?'

I try to think of a rational explanation; how Moss, in the 1950s, came by these suits and was duped. 'Moss must have been misled,' I say.

'Misled?' Dinah seizes the word vigorously. 'Who misled Moss?'

'Look,' I say, trying to climb out of the nightmare, 'it might not even have been deliberate – what I mean is, the person who sold them to him might have been taken in as well, because as she just said, they're haute couture quality.'

Dinah interrupts me angrily. 'What person who sold them to him? Coco Chanel? Of course they're couture quality! They're not copies! Let me tell you what they're doing, Fern. They want it for a cheap price so they can put a low estimate on it. You can't see that?' She throws the green jacket at Tallulah. 'They have *labels*!' she yells.

Tallulah hands the jacket to Cathy, who puts it with the others.

I put my coat back on for a quick getaway. People are looking at us. I'm trying to keep calm.

Dinah's eyes flash with anger. She pushes her chair back and the legs scream against the floor. 'I don't believe it. It's not possible. It's not *possible*.' She frowns and pats her lips. 'Moss bought them from Paris. He bought them from *Paris*, Fern. They have my measurements at the fashion house.' She's pleading with me to believe her. She winces in pain.

'Dinah, are you okay?' I say in alarm, afraid the shock is going to kill her.

'We went to Claridge's,' she says, pushing away a strand of dark hair that's falling into her eyes, 'and he told me . . .' She tails off and looks at me uncertainly, as though she can't trust this story anymore. She turns back to Cathy. '*All* of them are fakes? Every one?'

With obvious effort, she musters together her dignity and

stands up very straight. 'Well then, he couldn't have bought them where he said he did, could he? They came from somewhere else.'

All around us people are coming and going.

Her mind is working the same routes as mine did and she clutches her throat. 'Obviously, he lied to me about Paris. He knew they weren't genuine, right?' She blinks hard, squeezing back the tears.

Trapped in her drama, I feel frozen. 'I don't know, Dinah. I guess so.'

She takes in a deep, shuddering breath and looks through the window at a man pushing a buggy, a toddler kicking his chubby legs in the front. 'Okay, so they're copies,' she says bitterly, nodding to herself. 'As she says, good ones. Bah!' She gazes out of the window thoughtfully and strokes her chin with her elegant fingers. 'All that money for the real thing. So, if it's as good as the real thing, it might as well be the real thing – it's got the workmanship. That's what he told himself, isn't it? But where did he . . . ?'

The truth dawns on her and she raises her fine eyebrows. 'Moss made them himself,' she says.

Of course he did. Now I understand why he was so hostile, why he didn't want me to be friends with Dinah, why he didn't want me to see her wardrobe. It wasn't because he thought I was dishonest. It's because he was.

In a way, it makes it better. 'Dinah, think about it. He copied them for you, piece by piece. Think of the time he took, the attention to detail.'

'Bof! He cheated me,' she says, her voice hard. 'Don't tell me it's the same – it's not the same. Me in my home-made clothes, thinking I was someone! All these years he let me think I was worth something and I trusted him, I *believed* it,' she says with growing comprehension. She settles her intense tawny gaze on me and she starts to laugh, self-mocking and shrill. 'Look at me! I've been so proud of myself,' she says, 'and all this time I've been wearing fakes, and you know what? I am a fake! And Moss is a fake, too.'

'Dinah, let's just get out of here,' I beg.

A couple of old ladies carrying clothes in Selfridges bags edge past us disapprovingly to get to their table and she turns to confront them.

'Take a look at a fake!' she shouts at them, jutting out her chin, and they avert their eyes and pretend not to hear.

'Come on, please? Let's go.'

'He made a fool of you as well,' she says, turning on me, her voice high-pitched with denigration, her eyes feverish with tears. 'Curator of fashion!' she mocks.

In the force of her anger I feel my core self disconnecting, shutting down. I should never have taken her there. I've ruined everything.

As she gestures wildly, Dinah's hand catches in her necklace, snapping the thread, and the beads scatter to the floor. 'Oh!' she says in dismay and she grabs her red quilted bag, pushing past the people coming through the door.

I'm numbed by these developments and I feel frustrated and impotent in the face of Dinah's rage. I give orders to myself in a voice as stern as my mother's, feeling six years old again. *Put your coat on. Put the suits back in the garment bags. Zip up the bags. Put the garment bags in the suit carrier.*

This way, I leave the auction house. The air is fresh and I gulp it in gratefully. At the other end of the street, I catch the brightness of Dinah's red jacket, the gleam of her dark hair. She's not that far away and yet she's so distant that I convince myself I can never catch her up.

I don't even try.

# LOT 20

*Pale blue dolly-bird dress with elbow-length choirboy sleeves,*
*viscose, round neck, medium. Unlabelled.*

I repeatedly try calling Dinah but she doesn't reply. Back at
the market on Wednesday morning I fill David in on what's
happened.

'Fakes?' he says. 'Bloody hell! Don't look so worried, Fern.
They'll probably turn up today as if nothing's happened.'

'You think?' I ask hopefully.

He's completely wrong about this.

When Moss comes in he takes off his trilby and throws it
down on the table. 'You've destroyed our lives,' he says furiously.

I feel sick. 'I'm sorry. It was for a good reason; did Dinah
tell you that? She wanted to surprise you.'

He ignores me and I follow him to the back of the shop,
where he looks at the rail of dresses waiting to be altered. He
takes off his jacket, unhooks one, uncovers his sewing machine
and stoically sits down to start work.

'Look, how were we to know they were fakes?'

Moss looks hurt. 'They weren't *fakes*. They were the original
fabric, the original pattern, everything Chanel quality, apart
from the label. At that time there were four thousand of us

working for her and we worked for low wages and long hours until she shut the couture house in 1939, lying to us that it was because of the war. What were we to do? We kept the patterns. How else would we know how to copy? I wanted to give these gifts to my wife, gifts she'd value. Since when is that a crime? This is your fault! She was happy, but you tried to sell her happiness and now she wants to leave me. There's nothing left for me if she goes.'

'Come on, Moss, sit down, buddy,' David says. He pushes his fingers through the hair at his temples. 'I don't understand. What difference does it make who made them, whether it's Chanel or you? Neither Dinah nor Fern could tell the difference and she looks wonderful in them. You made them for her because you love her. Surely that's what counts?'

I rub the heel of my hand against my forehead. 'That's not really how it works in fashion.' Although, for the first time, I wonder if it should be.

'Where's Dinah now?'

'In bed.' There's a look of great sorrow and suffering in his eyes, which cuts me to my core.

The morning passes slowly. I'm wrapping up a dress for a customer, when I sense someone looking at me.

It's a middle-aged woman, with pale hair the colour of a latte and a solemn expression. She's wearing a beige polka-dot wrap-around dress and for a moment she's lost from view as people walk past, but then she emerges again as immovable as a rock in a river.

Blimey! I realise with a start. It's my mother!

As my customer writes her details in my client book, I give my mother a brief wave in the form of a gentle, almost imperceptible waggle of my fingers. Nothing too vulgar or ostentatious, you understand. She hates that.

My mother glides over, her skirt dancing in the breeze. She

looks at our shop with its universe on one side and rainbow array of dresses on the other.

As my client leaves, I say, 'Mum!'

'Annabel,' she corrects me, squeezing my upper arms in greeting and at the same time glancing over my shoulder to look at David. She has a radar for good-looking men.

'What are you doing here?' I ask warily.

'I've come to stay with you for a while. I've left my case at the flat. You really are neglecting it; it smells strongly of stale wine.'

'Does it?' How embarrassing. I avoid catching David's eye. I can't hide who I am when she's with me. 'Why didn't you tell me you were coming? I would have cleaned up.'

Still looking unsubtly at David, she says, 'I didn't want to put you to any trouble.'

I'm trying to interpret the words 'for a while'. In visitor language, the scale goes like this: a night, a couple of nights, a few days, a week or so . . . "A while" means indefinitely. If she'd said a week or so, my heart would still have stopped. As it is, I'm experiencing all the symptoms of shock: rapid pulse, dry mouth. If I had to have one of my parents living with me, I'd prefer my father, who's much less high-maintenance. 'Come and sit down,' I say when I can finally speak.

She sits next to David and gives him a brave and challenging pout. Her dress gapes gently, showing cleavage, her hair curves around her chin, and she looks poised and very beautiful.

David introduces himself. 'David Westwood.'

'Any relation to Vivienne?' she asks, sandwiching his beautiful tanned hand in her small, elegant ones.

'That's funny, it's exactly what Fern said when we first met.'

My mother doesn't find it at all funny. She looks at me accusingly, as if I've stolen her punchline. 'And *are* you?' she asks him firmly.

'No,' he replies equally firmly.

My mother responds to this by tapping him on his bare arm. I've seen her do this before – she pets men playfully. Not all men, obviously. Just the lovely ones. I hate her for manhandling my man. Or woman-handling my colleague. 'Won't Dad mind being on his own?' I ask treacherously, just to remind her that she's got a man of her own at home.

She avoids the question. 'Remember whose flat it is, Fern,' she says sharply. She turns back to David. 'Fern lives in our flat, you see. Jonathan used to spend the week in London and come to our place in Berkhamsted at weekends. Now he's retired he finds himself with too little to do. We have staff,' she adds unnecessarily.

It's embarrassing that my mother thinks this kind of talk impresses people.

'Fire them,' David says logically, folding his arms, 'and get your husband to do the work. It'll stop him from getting bored.'

I brace myself, because it's touch-and-go how she'll respond to this verbal sparring, but in the end she gives him another playful pat and he light-heartedly retaliates by giving her one back, a little less playfully, at least in my imagination.

My mother's very well aware of the effect she has on men. She gets to her feet and starts looking through the dresses, managing to put an extra sway in her step on the assumption we're watching her. Which we are.

Actually, I'm wrong. David's not looking at her; he's looking at me, eyebrows raised, suppressing a smile as if we're conspirators, which makes me feel better.

She's now looking at the light boxes. 'What are these?'

'What star sign are you?'

'Scorpio,' she says.

'The sign with the sting.' David selects a sheet of Perspex

and slots it into a light box. 'These are the claws and this large star in the abdomen, Alpha Scorpii, it's red, see? That's how you can identify it in the southern hemisphere, by its colour. Down here is the tail. The scorpion was sent by the Earth goddess Gaia to kill Orion when he boasted that there was nothing on earth that he wouldn't hunt.'

'The heavens have got such romantic stories,' she says softly, holding her face at the best angle to catch the light.

'Not all of them,' David says. 'There's the Chisel. And the Air Pump.'

'I've never heard of them,' she says suspiciously.

He's unaware that my mother hates being disagreed with.

'Haven't you?' He sounds surprised, as if this shows an unexpected level of ignorance.

I realise that not knowing there's a constellation called the Chisel isn't something that would bother most people, but my mother thinks he's mocking her and takes it as a personal attack. She walks away, scowling.

I'm meant to go after her, but I feel I owe David an explanation for her behaviour.

'She doesn't have *staff*,' I tell him, mortified. 'They've got an occasional gardener and a weekly cleaning lady, and every month someone comes to clean windows.'

He laughs and pats me on the head. Honestly, my mother's whole patting thing has gone viral.

My mother turns to see if I'm following her. She beckons me crossly.

'She's going to yell at you, isn't she?' David says.

'Yeah.' *Because of you.*

'Don't go. Ignore her.'

'I can't, she's my mother.'

'She's not your mother,' he grins, looking at me from under his eyebrows. 'She's Annabel.'

'Fern!'

Her voice barks across the yard and I feel a rush of anxiety. 'I'd better go.'

I catch up with my mother and she's predictably furious with me for allowing David to 'put her down'. I have learnt from experience that it's no use trying to be rational when she's in this state. My mother's feelings take priority, even if those feelings have arisen from nothing more than a misunderstanding or a failure in communication. The only way for me to deal with it is to freeze and wait it out and listen, penitent, to everything that she accuses me of, like my failure to succeed, or my failure to understand her, or my failure to give her the credit she deserves, or my failure to offer her the protection that she needs.

I'm not wearing the right outfit for this; I need Eighties shoulder pads, power dressing, not this cute pale blue dress with choirboy sleeves which makes me feel more like a doll than a dolly bird.

'Hey! Fern! Fern! Fern Banks!' David's bellowing to me. 'Come back! Customers!'

'Sorry, Mum, I've got to go back.' I pluck at the button on my dress apologetically. 'We're short-staffed.' I hurry back and it's true, I have got customers.

Now that I'm back, my heart is pounding. I can't look at David. I feel as if he's seeing me naked for the first time.

I retreat to the back of the shop and call my father urgently. 'What's going on with you and Mum?'

'Just let her stay for a few days,' he says.

'You haven't answered my question.'

'Nothing's *happening*. We need a break from each other, that's all, darling.'

'Can't she go to a spa or something?' I ask desperately.

'She wants to be with you. She thinks you'll understand.'

'Understand what?'

'Understand her, I suppose.'

'I do understand her, but it doesn't make her any easier to live with.'

'Do your best,' he says unhelpfully.

# LOT 21

*Burberry Classic trench coat, beige, 1960s, size M.*

When I get back home that evening, my mother has changed into a blue shift dress and she's still tight-lipped from earlier.

Determined to do my best to understand, as instructed by my father, I start the conversation. 'So,' I say decisively, going straight into the kitchen and opening a bottle of wine. I'm hungry, but she's eaten all the Marmite thins. 'What *are* your plans, exactly?'

'Fern, I need my own space,' she declares. 'I'm not used to having your father around twenty-four hours a day.'

'To be fair, there's more space at home than here.' I can see she's put her suitcase in my bedroom, so I'll be sleeping on the sofa for the foreseeable future. The wine is warm and cheap and I can trace its fiery path into my guts.

'But unlike your father, you're not around in the daytime, are you? You're in the market, selling second-hand clothes,' she points out logically.

I sit on the stool and clasp my hands behind my head to stretch the tension out. In a couple of hours I can legitimately say goodnight and go to bed, and that's the thought I'm hanging on to.

But my mother hasn't finished yet. She gives a shrill, brief laugh. 'Second-hand clothes!' she repeats and takes a mouthful of her drink. 'You've never been able to stick at anything, have you? You decide not to be a fashion designer. You get fired from your job. You set fire to the flat. You lose your boyfriends. You have no sense of responsibility. You've squandered every privilege you've been given. What *have* you achieved in life?'

I try to answer, swallowing the panic rising in me. 'I'm good at – I'm good at finding clothes that suit people.'

'Then go back to being a sales assistant and bring in a regular income so that you can afford a room of your own. Think about the future. What about a husband? Children?' my mother asks. 'This is hardly a secure basis for a good family life.'

I finish my drink in one. After the initial shudder the injustice rises up in me.

Alcohol. The insidious false bravado, the loss of mental restraint. At the same time there's a small sober part of me begging me to keep quiet for my own good because I've never faced up to her before. 'Family life?' I say scornfully. 'Like ours, you mean? We were never a family.'

'Of course we were!' She turns furiously to face me. 'We *were*!'

This is what my childhood was like: I was dressed up and paraded around by my mother while my father kept away from us both in this very flat, even though our house was only commuting distance. I was more like a doll for her to play with than a person in my own right, with my own thoughts and feelings. A good family life?

I hook my hair behind my ear. 'And when I started getting the attention from men instead of you getting it – attention I didn't want, because I knew it was going to make you angry with me – that was it for you, wasn't it? So it's easier for me to keep men at a distance and let you steal the limelight. When you talk about me having a husband and children, I haven't got much chance of that happening, have I?'

There's a fearful pause, and I brace myself and count the seconds, waiting with self-loathing for that ominous gap between lightning and thunder.

'You want to take a good look at yourself,' my mother says in a voice that's dangerously low. 'You've never had the male attention that I've had. I make sure I always fulfil my potential, unlike you. So don't blame me for the way your life's turned out.'

And there it is, her truth versus my truth.

What did I expect? I'd expected her to apologise and hug me and beg forgiveness, but for that to happen she'd have to see it from my point of view.

My throat's tight from the tension and my heart's pounding with anxiety, but my tears recede before they can spill and I'm bitterly grateful for that.

'And the reason that I dressed you up was that you were such a shy, insecure little thing, I wanted to make you more confident,' she says as she gets to her feet. 'I'm going to bed.'

It's been a pretty shit day all round. I can't breathe properly. I bend over and hug my knees until the blood comes back into my head.

What have I done with my life? I've tried to cure people with fashion. Alexa's comment comes back to me and in my mother's voice I can hear her saying: *Have you any idea how trivial you sound?*

My mother slams the bedroom door. I lie on the sofa and wrap myself in my Burberry trench coat, designed for soldiers fighting in the Great War, and try to sleep.

# LOT 22

*A Givenchy midnight-blue, full-length evening coat, ¾ sleeves,*
*frog-fasteners, couture-labelled, sold as seen.*

My mother and I are living like flatmates who steal each other's yoghurts: we're icily polite.

I'm about to get settled on the sofa for the night, when I get a frantic phone call from Moss telling me that Dinah's very upset and he doesn't know what to do. He sounds so desperate that I get dressed again, pulling on a midnight-blue evening coat that has the voluminous warmth of a comfort blanket, and catch an Uber taxi to Hampstead.

It's a dark, cloudy night. As I walk up their path I can smell a fire burning.

Moss meets me anxiously at the door in a navy silk dressing gown.

'She's out the back,' he says, 'destroying everything I made her. Come this way.' And he lets me down the side of the house and opens the side gate for me.

There's a fire burning at the far end of the garden and Dinah's silhouetted against the billowing smoke.

'Moss – what am I supposed to say to her?'

He raises his hands in surrender. 'She won't listen to me,' he says. 'God knows, I've tried talking.'

I walk over the soft, dewy grass with no idea how I can help her or how I can stop this desolate act of destruction. She hasn't seen me in the dark.

The fire flares and spits and in the dark heart of the flames I can see a garment, black and smouldering. Dinah's poking it aggressively with the handle of a yard brush.

'Dinah?'

I've startled her. She grabs my wrist.

'Look at it!' she says contemptuously. 'It doesn't even burn.'

I snatch the brush out of her hand and move away from the intolerable heat of the fire. Muslin garment bags are piled in a wheelbarrow and I feel sick to my soul to see them. 'That's your answer, is it? You're going to burn all of your clothes, your collection, your history?'

'It's worthless, so who cares?'

'I care! You've got to stop this. Think of Moss.'

She coughs and fans the smoke away with her hand. 'Why should I? This is all I've got to show for my life. What use is it? In the end it's all ashes anyway.'

'Don't say that! Don't destroy them out of anger – it's just – *wasteful*. Burning everything isn't the answer.'

'It's *my* answer,' she says defiantly. 'Pah! I'm finished with it all.'

'But you looked gorgeous in them. They were perfect for you, you always looked amazing.'

'You don't know what you're talking about,' she says, pulling my arm. 'Give me my stick back! They're all fake. His love was fake. Our marriage was fake. What have I got to look forward to?' She shrugs. 'I'm eighty-nine. My life's over.'

I don't know how to deal with emotion except by shutting myself away from it and I wrap my coat tightly around me. My eyes are stinging with smoke and tears. What the hell? Maybe she's right and in the end it is pointless, trivial and all for nothing.

She stabs the burning jacket and holds it up high. Her gleeful contempt breaks my heart and suddenly I've had enough; I can't cope with her anger. 'Oh, why should I care? They're your clothes. Do what you want with them.'

'I will!' She picks up a garment bag and holds it towards the flames, watching me defiantly, daring me stop her.

I start back to the house; the windows throw squares of light before my feet.

'I *will* do what I want!' she shouts after me. 'I don't need your permission for that! Who cares? Who cares what *I* do?'

Let her deal with her own problems, because I can't. I'm shivering with tension despite the warm night and as I get to the steps, Moss is looking out of the kitchen window, his hands cupped around his eyes, trying to make us out in the dark.

Behind me, Dinah starts crying – a heart-rending wail of melancholy, of grief.

I'm so close to leaving and I can't wait to go, but I can't leave her like this, I can't ignore her.

And so I turn and make that dread trudge down the smoke-hazed garden, dragging my reluctant shadow back to her.

She sees me coming. 'What are you doing back here? I don't need you! Leave me alone!' She kicks a burning log back onto the fire.

But I can't go. I owe her. All this time we've been together and I haven't told her what she did for me, how much it meant. 'I can't, Dinah. You changed my life ten years ago,' I tell her, 'when we first met. I've never thanked you for it.'

Dinah's silent, looking at me now, all darkness against the flames except for the steady light of her gaze. The wind shifts the smoke towards us in the damp garden.

She puts the stick down and leans on it heavily, weighed down with age and emotion. She shields her eyes from the glow of the window. 'No. You and me? We met before?'

'Yes. In Stables Market. It was a sunny May morning. Warm. The cobbles were gleaming like black pearls. It was sleepy at that time of the day; many of the stalls weren't even open yet.'

'It's true; I like it best in the morning,' she agrees.

'Yeah. Me, too.' That's something we share. 'I hadn't slept. I'd been worrying about my future, after uni. They tell you that you can be anything you want, that there are no limits to what you can accomplish if you put your mind to it, but it's not true.' I can feel the pressure of failure crushing me like I felt it then. 'I'd seen a dress in the market. It was beautiful and it lifted my spirits. It was the one thing that reassured me I still had some capacity for happiness. I'd gone to look at it three or four times and each time I was scared it would have been sold.'

'You should have bought it!'

'I couldn't.' The smoke stings my eyes. 'I didn't deserve it.'

'Oh.' She shifts position and her face is lost in the dark. 'This dress, what did it look like?' she asks keenly.

'Sleeveless, with a lime green knee-length skirt and a turquoise bodice with a keyhole neckline. The neckline and hem have square-cut faceted turquoise crystals and the fabric, it's two-tone, turquoise and green.'

'I remember you!' she says suddenly. 'All in black and very annoyed when I looked at the dress, like you wanted to kill me. You hated it that an old lady talked to you.'

'Yeah, you made it worse – you were everything I wanted to be: sophisticated, worldly. I hoped you'd walk past and leave us alone. Me and the dress, I mean.'

At the time I thought I was safely hidden in the shadows of her superiority, but her heels stuttered to a halt beside me.

'Beautiful colour,' she'd said approvingly, nodding at the frock.

I'd hung it back on the rack, in the middle, hiding it where it was less likely to catch someone else's eye.

'I told you it wasn't my kind of thing – save you thinking I was delusional. But you didn't go away. You came around in front of me and stepped right into my line of vision, looking me up and down through your sunglasses, your red lips the same colour as your suit. You walked your fingers along the hangers and found it again, the lime green-and-turquoise dress, and unhooked it from the rack, lifted it up to the sunlight to admire. '*So* beautiful,' you murmured.

She'd balanced the hook of the hanger on her finger and let the frock dangle. In the breeze the weight of the crystals and the built-in shaping made it flash and dance under the spotlight of the sun. The crystals sprinkled light around us like confetti.

'I thought you were going to buy it.' If she'd bought it then, in front of me, I swear I would have killed her.

But after admiring it for herself she made room for it again in the middle of the rail and closed the other dresses around to hide it, just as I'd done, and regarded me over the top of her shades. Her eyes were dark and intelligent. She seemed to look at me for a long time and I didn't look away – I trusted her in the same way that I'd trust a doctor who'd called me in urgently and was studying my notes, with that same sense of fatalism, of my future being in her hands.

'Don't do it,' she said.

'No, I'm not going to. It's too small.'

'Not the frock. I mean your plan. You have a plan, don't you, that you want to carry out? I'm telling you. Don't.'

I shook my head, ashamed and confused. It was as if she could see the paracetamol that I'd been popping out of the blister packs into my jewellery box, to see me through my lonely evenings. 'I don't know what you mean.'

Dinah Moss pushed the handles of her bag up to the crook

of her elbow and put her hand to the pearls at her throat. 'My mistake. I apologise.'

She glanced at her watch and seemed surprised by the time. The gesture seemed overdone, just for my benefit. I shield my eyes from the fire. 'You said to me, "Buy the dress. It's waiting for *you*. It'll change your life."'

Dinah chuckled. 'Was I right?'

'Yes. And that's why I'm here. I owe you a future,' I tell her. 'Thank you.'

I'm breathing deeply, as if I've been running.

Dinah is silent, looking at me now, a steady gleam in her eye. The wind shifts the smoke towards us in the damp garden. 'So I did that for you, long ago,' she says, marvelling. She rubs her eyes. 'And now, you and I, we are friends.'

'Yes. Strange how things work out, isn't it?'

The burning wood pops, releasing a shower of red sparks, and she turns and prods the remains of the jacket, sprawled black in the embers.

Her anger has burned off. The relief feels like the freshness of the air when a storm has passed. 'Let's take these clothes back inside.'

We carry them between us and climb the steps. On the doorstep we lay them down to take off our shoes.

She goes inside and I hear her say something to Moss. He's still leaning heavily with his forehead pressed against the window, looking out into the garden.

Dinah puts her hand on his shoulder and he drops to the floor like a felled tree.


Moss is on a trolley in a cubicle in A & E at the Royal Free Hospital when Dinah and I get there in our Uber. His eyes are closed.

A young guy in a pale blue tunic stops by. We look at him

eagerly. He could be a doctor, a nurse or a cleaner for all we know.

'It's good that they're keeping an eye on him,' I say to Dinah. She's picking mud off her jacket. We both smell strongly of smoke.

'Ha! Good for whom?' She looks at her husband. 'Look at him! He doesn't want to be in here. It's not safe in hospital. Too many sick people in one place.'

'Yeah, that's the idea.'

Dinah brushes a stray hair from my shoulder. 'Dahlink, you don't want to know what goes on in these places. He's under *observation*.' She makes it sound sinister. 'They're doing tests with his blood.'

'He's been working hard.' I get a pang of conscience. 'Dinah, you'd tell me, wouldn't you, if it was too much for him?'

'Bah! Work? Don't worry; it's not the work. They think it's a virus, maybe. Give me your phone to call David. He'll want to be here.'

David joins us twenty minutes later. His hair is mussed up, as if he's just got out of bed.

'Hello,' he says distractedly, coming inside the blue screens with us and looking at Moss, who's propped up by pillows. 'Poor guy. Do they know what's wrong with him?'

Dinah pats a footstool for him to sit on. She smooths her skirt over her knees, covering the holes in her dark stockings. 'A virus, they think. They're doing tests,' she says.

'Tests. Good. How are you bearing up?'

'I'm fine. I called you not for help but because it's good for you to keep busy. Take your mind off your broken heart.'

'Off my . . . ? Yes.' He turns his attention to me. 'Are you okay?'

'Yes, thanks.'

'You've got these . . . black smudges on your face.'

I get out my make-up mirror. Crikey. 'Smuts,' I explain. 'Dinah was having a bonfire.'

He looks at me quizzically.

Dinah takes her husband's limp hand and strokes his fingers tenderly. 'I'm thinking we can move into the Otto Schiff care home for the elderly. Where you go, I go.' She turns to us. 'You know Otto Schiff?'

David and I shrug. 'Sorry.'

She's surprised we don't know him. 'Otto Schiff helped us to come to this country as refugees. He was a lovely man, very English-looking, in a nice, sober suit, of German origin but looking very British, very understated, apart from the monocle. The first thing he gave us when we got here was a little blue book, a handbook: *Helpful Information and Guidance for every Refugee*. Written by German Jewish refugees who knew the ropes. You remember the handbook, Moss?' she asks, shaking his hand.

Moss's breathing doesn't change.

'It was important not to be a burden on our new country. We wanted to integrate. The Jewish community supported us, every last penny. Coming here, I was fifteen, still a child really. I'd left my country, my home, everything – and now I was in a new land feeling . . . what can I say? Not just relief, but also self-pity. This handbook, it told us how to behave so that we'd fit in and be treated with respect, and it was a very good handbook except for one thing.'

David and I sit forward in expectation.

She holds her hands up in the air. 'It advised us not to dress in a way that would catch the eye! We were guests here, you see, and like now there was anti-Semitism; it was better for us not to attract attention to ourselves.' She chuckles to herself. 'After all we'd been through! Don't catch the eye! It's crazy! But you know, it was helpful.'

She straightens the sheet covering Moss's chest and she sighs.

After midnight, Moss is moved to a ward and put on an intravenous drip.

Once he's settled for the night, Dinah asks David wearily if he'll take her home. I walk with them to his car, which is parked around the corner, in Fleet Road.

'Jump in, Fern. I'll drop you off afterwards,' he says to me.

At Dinah's, the grey smoke is still drifting up behind the house and I go with her to her door. She flexes her shoulders and puts the key in the lock, hesitating before opening it. She grips my wrist and looks up into my face anxiously. 'Who would think that this day would end like this?'

'I know.' I feel a rush of love for her. 'I hope you get some sleep. Call me if . . . well, for any reason,' I tell her.

She pats my hand. 'I will. Good girl.'

I'm touched; it's a long time since I've been called that.

As I get back in the car, David turns to look at me.

I can see part of his face lit up by the street lamp.

'Where to?' he asks.

'What are the choices?' I reply, half joking, raking my smoky fringe out of my eyes. 'Fancy going clubbing, do you? If I stay out long enough, my mother'll be in bed when I get back.'

'You mean Annabel.'

I laugh. 'Yes, Annabel.'

He looks serious. 'You don't have to go back, Fern. You could stay at my place.'

I feel a sudden adrenaline rush. 'What?'

'I've got a spare room.'

'Phew, ha ha,' I say, trying to sound normal in a 'good old Fern' way. But, oh, the thought of a real bed, of actually lying

307

flat for a few hours' sleep instead of bent up on the sofa, is so appealing. 'That would be brilliant.'

'Yeah?' He grins. 'Let's go, then.'

He drives towards Chalk Farm and turns left down Harmood Street before pulling up outside a small house with a red front door flanked by two olive trees in terracotta pots.

'This is it,' he says.

I look at the house through the car window and time seems to slow. I've got butterflies in my stomach. It looks so neat and he's so warm, and now the idea that I'm going there so that I can lie in a spare bed by myself shows a woeful lack of imagination.

I lean back against the headrest and meet his gaze. His eyes search mine and linger in a way that goes deeper than friendship.

'Fern,' he says softly.

I touch the hook at the throat of my blue velvet evening coat and undo it because it's suddenly too restricting. 'Yes?' I can feel the heat between us as I hold his gaze.

'Let's go inside,' he says.

*This is it.* My heart is pounding. We open the car doors at the same time and, choreographed under the lamplight, we step out over our shadows and walk across the road, footsteps beating rhythmically in sync. He points his remote at the car and it peeps and flashes its lights coyly. From his house there's a loud eruption of noise: a dog starts barking . . .

'Shit!' I say, stopping dead while David carries on up the path alone, keys now jingling in his pocket.

I feel a rush of adrenaline, and escalating panic. I'd forgotten about the dog.

I am overwhelmed by a sense of danger. It's barking as if it's using an amplifier.

It's barking a warning bark, a get-off-my-property message, a clear leave-my-owner-alone threat.

It's barking with a rage that's directed at me, so vicious that I can feel myself shrinking, powerless and vulnerable.

I quickly pull the metal gate closed with a clang. I've got to get away before David opens the door, because once that door is open that dog's going to come rushing out, motivated, impelled, galvanised to attack me by the smell of fear – and that gate's not going to stop it in its tracks.

I run back as fast as I can towards Chalk Farm Road, coat flying, my vision pulsing with the throb of my heart, hoping I can find a bar still open in which to take refuge. Reggae music is playing up to the right, so I bowl into Cotton's Rhum Shack and push into the crowd at the bar, into safety, my breath sobbing in my throat.

'Slow down, lady,' the barman says over the sound of steel drums. 'We're not closing yet.'

I put a tenner on the bar. 'JD, no ice, please.'

'Bad night, huh?'

'I've escaped from the jaws of death,' I tell him, getting my phone from my bag to find David's number to explain the truth about why I ran away.

But then I stop and think about it, because this is how it'll go. If I call him, David'll ask me what just happened and I'll have to explain to him that I'm scared of dogs. He'll laugh and tell me that his dog is an old softy who just wants to play. He'll then want me to go back and make friends with it, not knowing how much I hate dogs and how much they hate me. Only I know that and because of that I won't be able to do it. I won't be able to force myself to do it because my fear will cause every nerve in my body to scream at me to get away for my own protection.

'Here you go.' The barman slides my whisky to me.

'Thanks.'

I clutch my drink, feeling sick and empty. Never tell a dog lover you're scared of dogs, that's what I've learnt.

I message him instead:

Just to let you know I'm okay and thanks for the lift.

I add an *x* and then delete it again.

After a few moments he replies:

Thanks for letting me know.

The whisky is mellow in my mouth and I can feel the beat of the drums in my bones. I put my phone back in my bag. I'm an idiot. Knowing that doesn't stop me from hating myself. It wouldn't have worked anyway, with David and me.

I'm never going to be real enough for him and he deserves someone genuine, not someone like me who hides behind clothes.

# LOT 23

*Black leather biker jacket, Topshop, 1990s, zip front,*
*stud detail, size 12.*

Next morning, on my way to the bathroom, worrying about Moss and embarrassed about David, I fall over the footstool that my mother has moved from its usual place in front of the television.

As I shower, I can see she's slowly reclaiming the flat for herself and edging me out. Her cosmetics take up most of the bathroom shelves.

I can't find the cereal because she's rearranged the contents of the kitchen cupboards so that nothing is where I think it is anymore. I'm the apologetic guest who's outstayed her welcome.

She's right, though. It is time I moved out and stood on my own two feet. Being dependent on them is a lot more stressful than getting a regular job and it's a high price to pay for sleeping on a sofa when I could find a flat-share.

A regular job . . . this is the way I look at it. I've given self-employment a shot, but it's time to move forward. I come to my decision; the mature option, the only one I can make. I'm giving up the stall.

I wonder how Moss is. It's too early to call Dinah because

hopefully she's catching up on her sleep. In an hour's time I'll be facing David with some kind of explanation for my wild dash into the night. So I start googling Ideal Flat-Shares, when I hear the friendly sound of Lucy walking around over my head.

Like a vengeful fury, my mother bursts in from the hall with a Super Mop and bangs furiously on the ceiling. The footsteps above us go silent and I can imagine Lucy tiptoeing around up there, wondering what exactly my mother's on.

'Morning,' I say.

My mother hasn't got time for pleasantries. 'What kind of flooring has she got up there?'

'Ooh, er, I'm not sure,' I reply vaguely.

'It's supposed to be carpeted. Is it carpeted?'

'Yes, carpeted,' I lie and change the subject. 'Are you and Dad getting a divorce?'

'No. We like each other better at a distance, that's all.'

*Same goes*, I want to say.

'What are you doing on that phone?' she asks sharply.

'Looking for somewhere else to live.'

It's the right answer. I can see her relax. Good. I want her to look at me in a new light.

'You'll need to have a regular income,' she says, straightening a mirror that she's put up in the lounge. 'The sooner you leave that market the better, because the truth is, Fern, you never did have a head for business and you should have understood that by now. You're useless without me. I'm going for a shower.'

While she's in the bathroom I go into the wardrobe in my bedroom and take out my black leather biker jacket and Dr. Martens, black T-shirt, black skinny jeans. Her contempt corrodes like acid. I grab my largest sunglasses from my bedside drawer. Times like this, I need all the protection I can get.

Walking along the canal with the water winking in the sunlight, I keep thinking over all the things that have happened in the last few days, like taking the fakes to Tallulah Young's, and wondering about all the chances I've squandered without achieving anything in life.

I'm anticipating with dread some kind of hideous scene with David, where he demands an explanation and tells me he was worried sick the previous night. I'm prepared to apologise in all sorts of different ways with increasing servility; I can do it until I feel as if I'm dragging myself along the ground, the lowest of the low.

So when I get to the market it's a bit of a surprise to find him sitting in his chair in his usual place, wearing a white shirt with the sleeves rolled up, reading his astronomy book. I take my sweaty hands out of my leather jacket to face him. 'Hello.'

'Hello,' he says, perfectly normally, using his finger as a bookmark. 'Any news about Moss?'

'No. You?' What a stupid thing to say. Of course he hasn't had any news, or he wouldn't have asked me if I'd had any.

He doesn't point this out. He says, 'No.' And then, after a moment, 'Who are you today? Britney Spears?'

This is quite funny. I feel the dread lifting and I take off my sunglasses.

Across the way, the antiques dealer is opening up, and he turns and gives us a wave. I love it here, I think with a pang. I don't want to leave.

I unfold my chair and put my sunglasses back on, propping my legs in front of me, and I stare at the shine on my boots. 'David?'

'Yes?'

'My parents are worried that I'll never amount to anything because I'm wasting my life.'

He squints at me in the sunlight. 'Oh yeah? What did they have in mind for you?'

'A good job, a nice marriage, children.'

He shrugs. 'That's probably what all parents want for their children and what most people want for themselves, eventually. I thought you were going to say they wanted you to go into politics or something completely out there.'

'Yes, well, they'd prefer it to a market stall and second-hand clothes, that's for sure. When it comes down to it, I know that fashion is about as trivial as it gets, but when Lucy's flat was on fire, I risked my life to save those dresses. And when Tallulah Young told us that the suits weren't made by Chanel, I felt physically sick. And then when I saw Dinah trying to burn that suit, so angry and inconsolable, I thought – it can't really be that important, can it?'

One vertical crease pinches between his dark eyebrows.

Before he can say anything, I help him out. 'You don't have to answer that. Anyway. I'm going to look for a job as a sales assistant.'

'What? You're going to quit the market?' he says, shocked.

As if I don't feel bad enough. 'If I give you a month's notice, does that give you enough time to find someone else to share the space with?'

He slumps back in his seat looking baffled and shakes his head. 'Fern, is this your mother's idea of you getting on in life?'

'It's not a regular job with a regular income. She says I haven't got a head for business.'

'Your business is doing fine, from what I can see.'

'But I've got to think of the future,' I say lamely. When he doesn't reply, I stand on the chair, unhook the Bespoke Tailoring and Alterations sign and roll it up. 'I'll be at the back of the shop; I'm going to make a start on Moss's alterations.'

'I didn't know you could sew.'

'My degree is in fashion. I had to make my own designs, obviously.'

'Obviously,' he repeats as if he hadn't thought about it before.

All in all, that wasn't so bad, was it? I feel like crap, though. At the back of the shop I start sorting through the clothes on the rail. It's like revisiting old friends; I know these clothes and I know their new owners, too. Moss has pinned some of them, so it's obvious what needs doing. But there are also ones that only Moss knows what's meant to be done with them. Or maybe they've already been done? I look through my client book, putting asterisks next to the women I need to call later to check, and then I take off my jacket and get started.

I work until late morning and when I hear voices at the front of the shop, I assume that they're customers of David's. But after a few minutes, to my delight, Kim appears. He's wearing a lemon cotton skirt suit with boat shoes and he looks as refreshing as a cold drink. I switch off the sewing machine, straighten up and rub my back. He's got two well-dressed friends with him, and he introduces them as Betty and Mercia. The three of them look wonderfully fresh and summery.

'We're having lunch on the My Fair Lady restaurant boat at Walker's Quay and we thought we'd drop by to say hello,' Kim says. 'Any news on Moss? David tells me he's in hospital.'

I fill him in on recent events and he's shocked.

'She was burning her lovely *suits*?' he asks avidly, then he turns to the two women to explain. 'Dinah's the most stylish woman you could ever meet. Who cares if her suits aren't really Chanel? I'd buy them.'

'I always buy Hobbs,' Betty says. 'I like a print. This is Hobbs,' she says, holding out the skirt of the dress as if she's about to curtsy. 'Mercia can't wear Hobbs. You can't wear Hobbs, can you, Mercia?'

'I'm too short for Hobbs. They give me a hump. I need a petite in dresses. I'm short-waisted.' Mercia catches sight of herself in the mirror in the dressing room and turns sideways on. 'No hump, you see?' She glances at her watch. 'Kim, we've got plenty of time before embarking, so we're going to browse,' she says.

While she and Betty look through the rails, Kim sits on the edge of the table and asks which hospital Moss is in.

'The Royal Free,' I tell him.

'Are you going to see him tonight?'

'Yes, I'm going to call in after work.'

'I'll come with you,' he says, suddenly distracted by Betty and Mercia going into the dressing room with several dresses each.

We watch the curtains bulge out occasionally as they get changed and then they push aside the curtain for the big reveal, posing with aplomb.

Betty comes out wearing a black-and-white gingham check shirtwaister. Mercia's found an orange cheesecloth kaftan with turquoise beading at the neck that doesn't give her a hump.

Kim claps in admiration. 'My word! You look like models,' he says fondly.

To my happy surprise, bearing in mind they were browsing, they buy the dresses.

I wrap up their new purchases and get out the card machine. They pay and sign the client book and off they go for lunch, with Kim gallantly carrying their bags, his lemon skirt billowing in the breeze.

I go back to my sewing and when I've done enough to take a break, I look for the book so as to call the owners of the unmarked dresses. Bizarrely, I can't find it anywhere. Increasingly frustrated, I decide to stop looking. Sooner or later, it's bound to turn up.

# KIM

On the narrowboat, Mercia, Betty and I are having the Boatman's Buffet.

'Looks wonderful,' Mercia says.

'As long as the boatman doesn't mind,' Betty adds, laughing.

I'm looking out at the green canal banks; we're motoring slowly past joggers and cyclists and dog walkers and tramps, and I'm thinking about Moss's collapse. For some reason, it strongly reminds me of the game of British Bulldogs, where after each run from one end of the street to the other the players thin out until there are more bulldogs than players. We're in our eighties and Moss is even older than us. We're thinning out, too.

It's not the only thing on my mind, though. David told me that Fern is giving up the stall. It bothers him and it bothers me, too. I feel a sense of responsibility for her. More than that – I feel regret for a wasted talent that's nothing to do with her love of clothes but more about her ability to see people looking their best. Trivial is the word David said she used. Trivial! I wouldn't call it that. But watching her working at the back of the shop, dressed all in black with those solid workmen's boots, she looked as if she were at a funeral for her own dreams.

'Wine! Oh yes, wine! Kim? Ship's white, or ship's rosé?'

We opt for the ship's rosé and our food is wonderful,

poached salmon and three salads, just the thing for a hot day, with a choice of desserts to come.

'You're awfully quiet all of a sudden, Kim,' Betty says to me.

'Betty, how would you go about convincing someone that the course of action they're taking isn't the right one?'

'Who are we talking about?'

'Fern Banks. She's going to give up the stall to be a sales assistant.'

'What a shame! Just when we've discovered her!' Mercia says in dismay.

Betty looks thoughtful. 'In answer to your question, Kim, I don't think you can convince anyone to change their minds once they've made them up. I don't think you've got a right to.'

'That's pretty well what David said.'

'I do think David's rather good-looking, didn't you, Betty? He reminded me of Bertie. The same build. I'm talking about when he was young, of course. Did you see his light boxes?'

We're just passing London Zoo and Mercia says she can see a giraffe. I like listening to Betty and Mercia talking. We talk a lot when we're together. Like me, they live alone, taking full responsibility for themselves, which is no mean feat as I've discovered. It takes a surprising amount of discipline to live decently and eat regularly, and do the dishes, and make the bed just for oneself.

'This salad is wonderful. I love beetroot, don't you? I'd have liked one of the light boxes but I'm decluttering.'

'So am I. I'm having Cato back,' Betty says decisively. 'I'm going to see if he'll take the Turkish kilims that we bought from the rug shop in Kentish Town. They're curling at the edges and I forget and trip up. It's age, I suppose. They're a potential deathtrap and I don't want to be remembered as the

Pensioner Killed by her Kilim. He's a nice boy, isn't he, Cato? And ambitious. He wants to be an auctioneer. Didn't you find him pleasant?' She's directing the question at me.

'Oh yes, very pleasant,' I reply.

She tilts her head curiously. 'You're still thinking about Fern Banks, aren't you?'

'Yes, I am. I'd like to do something nice for her.'

'Such as?'

'I'm not sure yet.'

'She has some beautiful things. When we came out of the dressing room, you said we looked like models,' Mercia remembers coyly.

I laugh. 'It's true! You did! You had the look!' Then I look under her table. Her frock is tucked under her chair in the bag.

'What are you doing down there? Top him up, Mercia,' Betty says, 'he's fun when he's tipsy.'

'Tipsy! I'm outraged!' I roar. She's right, though, I am, rather.

'We should have a demonstration outside her shop, looking our best selves, to convince her to stay,' Mercia says.

'With placards,' Betty says. 'Save Fern Banks!'

'Exactly. Mercia, please could you pass me your carrier bag from under your chair?'

Mercia laughs. 'Kim, you're serious, aren't you? Here you are!' She passes it to me under the table. 'Whyever do you want it?'

'I've done something rather underhand,' I admit, reaching into the bag. 'I'm afraid I've gone and borrowed Fern's client book. I want to see who's interested in joining me in some kind of tribute to her. Where shall we start?'

# LOT 24

*Brown fitted jacket, viscose, with belt, narrow lapels,
silk-lined, small.*

When I get home from the hospital that night, my mother's
in a bad frame of mind. She's sitting at the table with her
head in her hands, her fair hair spilling dramatically over
her eyes.

We quickly reach a stalemate, both waiting for the other
to make the first approach.

When I don't greet her, she looks up grudgingly.

'Oh, *there* you are,' she says, as if we've been playing a long-
drawn-out game of hide-and-seek.

'Good evening,' I say patiently. 'How's your day been?'

She seems to be examining the question for sarcasm or
other signs of subordination but she decides to treat it at face
value.

'Hideous,' she says. 'You've made me like this.'

'How so?'

'I had lunch with Ruth Bennett.'

Intriguing. 'How is she?' I ask innocently.

'She asked after you. She wanted to know what you were
doing. Of course, I had to tell her about the market and it
makes me feel *this* big,' she says, thrusting her thumb and

forefinger into my face. I retreat into the armour of my leather jacket.

'And then she asked about Jonathan. Of course, he got his side of the story in first, so there was no possible chance of her having any sympathy for me, was there? She thinks I should go home before some other woman insinuates herself into his life.'

I bite my tongue to stop myself from agreeing with Ruth. Anyone who's seen my parents together automatically has a soft spot for my father because he does act as if he's slightly henpecked and it makes them want to spring to his defence even if he's in the wrong, which he quite often is. But instead of pointing out his mistakes quietly, my mother will speak to him sharply and suddenly – he's the good guy even if the misdemeanour actually was his fault.

My mother looks at me dolefully. 'You don't think another woman has insinuated herself into his life already, do you?'

To be honest, I do think it's weird that he hasn't come looking for her.

And it's worrying that he seems quite happy without her. Every now and then I find myself wondering what his yoga teacher looks like. That's the first thing I would have checked out.

My mother's still waiting for an answer and the right answer here is: of course not; why would he look elsewhere when he's got you?

But the honest answer is: in the circumstances, maybe.

'Have you asked him?'

'Of course not! I'm not that needy!'

'I bought some cold chicken and a salad for supper,' I tell her, putting them on the worktop.

'I'm not hungry,' she says stiffly.

Suddenly, I'm not, either, and I put them in the fridge.

Somebody comes down the outside steps and rings the doorbell, and I hurry to answer it, glad of the diversion. It's Cato, with a black bin liner of clothes over his shoulder – I assume they're clothes. From his general tweediness they could just as easily be pheasants.

'Who is it?' my mother asks, coming to see and preparing to disapprove, probably thinking it's Lucy from upstairs.

'Cato Hamilton, meet my mother, Annabel.' There's no getting round the 'my mother' bit. 'Cato deals in antiques.'

'How do you do?' Cato says, wiping his feet on the doormat and summing up my mother in a glance as a person who wouldn't appreciate a 'Yo!' as a salutation.

'Come in,' my mother says to him, and for the first time she notices the bin bag over his shoulder and turns her warmth down a notch, glancing at me quizzically.

I block his way. 'Cato – I meant to call you. I'm giving up the shop because—'

'She needs a regular income,' my mother finishes for me over my shoulder.

'I see. So you don't need any more stock,' he says to me.

'Yeah, that's right.'

'No problem. Goodbye, Mrs Banks.'

I'm gutted as he turns away and I have serious second thoughts about my willpower. 'Hang on, Cato. Anything interesting? What's the provenance?'

'They belong to a hypnotherapist, Alexandra Booth. She was given a Marie Kondo book for her birthday and she's had a clear-out. Clothes, silver, paintings. I've got a van full of her stuff. These are great times, Fern,' he says cheerfully. 'This is going to be known as the Year of the Great Uncluttering. And when everyone decides that it's just not a home without knick-knacks, the next big thing will be people flocking in their droves to buy everything back.'

He does make me laugh.

'I wouldn't mind having a quick look,' I tell him, desperately feeding my addiction.

Throughout this conversation, my mother has been standing behind me, close enough for me to step on her foot if I wanted to. Predictably, she wants to argue against having any more second-hand clothes in her flat, but Cato Hamilton hasn't felt the full power of her charm yet, so she's torn. Not for long, though, because a few seconds later he dumps the clothes on the sofa.

There are a couple of short, animal-print dresses with flounces around the hem, a sleeveless pink-and-brown pleated dress, a formal, backless, full-length column dress and a jacket of a glorious, glossy, milk chocolate brown with shoulder pads and a narrow belt that would be just perfect for my interviews to come. I try it on and look at myself in my mother's new mirror.

It's a perfect fit. If I saw anyone wearing this jacket, I'd hire them on the spot.

When I turn back, my mother's holding up the pleated dress against herself.

'Very becoming,' Cato says to her.

'Do you think so?'

'Oh, absolutely.'

I'm beginning to realise what my father feels like and why he wants her to find an interest of her own. She seems so aimless, somehow, as if she hasn't so much got interests as distractions.

'Fern?' she asks.

'Fantastic. Try it on.'

For a moment I have a brief fantasy that we'll bond over this dress, that this'll be the moment our relationship changes and she begins to understand the way I feel about my clothes.

But she drops it on the sofa as if she wishes she'd used tongs and tightens up her mouth in distaste.

'I'll have the jacket,' I tell Cato and we fold the rest of the clothes back into the bin bag. I walk with him up the steps and pay him for the jacket by his van, out of earshot of my mother.

'The business not working for you?' he asks.

'It's not that; it's going all right, actually. It's just that I need something a bit more stable because I need to get another place, before we drive each other crazy.'

'Sorry to hear that. It's a shame.'

'Fern?' I can hear my mother calling again.

He fist-bumps me and gets into the van.

Back in the flat, my mother's annoyed that I went outside with Cato, so I put the brown belted jacket back on and look at myself in the mirror to calm myself, reinvented once more.

# LOT 25

*A post-war make-do-and-mend parachute silk wedding dress, 1949, fit and flare, with long sleeves, sweetheart neckline, short train. Size 8/34*

I'm kneeling on the floor in the shop wearing a neon pink dress that outdazzles me, neatly marking out Closing Down Sale on the reverse of the Bespoke Tailoring and Alterations sign, when Alexa and Jenna turn up bright and breezy in sports gear, hugging David like a long-lost friend. I get to my feet awkwardly, not sure what to expect after Alexa's previous visit.

'Where are you off to?' David asks them.

'We've just come from Pilates,' they say together.

'We've got a new teacher,' Jenna adds. 'Gigi's gone to Spain.'

'And not with Max, either,' Alexa adds.

David rubs the edge of his jaw and his eyes narrow. 'I know. I heard.'

Alexa turns to me. 'Fern, I'm sorry I was such a bitch last time we met,' she says. 'Emotionally, I was a mess.'

'She's not usually like that,' Jenna says. 'It's been on her conscience.'

'It has,' Alexa agrees.

'Oh, sure, yes, that's okay, forget it,' I say, trying not to wonder how David knows Gigi's in Spain. Not that it's any of my business, obviously.

'Max wants to come back home,' Alexa says.

'What an idiot,' Jenna comments, but there's a wistfulness in Alexa's eyes that tells me she's thinking about it.

'Bloody hell, it's the runaway bride,' Alexa says suddenly, pointing across the yard.

Stuck in the archway from Gilbeys Yard is Dinah, wearing an ivory wedding dress, looking like one of those touchy, snobby old ladies that you see in Claridge's, holding their chins high to smooth out their necks. Also, slightly crazy. I wonder with great trepidation whether recent events have tipped her over the edge.

I run over to help her. 'Dinah, what are you doing?'

'The way people stare,' she says indignantly, 'you'd think they'd never seen a wedding dress before. So let them, it's a free country last time I looked.' She adds, with some satisfaction, 'I took up a whole seat on the bus for myself. Fern, where's my chair?'

I fetch her a chair and she sits happily in the front of the shop in her frothy nest of silk. Who doesn't like an audience?

'This is the dress that Moss made for me to be married in. It's based on Norman Hartnell's design of Princess Elizabeth's wedding dress. You recognise the sweetheart neck and the long sleeves, of course.'

'Absolutely,' we agree.

'It's made from parachute silk,' she tells us. 'I'm thinking, this dress has brought me seventy years of happiness and Moss made it with his own hands.'

I can see where she's going with this, her rationale. 'So you're going to forget about the Chanels?'

'Bof! I can't forget,' she says irritably, frowning at me.

'Wouldn't that be convenient? But I am choosing to forgive him. My choice.'

For a moment it doesn't seem as if she's sitting down and we're standing around her.

It's more as if she's way above us and we're sitting at her feet, because none of us says anything at all, it's that simple and that profound.

David seems miles away.

'Yeah,' Alexa says at last, breaking the silence. 'Like you said. Your choice.'

'You,' Dinah says, pointing at David, 'and you,' pointing at me, 'are coming with me to the hospital after work.' She spreads her hands, encompassing Jenna and Alexa. 'I don't know you, but you look like decent people and if you want to come with us to visit an old man, a stranger, I won't stop you.'

After we close, David, Dinah and I get the number twenty-four bus to the hospital, Dinah causing a stir in her wedding gown, and we go to see Moss. This journey has become familiar; we go up the steps, into the lobby, queueing for a lift and watching the floor numbers change with everyone else.

Moss is asleep when we get there. He's not attached to the drip.

'You know how he is,' Dinah says. 'No change. Always asleep.' She drags her chair nearer to him. 'Moss, it's me, your bride.'

The green sheet is rising and falling slowly with his breathing.

'Look at him! So thin!' Dinah tells us loudly, pushing me forward. 'He won't eat. I've tried pressing food against his teeth and he keeps his mouth shut, breaking my heart. Enough.'

Moss isn't thin. But his head is resting back on the pillows

331

and his jaw has dropped open, so he doesn't look good, either.

'He's giving up,' Dinah whispers, playing with the neckline of the dress and staring at him intently with fear in her dark eyes. 'This is something that I've seen before. Death doesn't take you; it invites you home and every day we march towards it, that bit closer, and look behind us to see how far we've come. Oh! Not far at all! It's all there still, everything that we thought we'd left behind.'

David frowns and catches my eye.

Moss grunts in his sleep as if he's heard her. 'Dinah, where is the girl?' he asks suddenly, and we all sit upright and pay attention. His eyes are closed but the words are strong and fluent.

'Hi, Moss, I'm here,' I tell him, sitting forward, and his eyes snap open, dark brown eyes edged with a perfect halo of pale grey.

I've annoyed him, I recognise that scowl. I'm not the girl he's looking for. He shakes his head, defeated.

'Don't worry. Sleep, dahlink,' Dinah tells him softly, rubbing his hand. 'Fern, to think I burned the precious clothes that he made for me with these hands. It makes me ashamed.' She lays his hand back down on his lap. 'So. Now, let's talk business. Have you got your new job yet?'

*Thanks a lot, Dinah, for bringing it up.* 'I've got an interview tomorrow. I was going to tell you.'

'What's this wonderful job you want to leave us for?' Dinah asks.

'Stockroom assistant in Topshop.' The words stick in my throat. 'The thing is,' I say, justifying it, 'they've got a vintage line.'

'Who cares about that? You've got your own vintage line, haven't you?' Dinah bats her hand at me crossly as if she's swatting away a fly. 'Of course, we can't stop you, can we, David? We wouldn't want to.'

*Good,* I think stubbornly. My gaze roves around, from the plastic jug of water on the locker top, to the screen folded back, the felt-tipped name of the consultant on the clipboard, *Mr Khan.* The clock ticks loudly. The neon of my dress leaves after-images on my retinas. I get the feeling I can't win. On the yelling front, that'll do me. I get enough of that at home.

Dinah crosses her legs and her beautiful shoe dangles from her toe. She examines it for a moment before looking up. 'But Fern, if you could just politely explain to me why?'

'Because the perfect fit is superficial and trivial.'

'Oh!' Dinah jumps to her feet. 'Superficial and trivial?' She's as angry as if I've insulted her parents. She turns to David in appeal. 'Can you hear her?'

David has the apprehensive expression of a man who's just realised he's walked into a wasp nest.

'Listen to yourself! It's not trivial what you do! The perfect fit, you call it, but there's more to it than that. Look – you can even make ugly clothes fit. It's not the point, to *fit.* What do you *do?*'

Her anger confuses me. I'm not sure what on earth I do at this very moment. It's like the interview from hell. 'I try to make people look good in their clothes.'

'Look good? Nooo! Come here.' She beckons me.

'What?'

'Come! Look at me!'

As I bend towards her she rubs her fingers roughly against my mouth, startling me. 'Ow!'

She holds her hand in front of my eyes for me to see. Her fingers are red. 'What's that?'

'Lipstick?'

'Just lipstick?'

I nod.

'Pah! Lucky I'm here to tell you that you're wrong. It's not "just" anything. I'm going to tell you something important for you to understand. What does nineteen forty-five mean to you? David?'

Confused, he sits up in his plastic chair like a kid caught out by his teacher. 'The year the war ended?' he asks hesitantly, wondering, like me, where this inquisition is going.

'Exactly. I was in a camp. The camp was Bergen-Belsen.'

My stomach contracts and my skin tightens, chills. *Oh, Dinah.* 'I didn't know.'

She glances at me and plays with her pearl earring. Her eyes soften. 'How could you? I never talk about it. I wasn't in there long, lucky for me. I was there for one winter.' For a moment she's distant; lost in thought.

The tick of the clock, Moss's rasping breath.

'It was long enough to starve, but by some miracle, not long enough to get sick.' Her gaze returns to mine, intense and ageless. 'Day after day we prayed for it to be over, you know? We prayed for the strength to carry on a little longer, not too far ahead, just for one more day because, you know, that's what we were urging each other, we must go on a bit longer.' She sighs deeply. 'Always rumours, that Germany might be defeated tomorrow or the next day or the next month, if we can just hang on. And one day it *was* over.'

Dinah looks down and rubs her fingers distractedly, wiping my lipstick off them. Her lips tighten as she holds back her emotions.

'When the Allies came, we welcomed them in triumph. They were our saviours! We were free!' Her voice drops. 'But Fern, you see, it wasn't over. We were still dying. The horror camp, the British called it, repelled by the inhumanity that had done this to us, made rubbish heaps of human beings, living, dead, the infected and the infectious, lying in our own filth.' She looks from me to David, and we flinch. 'Do you understand? Nothing had changed.' David rubs the bridge of his nose.

For both of us, it's hard to listen to and impossible to comprehend. We've grown to love her. We'd assumed that she and Moss were refugees who'd managed to get themselves here before it got too bad; the ones who'd found a home here before war broke out, the lucky ones.

Dinah shrugs and her mouth turns down. 'There was no great deliverance, after all. We were still hungry, still dying.' She gives a faint smile. 'Then the Red Cross came.' She claps her hands. 'Hooray! We needed medication and food. You know what they brought?'

I shake my head.

'Something that was better than food, and better than medication!' She pushes her sharp little face into mine, puckers her red lips, traces her mouth with her finger and holds it up for me to see. 'Look! This is what they gave us! Red lipstick!' And she bursts into gleeful laughter. 'Red lipstick!'

David and I stare at each other, and then we start laughing feebly with her, not getting the joke.

'They brought lipstick for you?'

'Hundreds of them! The Red Cross brought them! Of all the things that we needed, well, we got these scarlet lipsticks. So now the British medics are grumbling. Well, you can imagine – how crazy is this? Who would send something so trivial as this? So now,' she grips my wrist tightly, jerking me closer to her, 'and this is the important thing I want to tell you, Fern, so listen to me. Those lipsticks were better for us than medication and they were better than any food! We forgot about our hunger altogether. My friend died of typhoid in my arms two days after liberation clutching her lipstick in her hand. Those lipsticks did more for us than all the doctors

335

put together.' She reaches out and pinches my cheek. 'You know why?' Her eyes are eager, willing me to understand. 'Because they made us human again.'

Her eyes are shining with tears. She is silent for a moment, staring into space.

Blinking, I look towards David. He is rubbing his jaw grimly.

'The British soldiers held a dance in the camp,' Dinah continues. 'It didn't matter that during the clean-up, the officers, the Eton chaps, had cleaned the excrement in our stinking huts – those same soldiers put their gentle arms around our skinny bones and we rested our shaved heads against their sweet, boyish shoulders, and oh! It was wonderful, such courtesy. This inmate, Moses, he asked me to dance and we were skin and bone and angles, but I was a girl again and he was a boy.' Her voice tightens as if it's being squeezed. 'So now, Fern, I'm asking you. What did those lipsticks do? Did they transform us? Did they change the way we looked?'

'No,' I whisper, shaking my head but understanding her, and it's a revelation, a justification, a flash of comprehension. 'But they changed the way you felt.'

'Exactly so.' Her smile is kind. 'And is that trivial?'

I shake my head. 'No.'

'So there. That's how it was. And now you know.' She nods and gets to her feet, then bends over her husband. His head dents the pillows and she puts her hands either side of his face and holds him lovingly. 'That's how I met this boy of mine, my Moses.' She kisses him on the mouth.

It seems unbearably poignant and I'm about to look away, when I see Moss has opened his eyes a little, enough to let the light shine out.

'My bride,' he says hoarsely, and his words are muffled against her mouth.

Dinah straightens up. 'I kissed you awake!' She looks at us in astonishment. It's incredible, miraculous!

David gets to his feet, trying to compose himself.

Dinah gets onto the bed and rests her head on her husband's chest, and she looks so relieved, and so beautiful in her wedding gown.

I glance at David and he nods back at me, and we leave them be.

# KIM

Computers are miraculous things. The World Wide Web means I have the world at my fingertips. I'm rushing along in the full flow of information, working through Fern's book and sending emails to her clients, and I'm enjoying the replies that I get back. I get one from a woman who went to a wedding and came home with a boyfriend; a girl who went to a school prom and made up with her estranged mother; a young woman with sight problems who's up for promotion – all sorts of lovely tales. And they all have their ideas for the thank-you party – most vociferously, Betty and Mercia, who fancy themselves as models.

'After all, Daphne Selfe's a model, and she's older than we are,' Betty tells me.

'If you're wearing Fern's clothes for the party, I suppose you will be modelling them,' I reason.

We're helping Cato to roll up Betty's kilims.

'That's not modelling,' Mercia says, keeping out of the way. 'That's just wearing them. We need a catwalk to strut down.'

'I can't see the point of modelling the clothes she's sold you,' Cato says. 'You want to model the clothes that she's got left, the rest of the stock, because she'll have to get rid of it all when she closes.'

'They won't necessarily fit us.'

The kilims, despite being what Enid would describe as a mat rather than a rug, are incredibly heavy. I help Cato to carry them out to the van and we shuffle along with them, dead weights. It's like carrying a body out of the house.

Back inside, Betty has made the tea and a plate of home-made shortbread biscuits.

'We could have an auction,' Cato says. 'I'd willingly be the auctioneer. It's an ambition of mine. It could be a charity auction.'

'And how would that benefit Fern?' Mercia asks.

'Publicity,' Cato says.

'Why does she need publicity if she's going to work in a high-street store?' I point out. We seem to have drifted a long way from the thank-you party that I'd envisaged. 'But I do like the idea of a catwalk.' I can see myself on it, in my blue dress, with a spotlight on me.

'You know her better than we do,' Mercia says. 'What would Fern want, do you think?'

'That's what it all boils down to,' I agree. 'It's not what we want, it's what she'd want. That's what we've got to think about.' But the truth is, I know exactly what she'd like. She'd like to see us being our best selves, as we look through her eyes.

It would be the perfect tribute.

# LOT 26

*Men's black cashmere sweater, medium.*

'Let me look at you,' my mother says as I'm about to leave for my interview in the luscious, fitted brown jacket that I bought from Cato.

I'm half expecting her to spit on a handkerchief and wipe my face with it.

'You'll do, I suppose,' she says. 'Try to look animated, at least.'

I bare my teeth at her, a fake grin.

'Better,' she says. 'Off you go. Do your best.'

I climb the steps from the flat and outside, the sun shines and the world is waiting for me. I think of David and I'm so excited, my stomach flips.

I tuck my hands in my jacket pockets and close them over the business card belonging to Alexandra Booth, the hypno-therapist.

I take it out and read it again.

*Phobias.*

Last night, after seeing Moss wake up, David and I didn't go straight home.

Dinah's story had such a profound influence on us that we felt we needed to be quiet together, to share it and absorb it.

I knew he felt the same as I did, because once we were out of the ward, David pushed up the sleeves of his black cashmere sweater. He said, 'Fern, that was intense. It was as if Dinah brought him back to life. Drink?'

I have seriously never wanted one more. 'For sure.'

We caught the bus back to Chalk Farm and headed to Camden Beach on the roof of the Roundhouse venue.

The evening was cool and we lay back in stripy deckchairs with our feet in the sand, listening to music and drinking mojitos. The sky was streaked with turquoise and pink.

I felt vindicated, as if Dinah had given her blessing to my life choices, for want of a better phrase. I could see things more clearly now.

I was thinking of Dinah telling her story so matter-of-factly, but so determined to get the message over to me, that she gave me the confidence, I suppose, for me to be honest with David in turn.

'The night we were going to your house and I ran away, it was only because . . .'

He turned his head to look at me and the evening sun gilded his lovely face. 'Because?'

I looked into his eyes. 'I was afraid of the dog.'

For a moment, he stared back blankly and then it dawned on him I was telling the truth.

'Oh. I get it. You were scared of the dog, not me. I thought I'd come on too strong.' Then he grinned, as I knew he would; as all dog owners do. 'Seriously? You're scared of Duncan?'

'Yes.' I slumped back in the deckchair and looked at the beautiful pink-and-blue sky, feeling like an idiot. Here we go. This is the point in the conversation where the dog owners tell you you've got it all wrong and push their dog with its mouthful of sharp teeth in your face to show how cuddly it is.

'Fern, don't worry about it. It's fine.'

'Is it?'

'Sure. I'll find him another home,' David said, bumping his fist against my shoulder.

I laughed, loving him for saying it, even though I knew it was a joke.

His gaze was full of understanding. 'What started it? Did you have a bad experience once?' he asked.

'Not just once. I was a timid kid.'

'Are you scared of all dogs? Chihuahuas?'

'Just dogs with teeth. I try not to let them smell fear. My policy is to avoid them.'

'Aw, Fern, the whole country's full of dogs,' he said sympathetically.

'Yeah, I know.' We were having this conversation semi-seriously. I was laughing a bit at myself but at the same time it was all true. I scooped up a handful of sand and let it trickle slowly through my fingers.

'Why didn't you tell me that night? I would have put him out in the garden.'

'I didn't think you'd understand.' But actually, I was wrong about that.

'If it's any consolation, you hide it very well,' he said after a moment. 'You always look confident.'

I was pleased he was impressed. Hiding was one thing I was really good at. I took a sip of my mojito and the ice cubes chinked against my teeth. 'You had the dog with you the first time I met you.'

'So I did.'

'I was wearing that Fifties-style suit with a pencil skirt. Did you like me when you first saw me?' I asked, knowing that people's impressions of me are usually superficial judgements which, to be fair, I've always encouraged.

343

'I didn't know you then,' he replied with his customary honesty. 'But I liked you when we went to the Cotswolds.'

'Did you?' I ask hopefully. 'What did you like about me?'

'You weren't pushy.'

'Oh. That's a negative. What positives did you like about me?'

'You fitted in, I suppose.'

'And that's why I didn't tell you about the dog, because I wanted to fit in here, too.'

I wonder if he's ever looked at our star signs for compatibility, even if just out of curiosity, even though I don't believe a word of it. If we were governed by our star signs the world's population would be divided into twelfths. We'd all be doing the same thing in the same week, and the whole idea is completely ridiculous).

A blue beachball bounced our way and David kicked it back. 'I've seen the way you look at people,' he said. 'It's as if you get inside their heads and know just what they need to feel better about themselves. It seems like a heavy gift to carry around with you.'

'Why? It's nice.' I turned to look at him. I'm not sure how serious this conversation was. I didn't know whether it was influenced by Dinah's story and the way she woke Moss, or the mojitos. 'As for Duncan, I suppose I could try facing my fears rather than avoiding them. When I imagine a dog jumping on me I can feel its paws on my shoulders and smell its breath in my face as if I were a kid, but Duncan's not a very big dog and he'd probably only come up to my waist.'

'That's because you're a grown-up now,' David said logically, reaching for my hand.

He brushed the sand from my palms and I felt a surge of excitement, which tempered the dread from the dog talk, and I tightened my fingers in his.

'Am I? I'm always hiding behind my clothes,' I said.

He thought about this, and he smiled. 'That's not how I see it. I like the way you let your clothes speak for you,' he said.

*Phobias.*

Now, standing on the pavement outside the flat all ready to go for my interview, I'm looking at Alexandra Booth's card and wondering: am I grown-up? The question is quite depressing.

Harnessing my inner adolescent, I throw it to the fates and dial the hypnotherapist's number. If Alexandra Booth answers, I'll go and see her. If I get her voicemail, I'll go to the interview.

I don't have to worry about it for long because she picks up on the first ring.

'Hello? How can I help you?' she asks.

# LOT 27

*Baby Dior size 6A silk crêpe dress with full gold net skirt,*
*114cm, 1990s*

First of all, I don't know if hypnotherapy works but I'm willing to give it a go on the basis I've got nothing to lose.

I reschedule my interview at Top Shop and meet Alexandra Booth in St John's Wood. She has a consulting room in an office block. She's in her forties, kind and calm, dark hair and a short bob, and she's wearing a well-cut charcoal-grey suit with high-heeled shoes, so already I have a lot of faith in her.

She admires my jacket and tells me that she, herself, had the exact same one.

I laugh – well, actually . . .

So already, it's nice that we have a bond.

She makes a steeple of her fingers while I sit in her claret armchair and tell her about my fear of dogs.

As I lean back in my chair, relaxing and gazing at a spot on her oatmeal wall, she asks about my first memories of being afraid of a dog. I close my eyes and relive the time I was six and chased by an Alsatian in Regent's Park, when I got knocked face down in the mud in my gold tulle party dress.

I was, as my mother has said, a shy and timid child.

And to my surprise, and probably Alexandra Booth's, as I relive it, I start to cry. I feel as if my heart is breaking. Every dog that I've ever encountered since then has been that dog and every fear of being knocked down has been that fear.

I remember the jangle of its collar getting louder in my ears and running as fast as I can, running like the wind but at the same time experiencing the terror of knowing without a doubt that it's going to get me. WHAM! It does. It barges into me, stands over me, pinning me down in the cold mud, panting its hot, meaty breath in my ear.

And that's where my memory ends, right there, as if that was the end of the story and I'd died at that moment. When I see a dog, I've died at that moment ever since.

But it's not the end of the story. When Alexandra Booth lets me carry on viewing my memories in black and white in the cinema of my imagination, I can see my loving, furious mother running to me, picking me up, cleaning the mud and its grittiness out of my mouth with her manicured fingers. She yells at the dog's owners and at me for the state my dress and yes, it's true, I have spoilt it, ruined it, trashed it, sullied it. And in my distress and confusion, I'm not crying from the shock of being chased but for my gold dress, my lovely dress, which I've failed to protect as my mother has failed to protect me.

I replay the scene again and again in my mind until I can watch it without crying, until its power is weakened and the memory slides gradually from the present to the past.

Alexandra Booth asks me about my relationship with my mother.

'She's a bit self-centred.' I've edited the story in my head and left out the important bits.

I tell her the facts. My mother's parents were in the army, which was how she came to go to boarding school, which she hated. Her parents had an intense relationship. They loved her, but she always felt the outsider. So as soon as she was able to, she looked for someone of her own to love.

What my mother wanted was to be adored. It shouldn't have been hard. It was why she became a model. She had the kind of looks that attracted people, the kind of face that never took a bad photograph. She had a mouth that curved up at the edges as if she were always on the brink of a smile, as if her thoughts were always sweet and pleasant. Her hair was pale and glossy, wavy, large eyes looking through a heavy fringe.

I know from photographs that I was a beautiful child, a miniature version of my mother, with the same cleft in my chin and my upturned mouth denoting perpetual enjoyment. Our mouths are a quirk of fate, the stamp of genetics, because obviously neither of us was perpetually happy. Having said that, we were *mostly* happy, that's how I remember it, to the delight of my father.

She had the world at her feet, my grandmother liked to say, as if she could have been anything she chose and made a success of it. Which really isn't true. She liked the parties, the fashion, the runway, the attention, but she didn't apply herself.

In her opinion, life was about her looks. She was never interested in the bigger picture.

Despite the circles that she mixed with in that time, she chose my father because he could see no fault in her. She was perfectly beautiful. And then they had me and I was an appealing child, and she and I were all his. He disappeared to work on a Monday and when he reappeared on a Friday he'd shout, 'I'm home!' And his face would light up at the sight of us and he'd stretch his arms wide and we'd run into them – we, his girls, his beautiful girls. As a result, I spent my early childhood feeling totally loved and totally secure.

If I was a reflection of her, the perfect mirror to begin with, it began to warp and distort as I grew up, like a funhouse in a fairground. It didn't reflect what she wanted. She didn't want me to be myself if it meant thinking differently from the way she did. She had needs and expectations that I didn't know how to fulfil. Her anger frightened me. I made choices based on what I believed her choices would be, which was as useless as second-guessing a quiz in a magazine. She was vocal in her disappointment. I'd sit frozen in my lovely clothes, letting her anger flood over me, enduring it, waiting for it to burn itself out.

If I were a different person, it wouldn't happen to me.

It wouldn't happen to me if I transformed myself into someone else.

That's the whole story of my early years.

I drift back to the present.

Alexandra Booth is talking about my experience with the dog and my instinct to run away from it, which may be a result of my fear of my mother's criticism, which has made me hypersensitive to threat. 'But you might also find that you're more sensitive to other people's feelings,' she remarks, crossing one leg over the other. 'You may be more attuned than most to other people's needs and consequently, they'll be drawn to your empathy. Some people are like orchids and some are like dandelions,' she says.'

It's a consoling thought. 'So it's not all bad?'

'Not by any means. And I want you to remember that dogs bark because that's what dogs do,' she's saying. 'And you'll find, knowing this, that you don't mind it.'

I let my thoughts drift to a shaggy brown dog on a pink

lead and David Westwood in a pink floral shirt standing with my suitcase on Chalk Farm Road.

'In fact, it makes you feel warm and friendly.'

She counts me back to the present and I open my eyes and look around the oatmeal room.

'How do you feel?'

How do I feel? 'I'm not sure,' I say truthfully. 'I suppose I'll have to test it out before I know whether or not it's worked.'

I give her back her empty Kleenex box and leave, clutching the last of the tissues in my damp hand.

Obviously, I'm testing out my dog-worthiness at David's house. I'm wearing a nude mididress, because that's the way I feel, as if I'm missing a layer of confidence. I'm standing outside the red front door between two olive trees in terracotta pots and he's waiting inside for me – the perfect incentive.

I'm mustering up the magic mantra the hypnotherapist has given, that when a dog jumps and barks, it's just being a dog.

I ring the doorbell.

The dog barks and David comes to the door. 'It's okay, Duncan's in the lounge,' he says.

I clutch his blue shirtsleeve. 'Hang on, just checking – if Duncan does savage me, you'll pull him off, won't you?'

David takes me perfectly seriously; there's not a hint of a smile in his eyes. And isn't that what we all want, to be understood?

'Of course, Fern. You can rely on me.'

I can. I know I can. I flex my shoulders. 'All right then. I'm ready.'

David opens the door and goes inside the lounge first, with me following close behind him on the grounds that if there's any savaging going to occur, the dog will get him before it gets me. Obviously, he's a nice guy and I don't want him to be savaged, but if it happens I'll be in a good position to run for help.

The flat is painted white and it's extremely neat.

Duncan, the shaggy brown dog raises his blond eyebrows to look amiably at us. He licks David's hand and David scratches behind his ear with a rueful smile. 'Sit.' The dog sits.

So far, so good.

David looks up at me. 'How are you feeling?'

'I'm not sure.' On the other hand, I know what I'm not feeling – I'm not feeling scared to death. My heart rate is normal. I look at the dog and the dog looks at me with that expression of benign expectation that I recognise from before. And I'm not afraid. I *could* be afraid. The memory of fear isn't far away and I could revive it with a snap of the fingers if I wanted, but currently I'm not. I'm just not.

'Coffee?'

'Yes, please.'

In the kitchen there's an empty light box. I pick it up and look at the construction of the dovetail joints. 'Will you always just make these?'

'Well, I enjoyed making the chopping board. I might try making another one for someone who'd appreciate it,' he says with humour. His eyes meet mine for a moment. He takes a cafetiere out of the cupboard and measures the coffee accurately with a scoop. He does it as carefully and precisely as he does everything else.

'But you like these best?'

'I like these best,' he agrees, pouring the hot water.

'Is it because you're romantic, or just because they're nice gifts for people?' I say, leaning on the worktop, trying to help him out because I don't want him to feel I've put him on the spot.

'I'll tell you why,' he says, handing me the coffee and looking into my eyes. 'The universe is so immense that it puts my life into perspective. And the stars are orderly, a constant, millions of years old while we spin around them. When I'm down, the whole world seems dark, but then I look at the stars and I realise I'm nothing but an infinitesimal spark of energy, nothing more than that.'

'You've been unhappy?' I don't need a difficult mother for this particular insight.

'Yes. I was for a while. Something was missing in my life. I thought Gigi might be the answer, but it went deeper than that. Anyway, I'm better now. My life's good. You make it easy, Fern.' He goes into the lounge and comes back with two pieces of Perspex, which he slots into the light box side by side. 'This is for you.' He puts it on the worktop and plugs it in. He points to the left one. 'It's Virgo.'

'Aww,' I say, staring at the constellations, touched by the gift of my very own piece of the night sky. Then I start to laugh. 'David, I'm not a Virgo.'

'No, but I am.' He smiles at me and his eyes crease, and his mouth is on mine and it's such an incredible kiss that I feel I can take on the world.

# LOT 28

*White ostrich-feather bolero. Cream satin lining.*
*Coast. One size.*

Before I can take on the world, I have to take on my mother.

And I'm going to try not to be too fearful or anxious about her response. It's not only dogs that bark, my mother barks, too. It's what she does.

After leaving David's with my light box, feeling pretty buoyant about things, I hear someone calling me on Chalk Farm Road and it's Lucy, who's sitting outside Cotton's looking gorgeous in the Le Smoking-style trouser suit, with gelled-back hair and a white silk evening scarf.

She's been given a part in an all-female remake of *The Great Gatsby* and she's on a high.

She finishes her coffee and as we're walking home together along the canal, which is so dense with duckweed that it looks as if it's lined with artificial grass, I apologise for my mother's habit of banging on her ceiling with the mop.

'Don't worry, I've got used to it,' Lucy says. 'She's a funny old girl, isn't she?'

I give a rueful smile. No one has ever described my mother like that before. The hypnotherapy has made me think a bit

355

more about what my mother's done with her life, which is basically to look good. And she does look good, in a sphinx-style kind of way. I start to wonder if she's actually not been putting me down all this time but trying to spur me on in her own weird way.

I ask Lucy what she thinks about this theory.

Lucy gestures with her white gloves, which makes her look like a mime artist. 'Could be. She admires achievement in others. That whole Malcolm McDowell thing. Remember? When she thought I was starring with him in The Gatehouse?'

'Yes. That's true.'

'I wouldn't worry about it. She's ambitious for you. It's natural that our parents want us to do better than them.'

'That's what David said. Something like that, anyway.' We stand aside to let a wobbling cyclist pass.

The sound of plaintive mandolin music drifts towards us. It's the music punt, sitting low in the water, with a group of tourists looking happy as they're serenaded through the weed towards the lock.

'You've got to give the folks something to be proud of once in a while and throw them an achievement now and then,' Lucy says. 'It keeps them going for ages, and they feel they've done something right and they're not total failures. They're an insecure lot, parents.'

That my parents might be insecure has never occurred to me. They act as if they've got all the answers. 'How do you know so much about it?'

'Well, I've had mine ages,' Lucy says airily. 'Since before I was born. How about you?'

'Same.' We seem to have got incredibly wise all of a sudden.

We leave the canal by the horse stairs and cross the road towards our street.

'So, what's in the bag?'

'It's one of David's light boxes.'

'Oh, yeah?' She turns her full attention to me. 'Fern Banks! Do tell.'

'He's a Virgo.'

'Ah, a Virgo. Neat, self-motivated, cautious, sensitive?'

I laugh. 'All of those.'

'You'll suit each other,' she says. 'Good for you, Fern.'

We're now outside our house.

Lucy goes up the three steps to her flat. I go down the steps to mine.

I can hear voices inside. My mother: laughing merrily.

And a man, laughing heartily.

But it's not my father's laugh.

My stomach crunches into a ball.

Well, it's all clear now, isn't it, the reason she left home? She's got herself a love nest and like a cuckoo, she's manoeuvring me, the little chick, out of it. Right.

I make as much noise as possible as I open the front door. Then I stamp vigorously on our new Home, Sweet Home doormat until I practically wear the tread off my shoes.

'Darling!' my mother cries effusively, coming into the hall. 'You do have the nicest friends!'

Do I?

And sitting next to each other on the red sofa, Bloody Marys in hand, is Cato Hamilton in his tweeds and Kim Aston who's wearing my mother's white ostrich-feather bolero.

It turns out that they haven't come to see my mother at all, they've come to see me, but my mother, sorry, Annabel, has invited them to wait. They must have been waiting ages, because Cato and Kim look pink and rosy, and my mother looks extremely merry in a beige cashmere dress slit to the knee. She's chewing on a stringy celery stick.

'They've come about the fashion show,' my mother tells me.

Seriously, how long have I been out of the house? 'What fashion show?'

'Fashion show and *auction*,' Cato says, undoing the top button of his tweed waistcoat, thereby recklessly breaking with sartorial tradition.

'Yes, fashion show and auction,' Kim agrees.

I honestly have no idea what they're talking about. 'What are you auctioning?'

'Dinah's fake Chanels and special frocks your clients have bought from you that have made a difference to them,' Kim says. 'Proceeds to a charity of your choice.'

'Really?' I ask, deeply touched, fingering the neckline of my nude dress. I can feel my throat tighten.

'Yes, everyone wants to get involved – it's the best way we could think of to thank you.'

I'm stunned, overcome with gratitude.

'Oh,' he adds, fishing for something on the sofa, 'that reminds me – here you are, Fern, here's your client book back.'

I'm astounded. 'I wondered where that had gone!' I take the book from him and flick through the names that bring warmth to my heart and I look at Kim again, my eyes blurring. 'I can't believe it.'

'I'm going to teach the models the catwalk strut,' my mother says, hanging on to her glass and wobbling to her feet to demonstrate. 'Look at me! I've still got it!' she declares triumphantly, holding onto the wall for support.

Kim raises his glass to her.

'You know what your business USP is, Fern?' Cato asks me. 'Customer service. The personal touch. Everyone talks about it. That's why your clients keep coming back.'

'Do you really have to go back into a department store?' Kim asks kindly, extracting a stray feather from his mouth.

'No,' I admit, glancing at Annabel.

'I should think not, Fern. Why on earth would you? You're making such a success of things,' my mother says in such a brazen turnabout that I'm once again lost for words.

# LOT 29

*From Christian Dior's first collection, 1947, la Ligne Corolle, the iconic 'Bar' suit comprising a corseted waspwaisted skirt suit of Shantung silk and wool crêpe pleated skirt, with padded hips. 10/36, from the collection of Dinah Moss.*

Moss is sitting outside the shop, recovered from his viral infection. He's having a coffee break in the sunshine to top up his vitamin D while he reads the Jewish Chronicle. The top button of his white shirt is unbuttoned, his sleeves are rolled up and his jacket is folded carefully over the back of his chair.

David is sitting at his table, meticulously personalising a light box for a wedding anniversary. Sensing my longing gaze on him, he looks up at me and smiles. I smile back with a sudden rush of heat and the sensation makes me melt with pleasure.

I don't know if there's anything in the whole astrology business, but Lucy called it perfectly. He's neat, self-motivated, cautious, sensitive. And good-looking, *very* good-looking. I'd be crazy to leave that fact out.

The aroma of stirfry is wafting over from the food stalls. My frocks are quivering on their rails in the summer breeze and passing women are coming to look at them like butter-flies attracted to flowers. I'm wearing an electric-blue dress with wide Eighties shoulder pads that makes me feel like an American footballer, able to tackle anything, which is lucky because I've got my notebook on my knee, and I've been given the task of compiling the auction catalogue using Tallulah Young's post-sales reports as a guide to the estimates.

I'm still working on it when my mother unexpectedly turns up at lunchtime in her taupe Sweaty Betty gym gear, cream hair in a ponytail, looking remarkably pleased with herself. Commanding our attention with her hands on her hips, she says, 'Hello everybody, guess where I've been?'

I close my notebook. 'Taking a wild guess here – the gym?'

'No.' She sits on the edge of David's table. 'Just for the record, darling, Ruth Bennett was completely wrong,' she says, loosening her hair so that it falls around her face. She looks at David over her shoulder. 'Hello.'

'Hello,' he replies cheerfully.

'Wrong about what?' I ask eagerly, wondering what accounts for her good mood.

'Your father's yoga teacher is *not* a femme fatale.' She smirks. 'He happens to be a chap in his sixties from Amsterdam. The class is for retired men.'

'Uh-oh,' I laugh, 'don't tell me – you crashed it, didn't you?'

'I did,' she says smugly. 'I was asked to leave.'

I grin, sensing from her tone there's more. 'And?' I prompt her.

'And then Jonathan came rushing out after me,' she says, suddenly as breathless as a schoolgirl on her first crush. 'He's desperate for us to talk things over. But of course, I had to get back here, because I'm teaching Kim how to walk in heels. Oops!' She covers her mouth with her hand. 'You didn't hear it from me, darling; it's supposed to be a surprise.'

This is news to me. 'Wow. It's literally going to be a whole new step for Kim.'

'I honestly could not have that man striding down the runway in flats. My reputation depends on it.'

She has sent invitations out to fashion magazines, dailies and supplements, name-dropping wildly.

That's interesting, but I bring her back to the main topic. 'So . . . how did you leave things with Dad?'

'Let's just say he's taking me to dinner tonight and I've decided to give him a second chance. The fashion show has sparked up old memories of my modelling days, if you know what I mean.' She looks over her shoulder at David. 'For your information, David, old is a figure of speech, I'd just like to point out.'

'I know that,' he says mildly.

David remains wonderfully impervious to both her charms and her moods. I'm getting better at coping with them too; I'd say my current transformation is from a wilting orchid to a thriving dandelion, which is never a look I thought I'd go for.

Moss lowers his newspaper. 'Annabel, listen, anyone asks, tell them you're over twenty-one,' he advises my mother soberly.

She's flattered. 'You're right, Moss,' she says. 'That's all anyone needs to know about me. No Dinah today?'

'My bride will be here soon,' Moss replies confidently, looking at his watch. He folds up his newspaper and gets slowly to his feet. 'This fashion show and auction. The proceeds are for refugees, no?'

I nod. It wasn't a difficult decision, seeing as the main

attraction will be Dinah's 'Chanel-style' suits, as I've cautiously described them. 'Why?'

Moss's worn face creases into an enigmatic smile and he taps his nose.

My mother gets up from the edge of David's table. 'I'm going to start holding deportment classes. Our models might not be all model-shaped, but I'm making damned sure they'll walk like them,' she says nobly. She waggles her fingers at us. 'See you later,' she adds as she struts away.

I go back to my pricing, scratching my head with my pen.

'Good afternoon,' Dinah announces moments later, bull-dozing her way through the crowds, pushing a large, shiny silver suitcase. She's wearing a pink and cream tea-length dress and a little cream jacket with strings of pink faux pearls. She looks as cool as an ice cream. 'Where's *mein mann*? Oh, there you are.'

David and I exchange glances, because she and Moss are so obviously up to something.

However, she seems to have a crisis of confidence because she clasps her hands together and says to Moss, 'You tell her.'

'Very well.' Moss puts his black jacket on, as if he suddenly feels improperly dressed. He fastens the top button. 'Fern, we have an additional item for the auction. My bride and I have decided to sell Christian Dior's 'Bar' Suit,' he announces with gravitas.

It's like being punched in the chest. This is huge! I'm astounded, and speechless. This is the 'New Look' waspwaisted skirt suit of Shantung silk and wool crêpe that Dinah showed me the first day I went to her house.

'It's a very sexy ensemble,' Dinah adds for David's benefit, playing with the beads around her neck. 'Dior was a sexy man – he died having sex,' she explains to David matter-of-factly. 'Trust me, dahlink, don't you believe what anyone else says;

that he choked on a fishbone. The fishbone story is all nonsense because he hated fish, he told me so himself. Anyway. We want to give this ensemble to the auction.'

Moss adds, 'Also we would like it to be labelled From the Collection of Dinah Moss.'

Despite the sunshine, I can feel the warmth draining out of me. I'm in a state of shock. 'Moss, I'm telling you, this is something else. This a game changer.'

Moss jerks his head. 'Don't you worry,' he says gruffly, 'we already know how much it's worth. Kim has a google. Six figures, he says. Now you tell her,' he says to Dinah.

Dinah clears her throat and steps forward, pushing the shiny suitcase towards me. 'In here we have a gift for you. Keep the case, too and get rid of that old noisy one.' She frowns. 'You still have it?'

'Yes.'

'Anyway.' She waves at the case. 'Go on! Open it.'

I crouch down on the cobbles and open it nervously.

Wrapped in tissue is the Grès ivory one-shouldered Grecian-draped full-length couture gown that I'd tried on in her dressing room. It's too much. Overcome by their kindness I try to control my emotions. 'Thank you both so much.'

'Come. Get up. Don't cry,' Dinah says kindly, reaching for my hand. Her fingers grip mine tightly. 'It's for you to wear at your wedding. It will make you happy.'

I get up slowly, holding the dress in my other hand, glad that that my hair is loose and hiding my flushed face, and risk a glance at David.

The situation between me and David is that despite spending our spare time in his bed like two people who have been separated from each other for way too long, I am still spending my nights on the sofa in the flat.

I know he's not on the rebound from Gigi, because he's told

me so. But I don't want to move in with him for the wrong reasons, because it's expedient, or even if it just seems that way. So marriage isn't anything that we've talked about and I don't want him to feel forced into it by Moss and Dinah's romantic dreams.

He's watching me with a smile as I clutch the gown. He mouths, 'I love you' at me, and then he covers his eyes. 'I don't want to see it yet,' he says. 'I want you to surprise me.'

# KIM

I'm in Betty's parlour, wearing navy stilettos and a Jean Muir navy jersey dress with plenty of stretch, hopping from one foot to the other because my toes are crushed together, tortured and squashed unnaturally into tiny cones of leather, hurting like they've never hurt before.

'Kim, don't be such a baby,' Annabel says briskly, flicking her pale hair away from her face. 'Are you ready? One more time!'

For some reason, Mercia and Betty, who I normally think of as my friends, find this all very amusing, but Annabel is unsympathetic. She starts the music again, issuing orders.

'Go! Swing your hips, Kim! Don't slump! Keep your head up! Strut, don't mince! That's better! Keep going! Aim for the window! Stride, stride, stride, stride . . . No, no, no. That won't do at all. Watch me!'

I'm ruing the day that Betty got rid of the kilims because I would happily break my ankle at this moment so I'd never have to swing my hips again.

'I'm just going to put the kettle on,' Betty says, taking pity on me, and I gladly kick off my navy shoes and slump next to Mercia on the sofa.

To my surprise, once the shoes are off and I've propped my feet on a stool in the shape of a carved elephant, my mood improves and life immediately starts looking up again.

'This is my reputation on the line,' Annabel explains, by way of apology. 'The whole world will be watching us!'

Not the whole world, but fashion archivists from museums in Japan, the USA, France and the UK have all expressed an interest in Dinah's Dior gown, a gown which I am told changed fashion forever.

I can't say I'm surprised. Thanks to Fern, I already know the incredible power of a frock.

As I rest my feet, I notice that Betty has one of our invitations on her mantelpiece.

### Fern Banks Vintage and Cato Hamilton Auctioneers.

*You are cordially invited to a charity vintage designer fashion show and auction in the West Yard, Camden Lock for Refugee Aid.*

*Lots include Christian Dior's 'Bar' Suit 'New Look', 1947 from the collection of Mrs Dinah Moss.*

*Viewing from 10 am to 5 pm*

*Fashion show and auction from 7 pm*

We have unleashed a monster, as Mercia puts it and she's not just talking about Annabel.

Cato has been in his element, hiring sound systems and lighting for the fashion show part of the evening, setting up phone lines, internet connections, renting marquees, measuring rostrums. He talks about hammer prices and valuation contracts, and then, at a meeting we had yesterday at Dinah's, he slipped in the astonishing fact that the buyers' premium of 20 per cent on commission bids comes to a decent five-figure sum on the Christian Dior alone.

Who'd have thought?

Once we'd grasped the enormity of it, Dinah and Moss decided that this should, after expenses, be split between them, me, Cato and Fern. We argued of course, but they took offence at our protestations. They said we were family to them now. And so we are.

Betty brings the tea through and I move my feet off the elephant stool so that she can put the tray on it.

'I bet Enid would know how to strut,' she says.

I realise that the whole day has gone by without me thinking of Enid once, and I'm happy to be reminded of her. 'Would she?'

It makes me smile. I like the thought of Enid strutting.

It's quite extraordinary. I didn't think my life would turn out like this.

When she died, I could only see the part of my life that was over. I didn't realise then that it was the beginning of something different, and new.

# Cato Hamilton Auctioneers & Fern Banks Vintage Auction Catalogue

Outside in Camden Lock West Yard, it's getting dark. The brightest stars are gleaming. The Christian Dior outfit, star of the show, is featured on the screen.

I go back into the marquee. It's buzzing. I'm buzzing. The models are wearing the outfits that they're donating to the auction, the clothes that mean something to them, the garments that made a difference to the way they saw themselves.

My mother waggles her fingers at me. She's chosen the cashmere dress that's split to the knee. She's got a tremendous amount of energy and she's in her element, and as a result, my father is besotted with her once more.

I've taken Lucy's advice to throw her some achievement from time to time, like the fact that Holly Willoughby's in my client book, but this event has gone a long way to smoothing things over with Ruth Bennett, thus saving her from feeling a failure on my behalf.

Dinah is wearing the black-and-white cotton tweed suit that she had on the second time we met. 'Dahlink, how do I look?' she demands, winding down her red lipstick.

'Stunning,' I tell her.

'I'm nervous,' Kim says, wearing his first frock with the feather trim.

'You seem so different now,' I tell him fondly, thinking of

the anxious man in the personal styling suite who'd decided he didn't want to stay.

He looks surprised. Then he says, 'Fern, I *am* different.'

Kim and Dinah – they look so gorgeous and I hug them impulsively in a rush of gratitude for my great good fortune in having them as my friends. 'I'll never forget this, what you've done for me,' I tell them.

'Pah!' Dinah says, brushing it off.

I take a look outside the marquee. It's incredible, the way Cato's organised it. Crowds have gathered all around Camden Lock. Our banners are strung up around us.

It's coming up to seven o' clock and I'm checking my models as they stand in line, waiting to go up. Kim, his white hair spiked and gelled, Dinah winding a camellia print scarf around her neck, Lucy in Donna Karan. And Alexa, Bethan, Hannah, Daisy, Jenna, Betty, Mercia all waiting to go on, their faces illuminated by neon lights that read *#perfectfit* and *#passiton #refugeeaid*, and the lights are flashing and the music is blaring.

We cluster nervously near the entrance and the music changes. Kim's rubbing his hands together nervously, waiting for his cue.

'Get ready, Kim,' my mother orders. 'Head up, shoulders back, and STRUT!' She winks at me and I grin back at her because we are once again members of the same tribe.

Cato is on the podium with his gavel and the auction catalogue in his hand.

'Go!'

Kim strides onto the catwalk in his heels with style.

'Lot one,' Cato announces through the PA system. 'Sky-blue Sixties-style dress, unlabelled, with bracelet-length sleeves and feather trim to neck and hem. Who'll start the bidding at fifty? Fifty bid . . . ?'

Sitting in the front row, Moss and my father jump to their

feet and clap as he moves past them. Kim turns, pauses and swivels on his heels like a pro as Dinah moves forward towards the catwalk with her superior, jaunty walk and blows a kiss to the crowd.

'A Chanel-style black-and-white cotton tweed suit with bracelet-length sleeves, double "C" gilt buttons, chain-weighted hem and matching skirt, together with a black and white camellia print scarf. Who will start me at eighty pounds? Eighty bid. Eighty-five? Ninety . . .'

I go to the Roving Bridge to join David.

He's wearing a blue floral shirt. He's got Duncan on a lead and I can feel the heat of his arm against mine.

We are standing under the giant light box of the night sky. The floodlights are bouncing colours off the smooth skin of his face; blue, white and red and David turns to face me. He traces his finger down my forehead, down to my lips.

I put my arms around his waist and his hands are stroking my back through my favourite frock; I can feel the music beating through his rib cage and we are thigh against thigh and hip against hip and his mouth is on my mouth and I know the power of the perfect fit.

# Acknowledgements

Stories come from many different sources and ideas, but this one has been easier than most to pin down. I've been kept afloat by many acts of kindness in recent months and by my wonderful sister, Elaine, who's steadfastly good and true. The idea for a story about vintage fashion came from my brilliant agent, Judith Murdoch. It's been honed by editor Rachel Faulkner-Willcocks, championed by Sabah Khan and Elke Desanghere, and whetted by Sarah, over weekly coffees and lists. My husband, Paul, is my sounding board, best friend and hero of all of my stories, and our son Joe is a constant source of joy.

My friends, family and readers, you've given me many unexpected reasons to be happy even during the sad times and I'm so grateful to you.

With thanks,
Sophie

Follow me on Twitter: @sophiejenkinsuk
www.sophiejenkinsauthor.com

*Sometimes happiness can be found where you least expect it . . .*

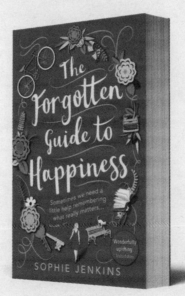

If you enjoyed *A Random Act of Kindness*, you'll love Sophie's gorgeous debut.

**Out Now!**